Four

Jane Blythe

Bear Spots Publications
Melbourne Australia

bearspotspublications@gmail.com

Paperback
ISBN: 0-9945380-2-2
ISBN-13: 978-0-9945380-2-4

Cover designed by QDesigns

I'd like to thank everyone who played a part in bringing this story to life. Particularly my mom who is always there to share her thoughts and opinions with me. My awesome cover designer, Amy, who whips up covers for me so quickly and who patiently makes every change I ask for, and there are usually lots of them! And my lovely editor Mitzi Carroll, and proofreader Marisa Nichols, for all their encouragement and for all the hard work they put in to polishing my work.

JULY 19TH

She was running late.

Again.

That seemed to be the story of her life.

Jordanna Milford had never expected her life to turn out like this. She was thirty-five years old, married, with four kids and an elderly and ailing father who required daily visits. Jordanna had always imagined she'd make her fortune in real estate and then live a life of luxury. Instead, she had gotten pregnant at eighteen, married the baby's father, and been forced to give up her dreams of really making something of herself to instead becoming a wife and mother. Sure, she had a job as a secretary at the local pediatrician's office, but mainly her life consisted of ferrying her children around, cooking, cleaning, laundry, and the mundaneness of family life.

She loved her kids, of course. She just wished she'd waited, not messed up her life with one night of sex with a guy she knew at the time she didn't love and was now stuck with.

Now to top it all off, Jordanna made daily trips to her father's place to help him shower, prepare meals, organize his medications, and do a general tidy-up. He needed to be in a home, she knew that, and even though she hated the daily visits, he was still her father and she couldn't face doing that to him.

Still, on days like today, it was particularly difficult. She'd been up late last night helping her nine-year-old with a science project she'd left till the last minute. Then the four-year-old had awakened her at three in the morning, claiming the monster under

1

her bed was singing nursery rhymes. In the car this morning, on her way to drop the three older ones at the bus stop then take the youngest to preschool, she'd had an argument with her seventeen-year-old who wanted permission to attend a college fraternity party. And now, running late as always, she was on her way to her father's place before heading to work.

It was days like this that Jordanna thought about divorcing her husband, leaving behind her kids, and starting on the life she really wanted. She was only thirty-five. She'd managed to keep her figure despite four pregnancies, and she knew that men found her attractive. She was tall with long legs, long blonde hair, and big green eyes that she could bat at any male and get her way.

Unfortunately, Jordanna believed in following through with the choices that you made, no matter how things turned out. She had chosen to marry Barry and raise their son together, she had chosen to add three more children to their family; she had chosen this life, and she was stuck with it.

Sighing as she pulled her car into a spot outside her father's apartment building, she turned off the engine and trudged up the sidewalk and into the building. She ferreted through her bag searching for the key. As she slid it into the lock, Jordanna sensed immediately that something was wrong.

At first, she wasn't sure why she felt that way.

Nothing in the hall appeared out of place. And Jordanna convinced herself it was just her imagination.

"Dad?" she called out as she set her handbag on the table by the door and carried the grocery bags toward the kitchen and living room, which were at the end of the hall.

There was no response.

Her anxiety edged up another notch. "Dad? It's Jordanna."

The doors to the apartment's two bedrooms were open and as she glanced inside, she could see that both were empty.

Subconsciously, her steps slowed as she neared the closed door at the end of the corridor.

What was waiting for her on the other side?

Had her dad had a heart attack? A stroke? A fall?

He could be lying on the other side of the door, dead.

Jordanna was not good with dead bodies. She'd only ever seen one before. Her mom's. Shortly after she had given birth to her first son, her mom had taken a fall from a ladder while cleaning out drainpipes. She'd broken her neck, died instantly. Jordanna had been the one to find her body. She hadn't even been able to touch her mom to check if she was still alive.

She couldn't even touch a dead animal. When the family pets died, her husband had to deal with them.

She couldn't even pick up a dead insect.

With a trembling hand, she reached for the door handle.

She was almost too scared of what she would find on the other side to actually turn it once her hand grasped it.

"Dad?" she called one last time.

Expecting no response, she got none.

Anxiety was starting to cause the hairs on the back of her neck to stand up.

Something was wrong. She could feel it.

The apartment had a creepy air to it. Usually, Jordanna just found this place depressing, but today it was more than that.

Knowing she couldn't put it off any longer, she opened the door.

All the air left her lungs in a rush.

Instantly lightheaded, she swayed unsteadily as she surveyed the room.

It wasn't what she had been expecting.

But who would ever suspect this?

Suddenly nauseous, Jordanna turned and stumbled toward the bathroom. She dropped to her knees once inside, just managing to lift the toilet lid before she threw up.

* * * * *

8:49 A.M.

As he approached the apartment building, he couldn't help but sigh.

Another murder.

He was so sick of murder.

More so than ever the last six months.

Still, murder was a part of his life. There was nothing he could do about that. It was the life he had chosen, so there was no point complaining about it.

"Hey."

A woman appeared beside him. Early thirties, tall, red hair, green eyes, pretty. She should be tired of murder, too.

"Jack? You okay?" The green eyes that studied him were now tinted with concern.

He uttered another weary sigh. "Yeah." With that, Detective Jack Xander resumed his walk toward the building where another dead body laid waiting.

The woman fell into step beside him. "We both know you're not," his partner commented mildly.

"Not what?" he asked, pretending he didn't know what she was talking about. Jack hated that his growing depression was obvious to those around him.

"Not okay," Rose Lace replied patiently, narrowing her eyes at him.

"We don't both know that," he lied. Of course, they knew he wasn't okay. In fact, it wasn't only the two of them who knew it. Rose wasn't the first person to point out to him that he wasn't doing so great these days.

"I think we do," Rose contradicted him, then she too sighed. "I wish you'd talk to someone. Me or one of your brothers or a professional, but you need to talk to someone."

"I don't need a shrink," he protested immediately. For one

thing, he didn't have anything to say to one. Some things were better left unsaid.

"Never said you did," Rose replied.

He was irritated that Rose couldn't be provoked into an argument and annoyed with himself for being irritated about it. Jack didn't really want to argue. He just wanted to feel something other than depressed. Maybe he did need to talk to someone. He just didn't know whom he trusted enough.

"Look, we're at work," he reminded his partner, "can we just drop this conversation?"

"Sure," Rose smiled agreeably. "For now."

Rolling his eyes, he knew that was the best he was going to get out of his partner. "Victim is sixty-six-year-old Tarek Milford." He changed the topic to the reason for their presence here.

"Who found the body?" Rose asked.

"Daughter," he replied. "She's waiting for us inside. First responders said she was nearly hysterical by the time they arrived, so they called an ambulance."

"Think we can get anything out of her?" Rose asked.

"Worth a shot," he replied, not really thinking it was particularly likely. The woman had just found her father's dead body; right now she probably wasn't going to be able to give them any information that would help them find out who may have committed the murder.

"Mmmhmm," Rose agreed, sounding about as confident as he felt.

As they entered the large apartment complex, Jack noted the secure doors, the doorman, and the security cameras. Breaking into this place wouldn't have been easy. Which no doubt meant their killer was a pro. He stifled a sigh; that was all he needed.

There was no need for directions to find the right apartment; all they had to do was follow the hubbub. Rounding a corner, they spotted a woman, sitting huddled on the floor, propped up against the wall, close to the only open apartment door. An officer stood at the open door. A pile of CSU equipment sat nearby, and crime scene techs and officers bustled about.

No one paid the woman much attention. Although another officer was standing nearby and had obviously been told to stick with her. The lack of attention from those around her didn't seem to bother Jordanna Milford. Her head was tilted back to rest against the smooth white wall. Her eyes were open but appeared to be staring sightlessly into space. Her hands were clenched tightly together in her lap.

"Ms. Milford?" Jack called out softly as they approached.

Big, round, green eyes looked back at him. They were brimming with tears and glazed with shock.

Reaching her, he dropped down into a crouch at her side so they were eye to eye. "I'm Detective Jack Xander," he told her, "and this is my partner, Detective Rose Lace. We were hoping to talk with you for a moment, if you don't mind?"

"Okay." Her voice trembled, but she met his gaze squarely.

"Mind if I sit?" Jack asked.

Jordanna gave a shake of her head.

Moving to sit beside her, he propped himself against the wall as she had done, while Rose took a discreet step back. He was always the one to interview victims. Especially traumatized victims. Apparently, he had a gift for calming them, helping to pry more out of their dazed subconsciousness, getting them to trust him. It was a gift that had helped him many times in the past. As was his unflappable calm. If you asked anyone who knew him to describe him, they would say calm, good with people, and quiet. His two younger brothers may add bossy to that list, but Jack always thought that being the oldest entitled him to be a little bossy with his siblings.

"Has someone called a family member for you?" Jack asked, focusing his attention solely on Jordanna Milford and blocking out the bustle of activity around them.

"My husband," she replied. "He's on his way here. Someone

killed him," she blurted, her scared eyes looked over at him, pleading with him, as though he could somehow change that fact.

"I know." He nodded sympathetically. "I'm so sorry for your loss. I can only imagine what you're feeling right now, but we really need to ask you a few questions so we can find the person who did this. I know it's hard," he added, "but anything you tell us could be really helpful."

"Okay." Jordanna tried to visibly pull herself together and focus.

Giving her an encouraging smile, he asked, "When was the last time you saw your father?"

"Yesterday morning. I come by every day. Usually in the morning, unless I'm running really late. My dad had a fall about eight months ago. He broke his hip. Then developed an infection. He can't get around like he used to anymore. He needs help with pretty much everything. He kind of became depressed after the accident. Stopped looking after himself, stopped eating and showering, just kind of sat there, watching TV and doing nothing." Jordanna's voice grew stronger and more confident with each word. Reciting facts was helping her to calm down, to distance herself a little from the horror that lay just beyond them.

"And everything seemed in order when you left?"

"Yes, at least I think so." She hesitated a little. "I was in a hurry; I had to go out and get some stuff for a project my nine-year-old had to have in by today."

Not wanting her to distract herself with worry and guilt, he pressed on. "How many kids do you have?"

"Four," Jordanna replied, all traces of guilt fading from her face. "The oldest is seventeen, then I have an eleven-year-old, a nine-year-old, and a four-year-old."

"Sounds like you have your hands full." Jack squashed a sudden shaft of jealousy. He was thirty-one now, unmarried—not even involved—and he was beginning to despair of ever having a family of his own. Realistically, he knew that thirty-one wasn't that old. That he had plenty of time left to meet someone, fall in love, get married, and have kids, but the fact that his brothers were busy with families of their own had been fueling his loneliness lately.

"Yeah." A small smile lit her lips.

"Plus, taking care of your dad," Jack continued, "you must be run off your feet most days."

"He probably should be in a home," she admitted, guilt crept back into the eyes that stared back at him.

"But he's not, because you take such good care of him. He was very lucky to have a daughter like you," he said gently. "You came here every day to look after him, to make sure he was okay, to make sure he had everything that he needed. Has anything seemed out of place lately, anything odd or unusual or concerning?"

"No, everything has been the same," she replied.

"Has your dad mentioned anything out of the ordinary?"

"No, but he never said a lot, he was so quiet these days." Jordanna began to twist her hands tighter together in her lap. Tears started to spill out and trickle down her cheeks, but she didn't seem to notice.

"Is there anyone you can think of who may want to hurt your dad?"

"No," She lowered her gaze so she was studying her hands.

Jack caught the hesitation in her voice. "Jordanna?" he pressed gently, reaching out a hand to cover hers and still them. "Is there anyone with a grudge against your father who may have wanted to hurt him?"

She continued, her voice a mere whisper. "My dad was a parole officer. I'm sure there are any number of criminals he supervised who could theoretically have a grudge against him."

That was enough for now. They weren't going to get any more out of Jordanna; adrenalin was ebbing from her system, leaving her drained and exhausted. At least they'd gotten a potential avenue to investigate. As soon as they were done here, he and

Rose would start searching through his old cases.

"Okay, Jordanna," he kept his voice gentle, "you did really good. Officer ..." He paused, casting a glance at the name tag of the closest officer. "... Biggs will stay with you until your husband gets here. If you need anything—anything at all—give us a call." He released her hands and pulled out a card, sliding it into the trembling hand she held out. "Can I help you up?" Jack pushed to his feet and extended a hand.

She looked as if she were about to protest, then Jordanna gave a weary sigh and let him grasp her hand and pull her to her feet. She staggered a little, and he moved his hand to hold her elbow, steadying her until she got her bearings. "Thank you, Detective Xander." She shot him a grateful, albeit shaky, smile.

"You're welcome. Take care of yourself, and let your family take care of you, too; they'll want to show you they love and care about you by taking care of you." As he watched her walk away, Jack wondered why he didn't take his own advice. He'd never even told his family when he needed their help and support, let alone actually let them offer it. Jack guessed he could add hypocrisy to the list of things that summed him up.

"That went well," Rose said quietly as Officer Biggs led Jordanna Milford away. "Maybe we'll luck out and find one of his old parolees who had an axe to grind with Mr. Milford."

"Yeah," Jack agreed halfheartedly. There would be hundreds of old parolee cases to go through. Finding the one they wanted would be like looking for a needle in a haystack, if indeed it was even there at all. This could have been random. It could have been a family member. It could have been a robbery gone wrong. It could have been anything.

Somewhat reluctantly, he followed Rose into the apartment. He was contemplating taking a break when all his current cases were closed. He needed a break. A vacation. Maybe he'd do some travelling. He just needed to do something other than watch his brothers enjoy their families while he went home alone, and watch life after life be destroyed by crime.

Right now though, he had a job to do. And do it, he would.

"Rest of the house looks undisturbed," he commented to Rose as they made their way down the hall to the living room.

"Probably rules out robbery," Rose noted.

He nodded his agreement. "Wife is dead, only the one child. I didn't sense it was the daughter, although we can look into her. Unless it's the son-in-law, I'm thinking it's not family related either."

Rose didn't answer because they had entered the living room. Instead, they both surveyed the scene before them. The room was a good size. A small kitchen in one corner, and a round dining table with six chairs was set beside it. A large screen TV took up most of one wall; two, three-seater sofas and a two-seater were grouped around it. Another wall had bookshelves built into it, crammed with hundreds of books. Over by the window was an armchair and a small table. In the armchair sat Tarek Milford.

However, what drew Jack's gaze was what was on the ceiling.

"That what I think it is?" He addressed his question to crime scene tech, Stephanie Cantini. He'd been working with Stephanie for years and considered her a good friend. She had just turned forty. She was sweet and fun and hardworking, and when she wasn't busy with work and her fourteen-year-old adopted daughter, she was an obsessive skydiver.

Pausing from her task, she looked up. "Yep, it is," she confirmed.

"What do we make of that?" Jack asked Rose.

Red brows raised in surprise, Rose said, "I have no idea."

"I'm hoping to get some prints on them," Stephanie informed them. She was perched on a ladder, pulling glow-in-the-dark stars off the ceiling. Jack and his brothers had had similar stars on the ceilings of their rooms when they were kids. He had loved looking at them as he fell asleep, and then their comforting green glow if he happened to wake during the night.

"He could have used gloves," Stephanie continued, "but they probably would have made it more difficult to peel off the stickers and stick them onto the ceiling, so I'm hopeful we'll get some good prints."

That at least was good news, Jack thought. A good print could wrap this case up by the end of the day. "Anything else?" he asked Stephanie.

"I started up here since I thought it was our best chance of prints, but I'll sweep the rest of the room when I'm done," the CSU tech replied.

Turning his attention to medical examiner, Francesca Marks, and the body of Tarek Milford, he asked, "Cause of death what I think it is, Frankie?"

"Exsanguination from a single knife wound to the heart," Frankie summarized. "I'll have to confirm it, of course, once I get him back to the lab, but given the knife is still in his chest and there's blood everywhere and no other obvious injuries, I'd say it's a safe bet."

Jack had also worked with Frankie for years and had been thrilled for her and her husband when they had finally had a child after twenty years of trying. Little Tania was approaching two now and was an adorable and bubbly toddler with her mother's big brown eyes.

"We may as well head back to the station," he said to Rose. "Start going through Mr. Milford's old cases, see if there was anyone who ever threatened him. Or anyone who had any sort of fascination with stars," he added with a glance at the ceiling. "Steph, Frankie—call us if you get anything."

As he and Rose exited the room, Jack hoped that this case would wrap itself up ASAP as he was already planning where he was going to visit on his much-needed vacation.

* * * * *

9:24 A.M.

Laura sat at her window watching what was happening below her.

She didn't want to watch.

And yet somehow, she couldn't seem to look away.

Police cars and crime scene vans filled the street outside her apartment building. It seemed like half the residents were milling around, for some reason enjoying the hubbub that always accompanied a crime scene.

Laura could never understand why people were drawn to watching the aftermath of violence.

Why would you want to watch as the police scrambled through the remnants of someone's life, trying to figure out who had cause to hurt them and why?

And sometimes there was no why.

She wondered what particular tragedy had befallen one of her neighbors.

Obviously, it was something serious, judging by the number of cops and crime scene personnel who had responded.

She would never find out, though.

She didn't watch the news.

She didn't read the papers.

She didn't use any website that showed any news articles.

And she never left her apartment.

Never ever.

It had been ten years now.

Ten years that she had spent inside these walls.

Ten years since she last felt the sun or the breeze on her skin.

Ten years since she had spoken to someone face-to-face.

Ten years since she had shut down her previous life and locked herself away.

Ten years and she was no closer to ending her self-imposed exile.

* * * * *

4:45 P.M.

"I can't go through another file," Jack announced wearily, pushing away from his desk. He and Rose had been going through Tarek Milford's files for the last six hours. They hadn't even stopped for a lunch break.

"Yeah, I hear ya," Rose agreed, stifling a yawn and setting down the file she was holding.

"Make any progress?" he asked as he stretched his back, trying to erase the kinks from sitting too long in the same position.

"I have three piles," Rose replied. "The definite nos, which are mainly his non-violent parolees; the maybes, which was basically anyone who had committed murder, and those who had made any threats to Mr. Milford." She pointed to each pile as she spoke.

He had used a similar system. "I have four who made threats, how many did you get?"

"Two," Rose replied.

"That's not so bad." He was relieved there hadn't been too many; six was manageable. "We should check those offenders out before we go, see what they're up to these days. You get anything related to stars?"

"Nope." Rose shook her head, sending her red hair, which she had taken out of its ponytail a few hours ago, flying around her head. "Is the daughter sure they weren't there before? He does have grandkids—maybe he put the stars up for them."

"She said they weren't there when she was at the house yesterday. The killer did it. But why?" Jack had seen a lot of unusual things in his time as a cop, but these glow-in-the-dark children's star stickers were really baffling him.

"I have no idea, but I'm guessing once we figure that out, we'll know who the killer is," Rose answered.

"We should run the MO—see if it pops up any similar crimes," he suggested.

"We'll do it first thing in the morning," Rose agreed.

"I'll do it tonight, after I look into the parolees who made threats against Mr. Milford," Jack said. He had nowhere to go and nowhere to be tonight, so he may as well work.

"He supervised a lot of murderers and violent offenders—any one of them *could* have killed him." Rose was looking thoughtful. "But what would be the point? He's retired, and even if he wasn't, killing their parole officer would have only gotten them more time and ultimately, if they ever got back out, another parole officer. And most of the murders were drug or family violence motivated."

"Anyone who killed just for the sake of killing?" There had been no one in his pile of cases, but maybe his partner had come across something.

"Not yet, but we still have more files to go through tomorrow."

"Any of the neighbors report hearing or seeing anything suspicious last night or over the last few days?"

"They haven't finished interviewing everyone yet, but so far nothing," Rose replied. "Doorman says there were no unaccounted-for visitors last night. Just residents, a few family and friends, and a couple of delivery guys, all of whom left the building."

"Maybe he got in a window, then?" Jack pondered. The building was secure. One of the most secure he had ever seen. Breaking in wouldn't have been an easy task.

"Or he lives in the building," Rose put forward.

"Possible," he nodded slowly, "but super risky. It's like inviting the police to your back door. Still, we can't discount it."

Rose's phone pinged and she glanced down at it and then back up at him, a huge smile on her pretty face. "That's Steph, she says she got a few prints from the stickers, she's running it through

AFIS right now. Maybe we'll get a hit. Wrap this case up right away."

Jack could only hope. Before he could comment, his own phone beeped. He quickly skimmed the text. "Frankie says COD was exactly what we all thought. Once we finish with the parolees who made threats, we should go through anyone who killed with a knife."

"A knife to the heart seems personal," Rose mused. "Maybe we're off base with this parolee thing. Just because Tarek Milford used to work as a parole officer doesn't mean it has anything to do with his murder. Maybe we should be looking at a jilted lover."

"I don't know." He considered this. "I agree the knife to the heart is personal, but Jordanna said that he had been in poor health since his fall. Physically and mentally. She said he had been depressed. I can't see him being involved with someone. Besides, Jordanna didn't mention anything about a girlfriend."

"Could have been broken up for a while," Rose countered. "And maybe the daughter didn't know about it."

"Maybe." But he doubted it.

"Maybe it was a one-sided thing," Rose suggested.

"Like a stalker?"

"Could be."

"Okay," Jack acknowledged. "Worth looking into. We'll talk to Jordanna again in the morning. Hopefully she'll have calmed down by then and we'll be able to get more out of her. Maybe Tarek was involved in gambling or something else that might have gotten him killed."

"All right, I'm calling it a night," Rose announced as she stood and began to gather her things. "You should, too."

"I will," he assured her. "I just want to do a few things first and then make a list of everything we need to do tomorrow."

Rolling her eyes, she said, "You and your lists."

"I'm an organized guy," he protested.

"That's not all you are."

Playing dumb, he asks, "And what else am I?"

Rose rolled her eyes again; this time, because she knew he knew what she was talking about. "You're stubborn, that's what you are."

"If you say so." He kept his voice mild with extreme effort. Jack knew that Rose and his family cared about him, but he didn't like being hounded to do something he wasn't ready to do.

"I do say so," Rose snapped. Then in a calmer voice, she continued, "I really wish you would consider talking to someone."

Wanting to get her off his back, he responded, "I'll think about it."

"Okay."

He was surprised his partner had given up that easily. "Really?"

"That's progress, and the best I'm going to get out of you right now. Jack, you've been depressed for months now; it's time to do something about it before it gets any worse." Then she was gone.

Staring silently after her, Jack sighed. Maybe she was right; he did need someone. Just not a shrink someone.

He gave up on checking into parolees for tonight, but before he left, Jack made out a neat list of tasks to be accomplished the following morning. Completing the list, he surveyed it, wishing that everything in life could be so easily organized and worked through.

* * * * *

11:19 P.M.

He was very excited.

Stage one of the plan had gone perfectly.

Tarek Milford hadn't put up a fight. When he'd broken in, well technically not *broken* in since he had a key, one that he had acquired illegally, the man had done nothing. Nothing at all. Just simply sat there. Looking at him with dull, empty eyes. He hadn't begged for his life. He hadn't pleaded for mercy. He had just sat and waited.

Which, if he was honest, had taken a little of the fun out of killing the man.

Not that he minded too much.

He wasn't all that interested in killing.

Well, at least not indiscriminately.

There was one person he needed to see dead.

And that one was personal.

Hence the plan.

The knife to the heart had killed Tarek Milford instantly. It was also a symbolic gesture. *She* had pierced his heart, all but ripping it out with her callous actions. He would simply return the favor.

Then he'd had fun with the stars. The police would be baffled by them, of course. As they should be. The stars weren't there for them or for him or even for Tarek. The stars were a message. For her. And she would understand.

He wondered if she knew yet.

If she didn't, she would soon.

And she would be terrified.

The thought of that aroused him.

But he didn't have time to think about it right now.

Right now, he was on to stage two.

Stage two was going to be a little more fun.

Mainly because Judith Barclay was so hot. The twenty-year-old had big brown eyes, long brown hair, and an awesome figure.

He couldn't deny he was a little excited about what the evening ahead held.

Usually he wasn't a believer in taking a woman against her will.

Not that it was often an issue.

He was good-looking, charming, intelligent—he had no trouble getting women to willingly sleep with him. In fact, many threw themselves at him.

He only resorted to force when it was necessary.

And tonight, it was necessary.

He needed to send his message.

His recipient had thought she'd gotten away. She thought he had forgotten all about her, and about what she had done to him.

But he hadn't.

In eleven long years, he had thought about her every day. He had searched for her relentlessly. He couldn't allow her to get away.

His thorough searching had paid off. Finally, he had tracked her down. And now that he'd found her again, he was going to finish what he'd started.

Unfortunately for Judith Barclay, she was just a casualty of the plan.

Sliding his key into the lock, he quietly pushed the door open and tiptoed inside. The apartment was quiet. And dark. Judith no doubt already in bed.

Which definitely made things easier for him.

He checked the equipment in his bag. He had plastic zip ties, duct tape to cover her mouth, a ski mask, and a gun.

He had debated on whether or not to bring some cleaning supplies, to clean down both the apartment and the girl. In the end, he had decided it wasn't worth the trouble. He didn't have a criminal record, so even if the police got his prints or his DNA, it wouldn't help them find him. Sure, it would prove that he had committed the crimes if he got caught, but he wasn't planning on getting caught.

How could he?

There was nothing to connect him to his victims. They were simply a means to an end. And there would be no one to even notice when his intended victim ended up dead. In short, there was no reason for the police to ever even think of him, let alone suspect him.

Putting on the ski mask, he headed for the bedroom. No sense in hanging around any longer than he had to. He didn't want to tempt fate. Just because the police would never come looking for him didn't mean someone couldn't unintentionally stumble upon him.

In the bedroom, Judith was snoring away. Covers tossed to the side, dressed only in an oversized T-shirt. For a moment he just stood there, staring at her lithe body and drooling. Then he roused himself. No need to daydream; soon he'd be experiencing every inch of that perfect body.

With his gun in hand, he climbed onto the bed. One hand clamped over her mouth, the other held the gun at her temple.

At his touch, her eyes opened groggily. It took a moment but then she registered the feel of a hand on her face and the cold metal against her head. Her brown eyes grew wide as shock turned to horror.

"Don't be stupid, Judith," he warned.

Apparently, she wasn't stupid because she didn't try to fight him, but her entire body stiffened as though she had been turned into stone.

With quick, efficient movements, he yanked her hands behind her back and secured them with a zip tie, then added a strip of duct tape to her mouth. As he studied her terrified eyes, he wondered briefly whether he ought to say something. Offer an explanation. Or maybe some words of condolence. In the end, he decided against it. Really, there was nothing to say. She was simply a means to an end.

Instead, he pushed her shirt up over her head, revealing her naked body beneath. Then he removed his own clothes and got busy.

JULY 20TH

Running.

She was always running.

And yet no matter how much she ran it was never enough.

They always caught her.

It wasn't fair.

They knew the area better than she did.

Plus, they were better prepared.

Still, there wasn't time to complain. Or to contemplate the unfairness of it all. Or to cry. Or even to sleep. She couldn't remember the last time she'd slept. Or eaten. And all she'd had to drink since she got here was a couple of mouthfuls of water from a small stream she'd passed a while back.

She paused to catch her breath.

She knew she shouldn't.

It was too big a risk.

And yet, she couldn't run another step until she got her breath.

She crouched down behind a tree.

It was the best she could do for protection, and she knew it wouldn't do her any good. They'd find her. They always did.

She gave herself just a couple of minutes to pull herself together and then she was moving again.

She kept hoping that somehow, she could walk out of this.

Find a way to freedom.

But so far, she hadn't.

Maybe she was just running in circles.

She very easily could be.

She was hurt and tired and scared; she really had no idea where she was going.

What she did know was that she couldn't keep going much longer.

Her injuries were building up—both the ones that had been inflicted on her and the ones she had inadvertently inflicted on herself.

She ran again until her sides were burning, her chest heaving, her head spinning. Then she collapsed against a tree, letting it hold her up as she tried to calm her ragged breathing.

Again, just minutes later, she readied herself to keep moving.

Only this time her body wouldn't cooperate.

As she tried to take a step, her legs buckled beneath her.

Try as she might, she couldn't push back up to her feet.

Instead, she sunk down to the ground, resting her aching head on a bed of scratchy leaves. She needed to rest. Even just for a few minutes.

Closing her eyes, she prayed that they wouldn't find her for at least a little while.

She might not survive another round.

She wasn't doing so well.

She didn't think she could last much longer.

She roused herself once again when she heard the crunch of footsteps.

A hand clamped on her shoulder, and then rough hands were pulling her to her feet.

She thought about fighting back, but what was the point?

It hadn't done any good any other time.

They were simply bigger and stronger than she was.

"I missed you, Laura," a voice mocked.

And then she was screaming.

An ear-piercing scream.

The sound was so loud, she almost couldn't believe it was coming from her.

But it was, and it had snapped her awake.

She'd been dreaming, but her screams had traversed the line between the dream world and the real world.

It took Laura several minutes to calm herself enough to form any logical thoughts. She was ice cold and yet drenched in sweat. She was shaking uncontrollably. She hated nightmares. It had been a while since she'd had one. Months, maybe even a year or so. It was probably the police activity from yesterday that had gotten her subconscious thinking about it again.

This was exactly why she didn't watch the news or read the papers.

Even a single reminder about crime could get her imagination flying into overdrive.

Climbing from the bed, she headed for the kitchen to make herself some cocoa. It was about the only thing that could calm her when she got like this.

It reminded her of her childhood.

Of cozy winter nights when she, her parents, and her big sister would curl up on the couch. They'd collect all the blankets and quilts and pillows in the house and pile them all up in a huge snugly pile. Then they'd climb inside and drink cocoa and watch movies until she and her sister fell asleep.

Those days were long gone, though.

Her life wasn't like that anymore.

It had all changed in an instant.

She'd never realized before just how quickly things could change.

And now she wasn't sure if she could ever get her old life back.

She wasn't even sure she wanted it back.

Or deserved it back.

She took her mug of hot cocoa to the living room. There was no point in going back to bed. She wouldn't sleep. Probably wouldn't for days. And even if she did manage to fall into an exhausted haze, she would only have more nightmares.

Laura hated nightmares almost more than she had hated the original events.

Back then, she had hoped and prayed that things would end.

And miraculously, they had.

Only at the same time, they hadn't.

She still relived that horror in her dreams.

Which didn't seem fair.

It should be over by now.

Eleven long years and it should be over by now.

She so desperately needed it to be over.

Curling up in her favorite armchair by the window, she reached for her favorite book and opened it up. The blinds were closed and she contemplated opening them, but decided against it. She wasn't sure she could handle looking at the sky right now. The sky would just add to her stress. It was silly, she knew. The sky was everywhere. There was no point in being afraid of it. And yet, she was.

With a sigh at her own stupidity, she began to read.

And once again prayed that someday, someday soon, this real-life nightmare would truly end and she would be able to live again.

* * * * *

6:34 A.M.

"Why did we get this one?" Jack asked as he approached Rose.

Even though it was barely six-thirty in the morning, it was already nearly stiflingly hot. Summer had been brutal so far this year. They'd been getting hot weather since mid-March. Jack was a cold weather guy, not a hot weather one. He loved the snow. He had been skiing since he was three, had even done it competitively for a while in high school. Squirming uncomfortably in his shirt and cotton pants, he thought if he had to endure hot weather, he preferred to do it topless and by the pool.

"Because of the location," Rose replied, face tilted up to the sun. As much as he hated hot weather, his partner loved it.

"But it was a rape, not a murder," he protested.

"Yeah, but it happened at the same apartment building where someone was murdered just twenty-four hours ago," Rose reminded him.

"Could be a coincidence," he retorted. "Since when does someone go backward from murder to rape? Usually it's the other way around. Someone starts off as a peeping tom, then when they gain enough confidence, they move on to rape and then to murder. It doesn't usually go the other way."

"Well, given that someone was murdered at the same building, just one floor down from where a woman was raped, and both happened within the space of a day, Belinda wanted us to look into it. Check to see if there's any chance the two are connected."

Jack sighed but didn't bother offering another objection.

He couldn't really argue with the fact that it was a huge coincidence for a rape to occur in the same building, just one floor up from where a murder had occurred the day before.

However, coincidence was most likely all it was.

Theoretically, it was possible that if the man who had killed Tarek Milford was one of his ex-parolees and a sex offender that he had simply seen and latched on to Judith Barclay while he was in the building. Still, Jack couldn't help but feel that was unlikely.

"She been to the hospital?" he asked Rose as they walked into the lift.

"Yes, they did a rape kit," she replied.

"They discharged her already? What time did it happen?"

"She called it in around one."

"Hospital discharged her already?"

"She discharged herself, said she didn't have any injuries and there was no need for her to stay."

"Did she speak with someone from psych before she left?" Jack sincerely hoped she had—the longer you put off dealing with something the harder it got to deal with it at all.

"She refused." The look in Rose's green eyes indicated she had the same feelings on dealing with trauma as he did. "Maybe we can convince her otherwise, give her the names of some counselors."

"CSU already been here?"

"Stephanie just left," Rose answered.

"She get anything?"

"Fingerprints on the tape he put on her mouth. And apparently, he didn't use a condom, so there's DNA, too," Rose explained.

"Any hits in AFIS or CODIS?" Hopefully the automated fingerprint identification system or the combined DNA index system popped out a suspect.

"Nothing yet." Reaching Judith Barclay's apartment, Rose rapped on the door.

A minute later, it was thrown open by a pale young woman. Dazed brown eyes studied them for a moment, then cleared. "You're the cops, right? The hospital said that some cops would be by to talk to me."

"That's us," Jack confirmed with a smile. "I'm Detective Jack Xander and this is my partner, Rose Lace. Can we come in?"

With a defeated sigh, she shrugged and held the door farther open. "I guess. So long as you don't mind watching me pack."

"You staying somewhere else for a few days?" he asked as they followed her into the apartment.

"Nope." In the living room, she resumed what she had obviously been doing before their arrived—packing all her things into boxes. "I'm moving. I can't live here after what happened."

While he completely understood where Judith was coming from, it probably wasn't the best idea to be making major life decisions on the back of a major trauma. He was definitely going to push her on seeking help before they left. "Do you have someone you can stay with?" She shouldn't be alone right now.

"My sister. I called her from the hospital, she said I can stay with her as long as I need to." Judith proceeded to throw things into boxes.

Getting answers out of her while she was distracted wasn't going to work. "Ms. Barclay," he kept his voice gentle, "why don't you sit?"

"I need to keep moving," she protested.

"I understand, but we want to catch this guy, so we need you focused."

Judith continued to throw books and ornaments into boxes for another minute before she reluctantly paused. Then with a weary shrug, she gestured at the three sofas grouped together around the TV. "Let's get this over with."

"Did you hear about what happened downstairs?" Jack asked, wanting to search for any possible connections as well as ease into what had happened to her last night.

Nodding slowly, she replied, "Not until last night though. The cops who showed up when I called 911 mentioned it."

"You didn't see all the cops and forensic techs?"

"I wasn't home that night. Sometimes I stay over at my sister's when I work late, so I didn't get home until around eight last night," Judith explained. "Do you know who hurt Mr. Milford?"

"No, I'm sorry. But we have some leads and some forensics; so hopefully, we will soon," he assured the young woman. If Judith Barclay hadn't even been home when Tarek Milford had been murdered, then it wasn't very likely that whoever had attacked her last night was the same person who had killed Tarek. Veering the conversation back toward her assault, he asked, "Did you notice anything off when you got home last night?"

Judith gave a single shake of her head.

"Are you sure?" Jack pushed. "Anything, no matter how small, could be important."

Looking overwhelmed now, Judith gave her head another shake.

He decided to walk her though it. "Did you notice anyone following you home?"

"No."

"Anyone watching you when you came inside?"

"No, I parked in the parking lot under the building and then came up in the lift, I didn't see anyone at all."

"What about when you got to your floor? Did you notice anyone?"

"No."

"Was your door locked?"

"Yes."

"When you got inside your apartment, did anything seem off?"

"No, everything was the same as usual." Her brown eyes were looking back at him helplessly.

"What's the first thing you remember about your attack?" he asked gently.

She swiped at the tears that were welling up in her eyes. "A hand on my mouth and something cold against my head," she raised a hand and rubbed at her temple as she spoke. "At first I thought I was just dreaming. But then I realized it wasn't a nightmare; it was real. There really was a man in my bedroom. He was on the bed. On top of me. I wanted to scream, to fight him, but I realized the cold thing at my head was a gun. I was scared he would shoot me if I fought him."

"You did the right thing, Judith," he assured the girl. She would blame herself, it was all but inevitable, despite the fact that there was nothing she could have done to prevent what had happened from happening.

The look she shot him indicated she didn't believe him.

"What happened next?"

She drew in a shuddering breath before continuing. "He told me not to be stupid."

"Did you recognize his voice?"

"I don't know. I was too scared."

"Okay. Keep going, you're doing great." He offered her another encouraging smile.

"He tied my hands behind my back with a plastic tie. Then he put some tape on my mouth. Next, he pulled my T-shirt up, and he…" She paused and licked her lips. "… he raped me." Tears spilled out, trickling down her cheeks. "I didn't fight him. I just laid there."

He placed a comforting hand on the girl's shoulder. "It wasn't your fault, Judith. He had a gun. You did what you had to do to survive."

"I feel so dirty," she cried. "As soon as I came home, I got in the shower, but it didn't help." Sobbing in earnest now, she threw herself against him.

Feeling awkward, Jack held the girl as she cried. He may have some knack for eliciting trust from victims of crime, but that didn't mean he felt comfortable around traumatized people. He didn't. He felt completely out of his element. He wanted to palm her off onto a professional who knew what to say and do to help her while he focused on finding the man who had hurt her. Still, he did what had to be done. "Judith, have you told your family what happened?"

The head on his shoulder shook in the negative.

"Not even your sister?"

"I told her I was scared to stay here after the murder," her muffled voice explained.

"I think you need to tell them. You're going to need their support to get through this." As he said the words, which he truly meant, Jack couldn't help but feel like a hypocrite all over again. He hadn't told his family when he'd gone through a traumatic experience. He had tried to struggle through it on his own. He was *still* trying to struggle through it on his own—three years later.

"I don't know," Judith murmured. "I'm ashamed."

"There's nothing for you to be ashamed about," he told her firmly. "And your family would want to know. They would want to be there for you." Jack knew that if his own family ever found out what had happened to him, they would be extremely hurt that he hadn't told them.

"Yeah, maybe you're right." Judith sat herself back up and looked apologetically at the wet stain on his shirt. "Sorry about crying all over you."

"Nothing to be sorry about," he assured her. "You may also want to consider talking with a professional. The hospital said you didn't want to wait to talk with anyone there, but maybe we could give you the names of some people we know who work with victims of sexual assault."

Indecision battled in her eyes, but her common sense obviously won out because she nodded. "Yeah, okay."

"Good, we'll give you some names and numbers before we leave. Judith, can you think of anyone who would want to hurt you?"

She thought about this for barely a few seconds before her brown eyes grew wide as if realizing something for the first time. "He knew my name. When he told me not to be stupid, he used my name."

"So, he knows you. Did you get a look at his face?"

"No, he wore a ski mask."

"And you're sure you didn't recognize his voice?" Unless this was a stalker who had fixated on her over some minimal or imagined contact, Judith most likely knew her attacker.

"I don't know, like I said, I was scared."

"Is there anyone you know who might want to hurt you?" Jack asked again. Judith was holding something back; he was sure of it.

Chewing on her lower lip, her hands fidgeted nervously with the edges of the white bandages circling her wrists, covering the cuts she'd gotten from where the zip ties had gouged her flesh. "I was dating this guy about a year ago. He was cute and smart, and I thought he might be the one. Only, I wasn't ready to sleep with him yet. My freshman year of college, I slept around a bit. I wasn't proud of it. I promised myself I would wait until I was sure that the next guy I slept with was the one. But Harry got mad. He tried to pressure me, but the more he did, the more I knew I didn't want to sleep with him. Then one night, he turned violent. He knocked me around and tried to force me. I fought him, and I screamed. Mr. Milford from downstairs heard me. He came and he saved me."

He glanced at Rose, whose excited eyes told him she was thinking the same thing he was. "So, your ex saw Mr. Milford?"

"Uh-huh," Judith answered, brushing at fresh tears. "Mr. Milford knocked down my door. When he came in, Harry had me on the bed. Mr. Milford threw him off me. Harry tried to hit him, but Mr. Milford was tough. He blocked the punch and Harry just ran."

So, it was possible that the two cases were related after all. If Judith's ex had come back to finish what he started that night, he could have seen it as a two for one. Get what he wanted out of Judith and kill Tarek Milford for intervening. "Have you seen Harry since that night?"

"No."

"Did you report it?"

Cheeks reddening, she said, "No. I was embarrassed. And Harry had been drinking that night. And he didn't do much more than hit me a few times; all I had were some bruises. I just wanted to forget about it and move on. I should have, though. I just didn't think he'd come back. I thought he'd just leave me alone. And he did. I haven't seen or heard from him since, and it's been almost year. Mr. Milford told me I should report it, I should have listened to him."

"Do you think it could have been Harry who assaulted you last night?"

"It could have been. I never saw his face, but the man was the right size." Growing agitated, she raised her voice. "Do you think it was Harry who killed Mr. Milford? Because he stopped Harry from assaulting me that night?"

There was no point in lying to the girl. If it did turn out to be Harry who raped her and killed her neighbor, then she was going to find out at some point anyway. "Maybe," he answered gently.

She dropped her head to her hands. "This is all my fault."

"No, it's not," he told her firmly.

"If I had listened to Mr. Milford, then he might still be alive." Judith was crying again.

"There's no way to know that," he reminded her gently. "If Harry was determined to finish what he'd started, then there could have been no stopping him. Do you have Harry's contact information?"

Giving a shaky nod, she rattled off an address and phone number, which Rose jotted down.

"If Harry is the man who did this, we're going to get him, Judith," Jack promised. "We have DNA from your assault and fingerprints from Mr. Milford's apartment. If they match Harry's, then he's going to go to jail for a long time."

* * * * *

10:11 A.M.

"Think it's him?" Rose asked her partner as they watched the man in the interview room.

"I hope it's him," Jack replied. "If it's him, then this is over. No one else is going to get hurt. At least no one is going to get hurt by this guy," he added wearily.

Casting her partner a covert glance, Rose was worried about him. Had been for a while now. Everyone who knew him knew that something had changed a few years ago. He'd gone away on a vacation and come back different. But the last few months it had gotten worse. Rose knew that he'd been feeling lonely. Seeing both his brothers with families of their own now was leaving him feeling left out. And yet, no matter how many times she tried to set him up with someone, he always refused. She hoped he took his own advice and opened up to his family and friends and let them in—let them help him with whatever it was that had happened.

As much as Jack seemingly longed to be in a committed relationship, she, on the other hand, was happily single. She dated casually, sporadically, whenever she felt like it, or when she crossed paths with a guy who was too hot to pass up. However, that was enough for her. She wasn't interested in marriage at this stage in her life. She was only thirty-five and she had spent most of her life caring for her disabled mother. Now, she just wanted to get out there and enjoy life without the weight of responsibility hanging around her neck.

"So, you ready to go in?" Jack asked.

"Yep." Rose had already formed her mental list of questions she wanted to ask. While Jack was always the one to interview victims and witnesses, she was always the one to interview suspects. Her partner was amazing with people who had suffered a trauma. She'd seen plenty of cops conduct interviews, and she herself had done it hundreds of time. None of them seemed to say or do anything differently than what Jack did, but they never seemed to manage to connect in the same way he could. He seemed to be able to get victims to trust him in a way few others could.

Maybe it was his demeanor. Jack oozed calm, strong confidence. He was a big guy, over six feet tall, well-muscled, good-looking. So good-looking, in fact, that if they weren't partners and friends, then Rose would have him in bed in an instant. He had bright blue eyes, dimples, and blond hair that he kept cut really short.

He gave out an air of having everything under control and taking control of every situation, making victims and witnesses feel confident in his hands. He was a little bossy, too. She knew he thought he was only bossy with his younger brothers, but his bossiness often seeped over into other aspects of his life, like work. When they'd first become partners, it used to infuriate her, especially since she was older and had been a cop longer. But these days, she just let it wash over her.

Getting herself in the zone, she studied Harry Kinkirk through the one-way glass. To look at, he wasn't much. Tall and beanpole thin, he looked young, much younger than his twenty-four years—he could easily still pass as a teenager. His light brown eyes were wide and innocent; his brown hair worn a little too long and shaggy. Both belied the violent temper lurking inside him.

He hadn't put up a fight when they'd gone to his apartment. In fact, he had remained cool and collected when they informed him that they needed to speak with him and that they would be conducting their interview at the station. However, the flash of pure rage that had flashed through his eyes at the mention of Judith Barclay had revealed a glimpse of the real Harry Kinkirk.

Now he was sitting, calm and composed, and waiting for them in an interview room. He had declined to have a lawyer present during questioning, so they were free to start whenever they liked. Rose had elected to make him sit and squirm for a while before they began. Although Harry didn't look like he'd been doing much squirming.

She stepped into the room. "Good morning, Mr. Kinkirk; sorry to keep you waiting." Rose kept her voice just shy of insincere.

"No problem." Harry smiled congenially, with a small tilt of one eyebrow to indicate he knew perfectly well they had kept him waiting so long on purpose.

"Thanks for agreeing to come down here and answer some questions," she continued, taking a seat at the table and arranging her papers into a neat pile.

"Didn't seem like I had a choice," Harry shot back. "You said this had something to do with Judith?"

"Judith was attacked in her home last night," Rose told him.

"Yeah, so?" Harry looked bored, but the hint of anger was back in his eyes. He clearly still had unresolved anger issues regarding his ex.

"She was raped," Rose added.

"Yeah, so?"

"So, she told us an interesting story about you."

The lid broke off the bottle of his emotions and fury came bubbling out. "She's a liar," he growled. "Whatever she told you is just lies."

"And what is it exactly that you think she told us?"

"That several months back I tried to force her to have sex." Harry's features had contorted from schoolboy innocent to pure evil.

"You didn't try to force her to have sex?" Rose asked, raising a disbelieving eyebrow.

"No, I didn't," Harry spat out. "She was a tease. I knew her reputation. She slept with anyone, everyone. Then she decides to go all prude-like virgin on me? Uh-uh, I wasn't having none of that. She was playing games. She wanted it. I know she did."

"You hit her."

He shrugged disinterestedly. "I may have had a few too many drinks that night. I didn't like her playing games. I was only with her because I'd heard how good she was in bed. I put in my time. Dated her for a few weeks. Took her out to fancy restaurants, bought her flowers, made nice with her friends. I did my part; she was the one that wouldn't put out for what she owed me. That made me mad." He turned to Jack as though she wasn't getting it simply because she was a woman. "You know what I'm saying, right? Some girls, you do everything for them and then they hold back. It's not right. They shouldn't be allowed to play games and get away with it."

The glare Jack shot Harry's way was so cold, the young man actually shivered.

"She shouldn't be a tease," Harry repeated sullenly.

"So, you went back last night to collect what you believed she owed you," Rose continued. "You broke into her apartment and raped her."

"No. I didn't," Harry protested.

"Oh, come on, Harry." Rose gave him a disappointed frown. "You were angry that she wouldn't have sex with you. You tried to rape her once before, only you got interrupted. This time, Judith wasn't so lucky. This time there was no one to save her."

"I didn't rape Judith." Harry's face went dark with anger as he over enunciated each word.

"Of course, you did. You got your revenge on her last night, and the night before that, you got your revenge on Tarek Milford for stopping your first rape attempt."

"No, I did—wait," Harry looked confused. "Who's Tarek Milford?"

"He's Judith's downstairs neighbor. He's the man who stopped you that night. You were angry with him. Wanted revenge on him too. So, you killed him."

His face paled. "I didn't kill anyone."

"Yes, you did," Rose persisted. "You raped Judith and you killed Tarek Milford because you were angry with them."

"Really, I swear I didn't." All traces of anger were gone from his face and voice, replaced by fear. "I didn't rape Judith and I didn't kill anybody. Look, maybe I would have forced her to have sex that night. But I really thought she wanted to. I thought she was just playing games. Playing hard to get or something. It made me mad. But I swear I didn't go to her place last night and I certainly didn't kill anybody. Besides, I couldn't have done it. I have an alibi."

"An alibi?" Rose raised a skeptical brow.

"Yeah, an alibi. I have a new girl. Unlike Judith, she is totally into me in every way. We were together last night. All night. She didn't leave until like seven or eight this morning."

"We're going to need to confirm that with her," Rose informed him.

"I got no problem with that. How many times do I have to tell you that I didn't do anything to Judith or that man? I didn't rape anybody. I didn't kill anybody. I didn't do anything," Harry all but shouted at them.

She was beginning to doubt that Harry Kinkirk was their rapist and killer. He had been upfront about the night he had first assaulted Judith Barclay and yet he was vehemently denying raping her and killing her neighbor. "Then prove it to us. Give us a DNA sample and your fingerprints so we can compare them to what we found at the crime scenes."

His brow furrowed as though they were trying to trick him. "I've been to Judith's apartment tons of times. I'm sure my fingerprints are going to be there. My DNA, too."

"But your fingerprints won't be on the tape that was put over Judith's mouth. And your DNA won't have been found inside her," Rose reminded him. "And you said that you didn't know Tarek Milford was the man who stopped you from attacking Judith, so your fingerprints shouldn't turn up in his apartment."

"Sure, fine, whatever. You can take my fingerprints and my DNA," Harry agreed.

"You're awfully adamant that you didn't commit these crimes," Jack spoke up. "But did you get a friend to do it instead?"

"Why would I do that?" Harry threw him an irritated glare.

"Maybe you knew that Judith would talk, tell us all about the first time you tried to sexually assault her and implicate you as her attacker. So, maybe you thought it would be safer to get a friend to do your dirty work for you. Then you get your revenge but you won't go down for the crimes."

"Why would I go to all that trouble?"

"Who knows?" Jack shrugged. "Who knows why criminals do the things they do."

"Well I'm not a criminal," Harry retorted sulkily.

He arched a blond brow. "You beat up a woman and tried to rape her; that makes you a criminal in my books," Jack replied frostily.

"Let me say it again." Harry was looking frustrated now. "I did not rape Judith. I did not kill Tarek Milford. I did not ask a friend to rape Judith. I did not ask a friend to kill Tarek Milford. I don't even know anyone who would rape or murder someone just because I asked them to. Is that clear enough for you?"

A glance at Jack confirmed her partner agreed with her; Harry Kinkirk was not their guy. "Okay," Rose nodded slowly, "Let's say we believe you, which we won't until we get your fingerprints and DNA sample and find they're not a match to what we have," she warned. "If you're not the guy we're looking for, do you know anyone who might want to hurt Judith?"

"No, I mean yes, or maybe, I don't know." Harry looked confused and overwhelmed now. "I guess not, but I told you she slept around a lot, she had a reputation. That's the only reason I was dating her. Maybe someone didn't like her giving it up to so many guys."

"So, that's a no, you can't think of anyone who would want to hurt her?" Rose confirmed dryly. She was getting tired of Harry's attitude.

"I suppose it's a no," he somewhat reluctantly agreed.

"No one hanging around her, paying her an inordinate amount of attention, following her, sending her email or texts or calling her?" Rose prodded.

"Not that I know of."

Rose suppressed a sigh. They were back to square one. Harry Kinkirk didn't rape Judith Barclay or murder Tarek Milford. Forensics would confirm it, but she already knew it wasn't him. So, they were right back where they started. And they didn't even know if the two cases were related.

* * * * *

FOUR

6:00 P.M.

Jack's eyes were tired. Too many hours reading files and staring at a computer screen.

At least they'd made good progress today.

Well, maybe not *good* progress.

Really, they hadn't made any progress at all. But they had managed to clear almost all of Tarek Milford's old parolees. In the three years since he had retired, most of his old cases had either died or were back in prison. A few had managed to fix up their lives. And some were in between prison stints. So far, none of them seemed to be panning out as a viable suspect in Tarek Milford's murder.

They had also gone back and spoken to Jordanna Milford again. She had been calmer, and getting information out of her had been easier. She had been adamant that there were no crazy ex-girlfriends; in fact, she had said that there were no exes at all. Apparently, Tarek hadn't dated anyone since his wife had died nearly seventeen years ago. Jack wasn't quite sure that was true, but a search of Tarek' apartment hadn't turned up any evidence of any old girlfriends.

Which meant they might be looking at something random.

And that was worrying.

Anyone who would randomly kill a stranger wasn't going to stop. He was going to keep killing.

A serial killer was the last thing Jack wanted to be dealing with right now.

"All right, Frankie, you start," Lieutenant Belinda Jersey announced, turning her dark brown eyes to the medical examiner.

Frankie nodded. "Like I already told Rose and Jack, cause of death was exsanguination from a single knife wound to the heart."

"Seems personal," Belinda observed.

"We were thinking that," Jack told his boss. "Only, as far as we know, there are no jealous exes, and the guy was in an accident several months ago—*he never physically recovered and became depressed.*"

Belinda nodded once, then reverted her attention to Frankie.

"No defensive wounds anywhere on his body," the ME continued. "In fact, the only wound was the one to his heart."

"Might have gotten him by surprise," Rose suggested.

"Or threatened him," Belinda added.

"Or maybe he was depressed and ready to die and he just didn't put up a fight," Jack put forward. From Tarek's daughter's account of her father's mental well-being since his accident, Jack wouldn't have been surprised at all if the man had simply quietly accepted his fate and not fought back when he came face-to-face with his killer.

"Maybe," Belinda acknowledged. "Stephanie, forensics?"

"As you know, we got great fingerprints from the stars on the ceiling of the Milford apartment," the crime scene tech began. "So far, I haven't gotten any hits in AFIS."

"What about the DNA and fingerprints from the Barclay scene?" Belinda demanded.

"Same," Stephanie replied. "No hits in AFIS or CODIS."

"Didn't we have a suspect?" Belinda directed this question to Jack and Rose.

"We did, but we cut him loose," Rose explained. "He had an alibi that checked out for last night."

"Any alibi for the night of the Milford murder?" Belinda asked.

"Yep," Jack nodded. "He has a new girlfriend. They spend a lot of time together. Are we still working the two crimes as related, just because they happened at the same building?"

"Your crimes *are* related," Stephanie inserted. "I ran the prints from the stars at the Milford apartment with the print from the duct tape from the Barclay apartment and they were a match."

"And we're sure it wasn't the Kinkirk kid?" Belinda persisted. "Maybe he faked his alibi. Got his girlfriend to lie for him to get him off the hook?"

"Nope," Stephanie answered. "I ran his prints and his DNA against our samples from the crime scenes, and neither were a match. Harry Kinkirk is not your guy."

"But the same guy committed both the murder and the rape?" Belinda looked baffled.

"That's what the forensics say," Stephanie reconfirmed.

Jack hadn't really expected the forensics to prove that the same person who had killed Tarek had also raped Judith. When they thought it could be Judith's ex, he had considered it a possibility given how Tarek Milford had played into their relationship. But as soon as they had ruled him out, in Jack's mind, the two cases had once again separated. "I don't get what kind of killer starts with murder and then works backward to rape," Jack pondered aloud.

"It's definitely not the norm," Belinda agreed. "But maybe it's not about what he does to the victim but the victim themselves. Maybe he reacts to them based on his interaction with them. He sees Judith Barclay somewhere, she's a pretty young woman, he's attracted to her, he wants her, so he follows her home and rapes her. He sees Tarek Milford somewhere, perhaps they have an altercation of some kind, he's angry with him, and decides to kill him."

"I guess." It was a possibility, Jack acknowledged. "But Tarek hadn't been out in months, so this wasn't some spur of the moment thing. If he picked those victims for a reason then he's been planning this for months."

"We are going to have to go through their lives with a fine-tooth comb," Rose said. "Starting with workers and residents from the apartment building. See if anyone there has a grudge against both of them. Then see whether their lives intersect anywhere else. Someone has come into contact with both of them somewhere—once we find out where he saw them and how he fixated on them, then we'll find him."

"Tomorrow, though," Belinda announced, getting to her feet.

"Now everyone goes home, gets some rest and comes back fresh tomorrow. We want to find this guy before anyone else winds up hurt."

* * * * *

8:13 P.M.

She was on edge.

Laura couldn't deny it.

She had been pacing her apartment all day. Unable to settle at anything. She didn't even think she'd had anything to eat. Every time she tried to do something, she got all shaky and nervous and ended up abandoning the task to pace. Moving was the only thing that helped to calm her when she was stressed. And so, she paced. She had probably covered a couple of miles already today just by walking backward and forward across her apartment.

The police had been here again this morning. That made two days in a row. Two days in a row that something bad had happened in her quiet apartment building. At least, it was supposed to be quiet here. That was why she had originally chosen the building. And in the ten years she had lived here, it *had* been quiet.

Only now that seemed to be over.

A murder and a rape.

That's what had happened just a few floors away from where she lived.

Earlier today, Laura had given in to the need to know what was happening around her and had called downstairs and spoken with one of the doormen. She had lucked out and her favorite one was working. Connor was one of the few people who Laura still spoke to. He didn't know what had happened to her, but he knew that she was agoraphobic. Connor often helped her out, accepting deliveries for her so she didn't have to deal with the deliverymen.

He even left her things outside her door so she didn't have to speak to him in person. Connor knew that she couldn't cope with talking to people face-to-face.

Murder and rape.

Here.

In what was supposed to be her safe place.

What if something else happened here?

Two nights, two crimes—were they related?

Did it really make a difference?

Laura wasn't so naïve as to think that there was zero crime here in her building, but these weren't just a burglary or break and enter. These were major crimes. The worst crimes. And they had happened just a couple of floors from where she lived.

Should she move?

She had been debating it ever since Connor had told her what all the police activity had been about.

But would moving really be the answer?

Wherever she moved could be just the same as here.

Crime was everywhere. Laura knew that all too well.

Even if she decided to move, could she really handle it?

The truth was, she really didn't think she could.

Ten years of living alone. Never seeing anyone. Never talking to anyone other than Connor the doorman, and ironically, her patients. Well, not technically patients. She worked as a counselor for a helpline for kids. Before her life had fallen apart, Laura had been studying to be a psychologist. She had wanted to help kids who were in trouble, and even after everything that had happened to her, she had found a way to do it. She enjoyed it. It made her feel like she was making a difference in people's lives. Even if she'd let her own life get messed up beyond repair, she was helping others from making the same mistakes that she had.

But talking to troubled kids on the phone was not the same as talking to people face-to-face. And to move would involve a lot of talking. She would have to find a suitable apartment. She would have to sign a lease. She would have to hire movers. She would have to explain to another doorman that she couldn't go outdoors and ask him to handle all her deliveries.

And worst of all, she would actually have to go outdoors.

That scared her more than anything else.

She knew she couldn't handle that.

Her apartment could be falling down around her, and she still wouldn't be able to make herself walk out her front door.

So, she was stuck here.

She would just have to hope that the spate of violent crimes in the building was over.

Maybe there was a simple explanation for them, anyway.

Maybe, as much as she hated to even think it, the victims had in some way deserved what had happened to them. Maybe they weren't good people. Maybe they had gotten themselves mixed up in something dangerous. Maybe they hadn't just been innocently going about their lives when tragedy had struck.

Maybe they weren't like her.

She had never even met the men who had hurt her. She hadn't done anything to them to warrant what they had done to her.

They had hurt her simply because they had wanted to. They hadn't cared about the consequences for her or themselves.

What they had done to her had changed her entire life.

It had cost her everything.

And now, she didn't know how to get her life back. Didn't even know if she wanted it back.

There was another solution to her living situation.

She could always go home.

Home.

The word sounded foreign to her now. For ten years, this apartment had been her home. It had been her sanctuary. Her safety net. Because she had pushed away what should have been her real safety net.

She had pushed away her family.

44

They had been by her side throughout her stay in the hospital.

They had been by her side throughout those first days and weeks.

They had been by her side throughout the police interviews and the psychiatrist visits, as she told her story over and over again so many times that it began to feel like nothing more than a story, something that had happened to someone else.

They had been by her side throughout the nightmares and the flashbacks and the panic attacks.

They had been by her side throughout the trial.

And then she had simply left.

The day the guilty verdict came in, she had packed up the few personal belongings that she couldn't live without and rented this apartment. She hadn't told her family where she was going. She hadn't given them her address. She hadn't even told them goodbye.

Sometimes she wondered if they still thought about her.

Were they angry with her for disappearing?

Were they worried about her?

Did they think she was still alive, or did they think that she had committed suicide?

Suicide had been on her mind a lot those first horrible days. She had been in so much pain, physically and emotionally, that she had thought it would crush her. And yet, she had battled through it.

Because of her family.

They had given her strength when she hadn't had any of her own.

They had been there for her unconditionally.

And yet, she had run.

Run and hidden.

She just couldn't face being around people.

She hated herself, and she didn't want to be with people who didn't hate her, too.

She hadn't deserved her family's love and support.

She hadn't wanted it, either.

She had just wanted to be alone.

And alone was what she was now. Was what she would always be.

That didn't stop her from wondering about them, though. Wondering what her big sister was up to these days. Mary would be thirty-four years old now. Was her sister married? Did she have kids? And what about her parents? They would be in their early sixties now. Were they still keeping good health or were they starting to develop some of the problems that came with age?

Laura missed them. Sometimes so much, she physically ached with it.

Maybe she should reach out to them. Give them a call. Let them know that she was okay. Apologize for leaving the way she had. Ask them to let her come home. Ask them to take care of her again because she wasn't doing a very good job of taking care of herself.

Tears had welled up in her eyes without her even realizing it, and as she reached for her phone they began to trickle down her cheeks.

She should do it.

Call.

Even if they were angry with her, they would still be happy to hear from her. Wouldn't they?

Her finger hovered over the keypad.

Would they be happy to hear from her?

Doubt began to creep into Laura's mind. Just like it did every time she considered reaching out to her family.

She hadn't deserved their love and support back then, and she certainly didn't deserve it now.

She had made her choices. And now she had to live with them.

Slowly, she put the phone back down.

She wouldn't call them. She'd never call them. Somehow, no

matter how much she wanted to, she just couldn't.

Instead, she all but ran to her bedroom, threw back the covers and crawled into bed, then drew them back over her head.

Laura hated herself. She hated her life. She hated that she had nothing solid to hold on to. Nothing solid to keep her grounded when fear had her feeling like she was floating alone in a vast ocean.

Curling herself into a tight little ball, Laura cried.

*　*　*　*　*

9:21 P.M.

"Hey, Paige." Jack grinned at her as he opened his front door.

"Hi, Jack." She smiled back.

He kissed her cheek, then held her by the shoulders, examining her. "I haven't seen you in a while; you're looking good."

"Thanks." Paige was pleased that she was finally in a place where she was feeling good and looking good. It had been a *long* six months.

"Hi, Elias." Jack shook her husband's hand.

"Hey, Jack," Elias returned.

"Ryan said he invited you, but he wasn't sure that you would come." Jack held the door farther open for them to enter. "I'm so glad you did."

The reason her partner hadn't known whether she would come for dinner with their friends was because she had turned down a lot of invitations the last few months. At first it was because she just wasn't physically up to going out. And then it was because she wasn't emotionally up to going out. The attack that had almost killed her had left her completely shaken up.

Physically, she was finally pretty much back to where she'd been before her assault, but it had been a long road getting there. Her assailant had beaten her with a baseball bat, leaving her with serious head injuries, a broken arm, broken ribs, a punctured lung, and internal bleeding in her abdomen. She had been in a coma for eight days before finally waking up in the ICU. It had taken a while for her body to regain its strength, but lots of physical therapy had paid off, and she was now ready to go back to work the beginning of next month.

Emotionally, things had been a whole other board game. Paige was much better at dealing with physical pain than she was with emotional pain. An incident with her mother's stalker when she was a teenager had left her sensitive to stalkers. When someone had begun stalking her shortly before her attack, it had brought up some old memories. That had left her on edge. And that had led her to being distracted and subsequently assaulted. The knowledge that the person who had tried to kill her was still out there was terrifying. It had led to hypervigilance, trouble sleeping, and a pressing tiredness that made getting through each day difficult.

But by far the biggest thing she had had to deal with following her attack was learning that she would never be able to have children of her own. Still in her early thirties, that was a blow. Especially since she knew how much her husband wanted kids. Elias had assured her repeatedly that he didn't care–that he was just glad he hadn't lost her. That they could adopt when she was in a place where she was ready to do that. But it didn't change how she felt. She was devastated about it, both for herself and for her husband.

Other than Elias, the only other person who knew about her not being able to have children was Ryan. Her partner had been a rock for her these last six months. She knew that he felt guilty about letting her get attacked in the first place, even though it was obviously not his fault.

It had been her fault. She'd known that she shouldn't have been at work that day. She hadn't been sleeping, she hadn't been eating, and she'd been injured just a couple of days before. She had been distracted. And that distraction had almost cost her her life.

Ryan had also been the one to find her.

Actually, he had saved her life.

He had arrived in the middle of her attack and his arrival had spooked her attacker who had run away. Her doctors had told her that if she had received just a couple more blows, then she might not have survived.

The fact that her stalker was still out there was as upsetting for Ryan and his fiancée, Sofia, as it was for her. The man who had stalked her had only done so because he perceived her to be a threat to Sofia, who he had been stalking for the last couple of years. He had decided that she was cheating with Ryan, and as such would cause pain to Sofia, so he had decided to take her out of the equation.

Thankfully for all of them, the stalker had been laying low the last six months. Since her attack, he hadn't made further contact with either her or Sofia. But knowing he was out there was awful. And the fact that he knew where they lived and worked was terrifying. She wanted him caught, but they didn't even know who he was. Until he was identified and apprehended, she was never going to be able to truly move on.

"Paige, you came." Ryan stood and gave her a hug when they entered the kitchen.

"I told you I would," she grumbled, dropping into the chair he held out for her.

"No, you told me you'd think about it," Ryan corrected. "Hey, Elias, how's it going?"

"Things are going okay, although I'm not ready for Paige to go back to work next month." Elias cast her a concerned glance.

"Well, I'm going back, Elias," she told him. They'd argued about it numerous times already. Paige knew that her husband had been truly terrified that he was going to lose her. When she had finally awakened in the hospital, the first thing she had seen was

Elias' worried, drawn, haggard face. The relief that had washed over him when he'd seen her awake had communicated just how scared he'd been that she would never wake up. When she had announced a few weeks ago that she was going back to work, he had protested vehemently. Elias didn't like to let her out of his sight these days, let alone have her go back to work where she had been so violently attacked.

Unfortunately for her husband, Paige fully intended to go back to work. She didn't want to make Elias angry and she didn't want to worry him unnecessarily, but she needed to work. She couldn't spend any more time just sitting around. She was bored, and when she was bored, her mind wandered, and when her mind wandered it usually went to a bad place. And she had already spent enough time in that bad place; she didn't want to be in it ever again. Getting back to work would help her recovery. She was literally counting the hours until she returned.

"Don't worry, Elias; I'll look after her," Ryan assured her husband.

"I don't need you to look after me," Paige shot back.

"If you say so." Ryan grinned.

Rolling her eyes at him, Paige was about to make a retort when Sofia and Rose came bustling into the room.

"I got her back to sleep ... Paige." Sofia's pretty face lit up into a smile when she caught sight of her. "Ryan said he wasn't sure you'd come."

"Hey, Sofia," she returned the other woman's hug. "I told Ryan I would come, so I don't know why he was telling everyone he didn't know whether I would or not."

"No, you didn't." Jack's partner Rose also gave her a hug. "When I called you to see if you were coming to dinner, you said you hadn't decided."

Getting irritated now, "I don't see why you're all making such a big deal about dinner. We've had dinner together before and it was never such a big deal."

"Because we're worried about you," Ryan replied calmly. "You hardly ever go out these days."

Frustration fading away, Paige knew she was lucky to have friends who cared about her. "Because it's too stressful," she murmured tiredly. As a cop, she had always been aware of her surroundings, but this hypervigilance was exhausting.

"I know, honey." Rose wrapped an arm around her shoulders and squeezed. "It'll get better with time." She and Rose had been friends for a long time now. After Ryan, she considered Rose her closest friend. Rose had even been maid of honor at her wedding. She wouldn't have made it through the last few months without her friend. Rose had visited her every day while she was in the hospital, and pretty much every day after she was finally released. No matter how many cases she was handling, and how busy her days had been, Rose had always made time for her. Often bringing cases with her for them to discuss because she knew that Paige needed to do something to keep her mind off what she'd been through.

"Yeah, I know." Paige offered her friends a watery smile. "Was that Sophie you were putting down?" she asked, changing the subject from herself to Ryan and Sofia's baby daughter. Technically, the baby was Sofia's aunt, but with no other family to raise her, she and Ryan had taken the child on and were raising her as their own.

"Yeah, she's teething." Ryan smiled fondly. His little girl already had him wrapped around her little finger.

"I bet she's getting big; I haven't seen her in a couple of weeks." Paige knew she couldn't keep the hint of regret out of her voice. It still hadn't really sunk in that she was never going to get to have her own children. And yet, Sophie wasn't biologically Ryan and Sofia's and they didn't love her any less. For the first time since she'd found out she would never get pregnant, the idea of adoption didn't seem so bad. She wasn't ready for it yet, but maybe one day.

"Why don't you come and have lunch with me and Annabelle tomorrow?" Sofia suggested. "You can catch up with us and Sophie."

Paige was all set to politely decline, but the look in Sofia's silvery grey eyes stopped her. As guilty as she knew Ryan felt over her attack, she knew Sofia's guilt was a hundred times worse. Sofia blamed herself because it was her stalker who had then become obsessed with Paige. It didn't matter how many times Paige told her it wasn't her fault, Sofia believed it was. "Yeah, okay." She smiled at Sofia. "So, Ryan says you two have a new case," she said to Jack and Rose.

"Yeah, a doozy," Jack grimaced as he returned from the kitchen with dinner.

"Want to tell us about it?" Paige pressed.

"Can't wait to be back, huh?" Jack asked her, chuckling.

She shrugged. "I'm bored. So, tell us about your case."

"Elias?" Jack looked to her husband. "You mind us talking about work?"

"No, I don't mind. Working a case seems to help Paige relax," Elias answered.

She shot her husband a grateful smile. What he'd said was true. Working cases, working to fix other people's problems, made her feel better about her own.

As they all dished up spaghetti Bolognese onto their plates, Jack and Rose explained about their case. As she listened to them talk, Paige could feel herself slowly start to relax. Her mind took a break from worrying, from obsessing over paying attention to everything that happened around her, and she focused on the case.

Feeling eyes on her, she looked over to see Elias watching her. Sensing her tension ease, he had relaxed, too. Reaching over to grasp his hand, she was very grateful for her husband's unwavering support. Elias, her friends, and her work—that was what was going to get her through this.

JULY 21ST

Jessica Elgar was dreaming.

Pleasant dreams.

A hand pressing something to her face ripped her from sleep.

As her eyes popped open, she saw a face hovering above her.

A real face.

A real man.

Here in her bedroom.

The hand on her face was holding a cloth against her mouth and nose. With a sense of horror, she realized that this man was trying to knock her unconscious. The cloth on her face smelled sweet. Wasn't that chloroform?

Taking a breath, Jessica tried to hold it. If she could just not breathe in the chemical, then it couldn't affect her. But it didn't do any good. She couldn't hold her breath indefinitely and the man wasn't budging.

With a desperate whimper, she drew in a shuddering breath.

Why did this man want to knock her out?

Did he want to rape her? Kidnap her? Kill her?

Panic began to course through her, but before she could even think of trying to struggle free, her limbs began to tingle with numbness. Then her vision began to fade. And despite her best efforts to fight it, unconsciousness washed over her.

When Jessica ever so slowly began to be aware of her surroundings once more, it took her a moment to comprehend where she was and what was happening to her.

The room was no longer dark. The surface beneath her was no

longer soft. The room she was in was no longer her bedroom. Now she was in the kitchen. And the reason the surface beneath her was no longer soft was because she was lying on her dining table.

Why was she in the kitchen on her table?

Had she had too much to drink last night?

No, that seemed unlikely. She wasn't a big drinker; in fact, she usually didn't drink at all when they went out. Plus, it wasn't the weekend, and if she went out, she never did on a work night.

Maybe Jerry knew why she was here.

No, she reminded herself. Jerry wasn't sleeping here tonight. He'd been away on business the last few days. His plane wouldn't get in until tomorrow. Or today. Depending on what time it was.

Maybe she was sick.

But if she was sick, why would she be in the kitchen? Wouldn't she have gone to bed? Or at least be in the bathroom.

She had to figure out what was going on.

As she went to move, her shock addled brain had to finally accept what it had been irrationally denying. She wasn't drunk, or sick. There had been a man. In her bedroom. The man had made her inhale something to knock her out. Then while she had been unconscious, he had brought her into her kitchen and tied her to her table. Ropes secured her wrists and ankles to the table legs. The rough fibers tore at her flesh as she made what she knew was a futile attempt at freeing herself.

There was rope across her stomach, too, she realized, as she could feel it rubbing her skin as she wiggled and squirmed. She shouldn't be able to feel the rope on her skin. She was wearing pajamas. A glance at her body confirmed what she already knew would be the case.

Her pajamas had been removed while she was out cold.

Her underwear was still in place, though.

Maybe he didn't intend to rape her.

Maybe he had already raped her.

No. She forced herself to calm down. It didn't feel like anyone had invaded her.

If he had left her underwear on, then he wasn't going to sexually assault her. But he was going to do something to her.

No one went to the trouble of breaking into someone's home in the middle of the night, knocking them unconscious, then tying them up if they didn't intend to do something to them. Something bad.

Suddenly, it occurred to her to scream for help.

She tried to open her mouth to yell for help, only to realize that she had been gagged. Something had been stuffed inside her mouth, and then tape had been used to keep her mouth closed. Try as she might, all she could produce were the quietest of muffled grunts. No one was going to hear that. Not even in an apartment building.

How had she not noticed the gag immediately?

Because she was in shock, she reminded herself.

Jessica's every instinct was to burst into fits of uncontrollable crying, but she couldn't. That would spell her death quicker than anything that man planned on doing to her. She couldn't afford to let her nose get stuffed up because she would suffocate. Suffocation could occur anyway. She would have to keep part of her focus on making sure whatever had been stuffed into her mouth didn't block off her airways. The rest of her focus would be on trying to get herself out of this.

How exactly she was going to do that, she wasn't quite sure.

Brute force wasn't going to get her out of these ropes. They had been tied securely, and fighting against them was only going to cause her further injury. Talking her way out didn't seem much of an option either. There was no way she could attempt to connect with her assailant when she couldn't even utter a word.

But she couldn't give up.

She never gave up.

And she had been through a lot in her forty-four years.

Her childhood had been rough. An absent dad and an alcoholic mother. No siblings to rely on, she had gotten out on her own as soon as she could manage. She worked two part-time jobs while studying. And the day that she had been offered a lecturing position at the university where she had obtained her master's degree was one of the happiest of her life. Second only to her wedding day. She hadn't dated much in her younger years; her priority had been forging out a good life for herself. But when she'd met Jeb Hughes, her life had changed dramatically. Married just six months after they met, for a while her life had been like a fairytale.

Until the day they had been mugged.

Walking back to their car after dinner at a restaurant one night, a teenager high on drugs had accosted them in an alley. He'd had a gun. He'd shot them even though they had given him everything he asked for. Her husband had been shot in the head; she had been shot in the back.

After that, life had never been the same.

Following months of surgeries and physical therapy, she had learned to walk again, but the pain of losing her beloved husband had never gone away. She'd become addicted to painkillers. Almost lost her job. But then she'd met Jerry Cutler. He'd helped her get clean. He'd helped her stay clean. And then he'd helped her move on with her life. She'd never forget, or stop loving Jeb, but she had found happiness again.

And now, she might lose it.

All because of some lunatic she didn't even know.

The face she'd seen in her bedroom before she'd passed out hadn't been familiar. She'd never seen that man before in her life. So why was he doing this to her? She hadn't done anything to him; she didn't even know him. What possible reason could he have for tying her up?

"Ah, Jessica, you're awake," a soft voice spoke.

The sound of it made her jump. Or would have, if she were

able to move her body. All she could move was her head, and she turned it in the direction the voice had come from. Standing beside the table was a man. To all intents and purposes, an innocuous looking man. If she'd come across him on the street, she would never have guessed he was some sort of sadistic maniac.

Slowly penetrating her terrified haze was the realization that he knew her name. Which meant he knew her. But she'd never met him, so how did he know her?

Jessica tried to talk to him. To beg him to let her go. To ask him what he wanted from her. To ask him why he was doing this to her. To ask him *what* he was planning on doing to her. But all she could muster were hysterical sounding moans.

The man chuckled and stroked her hair. "I can't understand you, Jessica."

She tried desperately to flinch away from his touch. She tilted her head as far away from his hand as she could manage, but it did no good. Her binds left her helpless. Helpless to do anything to save herself. Helpless to stop him doing to her what he wished. The thought made her feel physically sick. Desperately, Jessica fought the urge to throw up. Vomiting would cause her to asphyxiate.

As long as she was alive, she had hope. She had to cling to that.

"Okay, Jessica, we have to move quickly," the man announced. "Usually, I wouldn't do this in such a public place with so many people around us. But I don't really have a choice. I *have* to do this here. That's why I had to gag you. Usually, I'd be happy for you to scream as much as you wanted."

Panic was coursing quickly through her veins now. This man wanted her to scream. He wanted her to suffer. He'd obviously done this to others before. Just what did he have planned for her?

"Do you smoke, Jessica?" he asked as he pulled out a packet of cigarettes and a lighter.

He looked at her so intently that she realized he actually wanted an answer. So, she shook her head.

"Me neither, a disgusting habit," he continued as he pulled a cigarette from the packet and lit it. For a moment he just stood there, staring at the glowing orange circle. Following his gaze, Jessica too stared at the burning cigarette, allowing it to mesmerize her. Eventually, he roused himself. "They do serve their purpose, though."

Horrified understanding dawned as the man moved the lit cigarette toward her arm. He was going to burn her. The calm she had managed to cling to despite her terror evaporated and she completely lost it. She thrashed violently against her bindings, knowing it was pointless, but desperate to get away from this man and what he was about to do to her.

When the cigarette made contact with her flesh, the stinging pain had her shrieking as loudly as she could through her gag.

She was more prepared for the next burn, but that didn't make it hurt any less.

One look in the eyes that watched her had her heart dropping. This man was enjoying every second of inflicting pain on her.

Jessica knew she wasn't walking out of her apartment alive.

* * * * *

8:47 A.M.

"That's three now." Jack felt helpless. Three days in a row, three crimes, one location. That the victims themselves were the targets now seemed unlikely. What were the chances that someone had come into contact with Tarek Milford, Judith Barclay, and Jessica Elgar someplace other than where they lived? The building was the link. They knew it; they just didn't know why.

"He's all over the board, though," Rose said. "Murder, then

rape, then torture—it's impossible to get a read on him."

"He's not disorganized, though," Jack continued. "He may leave behind forensic evidence, but it's more because he knows it won't lead us anywhere than because he never considered it."

"I agree." Rose nodded. "He's smart and he's planned this out. He brought with him everything he needed, he didn't use things he simply came across in the victims' apartments."

"One violent crime and we assume it's about the victim. Two violent crimes in the same location and we assume there must be a connection between them. Three violent crimes in the same location and we have to assume the victims are not the perpetrator's primary concern. Apartment 1J, then 2J, then 3J, the connection seems to be the building, but he used Judith's name, so he knew her. And if he knew her, then he most likely knew Tarek Milford and Jessica Elgar, too."

"There's a personal element to the crimes, as well," Rose continued his theory. "The knife to the heart seems personal. And when he was raping Judith Barclay, he told her not to be stupid. He could have killed her if he wanted to, but it was like he didn't want to. He wanted to leave her alive so he didn't want her to be stupid and force his hand, make him kill her to protect himself."

"And the level of torture on Jessica Elgar, that was over-the-top and not in keeping with either of his other victims. It displayed a huge level of anger. Even if the connection is the apartment building, he still chose these victims for a reason. And his victimology is all over the map. He goes from old man, to young girl, to middle aged woman–he's not fixated on them because they represent a particular type of person. It's something else that brought them to his attention," Jack contemplated.

"He also gets in and out of the apartments without anyone seeing him," Rose added. "He's confident in his abilities. He's not worried that someone is going to come across him. There were no broken windows, no jimmied locks; it's like he just walked through the front door."

"Too bad the building doesn't have cameras in the hallways, just the entrance points and main foyer." Jack couldn't see an end to this case coming anytime soon. "Then we'd have an exact description of who this guy is."

"We had cops on the building last night, none of them reported anyone suspicious."

"We discussed the possibility of him being a resident of the building before, only then we thought it was too risky for someone to be killing in their own building, but I think now we have to look seriously at that possibility."

"I agree," Rose concurred. "I think we need to start running background checks on all the residents, see if anything pops."

"That's an awful lot of people to run checks on." Jack was feeling defeated before they even started. There would be thousands of people to have to check out.

"Well, we have to do something," Rose pressed.

"We need something to narrow it down. We need a direction to focus on. We should check out the doorman first; they would have contact with everyone in the building and the means to get inside the apartments."

"There're only four doormen—that's not too many to check out and we already have criminal checks on them. All four turned up clean. We should make appointments to talk with them though, maybe something will turn up."

"Paige suggested last night that we should check out the building's history. See whether there have been any other crimes that happened there that might be connected."

They'd all been pleased, and relieved, that Paige had come last night. Jack had been there the afternoon she'd been attacked, arriving shortly after Ryan had found someone beating her. She had looked as close to death as he'd ever seen without proving to be fatal. Getting her out of her house to do anything other than physical therapy was almost impossible these days. Everyone was worried about her, and Jack wasn't sure she was ready to go back to work next month, but he understood why she wanted to. When they'd been talking about the case last night, Paige had immediately begun to relax and seemed almost like her old self.

Only she wasn't her old self. No one could be beaten nearly to death and come out of it emotionally unscathed. Especially given Paige's history with a stalker as a child. When she'd been a teenager, her mother had had a stalker, who after repeated rejections had come to their house one night, tied up her mother and siblings before attempting to rape fourteen-year-old Paige. Her father had arrived home in time to stop it and had shot and killed him, but the damage had been done. Paige had been permanently traumatized and they were all concerned that recent events were going to push her over the edge. She had suffered a breakdown after the attack when she was a kid and no one wanted to see it happen a second time.

So far, she was managing to keep it together, but all the warning signs were there. She didn't sleep, she didn't eat regularly, she was hypervigilant, she had flashbacks. Everyone was watching her closely for signs of worsening post-traumatic stress disorder. Jack knew Paige's husband, Elias, was particularly worried about her, and that both Ryan and Rose visited her almost daily, and he made a mental note to do his part and try and check up on her more regularly.

"Not to get distracted," Rose interjected, her green eyes mirroring the concern he knew were in his, "but I don't think Paige is ready to go back to work. She's still avoiding. She won't talk about it at all. Not with anyone. Not Elias, not Ryan, not me."

"Is she getting worse?"

"No, but she's not really getting any better. She hasn't been back to the precinct since it happened—I don't know how she's going to cope when she finally does."

"Is she still seeing someone?"

Rose shook her head. "She quit a while back. She says she

doesn't need a shrink, she just needs to go back to work."

"Ryan will be keeping an eye on her when she comes back," he assured Rose. His brother was close with his partner, and Ryan felt guilty about Paige getting attacked in the first place. Paige would be lucky if Ryan let her out of his sight when she returned.

"Yeah, I know. Doesn't stop me worrying about her, though. Maybe she's right, maybe coming back to work will be good for her." Rose said the words, but her face remained doubtful. "Anyway, Paige is right, the location seems to be more important than the victims. He's just working his way up floor by floor. We need to check the database—see if anything similar ever happened there. For all we know, this guy's wife was murdered there and he's angry the police never found the killer, so he's making a statement."

Jack checked his watch. "We have an interview at eleven; that should be enough time to start looking into the building's past."

"Yeah," Rose agreed distractedly, obviously still thinking about Paige.

As they got to work, Jack eased his guilty conscience for not letting his family and friends know what was going on with him. They'd just be worried about him like they were worried about Paige. And his friends and family had enough to worry about. Between Paige, and Ryan's fiancée Sofia, who was still recovering from the second violent assault she had suffered in less than a year, and his younger brother Mark's seven-year-old son was due for his yearly checkup to make sure his leukemia had not returned, his family had enough going on without him adding to it.

* * * * *

8:47 A.M.

He wondered if they were on to him yet.

Not on to him as in hunting him, but on to him as in finally figuring out that his victims were immaterial.

He hadn't chosen them for any other reason than they lived in her building.

She lived in apartment 9J.

Hence the reason he had chosen to work the J apartments.

How long would it take the police to figure it out?

They hadn't yet. He'd already done floors 1, 2, and 3. Surely, they weren't that stupid. Surely they had to eventually figure out that he wasn't personally invested in his victims. That the only thing they had in common was the building they lived in. That his real target was another resident.

It had been fun last night.

A trip down memory lane.

And good preparation for what was to come.

Someone had messed things up last time.

Intervened before he was finished.

But that wouldn't happen this time.

This time, he was going to finish what he'd started.

He hadn't planned on waiting this long. Only at first, she was never alone. Someone had stayed by her side. Then the trial was on and it had seemed too risky to try to grab her again. He had intended to wait until the verdict was read and then grab her. Only, she had disappeared.

And it had taken him ten long years to track her down.

This time, she wasn't going to get away.

He had it all planned.

Exactly what he was going to do to her. Exactly what he was going to say to her. Exactly what she would say to him. Exactly how he was going to end it all.

He would have grabbed her immediately, only he knew he wasn't getting into her apartment. She never left it and he imagined she had a lot of locks on the door. Trying to keep out the bad memories as well as all the bad people, he suspected.

The only way he was getting to her was to scare her out of her apartment.

If he kept pushing, kept making this place as bad as the nightmares that he was sure still haunted her sleep, then eventually she would go running. And when she did, she'd go running straight into his waiting arms.

All he had to do was remain patient.

Besides, he'd already waited ten years; what was a few more days?

Any day now and she would be his all over again.

This time he would make sure that everything went smoothly.

This time she wasn't walking away alive.

He was going to play with her until he got bored and then he was going to kill her.

And then he would finally be able to move on with his life.

Right now, though, it was time to get ready for tonight.

He still had a few more preparations to make.

The residents of apartment 4J had no idea what was coming.

* * * * *

11:30 P.M.

"Sometimes I really hate this job," Jack murmured, more to himself than his partner.

"Yeah, I know." Rose shot him a sympathetic smile.

"It's just, I don't understand why people do these things to each other." Some days he just wanted to walk away from all of this and pretend that the world wasn't a completely depressing place.

"You want me to do this one?" Rose asked as they paused at the door.

He sighed deeply. "No, I can do it." He knocked on the door then opened it, since they were expected. A man in his early fifties met them in the hall. "Jerry Cutler?"

The man's face was drawn, his brown eyes filled with a mixture of horror and anger. Jerry Cutler had returned from a business trip to find his girlfriend, Jessica Elgar, covered in blood and tied to her kitchen table. "Yes. You're the detectives who I spoke with on the phone?"

"Detective Xander and Detective Lace," Jack introduced himself and his partner.

"This way." Jerry led them toward a closed door at the end of the hall. "Your CSU people said to stay out of Jessica's bedroom and the kitchen but that it was okay to come into the spare bedroom since they don't think that man ever came in here."

"Hello, Ms. Elgar." Jack greeted the woman in the bed as they entered the bedroom.

Dazed blue eyes looked back at him.

"I'm Detective Xander, and this is my partner, Detective Lace. Is it okay if we ask you a few questions about what happened to you?"

Jessica Elgar gave a shaky nod.

For some reason, whomever had attacked her had only wanted to hurt her, not kill her. Just like with Judith Barclay. Only unlike with Judith Barclay, Jessica had been brutally tortured. From what he could see, there were bruises on her neck, small round burns on her arms which were resting on top of the comforter, the pinkie finger on her left hand was taped to the neighboring finger, and her lips and the skin around them were swollen and blistered. She looked like she should be in the hospital. "Ms. Elgar, are you sure you don't want us to take you to the hospital?" Apparently, she had refused to go earlier.

"No, no hospital." Jessica's voice was hoarse but she sounded firm. "I told the paramedics I didn't want to go."

"Are you sure, honey?" Jerry asked her, perching on the bed beside her.

"I'm sure."

"Are you sure you're up to answering some questions?" Jack

asked. The woman didn't look as if she were.

"Yes," she shivered. "I know you have to, so let's just do it."

Grabbing the chair from the desk in the corner, Jack pulled it over to the bed, close but not too close, and sat down so they were eye to eye. "Can you walk us through what happened last night?"

"I guess." Jessica looked like she'd rather be anyplace but here.

Jack smiled encouragingly. "Take your time."

Drawing in a shuddering breath, she began her tale. "I woke up with a hand over my mouth."

Same as Judith Barclay, Jack thought, but didn't say it aloud.

"He held a cloth soaked in something over my face, it smelled sweet."

Probably chloroform; Jack made a mental note to check into it. He hadn't used anything to knock Judith out, probably because he hadn't needed to move her. Even with a gun, it would have been difficult to restrain Jessica while she was conscious; he couldn't have predicted whether she would have fought him or not, so drugging her was the safest option.

"I tried to hold my breath, but that was pointless. I felt my body start to go numb and then I passed out. When I woke up next, I was in the kitchen. He had tied me to the table. The ropes hurt my wrists and ankles when I tried to fight against them. And he'd put a gag in my mouth." Absently a hand moved to brush at her lips, which had been damaged when the tape had been ripped off. "He had put a handkerchief in my mouth and then tape over the top. I tried to yell for help but I couldn't. I was scared that I was going to choke." She paused to compose herself.

"Take a moment," Jack told her softly. "Do you want some water or something?"

"I'm okay." Jessica reached out a hand to grasp one of her boyfriend's. "He wasn't in the room when I first woke up. When he came in, he said, 'Jessica, you're awake'. He knew my name, but I didn't know him. How did he know my name?"

So, he knew both Judith and Jessica—it seemed safe to assume he also knew Tarek Milford. He may be choosing his victims based on the fact they lived in a certain apartment, but he still knew them. "I don't know, Ms. Elgar. Are you sure you've never seen him anywhere before?"

"I'm positive, I didn't know him, I'd never seen him before, but he knew me." She shuddered violently.

Jerry stood, walked to the closet, grabbed a spare blanket and took it back to the bed, where he wrapped it around Jessica's shoulders. "If you change your mind, I can drive you to the hospital." Jerry looked like he was a hairsbreadth away from throwing her in the car and taking her there, whether she wanted it or not.

Jessica merely shook her head.

"Do you think you can give us a description of him?" Jack asked; so far, they didn't have anything on what this guy looked like. Tarek was dead and Judith had never seen his face.

"He had blue eyes and brown hair, and his nose was kind of big," Jessica replied.

"Do you think you could work with a sketch artist?"

"Yes." Jessica nodded.

"What happened next?" he prompted.

"He touched me. Not like that," she added quickly when she felt her boyfriend tense beside her. "He had taken my clothes off while I was unconscious, but he didn't rape me, and he left my underwear on. He touched my head. But it made me feel sick. I was scared I was going to throw up, asphyxiate. I tried to breathe deeply through my nose and stay calm. Then he said to me that he had to move quickly. That he wouldn't usually do this in such a public place where people could hear us, but that he *had* to do it here."

"Did he mention why he had to do it here?" Jack interrupted her to ask. This man had a specific target in mind. Whether it had to do with the building itself or one of the residents, Tarek,

Judith, and Jessica had just been collateral damage on his way to his intended target.

"No, but it was obviously important to him. Then he asked me if I smoked; he pulled out a packet of cigarettes and a lighter and lit one of them. He told me that he thought smoking was disgusting but that cigarettes served a purpose. He burned me." She fingered the burns on her arms, eyeing them like she still couldn't believe they were real. Like she still couldn't believe all of this was real.

Jack was about to offer reassurances and whatever comfort he could, but Jessica resumed her recount.

"After he got bored with burning me, he took hold of my left wrist and the little finger. Then before I even realized what he was doing, he had snapped it." She stared at the swollen digit. "Next, he pulled out a small knife. I knew he was going to cut me with it, I just didn't know he was going to do what he did." Tears were trickling down her cheeks as she recounted the horror she had endured, but Jessica didn't seem to notice. "On my chest, he used the knife to write a word."

Jack already knew this and what the word was, but he wasn't going to push her to say it right now. "Did CSU get some photos of it?" he asked instead.

She wiped at her wet cheeks. "Yes."

Jessica was starting to look tired, he wanted to leave her be and let her rest but they needed to finish hearing her story. "What happened after that?"

"He put his hands around my neck," she began again. Once more, her hands went to stray subconsciously to the injury, but Jerry grasped them before they reached it and clutched them tightly. "He squeezed and squeezed. I wanted to fight him, but I couldn't. I couldn't move. I was just starting to pass out when he stopped. He'd wait till I finished gulping in air and then he'd do it again. I'm sorry," she said dully, "I don't know how many times he did it. Maybe five or so. Maybe more. I lost count after three."

Her hoarse voice was due to the repeated strangulations. She really should have gone to the hospital to be monitored at least for the next few hours. There could be further swelling in her throat that could end up obscuring her airways. "Did he leave after that?" Jack asked.

"Almost." Jessica rested back against her pillows and pulled the blanket tighter around her shoulders. "He said he was sorry that he couldn't drown me. He said that meant it wasn't exactly the same, but it was close enough. She would get the message."

"'She'?" Jack repeated, feeling the first real glimmer of hope that they might actually be moving closer to finding this guy. If they knew who he was after, they would be able to find him. Or at least be closer to finding him. "Did he say who the she was?"

Giving a weary shake of her head, Jessica answered, "No."

"He didn't give you any clues? A wife, a girlfriend, an ex, a daughter, anything?"

"He just said that she would get the message, and then he left. I'm sorry, maybe he said more and I just didn't hear it. I was a little out of it by that stage. I was in a lot of pain, and woozy, but I'm pretty sure he just left after that. I didn't know how long I would have to lie there until someone found me. I knew Jerry was coming home, but I didn't know if he was going to stop by his work first. I was scared. Almost more scared than when he'd been here. I wanted to cry, but the gag was still in my mouth. I almost couldn't help it, though. By the time Jerry got here and found me, I was about ready to give in," Jessica broke off as she dissolved into quiet tears.

Jerry took over the narrative. "She was covered in blood when I got here. I called for help, then I pulled off the tape and she started to cry. I used a knife to cut her free, I pulled her off the table. And then I just held her."

"I thought I was going to die," Jessica cried. "I thought that he was going to kill me. I truly thought that I was never going to leave my apartment alive. Why would he do this to me?" Her blue eyes sought his, desperately searching for answers so that she could attempt to make sense of what she'd been through.

"I don't know, Ms. Elgar," he answered honestly. "But we're going to find out. You know what's happened here the last few days, with your downstairs neighbors?"

"You think what happened to me is related to that?" Jessica's eyes grew wide.

"We're going to look into it. Do you know Tarek Milford or Judith Barclay?" Jack asked.

"No, I may have seen them around the building, but I've only lived here for a few weeks."

More confirmation that their guy wasn't choosing his victims for anything other than that they lived in particular apartments. His real target was the 'she' that he was trying to send a message to. A specific message. The murder, the rape, the torture—it all meant something to this mystery woman. Now they just had to find her. Before anyone else—including his real target—got hurt. "Have you noticed anything unusual going on in the building since you moved in?"

"I don't think so." Jessica appeared to be fighting to keep her eyes open now.

"All right, I think we have everything we need for now." Jack stood. "When you're feeling better, we'll send the sketch artist over to work with you. You should try to get some rest. Mr. Cutler, I assume you'll be staying with her?"

"She'll be lucky if I don't stay glued to her side for the rest of our lives." Jerry's eyes were fierce with protective concern.

"Take her to the hospital if she gets any worse," Jack advised.

"I don't need the hospital," Jessica protested, but her voice was faint and her eyes were already closed; she was drifting off to sleep. "Send the sketch artist today. I don't want this guy to hurt anyone else."

* * * * *

4:09 P.M.

"Sorry I was running a little late." Mr. Elijah Jonas came bustling through the door.

"No worries," Jack assured the owner of the apartment building. He was only nine minutes late, no big deal. After their interview with Jessica Elgar, they had done a little work and then taken a late lunch to Paige's. The fact that they'd been there to check up on her had been obvious, but Paige had been only mildly irritated. They had talked about the case while they ate, and Paige had seemed fairly relaxed when they left.

At least she would have to the casual observer.

However, both he and Rose had noticed how she jumped at every little noise. He didn't think it was a good idea for her to be home on her own all day. Obviously, someone couldn't stay with her all the time, but Paige had looked tired, and she was only going to hang around her house dwelling on what had happened till her husband got home. So, they had called Sofia on their way to their interview with Mr. Jonas and asked her to go and spend the rest of the day with Paige.

Hopefully the two women could help each other. Both were just avoiding dealing with what had happened to them a few months back. While Paige had thrown herself into physical therapy, Sofia had thrown herself into raising baby Sophie. They both needed to sort some things out, and if they wouldn't talk to anyone else, maybe they could talk to each other.

Despite his concerns over Paige and Sofia, Jack was feeling more optimistic about their case. The target was someone in that building. Or the target was taking a seat right in front of them.

"May I get you anything to drink?" Elijah asked as he pulled a bottle of water from a small refrigerator under his desk.

"No, thank you," Jack replied.

"Are you sure? Coffee, soda, water?" Elijah persisted.

"I'm sure, thank you," Jack reaffirmed.

Elijah looked to Rose, who smiled. "I'm fine, too, thanks, Mr. Jonas."

Elijah shrugged and opened his bottle of water, drinking several mouthfuls before setting it down. "It's been a long day," he told them. "Now, what can I do for you, detectives?"

"You know what's been going on in one of the apartment buildings you own." Jack intended it as a statement, not a question, but Elijah nodded anyway.

"Yes, it's just awful," he responded, his brown eyes wide with sympathy.

Jack viewed it more like fake sympathy. Elijah Jonas seemed like the kind of guy who would be more worried about how the recent goings-on at one of his buildings would affect him, rather than what the victims had endured. "A murder, a rape, torture." He paused to allow his words to hopefully sink in. "These are extremely violent crimes, Mr. Jonas. And all of them happened in one of your buildings."

"You think I was involved?" This time the man's eyes widened in genuine shocked horror.

Elijah Jonas was in his seventies, walked with a cane, and suffered from severe arthritis. He was an unlikely candidate. He wouldn't have had the strength to cart Jessica Elgar's unconscious body from her bedroom to her kitchen and tie her to the table. Nor did he match the description that Jessica had given. "No." Jack shook his head. "But it would be good if you could give us a DNA sample and a sample of your fingerprints, then we can positively rule you out."

"I should probably check with my lawyer first." Elijah looked hesitant.

"If you prefer, you can call your lawyer and have him meet us as the station where we can continue our conversation," Jack offered, standing.

"No, no, no," Elijah said immediately. "Here is fine, and I'll give you the samples."

"We don't think that you're involved, Mr. Jonas," Rose assured him. "At least, not directly."

Bushy grey brows knitted together in confusion. "What does that mean exactly?" Elijah asked.

"It means, Mr. Jonas, that we think it's a possibility that you are the intended target," Jack informed him.

"Me? Why would I be the target?"

"It's your building," Jack reminded him. "And the victims so far appear to be random?"

"How are they random?" Elijah asked.

"He's working up from the first floor. Apartment 1J, then apartment 2J, then apartment 3J. The only connection between them appears to be their apartments numbers," Rose explained. "We believe he's simply using them to make a point to his real victim."

"His real victim? And you think that's me?" Elijah looked shocked.

"You or someone you know," Rose replied. "He told one of the victims that *she* would get his message."

"You think he's doing this just to get someone's attention?"

"Not just to get their attention, but probably also to maximize the person's suffering—draw things out as long as possible, make sure they know what's coming," Jack explained.

"I hate to point out the obvious," Elijah began, "but I'm not a she. Are you sure that I'm the intended victim?"

"No, we're not," Jack confirmed. "But we have to look into it as a possibility, especially given that it's your building. Another possibility is that it's one of the residents, but right now we're looking at you. And yes, we realize you're a man, but you have to have some women in your life who this guy could be after."

"Well, my wife is seventy-four, and we've been married for nearly fifty years and I can't think of anyone who would want to hurt her."

"Children?" Jack prompted.

"We don't have any daughters, only two sons; one has never been married and the other has been divorced for nearly ten years now. We don't have any granddaughters. No grandsons, either."

"Any extended family?"

"Both my wife and I are only children, no siblings, so no nieces or nephews, and obviously, our parents are deceased. I really don't know who in my family this killer could be after."

"Any close friends?" Rose asked.

"None so close that someone would go through me to get to them," Elijah answered.

"I'm sorry, but I have to ask, but have you been involved with any other women over the course of your marriage?" Jack asked.

"No, absolutely not," Elijah stated firmly. "I have *never* been unfaithful to my wife."

"Any co-owners of the building?" Jack tried.

"No, just me. I also own several other buildings, and I haven't had any trouble at any of those," Elijah informed them.

"Has anyone made any threats against you recently?" Rose inquired.

"No, no one has ever made threats to me in my life. Look, I'm just a regular guy, I really don't think this guy is after me. I don't know anyone who would behave this way. I don't know anyone violent. I really don't think this has anything to do with me. I think it's just a coincidence that it's happening at one of my buildings," Elijah finished a little desperately.

"Have you had any problems with any of your employees?"

"None at all."

"Have any of your employees reported anything unusual at the building? Anyone hanging around who shouldn't be? Any residents reporting break-ins or people hanging around? Any problems at all?"

"Nothing that I'm aware of. I'm sorry, but I really don't think I can help you." Elijah looked like he was ready to dismiss them.

They'd gotten everything out of Elijah Jonas that they were going to. It didn't seem like he had anything helpful to offer them, anyway. It wasn't seeming likely that the intended target was Elijah or anyone in his family. "All right, thank you for your time, Mr. Jonas. We can see ourselves out," Jack informed him.

"Okay," Elijah nodded eagerly. "Once again, I'm sorry that I wasn't able to be more helpful. But please let me know if there's anything else you need to ask me."

They each shook Elijah's hand and then headed for the lift. "Stephanie texted me while we were in there," Rose told him once they were inside. "She said the fingerprints from Jessica Elgar's house match the other two crime scenes. Confirms this one is related."

"This guy isn't after Elijah Jonas," Jack stated.

"Agreed," Rose nodded.

"It's someone in the building," Jack noted.

"Yep. That would explain why he told Jessica that he *had* to do it there. And that *she* would get his message. She lives in the building."

"We're going to have to interview them all." Jack couldn't deny he felt a little daunted by the enormity of the task. There were twenty apartments per floor and fifteen floors—that made three hundred apartments. Interviewing all those people was going to take a long time. Time they didn't seem to have. This guy was nonstop. He was focused on his task and he wanted to get to his end game as quickly as he could while still inflicting maximum fear on his intended victim.

"But you're forgetting that he's working the J apartments," Rose reminded him. "I'm guessing that's for a reason. He's already done the first, second, and third floors; that means whoever he's after probably lives in a J apartment on the fourth through fifteenth floor. That narrows it down to twelve apartments to check out. Then if we're wrong, we can expand out and start checking out all the others."

That was true. Jack had just been too depressed about the prospect of interviewing thousands of people to think of it. "I guess we just have to hope that whoever this message is for actually gets the message. If this is some sort of psychotic stalker, then there's no guarantee that the woman we're looking for is even going to know that someone is after her."

Rose's phone beeped the second they left the lift. "Sketch artist is already at Jessica Elgar's, hopefully won't be too long until we get the sketch," she announced.

"Already? We only left Jessica's apartment a few hours ago."

"The sketch artist called her pretty much as soon as we left and Jessica told her to come right over. She really wanted to do it quickly, she's worried that he's going to hurt someone else."

"She's not the only one." Jack held the door open for his partner as they stepped out into the hot afternoon.

"I've been thinking about that," Rose told him.

He didn't like the tone of her voice. "Yeah?"

"Yeah." Rose looked at him out of the corner of her eye as they headed for the car.

"And what were you thinking?" he prompted when she didn't continue.

"We can't risk another attack in that building. We know he's coming back tonight. Apartment 4J, it's their turn. He's going to do something to whoever lives in that apartment."

"Most likely," Jack agreed warily. He was getting the feeling he wasn't going to like where his partner was going with this.

"What if we take the residents of 4J and put them in a motel or something for the night, and then I stay there as a decoy?" Rose paused at their car.

"No," Jack said firmly, climbing into the car and slamming the door. No way were they deliberately putting Rose in the path of someone who enjoyed inflicting pain and terror. Of someone who had killed and raped and burned and strangled and used a knife to cut words into someone's flesh.

"Jack," Rose wheedled as she joined him in the car. "We can't let him hurt someone else."

"So, we let him hurt you? No way." He glared at her.

"He won't hurt me, Jack," Rose soothed. "I'm a cop, I know how to take care of myself."

"Yeah, that worked great for Paige," he snapped snarkily. He felt a little bad for bringing what Paige had gone through into this. Jack knew that Paige blamed herself for her attack, and the rest of them blamed themselves in some way. He and Rose had been looking for whoever had been stalking her but hadn't found them. Ryan had known that Paige was distracted and tired and blamed himself for leaving her alone. Sofia blamed herself because her stalker had started stalking Paige. However, the facts were that none of them could have predicted that the stalker would suddenly escalate to violence. But what Rose was wanting to do was different. It was deliberately putting herself into a potentially dangerous situation with a man they knew was sadistically violent.

"Jack, that's not fair and you know it," Rose told him reproachfully. "What happened with Paige was completely different. Someone was stalking her, they wanted her dead, they deliberately came after her. This guy doesn't even know me. He's not coming after me. He won't even know that it's me there instead of the apartment's resident."

"He will as soon as he sees you," he reminded his partner. "He knows these people. He'll be expecting the real resident."

"He won't get close enough to me to notice. As soon as he's in and we establish that it's him, we arrest him."

"Or," Jack began, "we could evacuate the apartment building so he can't get to anyone in there."

"Evacuate the whole building?" Rose looked at him doubtfully. "He'd notice that. He won't even come inside."

"At least no one will get hurt," he reminded her.

"Yeah, but we won't get him either. He's not going to stop. He's invested in getting to whoever it is he's after. If we don't get him, he's just going to keep going after her until he gets her. This way, we can stop him."

"I don't like it," he growled.

"I know." Rose patted his arm. "But we have to do something and we can't interview everyone in that building before tonight. And he's almost definitely going to strike again—tonight. I can't just sit by and do nothing and let him hurt some innocent person. I'm not asking your permission, Jack," Rose said gently. "I'm doing this."

This was a bad idea. He knew it was. Just like he knew there was no way to stop it from happening. He was just going to have to hope and pray that everything went smoothly and Rose wasn't about to get herself injured or killed. Jack really didn't think he could deal with it if she did.

* * * * *

11:28 P.M.

Why was she doing this again?

Rose couldn't deny that she was on edge. Apprehensive even, and she didn't like to admit that she got apprehensive.

Now that she was actually here in apartment 4J, waiting for the killer to show up, she was starting to wonder just why she had wanted to make herself bait.

She liked to have fun, and she knew she had a dangerous job, but Rose wasn't usually one to take unnecessary risks. And putting herself directly into the line of fire of a vicious killer and torturer was certainly taking a huge and unnecessary risk.

She had been here since six-thirty. Around five hours. Five hours was plenty of time for her anxiety to inch up to a level where she now just wanted this man to turn up so they could get this over with.

The thirty-three-year-old woman who lived here had readily

agreed to let them use her apartment. Audrey Nichols had already decided to spend the night at a friend's. She had heard about what had happened in each of the apartments below her and had decided she didn't want to risk anything happening to her, too.

When Rose had arrived, she had cooked herself some dinner, taken a shower, and watched a little TV before climbing into bed. Now that she was simply lying here in bed in Audrey Nichols' spare bedroom, her mind was beginning to wander. Beginning to conjure up images of what the man they were looking for had in mind for his next victim. She was also imagining the overwhelming fear and terror that his victims had endured at his hands.

Would this man care that she was here instead of Audrey Nichols?

If he was simply choosing his victims because of the apartment they lived in, then chances were if he could get away with doing to her whatever he had been planning on doing to Audrey, he most likely would. The thought left her chilled

But, she reminded herself, he wouldn't be able to get his hands on her.

At least, Rose hoped he wouldn't.

Her colleagues were watching her. Rose knew that but the knowledge made her feel only slightly better. She was still in this on her own. After Audrey had left, CSU had set up some cameras and microphones throughout the apartment, but no one would do anything until the guy was in the apartment and they were sure he was who they were looking for.

Even though Audrey had informed them that no one but her mother had a key, they would still need something that would hold up in court to prove that the person who broke in here was the killer. Although her colleagues were just next door—they had commandeered the two neighboring apartments—they still might not get to her before this man had a chance to hurt her.

Jack had wanted to come and stay in here with her. But she

had refused.

They didn't know if the killer was keeping watch on the building or even if he was indeed one of the residents. A single woman lived in apartment 4J. If the killer saw two people in there, then he could back off.

They were already taking a chance that he wouldn't know until he was already inside that he wasn't going to find who he was looking for. He could have already seen the swap and decided to back off. Or to go after whoever it was in this building that he really wanted. They had officers all over this place to hopefully stop that from happening. But this guy was smart, focused, and he clearly had a plan.

Her partner wasn't the only one who hadn't liked the idea of her staying here on her own waiting to see if the killer was going to pop up. Paige had also volunteered to come and stay here with her. Of course, Rose had nixed that idea in the bud immediately. There was no way she was having her barely-recovered friend put herself in a situation that could get her hurt again.

It had been a low blow for Jack to bring up what had happened to Paige to try and talk her out of doing this. Since she didn't have any family left, her friends were very important to her; her friends were her family. Rose had never known her father. Her mother hadn't even known who he was. And her mother had been diagnosed with multiple sclerosis when Rose was eight, eventually succumbing to the disease a couple of years ago.

So, with no siblings, no extended family, and no wish to look for her biological father, her friends had taken the place in her life that her family would have taken.

And her friends certainly were a lot to worry about.

She wished she knew the magic words to say to ease Paige's constant fear of being attacked again. But she didn't. The best she could do was just be there, keep a watch on her friend to make sure she didn't get worse, and listen and offer advice when Paige needed it.

She taught her friend Sofia self-defense, wanting to give her the skills to at least give her a chance at defending herself should she ever be in a situation again where she needed to. Of course, Rose hoped she never was, but it was better to be prepared than sorry.

She kept a close watch over her partner. With his growing depression, she wasn't sure what the right thing was to do to help him was. He seemed to want to be in a committed relationship, and yet at the same time, he adamantly ignored any opportunities to date any woman who crossed his path.

Her friends were going to make her grey before her time. Luckily, her own life was pretty dull. But mundane was good. She liked it that way.

What she didn't like was lying in this bed waiting for some lunatic to break in here.

Restlessly, Rose climbed out of bed and headed for the bathroom. She didn't really need to go, she just needed to do something. In the bathroom, she splashed some cold water on her face, then studied herself in the mirror. Her green eyes had bags under them, she looked tense, her red hair hung messily around a pale face. She really needed to get all her friends back on track so she could start sleeping properly again instead of lying awake at night worrying.

She was just starting back down the hall to the bedroom when an arm wrapped around her neck, pulling her backward and pinning her against a hard chest.

Immediately, her training kicked in. Rose rammed her head backward, connecting with the man's face, getting him squarely in the nose.

The man cursed and let her go.

Rose spun around and headed for the door. But the man recovered quickly and grabbed her again.

Reaching for a glass vase on the table beside her, Rose swung it at him. It connected with his shoulder and shattered.

The man growled another curse and his grip on her loosened.

Taking advantage, Rose twisted sideways and managed to spin away from him. Unfortunately, he wasn't as stunned as she had hoped. He caught hold of her arm, and as she lunged forward, her bare foot came down on a glass shard. With adrenalin pumping through her body she barely felt it.

Stumbling, she lost her balance and landed hard on the wooden floorboards. Her hands and knees took the brunt of the fall and Rose could feel the glass slicing through her flesh.

Wondering where her backup was, she darted forward, hoping to regain her footing before the man, who had fallen with her, recovered and was on her again. But he recovered quicker than she'd hoped. His weight suddenly flung itself against her, flattening her down against the floor as he straddled her back.

Rose was thrashing frantically beneath him when voices and footsteps suddenly filled the air. The next thing she knew, someone had tackled the man off her.

"Rose?" Jack dropped down at her side. "Are you okay?" he rolled her over onto her back.

"Yeah." She closed her eyes and rested back against the floorboards, willing her wildly beating heart to slow.

"I see blood," Jack said doubtfully.

"It's nothing. A few scratches," she assured him.

"Someone call an ambulance," Jack called over his shoulder.

She opened her eyes. "No, I'm fine. I really am. I don't need an ambulance." Rose pushed herself up so she was sitting.

"Are you sure? Where are you hurt?"

"I'm sure. It's my foot and my hands and knees; I really only need a couple of Band-Aids." Rose tried to stand, but Jack preempted her by scooping her up. She wrapped a startled arm around his shoulders. "Jack, this really isn't necessary," she protested.

Jack merely carried her to the couch and set her down. "Stay put while I get something to clean and dress those cuts," he ordered. Then added with a glare, "I mean it; stay put."

Rose barely resisted the urge to say, 'yes sir.' Instead, she merely nodded and glanced toward the man who had attacked her. He was now lying on the floor on his stomach, his hands cuffed behind his back. He was shouting something, but Rose couldn't make out what it was. Adrenalin was slowly ebbing out of her body, leaving her feeling shaky and tired. She rested back against the soft sofa cushions and let her eyes fall closed, concentrating on calming herself.

"Sure you're okay?" Jack's voice rumbled beside her.

Opening her eyes again, all she could manage was a nod. Although she'd thought she could empathize with what Paige and Sofia had gone through when they'd thought someone was about to end their life, she hadn't realized until right now just how little she really had understood.

Her partner studied her through calm blue eyes as he gently bathed the cuts on her knees. "Does it feel like there's any glass in any of your wounds?" he asked.

She gave her head a shake in the negative.

Lifting her foot, he propped it on his knee as he washed the slightly deeper cut. "You're not staying at your place alone tonight," he announced.

"Jack," she objected, "I'm really okay."

He wrapped a bandage around her foot. "I can take you to Paige's, if you want," was all he said.

"No way," she insisted immediately. "This will completely freak her out. She already doesn't sleep. I'm not going to go to her house in the middle of the night and tell her what happened. I know she's going to find out, but not tonight."

"Then you're staying with me," he informed her in a voice that brokered no argument.

Nonetheless, she offered one anyway. "I can stay at a hotel."

"What would be the point of that?" Jack set her foot down and reached for her hands. "You'd still be alone, wouldn't you? The point was you shouldn't be alone tonight."

The truth was, Rose didn't want to stay alone tonight. But that embarrassed her. She was a cop; she knew she was capable of taking care of herself; she knew her job required her to put herself into dangerous situations, and she knew that she had deliberately put herself into a dangerous situation tonight. She knew all of those things. And yet, she was still shaken. That man could have killed her. If he'd had a weapon, she would have been dead before Jack and the others could get to her.

She wasn't just shaken, she was drained as well. Bordering on exhausted. She needed to sleep and she knew she wasn't going to sleep alone in her house tonight. The idea of not being alone was tempting, yet still she resisted it.

"Jack," it came out as somewhat of a whimper.

"Yeah, I know." He finished applying bandages to her hands. "Come on, let's get you to bed. Can you walk?"

"Yes," she answered quickly before Jack could pick her up again.

"We're going to my place," her partner warned as he took her elbow and helped her stand.

"Sure," she agreed.

As Jack helped her limp to the door, she cast another glance at the handcuffed man on the apartment floor. The night had been successful. They had their guy. No one else was going to wind up dead or injured. Hopefully, that thought would help her sleep.

JULY 22ND

1:19 A.M.

Sometimes, Laura wondered if she would ever sleep properly again.

She hadn't had a good night's sleep since the night before she had been kidnapped.

For eleven years now, she had been lucky to grab a couple of hours of sleep a night. And even then, most nights her sleep was plagued with bad or at least unsettling dreams. When she got really tired, she would usually pass out from exhaustion and sleep through the night, which gave her enough reserves of sleep to last a couple of weeks until once again her overtired mind would crash.

She had slept even less than usual the last few nights.

Ever since her apartment building erupted into chaos.

Something else had happened here last night.

She didn't know what. She could have called Connor to ask him, but she hadn't really wanted to know. She was regretting asking about the first two crimes here. She didn't want to know that someone had been murdered here in her building. And she certainly didn't want to know that some poor woman had been raped.

Against her will, images began to flood her mind.

Herself lying almost naked on the ground.

The dry scratchy grass beneath her.

Strong hands holding her down.

The big, empty sky above her.

A man forcing himself inside her. Oblivious to her cries of

pain and her pleas for him to leave her alone.

The wind, the rain, the sunshine—all seemed amplified against her bare flesh.

Then the man holding her down took his turn.

Despite her struggles, she couldn't get free.

Two of them against her had stacked the odds firmly in their favor.

She didn't stand a chance.

As quickly as they had come, the memories fled.

She wasn't out in the woods anymore.

Now she was back in her own home, tucked in under her blankets, in her bed.

The flashbacks left her breathless. Like they always did.

Scrunching her eyes closed, Laura put all her energy into calming her ragged breaths. Tears seeped from the corners of her eyes, but she didn't bother wiping them away. She rarely did. There was never anyone here to see her cry, so she usually did it openly and with abandon.

Giving up on sleep for another night, Laura headed for the kitchen. She'd make some cocoa, read a book, and hopefully get tired enough to doze a little later in the day.

She filled a saucepan with milk and set it on the stove, stirring it absently. Her mind kept darting back to the past. If she could have one wish, it would be to erase her memories so she never had to think about what happened to her ever again.

Scratch that. If she could have one wish, it would be to erase what happened altogether. Those men never would have grabbed her. Never would have raped her. Never would have hurt her. None of it would ever have happened.

Too bad there was no way to make that happen.

Instead, she was stuck with her reality.

And no amount of wishing was going to change that.

She was stuck with her past, just like she was stuck with a future of flashbacks and nightmares, memories and never-ending fear.

It wasn't fair, but then, life wasn't.

Realizing her milk had started boiling, Laura reached for it. Unfortunately, she was still shaky from the flashback. She lost her grip on the saucepan and tipped it sideways, sending the boiling liquid sloshing all over her hand.

The sudden burning threw her mind back in time once again.

She lay on the ground.

The day was warm.

He sat on her stomach.

The other one held her arms down.

They were both laughing.

The one sitting on her pulled a cigarette from the pocket of his shirt.

The one holding her arms placed his knees on them, freeing up his hands and he retrieved a lighter from his pants.

His knees dug painfully into her biceps as he leaned forward to light the cigarette.

Holding the glowing cigarette in one hand, the man on top of her pushed up her bra with his other.

Laura knew what was going to happen before they did it.

Still, she wasn't prepared for the horrible sting that came when he pressed the tip of the cigarette against the tender flesh of her breast.

Despite her best intentions not to scream again, since she knew they liked it, a scream was ripped from her lips.

"Is everything all right in there?"

The voice and the knocking on her door that accompanied it brought her back to the present.

Someone was at her door.

Panic had her heart thumping painfully in her chest, her breathing quickened almost immediately to a pace that had her worrying she was going to hyperventilate.

"Hello? This is Officer Byrns. Is everything all right in there? I heard screaming."

The doorknob rattled as the officer obviously tried to enter.

Forcing herself to calm down enough to speak, Laura hurried to the door. She didn't want him breaking in here, and if she didn't offer an explanation and assurances that she was all right, then she feared he would.

"I'm fine," she said through the door; her voice trembled but there was nothing she could do about that. "I just had a nightmare."

"Do you need us to come in?" the cop's voice had softened in sympathy.

"No, I'm okay," she assured him quickly. The last thing she needed right now was to have someone in her apartment.

"If you're sure." The cop still sounded doubtful.

"I'm sure," she said firmly. "I'm sorry I startled you."

"No problem, ma'am, that's what we're here for. Good night, and hopefully you don't have more bad dreams."

"Thank you," Laura whispered. She waited at the door until she heard footsteps receding. Then she leaned wearily against it.

That had been a close call.

Not only did she not like being around people anymore, but she particularly didn't like being around cops. It wasn't so much that she disliked cops, more that she had spent so much time around them in the days and weeks following her attack, being asked the same questions repeatedly, being made to tell her story so many times it had nearly killed her. She could happily go the rest of her life without ever having to see one again.

They were all over building, though.

Connor had called her earlier to give her a heads up that the police were going to be patrolling the building over the next few days given the recent spate of assaults.

Laura hoped they could find this guy before anyone else got hurt. She didn't ever want anyone to go through what she had.

Glancing down as she went to push herself away from the

door, she was surprised to see her hand red and already starting to blister. Laura had forgotten that she'd burned it.

Feeling drained, she headed for the bathroom to soak her hand in cold water and then dress the burn.

* * * * *

4:31 A.M.

They must have thought he was an idiot.

Well, the police were going to find out they were completely and utterly mistaken.

He was *not* an idiot.

Far from it.

Their silly little switcheroo was not going to work.

He'd been watching the building and noticed immediately when Audrey Nichols had departed. He knew her schedule, knew she never usually went out in the evening after she returned from work.

It hadn't taken a genius to figure out that the police had caught on enough to stake out apartment 4J.

It had been a risk, albeit a calculated one, to work up the apartments like that. But he had made the decision to focus on *her* rather than the police and what they may or may not think.

He was going to have to make his move soon.

Much longer and the police would figure out who she was. And once they did, they were going to spirit her away and lock her up some place where he wouldn't be able to get to her.

He would not allow that to happen.

This time, no one was going to take her away from him.

There was just one more thing he had to do before he was ready to get her.

Since the police were busy pretending to be Audrey Nichols, he had had to alter his plans slightly. Actually, they were making things easier for him. Now he wouldn't have to worry about being careful to avoid police detection like he had last night when he'd broken into Jessica Elgar's apartment. Now he could just take his time and enjoy.

Speaking of such, he parked his van close to Audrey's motel room and climbed out.

Moving confidently, as though he belonged here, he headed straight for her door. He didn't want to stand out should anyone see him, not that there was much chance of that—the place was deserted. Which, given the fact that it was only four-thirty in the morning, seemed completely reasonable.

At the door, he fiddled with the lock then swung it open. It always amazed him that most people didn't take their safety seriously. Didn't they know how easy it was to pick a lock? Obviously not, or people would make sure they added deadbolts and safety chains. The fact that most people didn't care about how safe their homes were certainly made his job easier most of the time.

Except with the one person he wanted to get.

If she wasn't such a safety nut, he would have just grabbed her and been done with it. Still, what he'd been doing in her apartment building must be getting to her by now. Pushing her to the edge of what she could bear. And when she reached her limit, she'd be forced to leave that apartment. And then he'd get her.

He stepped inside and quickly closed the door behind him. He didn't want to wake Audrey Nichols until he was ready for her. He took a moment to let his eyes adjust to the dark room and get his bearings.

Although he was all for fun, he wanted to do this as quickly and efficiently as he could. There would be plenty of time later to play.

Reaching into his bag, which still held all the essentials for breaking and entering and restraining victims, he pulled out the bottle of chloroform and studied it. Did he want to knock her out? Sometimes, that really dulled the excitement. But then on the flip side, an unconscious victim was safer to transport than a conscious one. And unlike his other victims, Audrey Nichols was coming with him.

This time he wasn't killing her, nor was he leaving her behind.

Audrey was going to represent the final piece of his message.

She was the last base to cover.

This should be enough to send *her* running right out of that apartment and into his waiting arms.

He refocused himself on the task at hand. Chloroform or no chloroform? He had his gun on him, so he could do either. And of course, he had plastic zip ties and tape. So, he could scare her into submission and then restrain her and throw her in the back of his van. It was what he'd prefer to do.

But of course, it was always a risk.

There were no guarantees that she would comply. Sometimes scared people did stupid things. Even with the threat of the gun, she could try to make a run for it. And then he might be forced to kill her. He didn't want to, but, of course, he would if it came down to it and she gave him no choice. That would be a hassle, though, because then he'd have to move on to apartment 5J, and a whole family lived there. He didn't really enjoy hurting kids, and abducting an entire family would be a lot more hassle than it was worth. Especially given the police presence at the building.

Still, the thrill of taking her while she was conscious was enticing.

What the heck, he decided, taking risks was what made life worthwhile.

Setting the bottle of chloroform back into his bag, he pulled out his gun instead. Then he crept toward the bed. The woman must be a cold sleeper. Despite the warm night, she was under several layers of blankets.

He sat on the bed beside her.

Audrey Nichols was pretty. Not as pretty as Judith Barclay, but still pretty nonetheless. She had smooth black skin, large dark eyes, and thick brown hair that she obviously straightened.

They were going to have some fun together.

Maybe he'd even keep Audrey alive long enough to meet her. Maybe he'd make her watch him kill Audrey. Show her what he was going to do to her once he was finished playing with her. He wanted to take his time, though. There was no need to rush. He had all the time in the world to enjoy himself. And enjoy himself, he would. With eleven long years to fantasize about everything he was going to do to her when he finally got his hands on her again, he was going to make the most of it.

He roused himself; he didn't want to get lost in daydreams and have Audrey wake up before he was ready for her. Besides, he didn't need to daydream—he was about to experience the real thing.

With a practiced hand, he clamped down on Audrey's mouth and held the gun to her temple.

Just like the others, she came awake with a start. Panic filled her eyes and she started to fight him.

"I have a gun at your head, Audrey," he whispered in her ear. "If you don't stop squirming, I'm going to blow your brains out."

This fact had the desired effect. The woman immediately went stone still. Her chest heaved as she struggled to calm herself.

"I'm going to remove my hand from your mouth and tie you up. If you make a sound, not only will I kill you, but I'll track down every member of your family and every one of your friends and kill them, too. Understand?"

It seemed to take a moment for his words to penetrate her terrified haze, but eventually she nodded.

Cautiously, he removed his hand. When she remained quiet, he nodded, pleased. Making quick work of securing her wrists and ankles together, he was about to put some tape over her mouth when she spoke.

"Are you the man?" Audrey's voice was so quiet, he had to

strain to hear it. "From my building?"

He saw no reason to lie to the woman. "Yep, that's me," he agreed cheerfully.

"Why?" her voice trembled and she started to cry. "Why are you doing this to me? Why did you hurt those other people?"

Now that, he didn't have time to answer. At least, not right now. Right now, he had to get Audrey out of here and tucked safely away. So, instead of answering, he cut a piece of tape and slapped it down over her mouth. Audrey mewed a protest, but the muffled sound wouldn't have carried outside the room.

Now to get her out of here and into his van. It was parked close to the door, and the early hour still meant there wouldn't be many people about. But on the off chance anyone was up already, he didn't want to be seen carrying a woman from the motel to his van.

The police would soon realize that Audrey Nichols was missing. And they would assume he was the one to have taken her. But he didn't want them getting a lead on his van. He still needed it. Not just to transport Audrey, but also to enact the last stage of his plan.

Carrying her was out; or, at least, the very last option. He needed something to move her in. He scanned the room in search of something suitable. His bag was too small, but he spied a suitcase over by the closet. It wasn't a huge one, but Audrey was a skinny little thing, so it might work.

Unzipping it, he dumped all the clothing onto the floor, then turned back to the bed. Amused, he watched as Audrey wiggled herself to the edge of the bed. She reminded him of a caterpillar and he couldn't help but chuckle. At the edge of the bed, she swung her bound legs over the edge, then tried to stand. With her ankles tied together, she couldn't really move, and she lost her balance, helpless to break her fall with her hands still coupled together.

Once on the floor, she began her caterpillar wiggle again as she headed for the door. As amusing as it was to watch her slow progress, he didn't really have time for this, so gun in one hand, to remind her just who was in charge here and what the consequences were of disobeying him, he went to retrieve her.

Throwing her over his shoulder, he carried her to the suitcase and put her inside. It was a tight fit, and she fought him, knowing that once he had her inside, her chances of escaping dropped to virtually zero, but curling her up in the fetal position, he managed to just fit her in.

With Audrey safely tucked away, he collected his supplies and repacked them in his bag. Then taking it and grabbing hold of the suitcase's handle, he wheeled it out the door, locking it behind him.

Now closer to dawn, there were a few joggers and holidaymakers out and about, but no one cast him a second glance as he wheeled the suitcase along behind him toward his van. Opening the back door, he heaved the suitcase inside, tossed his bag in beside it, then slammed it closed.

Climbing into the driver's seat, he started the engine, and pleased with the night's events, he drove off down the street.

* * * * *

8:47 A.M.

Rose was feeling much better this morning, and more than a little embarrassed about last night's little meltdown.

After they'd left the apartment building, they had stopped briefly at her house so she could grab a change of clothes and some toiletries, then gone straight to Jack's. As soon as they got there, she had jumped into the shower, standing for ages under the steaming hot spray. Then Jack had helped her redress her wounds and she'd crawled into bed, falling asleep as soon as her head hit the pillow.

She awakened when Jack had gotten up only a few hours later, but she'd felt fully rested, and despite Jack's protestations that she go back to bed and take the day off, she had dressed and come with him to work.

No way was she missing out on interviewing the man who had attacked her.

Now she was standing watching Kirby Tam as he sat inside the interview room waiting for them. The man was huge. Tall and extremely well-muscled, with a shaved head and small brown eyes. He reminded Rose of a kind of dark, angry version of Jack. As she took in his size, she realized that had she not had backup last night, she would not have gotten away from the man alive. He was simply too big. She was well trained in self-defense—she even taught classes from time to time–but skill and training only went so far. In the end, size won out every time.

"You sure you want to do this?" Jack came up beside her.

"Positive," Rose assured her partner. She wasn't intimidated by Kirby Tam. Sure, he may be bigger and stronger than she was, but she was smarter. And right now, sitting in an interview room at the police station, Kirby's size wasn't going to do him any favors.

Jack looked doubtful but didn't say anything else. They had argued in the car on the way here about whether or not she should even be in today. But, as far as Rose was concerned, there was no good reason for her to stay home. She'd been shaken last night, but some good sleep had taken care of that. The cuts on her foot, knees, and hands had stung last night, but a couple of Tylenol had done away with that and this morning she barely even felt them. What would be the point of her lounging around in bed all day when she could be here at work making sure that Kirby Tam never had the opportunity to hurt another person?

"Let's do this," she announced.

"I can do the interview, if you want," Jack offered.

"I know you're worried about me, Jack, but I'm okay. I really am. I chose to stay in Audrey Nichols' apartment last night. I chose to put myself in this guy's path. I'm not Paige and I'm not Sofia; I didn't just get attacked while going about my everyday life, and I didn't even end up with any serious injuries. I really am fine," she assured her partner.

"Okay," Jack agreed, sighing deeply. "But if you change your mind in there, just let me know."

"I'm not going to change my mind," she said stubbornly. Jack merely nodded and followed her as she strode into the interview room.

At the sound of the opening door, Kirby's head snapped up. As he looked at her, recognition dawned and a small smirk lit his face. "Hi, Detective," he drawled.

"Good morning, Mr. Tam," she replied calmly.

Disappointment had his smirk dimming a little, but still he kept his tone cocky. "Hope I didn't hurt you too badly last night."

Refusing to get drawn into Kirby's game, she merely kept her face impassive and took her seat. "Mr. Tam, you are being charged with murder, sexual assault, several counts of aggravated assault, and attempted murder of a police officer."

"I'm being charged with what now?" he snapped irritably. Kirby Tam hadn't lost his attitude throughout the night. He was still snippy and argumentative, and even the prospect of facing several extremely serious charges wasn't going to diminish that.

Patiently, Rose repeated the crimes. "Murder, sexual assault, aggravated assault, and attempted murder of a police officer."

"I didn't try to kill you." Kirby rolled his eyes as though the notion were ridiculous.

"You grabbed me, chased me, and were pinning me to the floor when you were dragged off me," Rose reminded him.

He snorted. "That's hardly attempting to murder you. I don't even know you. I was surprised to find you there. And who exactly do you think I murdered?"

"We don't *think* you murdered anyone. We *know* you murdered Tarek Milford," she replied.

"Who is Tarek Milford?" Kirby was looking at them suspiciously, as though he thought they may be trying to trick him.

"Tarek Milford lives in Audrey's apartment building. You do know Audrey Nichols, don't you, Mr. Tam, since you did break into her apartment last night?" Rose goaded.

"Of course, I know Audrey." Kirby gave them a withering glare. "But I didn't kill anyone."

"Mr. Tam, we know that you did, we are simply waiting for the fingerprint and DNA samples we took from you earlier to be compared to those collected from the crime scenes." Rose was wondering why Kirby Tam was denying his crimes. Maybe he was trying to play coy to get out of here and to whoever the woman was he was really after.

"You think I'm that guy who's been attacking people in Audrey's building?" When they both nodded, Kirby continued with a small, smug smile. "I was right. I knew you'd think it was him. If you hadn't been there," he snarled at her, "then it would have gone perfectly."

Rose exchanged a glance with Jack. "What would have gone perfectly, Mr. Tam?"

"My plan," he answered. "I didn't kill that old guy in Audrey's building, and I didn't rape anybody, either. But I had heard about the crime spree. I thought I'd take advantage of it."

"For what reason, Mr. Tam?" Jack asked.

"Audrey and I were married; our divorce was finalized a few weeks ago."

"Was it an amicable separation?" Rose asked, knowing that it wouldn't have been because Kirby Tam didn't seem to do anything amicably, but wanting confirmation.

"No," Kirby replied a little sullenly.

"Why did you separate?"

"Because Audrey is a control freak. She tricked me into marrying her. Pretended that she was cool, open-minded, that she wasn't going to be like other girls and freak out over everything I did. But she did. As soon as we were married, she started trying to monitor everything I did, everyone I talked to, every place I went. She wanted to change me. Nothing I ever did was good enough for her. I drank too much, I spent too much time with my 'loser' friends, as she called them. She didn't like that I flirted with beautiful women, she was jealous." Anger and resentment toward Audrey was seeping out of every pore in Kirby's body.

"Who ended things, you or Audrey?" Jack asked.

"She did," Kirby pouted. "She caught me sleeping with another woman, said she never signed up for that. Little witch was lying, though; she knew who I was before we got married. But women always think they'll change a man." Kirby glared at her as though she were personally responsible for every decision every woman had ever made.

"So, you were angry at her?" Rose continued.

"Of course I was. In the divorce, she thought she was entitled to everything she wanted just because I slept with a few other women. She convinced the judge in our divorce proceedings to give her everything, even things that were mine, things she didn't even want," Kirby raged.

"So, you wanted to do something about it?" Rose pressed.

"Yeah, I sure did. I didn't care about Audrey, she wasn't even that pretty. I can get women ten times more beautiful, but I wanted my stuff back. She shouldn't be allowed to be spiteful and get away with it," he groused.

"So, what did you intend to do about it?" Rose was wondering whether Audrey was the intended victim that their killer was after, and the others were the collateral damage along the way.

"I intended to get my stuff back," Kirby repeated as though she were an idiot.

"And just how did you intend to get it back?"

For the first time, Kirby started to look a little uncomfortable. "I was just going to tie her up. Maybe knock her around a little.

But I swear that was it." His brown eyes bounced from her to Jack, trying to gauge if they believe him or not. Apparently deciding they weren't convinced, he continued, "I was going to tie her up, blindfold her so she didn't know it was me. That was it. Then I'd get my stuff and leave. I thought Audrey and the rest of you would just think it was that guy who'd been hurting people in the building. I thought I'd get away with it. That no one would even be thinking about me. If I'd known you were going to be there instead of Audrey, I wouldn't have done it."

"Audrey said no one else had a key to her apartment, but you unlocked the door to get in." Jack was staring at Kirby Tam with a look that suggested he believed that Kirby was not the man they were looking for.

Rose, however, wasn't quite ready to believe that yet.

"I still had a key," Kirby replied tightly.

"She changed the locks after you moved out though, right? So, how did you have a copy?" Jack raised a blond eyebrow.

"I stole it, okay?" Kirby sighed.

"How?"

Another sigh. "I had a friend chat her up at a bar, then when she wasn't looking, swipe her keys. Then he met me in the bathroom, gave me the key and I went and had a copy made. Then I went back to the bar and slipped my friend the key. He put them back in her bag before she even knew they'd been missing," Kirby explained.

"I think you had more in mind for Audrey than just tying her up and stealing back your things." Rose watched Kirby closely for his reaction. "I think you intended to hurt her, maybe even kill her."

"That's crazy," Kirby growled. "I never laid a finger on Audrey when we were together, and even though I was angry with her, I would never have physically hurt her."

"You said you might have knocked her around a bit last night if she'd been there," Rose reminded him.

"Just to make it believable," he added defensively.

"I think you were just so angry with her, you wanted her to suffer. I think that you killed Tarek Milford, raped Judith Barclay, and tortured Jessica Elgar, just to throw suspicion off your intended victim. I think you wanted us to think there was some lunatic stalking the building, so that when you got around to Audrey we wouldn't even be thinking about you, then you'd be free to do to Audrey whatever you wanted."

"That's insane," Kirby roared. "Do you think I'm some kind of nutcase?"

Out of the corner of her eye, Rose saw Jack stand and move to a corner of the room, his phone in his hand. She kept her attention focused on Kirby. "I don't know if I'd call you a nutcase," she commented mildly. "You certainly planned this all out carefully. You knew exactly what you were doing. You organized everything perfectly. I'd say you're more like an evil genius than a nutcase."

Before Kirby could make a retort, Jack returned to the table. "His prints don't match," her partner announced. "DNA doesn't, either. He didn't commit the murder, rape, or torture."

"See?" Kirby smiled triumphantly. "I told you I didn't. I told you it wasn't me. I'm out of here." With that, he stood dismissively.

"You're not going anywhere, Mr. Tam," Rose informed him, stopping him with an outstretched hand.

"Why?" He looked confused. "You just said your forensics proved I didn't kill or rape anyone."

"Our forensics showed you weren't the perpetrator of the murder, rape, and torture that were committed in the building. But you will still be prosecuted for breaking and entering Audrey's apartment and for assaulting a police officer. You are not going anywhere. In fact, you won't be going anywhere, other than to prison, for a very long time," Rose finished with a smug smile of her own. Kirby Tam was really getting on her nerves.

"You witch!" Kirby threw himself at her, lunging across the table, sending his chair clattering to the floor, and the papers on the table flying.

He got maybe halfway toward her when Jack grabbed him, throwing him up against the wall and twisting his arm behind his back. Kirby continued to yell obscenities at her, even as other officers flooded the room.

"You okay?" Jack kept one hand on Kirby as another officer cuffed him.

"Fine," Rose assured him as her heart rate slowed back down to normal. Kirby Tam's little stunt had done little more than give her a momentary start. She wasn't afraid of him. And she doubted he was stupid enough to come after her if he got released on bail.

What was worrying her more was that another suspect had slipped through their fingers. Kirby Tam wasn't their guy.

Which meant their guy was still out there—somewhere.

And so was the woman he was after.

And they were no closer to finding either one of them.

Which meant they were no closer to ending this and had no idea how many more casualties were going to fall before this guy got what he wanted.

"I'll see you in court, Mr. Tam," she called sweetly after him as he was dragged, still yelling, from the room.

* * * * *

1:03 P.M.

"We've been wrong twice now." Jack tried to say it like a statement, but thought it probably came out as more of a dejected whine.

Both Harry Kinkirk and Kirby Tam, while neither of them were decent human beings, had turned out not to be the man they were looking for, based on the forensics. Jack was hoping there was some way the forensics could be wrong. He knew they weren't and yet still he hoped they were.

"Steph?"

"Hmm?" the crime scene tech looked up from her papers.

"Is there any way the forensics could be wrong?"

"Wrong, how?" Stephanie looked confused.

"Maybe the prints are just from whomever made or packaged the stars," he suggested, knowing he was clutching at straws with that idea.

She shook her head. "No one would have touched the stars before whomever put them on Tarek Milford's ceiling took them out of the package. And the prints are at all three crime scenes," Stephanie reminded him. "And not just on the stars; they're on the duct tape, the doors, light switches."

"What if the prints were faked?" Jack proposed.

"What do you mean by faked?" Stephanie had set down her papers to give him her full attention, her brown eyes inquisitive.

"What if he's planting them? Trying to set someone up?"

"Placements of the prints suggest they're genuine," Stephanie informed him.

"Wouldn't it make more sense to frame someone who already had a criminal record if you were going to go to all that trouble, rather than use someone's prints that we don't even have?" Rose put forward.

His partner was looking better than he was feeling this morning. Last night had been rough and left all of them a little shaken. Jack hadn't wanted Rose to go through with her plan of playing decoy in the first place. Then having to sit in the neighboring apartment, doing nothing, while they waited for their guy to show up had been excruciating.

Then watching as the man, whom they now knew as Kirby Tam, get off the elevator at the fourth floor, walk to apartment 4J, put a key into the lock and enter the apartment, while he had to sit there and do nothing but watch had taken every ounce of self-control he possessed. What he'd wanted to do was go running to the man and arrest him as soon as it was clear he was going to enter apartment 4J.

However, they needed him to enter. So, Jack had forced himself to remain still as Kirby closed the door behind him and headed straight for the bedroom, where he had expected to find Audrey Nichols. Instead, Kirby had been surprised to see Rose coming out of the bathroom. When he had wrapped an arm around her neck, Jack and every other detective and officer in the room had sprung into action.

Luckily, Rose hadn't received more than a few minor scratches. Kirby was a big guy; he could easily have killed Rose before any of them were able to get to her. His partner had been shaken at first, evident in the fact that she had agreed with minimal fuss to come and spend the night at his place. But by the time they'd picked up a change of clothes at her place, gotten to his, where she'd jumped immediately into the shower, she had already started to calm down. She'd gone straight to his spare room and into bed, where she had slept peacefully until he'd accidentally awakened her while getting ready for work. Of course, she had ignored his attempts to convince her to take the day off, saying she felt well rested and completely fine to be back at work.

Jack, on the other hand, had been too wired to sleep. He hated being put in a position where he had to watch something awful happening while being powerless to do anything about it. So, he had just laid in bed, staring at the ceiling and replaying the night's events over and over in his mind. He honestly didn't know how he would have coped had the outcome been different. Catching their killer, if it had cost him his partner, would not have seemed like a fair trade.

"All right, I get it, I'm stretching," he admitted, refocusing himself on his colleagues. "It's just that we've had two viable suspects–both with links to the building. Both with motives. Harry Kinkirk could have been getting his revenge on Judith and

Tarek, and Jessica was just collateral damage. And same with Kirby Tam—he could have thought he'd throw suspicion off himself when he went after Audrey by attacking Tarek, Judith, and Jessica. The only reason both of them weren't charged with the crimes was the forensics. Maybe one of them decided to muddy the waters by framing someone else."

"Interesting theory." Rose was looking thoughtful. "Maybe one of them decided to work with a partner. The fingerprints and DNA could be from them instead."

"Only there was no suggestion of a partner in either Judith Barclay or Jessica Elgar's statements," Jack pointed out. "Although, thinking of that, he covered his face with Judith but not with Jessica, maybe it was because he thought Judith could identify him. Could be further proof that he lives in the building. Jessica hasn't lived here long, so she might not have met him yet, but Judith has lived here a while, so she might know him. Could also explain why there were no defensive wounds on Tarek Milford—maybe he knew the guy, too, and didn't consider him a threat."

"I've been running any of the residents with criminal records to see if their fingerprints or DNA match our crime scenes, but so far, no luck," Stephanie told them.

"We still could get lucky. There's plenty more to go through," Rose commented.

"Also, back to your partner theory, Rose; we didn't find any fingerprints from Kirby Tam or Harry Kinkirk in either of the apartments. If one of them were the mastermind behind all of this and working with an accomplice then wouldn't the partner notice that either Kirby or Harry were wearing gloves and taking forensic countermeasures?" Stephanie pointed out.

"Good point," Rose acknowledged.

"It seems more like he just doesn't care about leaving his fingerprints and DNA behind. I think he knows he's not in the system, so we aren't going to have his prints on file in any of our databases; therefore, we're not going to find him through them," Stephanie said. "Of course, they're still useable for comparison when you do find this guy, but I'm thinking he doesn't anticipate you catching him."

"He's definitely smug—arrogant even; it's like he's flaunting it in our face that we aren't going to get him." The killer's attitude made Jack all the more determined to catch him. "Chloroform hard to find or make, Steph? I've never actually worked a case where someone used it. I thought it was too 'Hollywood' for real criminals to use."

"You can get anything these days on the internet, so I'm sure it would be available. And if you know what you're doing, it wouldn't be too hard to make. Instructions are probably available on the internet, too, but you'd need to be careful making it, so you'd probably need some experience," Stephanie explained.

"We need some sort of profile, some sort of indication of who we're looking for," Rose mused.

"Motive for the murder wasn't robbery, wasn't mob or gang related," he said. "Could be crime of passion or mental illness, but it seems too well executed and organized to be either. I guess it could be some sort of thrill kill, only there was no infliction of suffering on the victim. Although, I guess if we include the torture of Jessica Elgar into the equation, he definitely enjoys inflicting pain."

"He *definitely* enjoys inflicting pain," Rose agreed. "And he indicated to Jessica that he's done this before, and that he usually would use a more secluded location. That definitely implies he likes to take his time and ensure that they suffer."

"And," Jack added, "he told her that usually he'd be happy for her to scream as much as she wanted; that definitely indicated that he enjoys knowing and hearing that his victims are suffering. He feeds off it. It's important to him. He probably has kept his other victims for hours—days, most likely—maybe even weeks, before he killed them."

"What if we add the rape in?" Rose asked.

"Just another method of torture, another way to dominate them, unleash his anger," Jack replied. "I bet if he'd had more time with Judith and a more private location, the rape would have been a lot more violent. I think if we look at everything as a whole, then his motives are revenge. He knows his victims; this isn't just some random thing for him. It means something. He believes that his victims have done something to him deserving punishment. He's angry at this woman, he wants her to suffer, and he's prepared to use any means available to achieve it. You don't do that for a stranger."

"So, what are we looking for in the intended victim? I mean, other than she obviously has a connection to this guy."

He considered this for a moment. "I'd guess she could be an ex-lover who somehow got in the way of his plans. Maybe he hurt her and she went to the police, maybe she found out what he was doing, maybe she just left him and it made him mad. Or maybe she's one of his victims who somehow managed to escape. That would certainly make him mad, and given how methodical and organized he is about everything, he would certainly want to finish what he started."

"If he's done this before, as we believe he has, then we should look into finding his previous victims," Rose proposed.

"They may never have even been found," Jack commented. "He's highly organized, he probably made sure that the bodies were carefully disposed of. Still, we should look into it. He chose each aspect of these crimes carefully—murder, rape, torture— they each mean something; they're each a piece of the puzzle. I bet it's what he does to his victims, so the MO of the torture should link us to any other crimes that are in the system. Could give us a place to start in locating who this real target is."

Jack was extremely concerned about this mystery woman. Had she gotten the killer's so-called message? If she had, why hadn't she come to the police for help? If she knew him, then she had to know what he was capable of. And given what he had done to these random victims just to get a message across to this woman, whatever he had in store for her had to be much, much worse. Maybe she hadn't yet realized this was all about her. If she hadn't, then she wasn't going to be prepared when he finally made his move and came after her.

"I have bad news."

His, Rose's, and Stephanie's heads all popped up as Belinda entered the room. The lieutenant's glum face indicated that the news she had for them was worse than simply bad news.

"Audrey Nichols is missing," Belinda announced.

"Missing?" Jack repeated, his heart dropping.

She nodded dismally. "When I sent officers around to the motel to pick her up and bring her back here, she was gone," Belinda explained.

"Gone like, gone to work or someplace else to get away from the craziness at her apartment building?" Rose asked hopefully.

"Her car is still in the motel's parking lot, her cell phone and purse were still in the room, as were her clothes, minus her suitcase," Belinda replied.

"I better get over there." Stephanie stood and gathered her things. "I'll talk to you guys later."

"He got her," Jack murmured disbelievingly. "This one is our fault."

"We didn't know he would follow her to a motel," Rose reminded him.

"But we knew he was after someone in that building; it could have been Audrey and we left her alone and unprotected." Jack didn't want any excuses. It was their job to protect people and they had failed Audrey Nichols—it was as simple as that. "We should have had her stay in her apartment and just watched her, backed her up, like we did with Rose last night."

"We sent her away to try and keep her safe," Rose reminded him gently.

"Well, he got her, anyway." Guilt was gnawing at his stomach. "We didn't even send someone to keep an eye on her. We should have predicted he'd do this. He's been focused and organized the whole way along. We should have known we couldn't fool him. That he'd follow through with his plan no matter what we did."

"He knew she wasn't going to be in her apartment," Rose commented. "He never even tried to get in. He knew we were trying to set him up. He knew we made a switch. He must have been watching the building the entire time. It's the only way he could have known. If he'd been watching, he would have seen Audrey leave and could have followed her straight to the motel."

"Get busy interviewing those apartment residents," Belinda ordered. "We don't know that Audrey is who he really wants, she could easily still be just another pawn in his game. And if she's not his target, then we need to find this woman before he does."

* * * * *

8:24 P.M.

"So, playing decoy two nights in a row; seems like you need a life." Jack grinned at her.

"Ha, ha, very funny. You know you have no more of a life outside of work than I do," Rose shot back with a playful glare.

She and her partner were spending the night in apartment 5J. They'd sent the family who lived here, which consisted of a middle-aged couple and their two young children, a six-year-old girl, and a baby boy who was only four months old, to spend the night at a motel. Only this time, they were sending a police guard along with the family. And the two of them were going to stay here in the hope that their killer might make another attempt at entering what they were assuming was the next apartment on his list.

It had been her idea, and she had expected Jack to protest after last time. He didn't want her using herself as bait again. But instead, he had merely nodded, and said they'd both do it.

Again, they had backup in both the neighboring apartments and surveillance set in both apartment 5J and the hallways on this floor. They had played with the idea of evacuating the entire building, but ended up deciding against it. Last time, their killer had simply followed Audrey Nichols to the motel to abduct her. If he wanted any one of the residents in this building, it seemed more than likely he was going to get to them no matter where they were. And they couldn't afford the cost of putting twenty-four-hour guards on every single person who lived here until this case was resolved. So, it seemed best to at least keep everyone here where they could keep an eye on them.

Jack had taken Audrey Nichols' disappearance particularly hard.

For some reason, her partner had developed the habit of feeling guilty for every victim in every case they worked. Jack blamed himself. Acted as though he were personally responsible for the tragedies that befell those they encountered in their job.

And she was tired of letting him get away with it.

Tired of letting him get away with all of it. The depression, the personality changes, the refusal to have any life that wasn't related to work. She was done.

"That's it," she announced. Jack looked at her in surprise. "I've had it with beating around the bush with you, so I'm just going to come right out and ask you. What happened?"

Jack's blue eyes went blank. "What happened with what?" he asked innocently.

She narrowed her eyes at him. "No playing stupid," she warned. "What happened on that trip you took?"

"What trip?"

"I mean it, Jack." She bit back her frustration since she knew her partner would use it as an excuse not to open up to her. "Three years ago. You went away on a vacation with your girlfriend, and you came back minus the girlfriend and with a whole different attitude."

Jack couldn't quite hide the horrified surprise that flitted across his face. "I-I ..." he stammered.

"You what?" Rose demanded quietly. "Did you think I wouldn't notice? Come on, I'm not stupid. I know something happened on that trip. Something bad," she added gently.

"If you thought something bad happened, why didn't you just find out about it on your own?"

"Because I wanted you to tell me when you were ready. I didn't want to invade your privacy."

"Then what's this?" Jack pouted sullenly.

"This is your friend caring about you," she replied calmly.

Jack rolled his eyes, but his entire body was tense. Rose knew she was getting to him.

"I know you're lonely. I know you want what Ryan and Mark have. And yet, you refuse to do anything about it. And the last few months, you've been getting worse. You're getting depressed. You blame yourself for every bad thing that crosses your path. It all leads back to that vacation. What happened, Jack?" She pushed a little more; he was almost ready to open up, she was sure of it.

For a long moment, he just stared at her, as though he couldn't believe she was actually confronting him on this. Then he gave a resigned sigh. "All right, so I get a little jealous sometimes that Ryan and Mark are so happy with their families, but I don't resent them. I'm happy for them. I just wish that I had someone, too."

"Then why do you avoid relationships?"

Instead of answering that, he conceded. "Okay, you're right. Something did happen on that vacation, but I'm not ready to talk about it yet."

She attempted to cover her surprise that Jack had admitted she was right. Rose had hoped that he would admit it, but she hadn't really believed he would. Apparently, she failed in hiding her shock because Jack shot her a wry smile. She smiled back. "You're going to have to talk about it soon, though. Otherwise, you're going to wake up one day and realize that you let your whole life go by and you're still alone."

"Hey, you're alone," Jack reminded her.

"But I like being alone, and you don't," she countered.

"Did you tell Paige what happened last night?" he asked, abruptly changing the topic. "Because if you don't tell her, she's going to find out from someone else, and you don't want that. She should hear it from you."

Taking Jack's admissions as progress, she went along with his topic change. Although going from him to Paige was just exchanging one set of concerns for another. "Yeah, I told her." Rose grimaced.

Catching her grimace, he asked, "She didn't take it well?"

"You could say that," she agreed. Before she and Jack had met up here, she had gone to Paige's house to let her friend know about her run in last night with Kirby Tam. Usually doing that wouldn't have worried her; she would simply have slipped it into conversation, but Paige had been so sensitive lately that Rose had dreaded having to tell her.

"What did she say?" Jack asked.

"Nothing."

"What do you mean 'nothing'?" Jack looked confused.

"I mean, she said nothing," Rose repeated. "When I told her, she just freaked out and ran from the room. She refused to talk to me. Locked herself in the bathroom. Elias was working a night shift tonight, and I didn't want to leave her alone, so I called Ryan and asked him to go and stay with her. Jack, I don't know what I'm going to do about her."

"Hopefully coming back to work will help her to get back to her old self," Jack consoled.

"I hope so," she murmured, completely unconvinced. Dealing with Paige made her feel completely helpless. She wanted desperately to help her friend, but she just didn't know how.

Before Jack could respond, her phone began to ring. She dug it out of her purse pressed answer. "Hello. Detective Lace speaking."

"Detective, this is Connor Newman, one of the doormen."

"What can we do for you, Mr. Newman?" She remembered meeting him the first day they'd come to the apartment building. He was an older gentleman, in his late sixties, with thinning, grey hair and warm, brown eyes.

"You said to call you if anything unusual happened," he replied.

Excitement sparked inside her and she threw a quick smile at Jack. "What happened, Mr. Newman?"

"Well, one of the residents just came in and he said he saw someone hanging around outside. He said the person left a letter of some sort," Connor explained.

"We'll be right down, Mr. Newman." She was already heading for the door, gesturing at Jack to follow. "Keep the man who found the letter with you; we're going to want to talk to him," she ordered. "We'll be right there."

"What letter?" Jack asked the second she hung up.

"One of the doormen, Connor Newman, said one of the residents just came to him and said he saw someone outside leaving a letter of some sort," Rose informed him as they took the stairs down to the ground floor.

"Did anyone catch the guy who left the letter?" Jack asked. They still had officers both inside and outside the building.

"I don't think so, but I didn't get a chance to ask, I just wanted to get down there," she replied as they pushed through the stairwell door and jogged to the front desk where Connor Newman and another man were waiting for them.

"Detective Lace, Detective Xander, this is Mr. Christenson." Connor made the introductions as soon as they reached him.

"Axel Christenson," the man added.

"Mr. Christenson, do you know if any officers went to look for the man you saw?" Jack immediately inquired.

"As soon as Mr. Christenson told me what he'd seen, I reported it to the officer in the lobby and he went to see if the man was still out there, then I called you." Connor answered before Axel could.

"All right, I'll go see if they found anything." Jack glanced at her and she nodded her assent.

"Okay, Mr. Christenson, can you tell me exactly what you saw?" Rose asked once Jack had headed outside.

"I was coming home from work; my car is in the shop, so a co-worker dropped me off just down the street a little way. I was walking toward the front door and I saw someone—I think it was a man—who was dressed all in black. He was right by the front, near the sidewalk, and it looked like he was putting something in the bushes out there. Normally, I wouldn't have even looked twice, but given what's been going on here, I walked toward him. When he saw me, he ran off. I started to chase him, then thought maybe that wasn't the best idea. So, I stopped, found the letter, and came straight in here and told Connor," Axel summarized.

"Did you get a good look at the guy?" She hoped Axel Christenson could corroborate the description of the guy they'd gotten from Jessica Elgar.

"Not really," Axel replied apologetically. "It was dark and I didn't get that close. Maybe kind of my height, with darkish hair, I think. Sorry, that's the best I can do."

"That's fine, Mr. Christenson," she assured him. As soon as they were done here, she'd call Stephanie and get the letter tested for prints—that should confirm whether or not this was from their guy. "Did you touch the letter?"

"No, I left it where it was; I didn't want to mess up your forensics," he replied, a little smugly.

"All right, thanks, we'll call you if we need to know anything else," she informed him.

"I can go now?" Axel confirmed.

"Yes, thanks."

"You've got officers still here, right?" he queried.

"Right," Rose assured Axel Christenson.

"And you're making progress in finding this guy who's terrorizing our homes?" The look Axel gave her was stern.

"We're working this case as hard as we can," she promised.

Axel's face changed from stern to skeptical, but he nodded once and then strode off toward the lifts. Connor Newman was off to the side talking with another resident, so Rose headed straight for the front door. She spotted Jack down by the bushes at the sidewalk.

"Jack," she called.

He looked up and waved her over. "I was just about to open the letter," he told her once she reached him.

"Did you find the man Axel Christenson saw?" she asked.

"Nope, he was long gone. Probably in a car and off down the street before Axel even made it inside," he answered.

With gloves on, Jack carefully used a small knife to make a slit along the top of the envelope. Then he slid out a piece of paper, holding it out so they both could read it at the same time.

Greetings Detectives,

Congratulations! Finally, you caught on. Apartment 1J, apartment 2J, apartment 3J, apartment 4J—they were all just steps on my way to my goal.

For *her* sake, you better find her before I get my hands on her. But you won't. You'll never find her and you'll never find me.

Enjoy your evening.

P.S. Don't bother keeping the Zeke family out all night; I'm not interested in them!

"Well, he's certainly pretty cocky," Rose mused wryly.

"He's pretty confident we aren't going to find him, or her," Jack agreed.

"He was watching us again," she noted. "He knew the Zeke family wasn't in apartment 5J tonight."

"We have to find her, Rose," Jack said desperately. "When he gets his hands on her, he's going to torture and rape her until he gets bored and then he's going to kill her. We have to find her."

And if they didn't, then her partner was going to blame himself. Although on this one, Rose would probably find herself joining Jack in being swamped with guilt. This guy kept circling around them, darting in and out of this building despite their presence. He was like a ghost. And if they didn't get to this woman first, she was going to wind up a ghost, too. Literally.

JULY 23RD

7:56 A.M.

"All righty," Belinda announced, "let's get through this meeting quickly so we can get moving with our interviews."

Jack was tired. He hadn't gotten much sleep the last few nights. Last night, it had been close to two before he'd finally fallen into bed before rising at seven to grab a quick shower and come back to work. They had a lot to get through today.

At least it had been a quiet night.

Their killer seemed content with the fact that he had gotten his message across. He hadn't felt the need to go after anyone else—either another random casualty or his intended victim. But that wouldn't last.

This guy was having fun, but he was only just getting warmed up.

They had to find the woman.

There was simply no other option.

If they didn't find her, not only would she be killed, but she'd be horribly tortured first.

The knowledge left him with an unpleasant tightening in his chest that he was afraid would never go away if they didn't get to this woman first. He couldn't live with any more deaths on his conscience. And this one would weigh heavily.

They were close.

The letter confirmed it.

That woman was in the building.

They just had to find her.

What was really worrying Jack was that this woman might not

even know that she was the target. They were working the theory that she was either a previous victim of this man or else a previous lover. But that didn't mean that she had realized these crimes were related to her. And if that were the case, if this woman didn't know that this was all about her, then they could interview her, discount her, and move on.

"The prints from the motel once again match our samples from the other scenes," Stephanie was saying.

"So, it was definitely him. He has her." Jack felt his heart drop. They'd known this, but having it confirmed made it seem more real.

"Looks like it," Stephanie agreed dejectedly.

"We'll find Audrey, Jack. We'll find this mystery woman, too." Rose reached over and patted his hand sympathetically.

His partner seemed to sense his disproportionate guilt. In fact, she apparently knew a lot more about what went on inside his head than he'd ever realized. Perhaps he'd been naïve to think that no one would notice the change in his behavior after that nightmare of a vacation three years ago.

"Yeah," he agreed morosely. "But will we find either of them alive? Audrey could already be dead. He doesn't really need her. She was just a pawn."

"No, I think Audrey is still alive," Rose disagreed. "I think he'll keep her alive until he gets this woman he's really after. I think he'll want her to see him kill Audrey. Make sure she knows that Audrey is only dying because of her. He wanted this woman to suffer. What better way than making her watch him kill someone he took just to send her a message?"

"That's makes sense," Jack begrudgingly acknowledged. The idea that Audrey was still alive and they still had time to find her before he killed her should have made him feel better, but it didn't. Because they all knew that this poor woman would be subjected to horrible suffering. If the killer didn't plan on attacking anyone else from the apartment building until he made his play for the woman he was after, then Audrey Nichols was going to be his only source for fun until he claimed his real prize. That did not spell good news for Audrey.

"Did anyone report seeing anything at the motel the night Audrey was taken?" Rose asked.

"Not so far," Belinda replied.

"He probably went in early, while it was still dark and no one would be out and about," Rose commented.

"He would have made sure he looked like he fitted in," Jack added. "In case anyone spotted him, he would have looked like just another tourist staying at the motel."

"He has a real knack for blending in," Rose agreed. "We still don't know how he's getting in and out of that building or whether he's a resident there. Any way we can get a warrant to print everyone in the building?"

Belinda shook her head. "Not unless you get something to narrow it down or something that directly points to a particular resident. But so far, we don't have anything to prove he lives there so no judge is going to okay printing the entire building."

"What about the sketch of the guy Jessica Elgar described as her attacker?" Rose persisted. "Can't we at least print anyone who matches the description?"

"You've seen the picture, it's pretty vague," Belinda reminded her. "It could match nearly any man, I don't think it's enough to let us do the prints. Basically, we'd still be printing every male who lived in the building."

"We can ask them to volunteer their fingerprints and DNA, though," Jack suggested. "As we interview each apartment, we can ask the residents if they'd be willing to voluntarily offer up the samples so we can discount them. If they're innocent and have nothing to hide, they should offer them without complaint. Especially since they're all desperate to find this guy and end this so they and their families are safe. And anyone who refuses can go on our list as a suspect. It'll at least help us narrow things down."

Belinda nodded her consent. "We'll also go back over the apartments where the residents have already been interviewed and ask them to volunteer their samples."

"If we can locate this woman and get her out of the building, it'll mess up his plans." Jack paused thoughtfully. "Like it did with Audrey."

"It didn't seem to mess him up," Rose countered. "He simply followed her to the motel and grabbed her there."

"Yeah, but he had to use Audrey's suitcase," Jack pointed out. "He didn't have anything with him that was suitable to get her out of the building and to his car. If he did, he wouldn't have had to dump her clothes on the floor and stuff her inside her suitcase to get her out."

"That's true, he wasn't ready for that," Rose agreed. "He obviously had something different in mind if she'd been in her apartment, but, since she wasn't, he had to improvise."

"So, he's organized, and he can adapt, but then he has to improvise. If we can mess things up by removing this woman from where he thinks she's going to be, it would definitely give us the advantage."

"That only works if we can find her, though," Belinda said. "We're looking into Audrey's background, speaking with her family and friends, to see if she might have been the intended target. It seems feasible since he went to so much effort to get her."

"But we can't be sure that Audrey was the target, especially since the letter seems to imply otherwise," Jack reminded him.

"I don't see why he'd bother to come back to the building just to leave us a taunting note if he already had who he really wanted," Rose mused.

"It would be too risky," Jack agreed, "to come back there when he knows how many cops are going to be there, just to goad us. If it was Audrey he wanted, then he already had her. It would be stupid to come back. He would have just taken her and disappeared."

"That doesn't discount her as the intended victim, though," Belinda countered.

"But the letter does imply she wasn't. He congratulates us for realizing that his previous victims were just pawns in his game. And he includes Audrey in that. Then he also tells us that he doesn't care about the Zeke family. And then he tells us that for 'her' sake, we better get to her first, but he knows we won't find her or him. It wasn't Audrey he was after, the real woman is still out there somewhere," Jack summarized.

"Are we sure the letter is really from our killer and not just some nut after attention?" Belinda queried.

"Prints match, Steph?" Jack asked the crime scene tech.

"Yep, same as the prints from apartments 1J, 2J, 3J, and the motel," Stephanie confirmed.

"Okay," Belinda conceded. "We'll assume Audrey isn't the intended target, but I'll keep people looking into her past, just to be safe. You two," Belinda directed to Jack and Rose, "keep working through the 'J' apartments. That seems to be where we'll be most likely to find this woman."

"We know it isn't anyone in apartments 1J through 5J, and yesterday Rose and I did apartments 6J and 7J, so today we'll start with apartment 8J and keep working our way up until we either get through them or we find something viable." Jack was really hoping and praying that today would be the day they would finally make some definitive progress on this case.

"Okay, sounds like a plan." Belinda stood to dismiss them all. "Let's go find this guy."

* * * * *

9:33 A.M.

Ever so slowly, Audrey Nichols began the slow climb back to

consciousness.

At first, she wasn't sure where she was.

All she knew was that she was lying on a bed in kind of a hazy, surreal slumber.

Audrey tried to open her eyes, but they felt heavy.

Why did her eyes feel heavy?

She tried to move her limbs instead, but they too felt as though they'd been weighed down with lead.

She could twitch her fingers, though. And beneath them, she felt the soft, satiny feel of sheets. She was definitely lying on something soft and comfortable. And it felt like there was a pillow beneath her head. She was definitely in a bed.

So, the next question was, where was the bed?

It didn't feel like her own bed. The mattress was too soft. Audrey had a bad back, an old injury from her days as an equestrian rider. So, she slept with a firm mattress. Something as soft as what she was currently lying on wouldn't offer enough support.

That confirmed it, then. She was definitely not in her own bed.

Since she felt heavy and disoriented, maybe she was in the hospital. She could have been in some sort of accident. The way she felt now was similar to how she'd felt awakening in the hospital after her fall off the horse. She'd fallen plenty of times before. But that one had been different. That one had left her with a badly broken arm, swelling in her spine, and serious head injuries. It had also ended her career.

She had been in a coma for six long days. Well, long days for her family; she had known nothing of what was going on. When she'd finally awakened, she had been in the hospital. She'd felt sore and groggy and focusing on where she was and what had happened to her had been near impossible.

Maybe that was why she felt odd now. She was in the hospital again. She no longer rode, but maybe she'd been in a car accident.

But something was niggling at her.

Something that told her wherever she was right now and whatever had happened to land her here had nothing to do with a car accident. Nor did it have anything to do with any sort of accident.

She forced her sluggish mind to focus.

Audrey went with facts.

What was the last thing she remembered before waking up feeling like this?

The last few days, there had been a spate of violent crimes at her apartment building. A man had been murdered. Then a young woman had been raped. Then there had been a violent assault on the woman who lived in the apartment directly below hers.

The police had come to her, worried that she might be the next victim. They had wanted to have a police officer stay in her apartment as a decoy, so they could try and catch this assailant. Audrey had readily agreed to the plan. She had no wish to end up like her neighbors. So, she had gone to a motel for the night.

Was that where she was right now?

In a motel room?

It could explain why the bed she was currently lying in didn't feel like her own.

But it had to be more than that.

This couldn't just be the effects of sleeping in a strange bed.

Then with a sudden rush of all-encompassing horror it all came back to her.

She *had* gone to the motel. And she *had* gone to sleep in the motel bed. But then something had awakened her.

A hand.

On her mouth.

A gun at her head.

A voice telling her it would blow her brains out if she didn't do what it said.

She had been icy cold with terror.

Her every instinct had screamed at her to fight. To do

whatever it took to get away from this man.

If it had only been her life at stake, she might have considered risking it. However, he had threatened to go after her family and friends.

She had had no doubt he would do exactly that.

The complete and utter calm in his voice when he'd threatened her and told her that he wouldn't think twice about putting a bullet in her head and then doing the same to the people she loved, had conveyed how serious he was.

And so, she had complied.

She had laid still as he put plastic ties around her wrists and ankles. Before he had put tape on her mouth, she had risked his wrath to ask if he had been the man terrorizing her building. He had confirmed that he was, but when she had asked him why, he had refused to answer. Instead, he'd just covered her mouth with tape.

Despite the odds stacked so horrendously against her, Audrey couldn't just give up. That wasn't who she was.

So, when he'd briefly moved away from her side, she had made a desperate attempt at escape.

With her arms secured behind her back and her ankles tied together, moving had been difficult. Still, she had managed to get herself to the floor and start wiggling toward the door.

Her efforts had not only been fruitless but had also proved to amuse the man.

He had been chuckling as he picked her up.

He had stuffed her inside her suitcase and the overwhelming sense of claustrophobia had drowned out everything else, even the pain of being cramped and twisted inside the too small space.

He put her in a car and they had driven for what seemed like hours.

He hadn't spoken to her, but he had paused sporadically to check on her.

Each time, she had promised herself that she would try to

escape. If she could get away, she could get to the police and they could protect her and her family. Only, each time he unzipped the suitcase to look in at her, she had been so frozen with fear that she hadn't been able to force herself to move.

One time, he had opened the suitcase a little more and Audrey had convinced herself it was now or never. If he got her to wherever it was he intended to take her, then Audrey knew it was all over for her. But he had stabbed a sharp needle into her arm and the world had dissolved into nothingness.

Until she had woken up here.

Ignoring her heavy limbs, Audrey clumsily shoved herself up into a sitting position, her eyes popping open.

Her head swam, but she paid it no mind. Instead she took in her surroundings. She was in a one-room cabin. A fireplace was on the far wall, a couch set in front of it. A small kitchenette was in one corner, a large wooden table nearby. There was a door close-by to the bed where she was lying, and Audrey assumed it led to a bathroom.

There was only one other door in the cabin.

It had to lead to the outside.

Audrey headed for it.

For some reason, she wasn't sure if it was a good or a bad thing, he hadn't left any restraints on her. She was free to move.

Unfortunately, her legs weren't as steady as she had hoped and Audrey sank to the floor as soon as she stood. Without a second to spare, she levered herself back up into a standing position with the help of the bed.

Once she was on her feet, she staggered for the door.

The hope that had been bubbling inside her went flat as her hands grasped the doorknob and she tugged.

It didn't budge.

It was locked.

"No." She collapsed against the door. "No, no, no, no, no," she screamed.

It wasn't fair.

She hadn't done anything to this man, so why was he doing this to her?

She tried the door handle again and again, unwilling to believe that she was trapped inside this cabin.

"Help!" She started to bang on the door. If she couldn't get out maybe someone could hear her and would come to her rescue. "Hello? Can anyone hear me? I need help. I'm locked in here. Someone kidnapped me. Hello? Can anyone hear me?"

Audrey didn't know how long she spent hammering on the door and yelling for help. But eventually, she gave up, sagging in shock-induced exhaustion to lean once more against the door.

It was hopeless.

There was no one out there.

No one to hear her pleas for help.

That must had been why the man hadn't bothered to put a gag on her. He knew that there would be no one to answer her calls for help.

She roused herself. So, the door was locked. But that didn't mean she couldn't get out of this cabin. There had to be another way.

There were two windows. One on either side of the door. As quickly as her rubbery legs would allow, she hurried to one.

Her heart dropped as she got to it.

There were metal bars blocking her access to it.

Tears began to trickle down her cheeks, leaving warm little trails in their wake. If she couldn't get out the door and she couldn't get out the windows, then how was she going to get out of here?

Was she going to get out of here?

Was she ever going to get home? Was she ever going to see her family and friends again?

Footsteps sounded outside.

Instinctively, Audrey knew it was her captor.

She weighed her options. Should she try and rush him as he came in, try to get past him and escape? Should she try hiding? Should she go back to the bed and pretend that she was still drugged unconscious?

In the end, she was still standing like a statue by the window when the door swung open.

The man's gaze moved immediately from the empty bed to her, and a slow smile spread across his face. "Audrey, you're awake, how pleasant."

Audrey knew, *knew*, that begging with this man would not only be pointless but would also increase his enjoyment. This man got off on inflicting pain and terror. She'd heard the rumors circling her building about the way he had tortured that woman, Jessica Elgar. This man enjoyed making others suffer.

Despite all of this, she was begging before she even realized it.

"Please, please don't hurt me. Please let me go. I won't tell anyone, I promise. If you let me go, I won't go to the police. I won't tell them anything about you. I promise, I won't. I just want to go home. Please, don't hurt me," she rambled.

He chuckled. "*She* said that, too. But of course, it wasn't true. How could it be? It's your natural instinct to go running straight to the cops."

"Who? Who said that, too?" Audrey asked. Perhaps if she could get him talking, she could find some way to connect with him, convince him not to kill her.

"Don't worry, you'll meet her soon enough. She's the reason I'm doing all of this." The man locked the door behind him, pocketing the key, then he took a menacing step toward her. "While I really want to be doing this to her, you'll have to play her stand in."

When he wrapped a vice like hand around her arm, Audrey completely lost it.

She began to scream and thrash. She threw her body from side to side. She swung her free arm at him. She tried to kick him.

Remembering her self-defense training, she tried to aim for his groin, eyes, or throat.

A sudden burst of agony in her face sent her neck snapping back, and her brain felt like it was ricocheting around inside her skull.

He had backhanded her across the face; the force of the blow would have sent her sprawling to the floor if he weren't still holding on to her.

"You can scream all you like; in fact, scream as much as you can, but don't fight me, I don't like that," the man warned.

Audrey whimpered as the man dragged her to the bed and threw her down. Then she let her shock dissociate her mind from her body.

* * * * *

10:00 A.M.

"I hate these sorts of interviews," Jack complained as they headed for apartment 8J. "They always go the same way. They don't know anyone crazy. They've never met anyone crazy. They don't have any enemies. Their families don't have any enemies. They don't know anyone who would hold a grudge against them. They don't know anything ... period."

"They're regular people, Jack," Rose reminded him.

"Yep, I know." He uttered a weary sigh. He wasn't looking forward to the prospect of spending the day speaking with the residents of the apartment building. He wanted to find this woman. But she was only one person in a building full of hundreds. It felt like a waste of time to interview wrong person after wrong person when they desperately needed to find her. Except this was the only way they were going to find her.

"Maybe we'll luck out and she'll be in this apartment," Rose consoled.

"We can only hope," he agreed halfheartedly as he knocked on the door of apartment 8J. He was so tired of conducting useless interview after useless interview. They needed an interview that yielded some results.

A moment later, the door was opened by a young man in a wheelchair. "Are you the detectives?" he asked.

"Yes, that's us," Jack confirmed, forcing his voice to be calm and his lips to curl into an easy smile. "I'm Detective Xander and this is my partner Detective Lace."

"I'm Danny." The young man maneuvered his wheelchair backward so that he could open the door wider. Danny looked like he was in his early twenties; he had reddish brown hair, freckles, and light brown eyes. "Come in."

They followed Danny inside, sidestepping numerous piles of clothes and books and an assortment of other things, and Jack wondered how the man managed to navigate through everything in his wheelchair.

Danny led them to an equally messy living room and gestured at a sofa that appeared to be the only surface in the room not piled high with junk. "Grab a seat. Can I get you anything to drink?"

"Water's fine," Rose replied.

"For me, too," Jack added.

"Sure thing." Danny went to the fridge, retrieved three bottles of water, set them in his lap and wheeled over to the sitting area, handing each of them a bottle. "So, you still don't know who's been terrorizing us here?" Danny demanded.

"We're working on it," Jack assured him.

"Well, working on it isn't good enough." Danny shot them a stern glare. "Murders, rapes, abductions—who's going to be next? He's been working on the J apartments. Does that mean I'm on his list?"

"No, sir. We believe that his victims so far have just been to get someone's attention," Jack explained for what felt like the hundredth time. "He's really after a woman who lives in the building."

Relief washed across Danny's face. "So, why are you talking to me? I'm obviously not a woman."

"Obviously." Jack tried not to inject any sarcasm into his voice. "But I'm sure there are women in your life. Girlfriend, fiancée, sister, mother, et cetera."

"Mother is deceased, no sisters, only brothers, and no fiancée," Danny informed them.

"What about a girlfriend?" Jack repeated, noting that Danny hadn't covered that one.

He hesitated. "Nothing serious."

"Serious or not, we need to know about it," Jack told him.

"We've only been dating for a few weeks." Danny's cheeks had pinked slightly.

Jack wondered why he was suddenly being so coy. "That's long enough for this man to have noticed her. Has she been here? Stayed over some nights?"

"Yes," Danny answered slowly.

Jack was losing his temper. "Look, Danny, we're not trying to cause you any trouble; we just need to find this man before anyone else gets hurt. We also need to find this woman so we can protect her. So, tell us about your girlfriend."

"All right," Danny gave a defeated sigh. "We haven't told anyone yet that we're seeing each other because she used to date one of my brothers. She has stayed here once or twice, but she has her own place. And more often, I go there. If she was his target, I really don't think he'd try to get to her through this place."

That didn't sound very promising. Danny was right. If his girlfriend had only been here a few times and had her own apartment, and she was the killer's target, then he would have been playing this game at her building and not this one. "Is there anyone you can think of who would want to hurt you?"

"No." Danny shook his head.

"No one with a grudge against you, or maybe against your family?" Jack pressed.

"Nope." Danny gave another headshake.

"Is there anyone you know who could be doing this?"

"No, of course not." Danny looked horrified by the mere possibility. "I don't know any crazy people."

He fought the urge to roll his eyes; this interview was going *exactly* how he had envisioned. "What about the brother whose ex you're now dating, could he have found out?"

"My brother would *never* do this," Danny said, outraged. "And no, he doesn't know. We've been careful. We wanted to see where this was headed before we told people. No use upsetting everyone if there's no future between us."

Regardless of Danny's thoughts on the matter, they would look into it. Having a brother steal his woman could have made him snap, want revenge; it was worth considering.

As if reading his mind, Danny said, "My brother is engaged now. He's moved on, he might be hurt but he wouldn't be angry enough to do something like this."

"What about anyone from the building?" Jack moved on. "Anyone here that you know who seems a little unstable?"

"You think he lives here?" Danny looked positively aghast at the very idea.

"We think it's a possibility," Jack confirmed.

"I don't know anyone here who is capable of doing all of this," Danny replied. "But, of course, I don't know everyone in the building."

"And in the days or weeks leading up to the attacks, had you noticed anything unusual happening around here?" Jack continued, knowing the answer before he even asked the question.

"Nothing. Everything was just the same and then one morning there were cops everywhere and we all learned someone had been murdered."

"Did you know any of the victims?"

"Never spoken to them; I might have nodded hello if I saw them in the lobby or the lifts, but I couldn't have picked them out of a crowd," Danny answered.

Jack pulled out the sketch of the killer. "Does this man look familiar to you?" he asked Danny, again knowing what the answer would be. The same answer they'd gotten from everyone else they'd shown the picture to.

He gave the picture a quick once-over. "Sure," Danny nodded. "He looks like any one of a million people I've seen, spoken to, walked past."

Jack was ready to wrap things up and move on to the next apartment. "One last thing, would you be willing to voluntarily submit a sample of your fingerprints and DNA so we can positively exclude you?"

"What? No." Danny frowned irritably at them.

"Do you have something to hide, Danny?" Jack raised a blond brow.

"No, of course not. I'm innocent. I don't have a criminal record. I didn't hurt anyone and I shouldn't have to prove it to you. Besides," he glared, "I'm in a wheelchair."

"That doesn't positively exclude you, Danny; you look like a strong guy." Jack glanced at his partner. "Can you mark down that Danny refused to volunteer his samples?"

"Are you seriously going to list me as a suspect just because I won't give you my fingerprints? You know by law you can't force me to do it?"

"We know," Jack agreed. "But we're going on the assumption that people with nothing to hide will be happy to volunteer, given that these crimes are happening in your building and any one of you could end up a victim. Surely, you would want us to wrap this case up as quickly as we can so your lives can go back to normal." Jack didn't really think Danny was a viable suspect. The fact that he was in a wheelchair would have made committing the crimes difficult, but not impossible. However, it seemed likely that Jessica Elgar would have mentioned if the man who had attacked her had been in a wheelchair.

Danny exhaled a frustrated breath. "Fine. I'll give you the samples. Now I need you to leave; I have to study for a test. You can see yourselves out."

"Someone from the crime scene unit will be by soon to take a DNA swab and print you," Jack informed him, standing.

"Whatever," Danny snapped sourly.

"Another waste of time," Jack said as soon as they were back in the hall. "And I didn't like him."

"I would never have guessed." Rose smiled.

"On to the next one I guess." Jack was starting to doubt they were ever going to locate this woman. "Let's do the stairs." He nodded at the door to the stairwell, with all this sitting and interviewing he felt like he needed a little exercise. Rose took the stairs one at a time while he bounded up them with long strides taking them three and four at a time.

He was already knocking on the door of apartment 9J when Rose reached him. They waited in silence, and after a minute passed and no one answered, he knocked again.

"Coming," a timid, shaky voice spoke from inside the apartment.

When the door finally opened, his mouth fell open in shock. "Laura?"

* * * * *

10:43 A.M.

"Jack?"

Laura couldn't have been more surprised if she'd opened her front door to see a whale.

133

All morning, she had been trying to prepare herself for the inevitable visit from the police. Connor had called to tell her that they were going to be interviewing everyone in the apartment building in their quest to find who had been attacking the residents.

For obvious reasons, having people here in her apartment was not easy for her. More like a nightmare. But she knew it was unavoidable. If for nothing else than she wanted this man who had shattered her sense of calm to be caught. Even if she had tried to avoid talking with the cops, it wouldn't have worked. They would simply have kept coming back until she spoke to them.

So, all morning she had been readying herself for their impending visit. Doing the calming techniques a therapist had taught her many years ago, she tried to imagine what they'd ask her and how she'd answer. But no amount of preparation could have prepared her for this.

It was him, though. He was still tall and muscled. He had the same dimples and sparkling blue eyes that had first attracted her to him. The only difference from the last time she'd seen him was that his blond hair was shaved short.

Her shock melted into anger. "Get out," she screamed at Jack Xander.

Jack just continued to stand there staring at her. The tall, pretty redhead at his side was looking from Jack to her and back again.

Laura was attempting to close her door again when Jack suddenly bounced back to life. "Laura, wait, we have to talk to you." He put his hands on the door to prevent her from closing it.

"If you think I'm going to talk to you, then you are crazy," she shot back.

"Laura," Jack began in the same pleading tone she'd heard him use a million times before.

"No," she cut him off before he had a chance to speak. "I don't want to hear anything you have to say."

"Laura, please," he tried again.

"How are you not getting this, Jack? Get away from me." If he wasn't going, then she was, she turned and was going to go and lock herself in her bedroom, but he grabbed her wrist. That was a bad move. She didn't like people touching her. And she certainly didn't want this man touching her. Add to that the fact that she was terribly on edge and hadn't slept properly in days and she totally flipped. "Don't touch me."

Jack must have read the panic in her face because he instantly dropped her arm, his brows knitting together in concern. "Are you okay?"

"I'll be fine once you leave," she all but shrieked.

"Okay, okay." The redhead stepped between them. "You two obviously have history. Complicated history. But we haven't met, I'm Jack's partner, Rose."

She tried to calm her ragged breathing, focusing instead on Jack's partner. "Hi," was all she could utter.

"And you're Laura." Rose gave her an encouraging smile.

Laura managed a nod in response.

"Maybe we can come in?" Rose took a tentative step inside the apartment.

Giving up, she shrugged and she closed the door behind them, carefully relocking each of her five deadlocks. Laura wished desperately that there was some escape from this, but she knew there wasn't.

"Laura, I'm sorry." Jack's voice rumbled softly beside her.

"I know, Jack," she replied wearily. "You told me a million times already."

"Laura," his tone was so serious that she couldn't help but meet his gaze. "The baby died. She had a miscarriage."

Her eyes widened in surprise. That, she hadn't been expecting to hear. For a moment, it confused her. Had her mind spinning off into unwise territory. But then her common sense kicked back in. "That doesn't change anything, Jack," she said, her tone just as serious as his had been.

"But—" he began to protest.

"No," she cut him off again, "no buts."

"Laura, it's been a long time, you know I'm sorry." Jack sounded frustrated now. He was always so bossy and he hated that he couldn't order her into forgiving him.

"So, just because years have passed I should just forget about everything? Forget about what you did?" she demanded.

"Okay, okay," Rose once again inserted herself between them like they were two bickering preschoolers. "So, you two have issues. I get it. But we need to talk. Maybe you two can discuss your personal problems another time."

"You're right." Laura took a deep, calming breath. "I'm happy to talk to you, but no way am I having any conversation with him."

Jack sighed, but wisely refrained from commenting.

"I'd offer you something to drink, but I don't think you're going to be here for long, so hurry up and ask your questions so he can leave." Laura knew she was being rude, but couldn't summon enough energy to care.

Seemingly sensing that her discomfort ran deeper than just having to talk with the cops, and wasn't just because of her complicated history with Jack, Rose smiled again. "We'll be as quick as we can," she assured her gently.

"Okay," she whispered, all but dragging herself to her couch. No matter how quick they made this, it would never be quick enough. She wanted Jack and his partner out of her apartment immediately. She was wishing she hadn't even let them in.

Exchanging a look, Jack gave his partner a nod, and then hung back as Rose came to join her on the couch. "So, you know about what's happened to some of your neighbors?" Rose began.

An involuntary shudder ripped through her. It was as much to do with the crimes in her building as it was with the man standing in her apartment. Why, oh why, of all the cops in the city, did it have to end up being Jack Xander who was working this case? This was hard enough to deal with as it was, without adding Jack to the mix.

Blinking, she realized Rose was watching her with a little frown of concern. "Are you all right, Laura?"

She gave a shaky nod. "Yes," she replied in a small voice. "And yes, I know about what happened downstairs. At least, some of it."

"You haven't been following it?" Rose looked vaguely surprised.

"No, I uh, I don't like to know that kind of stuff," she explained.

"Did you know any of the victims?" Rose continued.

"No, I don't know anyone in the building."

"But you've lived here a long time," Rose prodded. "You don't know a single one of your neighbors?"

"No," Laura answered simply. She wasn't going to explain her agoraphobia to them.

"Why were you using a different name, Laura?" Jack asked. "Your name is Laura Opal, but the name on your lease is Laura MacArthur."

So no one could find her was the answer to that; but instead, she replied, "MacArthur is my mother's maiden name."

"I know that," Jack replied, reminding her of just how well he did indeed know her. He knew everything about her. Well, almost everything. He didn't know about her kidnapping, and if she had her way, he would never find out about it. "Why aren't you using your real name?"

Shrugging fitfully, she couldn't think up a convincing lie to that, so she just kept quiet.

"Are you scared someone's going to find you, Laura?" Rose asked gently. "Someone who might want to hurt you?"

"What? No, of course not." That at least was true. The men who had hurt her were in prison. It was her family that she didn't want tracking her down.

"If you need help, we can help you." Rose didn't look convinced by her denials.

"Thank you, but I don't need any help. Really. I didn't know any of the victims, and I don't have anybody in my past who would want to hurt me. Nor is there anyone in my life who would use me to hurt someone I know. I hope you find whoever hurt those people, but I don't think I'm going to be able to help you with that," she finished firmly. She needed them gone. Now.

"Laura, what happened to your hand?" Jack's gaze was fixed on her bandaged hand.

When she thought about it, her hand ached terribly. When she'd changed the dressing this morning, the burn hadn't looked like it was doing too well. She probably needed to see a doctor, but there was no way that was happening. She would just have to treat it as best she could and hope it healed on its own. Laura did not want to explain to Jack how she'd burned herself. If she told them she didn't sleep so she'd been making herself a hot drink when a flashback had distracted her and she'd injured herself, that would lead to a million questions she had no interest in answering.

"It's nothing. Really, Jack, its none of your business," she added when he looked ready to push the issue.

"I don't mean to invade your privacy, Laura," he spoke in an overly patient voice. "It just doesn't look like you're okay . . ."

"Of course, I'm not okay," she snapped. "*You're* here. You bring up all kinds of bad memories." Again, that was true. Jack did bring up bad memories. Memories that hurt her just as much as the memories of her assault. "It's time for you to go," she announced, standing to dismiss them. "I'm sorry I couldn't help you, and I truly hope you find this killer before he hurts anyone else."

Somewhat reluctantly, Jack and his partner followed her to the door. "Laura, I'm going to leave you my card." Jack pulled out a card and a pen and quickly wrote on it. "It has my cell phone number on here, so you can reach me any time. I know you're mad at me, and you have every right to be, but if you need help, call me and I'll be right here."

Laura refused to take the card, which didn't seem to surprise or faze Jack, who merely set it down on the small table by the door.

"Goodbye, Laura." His gaze on her was intent.

She leaned wearily against the door after she had locked it behind them. Her nerves were all aquiver; she didn't know what to do. She'd considered moving before, because of the attacks in the building, and now she was thinking about it again. Jack knew where she lived. Would he come back and try to talk to her again? From the look on his face when he said goodbye, that was exactly what he was planning on doing. She couldn't have him disrupting her carefully controlled life. And yet, even the thought of moving left her shaking so badly, she could hardly hold a coherent thought in her head.

Maybe Jack would just let it go. Just forget about her.

Only, she knew that he wouldn't.

He would find out what had happened to her. It wouldn't be hard. All he had to do was type her name into a police database and her case would pop up.

Sinking to her knees, she buried her face in her good hand and sobbed.

* * * * *

1:06 P.M.

"So, are you going to tell me what all that was about?" Rose demanded.

"Laura and I used to know each other," Jack answered vaguely; he had barely said a word since they had left Laura's apartment and come back to the station. He felt like he was in a dream, just as he had ever since he'd seen Laura standing in front of him.

That had been a completely unexpected blast from the past.

Although, when he'd looked at her, it was like no time had passed at all. With her milky white complexion, her long dead straight jet-black hair, her large violet eyes, she was just as drop-dead gorgeous as she'd been back then. And she was just as sweet and loving and caring and thoughtful as she was beautiful. He'd really missed her.

"Yeah, somehow I got that," Rose shot back dryly. "Are you going to tell me why she's so angry with you?"

Sinking down into his desk chair, Jack didn't want to think about how he'd hurt Laura much less tell someone about it. "We grew up together," he reluctantly began. "Her family lived across the street from mine; we've known each other since we were babies."

"That doesn't explain why she's mad at you," Rose said when he didn't continue.

"We dated all through high school. I'd had a crush on her since I was like, seven, but it took me years to get up the courage to ask her out. We were such great friends, I think we were both scared that if we dated and then broke up it would ruin our friendship and we'd end up losing each other."

"And you did break up," Rose prompted when he stopped once again.

"Oh, yeah." He nodded.

"What did you do?" Rose asked.

"I ruined things. I cheated on her. I was seventeen and stupid and I wanted to have sex and Laura didn't; she wanted to wait until she was married. But I got drunk at a party and let my hormones get the best of me and slept with this other girl," he explained in a rush.

"Oh, Jack." Rose sounded disappointed in him. But she couldn't be more disappointed in him than he was in himself.

"I know. It was stupid," he agreed. He had lost the single best thing in his life in one moment of stupidity.

"She found out?"

"I told her. The girl got pregnant; I knew it was going to all come out and I thought it would be better for her to hear it from me than someone else, so I told her," he repeated.

"It didn't go well, I take it?"

"You could say that," he agreed. "Laura freaked out, ended things immediately. I told her that I still wanted us to stay together, that it was a mistake, that I would raise the baby with Melissa as co-parents, but I had no intention of being in a relationship with her. I told Laura how sorry I was, but she was having none of it."

"You told Laura that the baby died—did Melissa have a miscarriage?" Rose asked, gently now.

"Yeah, about a week after I told Laura. I wanted to go to her, to tell her about the baby, to apologize again, but I was too scared she would reject me again." Letting Laura go had been the second biggest mistake of his life; the first, of course, was cheating on her. Jack had never gotten over her. She was the one true love of his life. In high school, they had planned their whole futures, promising themselves that they would be together forever. And he had ruined it. He had hurt Laura, and he'd never forgiven himself for it.

"Okay, I get why she can't forgive you. She was young and you broke her heart. She probably felt like you thought sex was more important than her, since you cheated simply because she wouldn't put out for you. But you were kids back then, you're not anymore—go try apologizing to her again."

"You saw how that went down today. She doesn't want anything to do with me."

"She was caught off guard. Try again once she's calmed down."

He might. But right now, convincing Laura to forgive him was not number one on his list of priorities. "Rose, I think it's Laura. I think she's the killer's target," he informed his partner.

Rose raised an eyebrow at him and waited for him to elaborate.

"That was not the Laura I remember. Did you see all the locks on her door?" He continued when Rose nodded. "She had them on the windows, too. She's scared of something. She's lived there ten years, but doesn't know a single neighbor. She doesn't want to know about the crimes. She was timid and jumpy and that is so not the Laura I used to know."

"But you haven't seen her in a long time. Not since high school," Rose reminded him. "Maybe she's just changed in all those years."

"But changed why? We were looking for a previous victim who escaped. What if Laura is that victim?" Jack's heart constricted so tightly at the very thought of Laura being raped and tortured by this man that he could barely draw a breath.

"Then look her up," Rose said gently. "If she was a victim of a violent crime, then there'll be a record of it in our system."

Jack's fingers froze over the computer's keyboard. Did he really want to know if Laura had been brutalized? Could he handle it? Could he make himself read the case files and look at the pictures of whatever had been done to her?

"You want me to do it?" Rose asked softly.

He gave his head a single shake. Jack felt that he somehow owed it to Laura to look it up himself. With grim determination, he typed in Laura's name. And almost immediately, an eleven-year-old case popped up.

"You find something?" Rose asked.

"Yes." His voice shook a little. He printed out the information contained on the computer; he would request the entire case file later. What he had was enough for now.

As he read, he was vaguely aware of the fact that his breath was coming in small pants. Laura had been grabbed entering her house when she was only twenty. She was taken by two men, Frank and Francis Garrett, to a secluded wooded area where they proceeded to rape and torture her for four days before she was found, close to death, by a group of hikers.

Reading what had happened to Laura was nowhere near as bad as seeing the pictures. Presumably taken just after she had been rushed to the hospital, they showed every horrible thing that had been done to her. There didn't appear to be an inch of her body that had been unharmed.

The bottom of her feet were covered in cuts; a mottled mix of yellow and green and purple and black bruises covered her body; there were scratches over her arms and face, and a large lump on the side of her head. Hand shaped bruises circled her neck. Cigarette burns dotted her body. Three of her fingers stuck out at weird angles. Two of her fingernails had been ripped out. On her back, three words had been sliced into her flesh. 'Bitch,' 'whore,' and 'slut.' Someone had had a lot of rage toward her.

"You have to breathe, Jack," Rose's voice spoke quietly beside him.

He drew in a ragged breath. "Are you seeing this?"

"Yeah, poor thing, looks like she suffered horribly." Rose's voice was heavy with empathy.

"This should never have happened to her. It's my fault," he intoned quietly.

"How do you get that?" Rose sounded surprised.

"If I hadn't cheated on her, then we would have still been together," he replied. Guilt crushed heavily down on him.

"That is the most utterly ridiculous thing I've ever heard you say," Rose snorted. "There is no way to know that. Even if you two had stayed together, this could still have happened to her."

He ignored her. Nothing was going to soothe his guilt at the moment. "This matches what was done to Jessica Elgar," he noted. "The cigarette burns, the strangulation, the broken finger and the cutting of a word into the skin. Laura is this guy's target. He's angry that she was rescued before he was finished with her."

Rose nodded slowly, considering this. "I'll give you that she seemed nervous and jumpy. She's scared. And the fact that she uses an alias does make it look like she's hiding from someone. But, Jack, the men who hurt her were caught—they're in prison—they can't be doing this."

Jack knew in his bones that Laura was at the center of this. "What Laura went through is being recreated in these crimes. He's working backward. Audrey was abducted just like Laura was. Jessica and Judith were tortured and raped just like Laura was, and I'm going to guess a knife to the heart was how he intended to kill Laura once he finished playing with her. There could have been a third man involved. One who was never caught. You can't deny the similarities, Rose. And she lives in one of the J apartments. It's her."

The thought that someone, especially someone who had already done such heinous things to Laura, was after her was chilling. Jack could barely think straight. The only thing he knew was that this man was *not* getting his hands on Laura ever again.

"We need to put cops on her door," he told Rose, already reaching for his phone to call Belinda and have her set it up. "I don't want her alone and unprotected. If I thought she'd let us in the door, we'd go straight back over there, but she's not going to talk to us again today. We'll let her cool down a little and go see her again in the morning."

He was going to find the man who wanted Laura dead, and then he was going to somehow convince her that he was sorry and get her to forgive him so that he could get her back. He still loved Laura, and he had a feeling, that despite her anger, deep down, she still loved him, too.

JULY 24TH

8:11 A.M.

"You know," Laura stated as soon as she opened her front door and saw Jack and his partner standing there. She could always tell when someone found out about her abduction. It changed the way they looked at her. Invariably, once someone knew what she'd been through, when they looked at her they saw a poor helpless victim. Their gazes were always full of pity. Laura had resented that at first. But now, she acknowledged that if the roles were reversed, she would look at someone who had been through what she had with pity, too. How could you not feel sorry for someone who had been repeatedly raped and tortured?

"Can we come in?" Jack asked her gently. Apparently, they had decided to treat her with kid gloves.

"I guess." She stepped back to allow them entrance, and Jack relocked the deadbolts for her.

"You look cold; go sit down and I'll make you a hot drink," Jack ordered.

Against her better judgment, Laura complied. She wasn't feeling so good this morning. Too many nights without sleep was catching up with her and leaving her feeling anxious and weak. Seeing Jack again after all these years had just added to the too full basket of stress she had already been carrying.

"I like cocoa," she informed him as she curled herself up into a ball in the corner of the couch.

"I know," Jack replied mildly, bustling about her kitchen as if he'd done it a hundred times before.

"Jack, make her something to eat, too," Rose told him as she

145

plonked herself down on the couch beside Laura.

Laura rolled her eyes. "You're as bossy as he is," she commented, closing her eyes and resting her head back against the pillows. She probably should eat something. She was feeling a little light-headed.

"Yep," Rose agreed cheerfully. "Keep your eyes closed and rest for a moment. Did you sleep last night?"

"No." Laura stifled a yawn.

Rose clucked like an anxious mother hen, even though she couldn't be more than a couple of years older than Laura herself. "You're shaking," Rose declared. "Where do you keep spare blankets?"

"Her bed has a built-in drawer underneath it; they're in there," Jack answered before she could.

"Jack," Laura opened her eyes to frown at him, "stop acting like you know everything about me."

"I do," Jack shot back unperturbed.

"No, you don't," Laura grumbled sullenly.

"Was I wrong?" Jack challenged.

"No." She didn't want to give Jack any more encouragement to get too comfortable around her. He was looking like he wanted to start things up with her again and she was not interested in that at all.

"Here you go, cocoa and toast with peanut butter, I know it's your favorite breakfast." Jack grinned goadingly as he stood before her.

Laura was too tired to bicker, so she simply accepted the breakfast and ate as much of it as she could manage. Jack and Rose let her be while she ate, speaking to each other in hushed voices Laura didn't even bother trying to decipher.

Jack frowned slightly when she set the plate down with three quarters of the piece of toast still remaining, but chose not to comment. Instead, he shot her a reproachful glance. "Laura, why did I never know about your attack?"

Taking the blanket Rose had retrieved from her bedroom, Laura wrapped it tightly around her shoulders, then clutched the mug of hot cocoa in her freezing hands. "Because I'm a rape victim, and the police don't release the names of victims of sexual assault. I would have thought you knew that," she replied.

"You know I didn't mean professionally," Jack admonished. "I meant, why didn't I know about your attack personally? Our families were close. Even after we split up, our parents continued to hang out."

"I told my parents not to tell anyone about what happened. Especially you," she added.

He looked offended. "Why especially me? We've been best friends most of our lives. I would have been there for you. Why wouldn't you want me to know?"

"Because I knew you would blame yourself and come running straight to my side. In fact, I bet when you found out about my assault, the first thing you did was blame yourself. If only you hadn't cheated on me with Melissa, then we would have still been together. And if we'd still been together, then I wouldn't have been abducted and none of it would have ever happened. Am I right?"

A glance at his partner's face confirmed that she was.

"I played the 'what if' game at first, too—almost drove myself crazy doing it. It didn't help any. What happened happened, and I can't change it and neither can you. But there was no way I was going to break up your family by having you leave them to come and look after me." Laura had wanted to call Jack in those first months. She had still been in love with him, and even though he'd hurt her, she still wished they could work it out. But there was no way she would have ruined that child's family. It was bad enough her own life had been ruined, but she wasn't going to spread her misery around.

"There was no baby, Laura," he reminded her.

"Well, I didn't know that then," she snapped.

"But you know it now," Jack noted meaningfully.

He wanted that to change things, it was clear; only for her, it didn't change a thing.

When she didn't respond, Jack sighed. "Laura, we have to ask you some questions about what happened to you. Do you want to call your mom or dad or sister to come over?"

Her heart clenched both at the mention of her family and at the prospect of the questions they were going to be asking her. "No."

He was puzzled for a moment, then comprehension dawned. "Are you hiding from your family? Do they not know where you are? Is that why you weren't renting this place under your real name?"

She nodded a yes to all of those.

"Why did you push them away? Laura, they would have done anything for you." Jack looked confused.

"I needed space," she explained. "They wanted me to go back to the way I was before, only I couldn't." Laura was dangerously close to tears. "I'm not the same person I was before. I can't even go outside, Jack. I'm agoraphobic now. I haven't been outside my apartment since I moved in here ten years ago."

"Oh, honey, I'm sorry." His eyes were pained, and his voice was hoarse with concern for her.

The desire to throw herself into Jack's arms and sob hysterically was almost overwhelming. As she looked at him through her watery eyes, she realized with a start that she wasn't angry with him anymore. She was still hurt, but her anger had gone. Jack was so strong and so confident and he always knew what to do. Jack would take care of her when she couldn't take care of herself right now.

"Honey, let me look at your hand. I'm a little worried about it; you don't seem to be able to use it properly. What did you do to it?" he asked, reaching for the injured hand.

His bossy tone snapped her back to reality. She couldn't go to

Jack for comfort. She didn't trust him anymore. "I burned it," she replied, moving her hand away before Jack could grasp it.

This earned her another frown. "How did you burn it?"

"I was heating milk to make cocoa the other night and I had a flashback and got distracted and spilled the boiling milk on it," she answered.

He winced. "Ouch. Well, if you won't let me check it out, will you let Rose look at it?"

"No, I don't need either of you to look at it, I can take care of myself," she informed them.

He raised a skeptical brow at that. "The flashbacks, do you have them regularly?"

"I used to, after it first happened, now I just get them when something reminds me of it," Laura explained.

"Like what's been happening here?" Jack asked.

Laura just nodded.

"You said you hadn't been following too closely what has been going on here, what do you know?" Jack leaned forward, elbows resting on his knees.

"Someone was murdered and someone was raped." She couldn't help the shiver that wracked through her.

"There was also a woman who was tortured and another woman who was abducted," Jack informed her gently. "We think that the man who's done all of this is really after you."

"Me?" she echoed, completely confused.

"The man has been attacking the people in the building because he wants to scare you. He's recreating what you went through. You're the one he really wants, Laura." Jack was looking at her anxiously.

"This can't have anything to do with me," Laura protested. "They caught the men who hurt me. They were two brothers. They're in prison now. And I know they weren't falsely convicted because I saw them. They never bothered to hide their identities from me."

"Laura," Rose began. "He's recreating *your* attack. The abduction, the rape, with one of his victims he strangled her, burned her with cigarettes, broke her finger, used a knife to cut a word into her skin."

Her gaze strayed to her body, where her many scars were hidden under the sweatshirt and sweatpants she always wore. Laura couldn't stand looking at her body. She showered with her eyes closed and she always wore clothes that completely covered her.

"I'm so sorry, honey, but he wants you. He wants you to suffer, he wants you to figure this out and know he's coming for you." Jack reached out a hand to take hers, then seemed to remember her bad reaction from when he touched her yesterday and stopped midway toward her.

"No." She shook her head adamantly. "You're wrong."

"We don't think we are," Jack said apologetically. "We think there was another person involved in your abduction who was never caught."

"No. No," she said again, as though saying it could make it true. She would quite simply not allow herself to believe that her ordeal wasn't over and finished with.

"Can we show you a sketch of the man we're looking for? One of his victims got enough of a look at her attacker to give us a vague description. The picture isn't great, but it's all we have. Can you have a look at it for us? Tell us if you know this man?"

"No," Laura said resolutely. There was no need to look at a picture because there was no other person involved in her attack.

"Laura?"

She turned dazed eyes to Rose; she couldn't seem to summon a word.

"The killer left stars on the ceiling of one of his victim's home. Does that mean anything to you?"

When she had been out in the woods, she would lie there while they were assaulting her and stare up at the sky, hating it. Hating the wide blue, powerful expanse. Hating the inky blackness with its millions of shimmering diamonds. But most of all, hating herself for letting those men hurt her over and over again.

"Laura," Jack said sharply, "put your head down. You look like you're about to pass out."

Instead of complying with what was probably a wise command, she bounced up to her feet. "You need to leave now." She caught the hysteria in her voice but was powerless to eradicate it.

Jack had stood with her, ready to catch her if her knees should give out she supposed. "Laura, you need to sit down," he told her.

"No. You need to go. *Now*. You need to go." She needed to be alone.

Apparently, deciding complying was going to upset her less than staying and arguing with her, Jack and Rose walked toward her front door. "Laura, I have cops posted at your door. Okay? No one is going to get to you. And you have my number. Call me if you need anything at all. I mean it, Laura. If you get scared, or you don't want to be alone, or you need to talk, all you have to do is call, and I'll be right here."

Once she was alone, she took a step toward the bedroom. Only her legs wouldn't hold her up for another second. She collapsed. Lying sprawled on the carpet. Panting as she struggled for breath and the world went spinning mercilessly around her.

It's over, she assured herself.

They were wrong.

There was no third guy.

What had happened to her was in the past.

It was over. It was over. It was over.

* * * * *

9:42 A.M.

"So, you think you've finally found the woman our killer is really after?" Belinda directed the question to him and Rose.

"Yes," Jack replied. "Her name is Laura Opal, she lives in apartment 9J."

"I understand you know her." Belinda was studying him carefully, seemingly trying to ascertain whether this was going to be a problem.

"We grew up together," Jack acknowledged. "We dated for a while until I cheated and we broke up."

Although, if Jack had his way, they would soon be back together. Being in the same room with her felt so right. Even after so many years apart, they still knew each other so well. They belonged together. They both knew it, even if Laura would deny it right now. She was warming up to him, though. Today she hadn't been angry with him, she hadn't been thrilled to see him either, but at least her anger seemed to have faded.

"Run down for me why you think Laura is the target," Belinda requested.

Jack opened his mouth to describe the similarities between Laura's abduction and assault eleven years ago and what was happening now, but found that he couldn't speak. When he thought of what Laura had suffered, it felt like his heart was breaking into a million pieces. She had been so young, so scared and alone. Was still alone now. His heart broke all over again as he thought of how she had cut herself off from everyone who loved her.

She needed someone.

Badly.

He hadn't wanted to leave her this morning. It had been clear to both him and Rose that Laura wasn't coping very well. From the moment she had opened the door, she'd been shaky and weak looking; three times he'd been afraid she was about to faint. Her eyes had held a glassy, faraway look in them, like she was disconnecting herself from reality. He wouldn't have been surprised if she'd broken down the second the door closed behind them.

Jack was now more desperate than ever to find this man before he got to Laura. She had been through enough—more than enough—more than any person should ever have to go through, and he wouldn't let this man hurt her again.

And yet, he still couldn't bring himself to put into words what Laura had suffered.

Rose came to his rescue. "Eleven years ago," his partner began, "Laura was grabbed as she was about to enter the house she and some friends were renting. Whoever got her must have been lying in wait for her because they killed one of her roommates and then got Laura just as she was opening her front door. She was reported missing promptly, when another roommate came home to find twenty-year-old Matilda Warren dead and Laura's bag on the floor by the door, signs of a struggle, including some blood and hair, which turned out to be from Laura, and no signs of Laura anywhere."

"Were there any leads or suspects at the time?" Belinda interrupted to ask.

"No. None. No one knew who had taken Laura. She was found four days later by chance by some hikers in the woods about three hours from where she lived. The three hikers who stumbled upon her said she was in pretty bad shape. Her body was covered in bruises from being repeatedly kicked, there were burns everywhere, she'd had three fingers broken and two fingernails ripped out. She had head injuries, her back was covered in blood from the cuts, she was having difficulties breathing, and she was badly dehydrated. She was dressed only in her underwear, she didn't have on any shoes and her feet were badly cut and bruised from running through the woods. The hikers said when they found her she was unconscious but she woke up and freaked out when they started administering first aid."

Which was no wonder, given the trauma she had just endured. Jack realized he had been clutching his hands into fists so tightly that his nails, short though they were, had begun to cut into his palms. Deliberately, he opened his hands and rested them on the table.

"Hikers called for help, Laura was rushed to the hospital, where she was treated for dehydration, exhaustion, shock, broken bones, a bruised larynx, pulmonary edema, and infections that had developed in several of her wounds."

Laura had had her head held repeatedly under water. Not to kill her, just to increase her suffering. As if they hadn't already done enough to her.

"The hikers all checked out?"

"Yes. When Laura was recovered enough to give her statement, she gave the names and descriptions of the men who had assaulted her. Although she didn't know their surname, only that they called each other Frank and Francis, they were quickly identified and arrested. Frank and Francis Garrett lived close to where Laura was found—they were virtual recluses who lived off the land. Their DNA was found inside Laura, and given her positive IDs, it was a slam-dunk case. Only, the Garrett brothers decided to plead not guilty by reason of diminished capacity. They claimed that they were raised by an abusive father and were not sent to school or allowed to socialize, and thus never learned right from wrong, and, as such, couldn't be held responsible for their actions. Which meant that Laura had to then endure a long trial. Luckily, the brothers were found guilty and are both still in prison."

"If the men who abducted and assaulted her are in prison, then why do we think that Laura is the woman our killer is after?" Belinda looked confused.

"We believe there may have been a third man involved," Jack jumped in. He knew that Laura was the target. He *knew* it. Knew it with an all-encompassing sense of desperation that their time was running out. If they didn't find this man first, then he was terrified that the price to pay would be Laura's life.

"Based on?" Belinda prompted.

"Based on the fact that the Garretts' truck wasn't used in the abduction. The police checked it out after they had the Garrett brothers in custody and they couldn't find any evidence that Laura had ever been in it. Given that whoever abducted her had had to knock her unconscious to take her. As evidenced by the blood and hair samples in her house, there would have been something in the van. The van hadn't been recently cleaned, either," Jack added, guessing what his boss was going to say next. "The police questioned the brothers on it, but they wouldn't say how Laura was taken to their place, and given that they had enough with the DNA and IDs, they didn't push the issue."

"So, you think that whoever transported Laura is this mystery third man, and the one who's committing these crimes now is trying get her back because he's angry that she got away the first time?"

"Yes." Jack nodded his agreement to his boss' summary. "The similarities between what he's doing now and what was done to Laura are too similar to be ignored."

"He knows where she is, why not just grab her?" Belinda put forward. "So, this might add some additional terror, but really, assuming he's going to recreate what he did to her the first time around, that would be terror enough."

"I was thinking about that since we visited Laura yesterday." Jack paused thoughtfully. "Laura is understandably traumatized by what she went through; she has five deadbolts on her door, breaking in there wouldn't be easy. Certainly not like breaking into the other apartments. And there is no way she would open her door to anyone. If the killer suspected that getting into Laura's place to grab her would be near impossible, then perhaps he thought he could scare her into leaving. Then once she came out of that apartment, he would be able to grab her."

"Not a bad theory," Belinda acknowledged. "Okay, I'm convinced. So, if we believe Laura is the target and in danger, why haven't you brought her into protective custody?"

"Two problems with that." Jack grimaced. Bringing Laura into protective custody was exactly what he wanted to do. He wanted to lock her away someplace safe until this was all over. In fact, the urge to simply throw her over his shoulder and carry her from her apartment had been near overwhelming when they'd been there earlier. "Laura doesn't think any of this is about her. She's convinced that there was no third man and that her ordeal is over. And she's also agoraphobic. She can't go outside. She told us she hasn't left the apartment since she moved in there. There is no way she's going to agree to leave that place, and I'm concerned about the effects—physically and psychologically—on her if we forcibly remove her."

"Okay, then let's figure out who is after her before we need to further traumatize her by taking her out of her apartment against her will. Which I will do if it comes down to it." Belinda shot him a warning glance.

"We'll speak with her family, see if they have any ideas on who could be after Laura." Jack tried to hide his wince as he said it. He was not one of Laura's parents' favorite people, given how badly he'd hurt their daughter. Hopefully, that wouldn't be a hindrance to the interview.

"We'll also go and speak with the Garrett brothers," Rose added. "See if after all these years, they're ready to be more forthcoming about who else was involved."

"Sounds like a plan." Belinda seemed pleased with their progress. "We found the woman, now let's find the man who wants her dead."

* * * * *

10:14 A.M.

It's over. It's over. It's over.

Laura had been lying on her living room floor repeating the mantra to herself ever since Jack and his partner left.

Frank and Francis Garrett were the men who had hurt her.

She should know.

They hadn't been worried about her seeing their faces because they had thought that she was never getting away alive.

They hadn't known that three hikers, who just happened to be passing by, would find her bruised, bleeding, and passed out.

The Garrett brothers had just finished another round of torturing her.

Francis had held her down while Frank had raped her so roughly that she had been left bleeding.

She had stopped fighting back by then.

What good did it do?

She was never going to beat them. They were bigger and stronger, and by that time, she was too weak and injured to do anything anyway.

Then Francis had wrapped his hands around her neck, tightening and tightening until no air could get into her lungs.

He'd done it before.

Many times.

Her vision would start to explode into hundreds of tiny white dots; her hearing would fade, and then just when she was on the verge of unconsciousness, he would let go.

And she would lie there, desperately gasping in each precious breath of air through her aching throat.

When they'd left her, laughing as they always did, she had tried to move.

Instinctively, she knew that moving, that continuing to search for help, was her only chance at surviving this.

But she had been unable to move.

Even an inch.

Her body had given up on her.

She had known it would at some point.

The trauma it had been through was severe.

Still, she had kept desperately trying to keep moving.

Even to drag herself along the ground, if she couldn't stand up.

But her body had been uncooperative.

So, she had just laid there.

And when unconsciousness had tugged at the corners of her mind, her exhausted body had given in immediately.

She had been ripped back to consciousness when she felt hands on her.

The Garretts were back.

She had made a somewhat feeble attempt at fending them off, before she realized the hands that were on her were different.

They were gentle hands.

Helping hands, not hurting hands.

As her vision had returned, she had made out three faces hovering above her. Two females and one male.

Kind faces.

Worried faces.

They had wrapped her up in warm blankets.

They had offered soothing words of comfort that she was safe now.

Her larynx was too badly damaged by repeated strangulation to produce any words, but her panicked face must have spoken volumes.

The man had pulled out a gun, and left the two women to tend to her while he kept watch, in case whoever hurt her had returned.

Content in the knowledge that she was safe now, she had rested in one of the women's arms, drifting in and out of consciousness until help arrived.

Then she had been sedated and rushed to the hospital.

When she'd awakened, hours later, her mother had been sitting at her bedside, clutching her hand.

Laura had cried. Her mother had cried. Laura had tried to tell her that she loved her, but her voice still wasn't working properly.

The police had arrived shortly after she had woken up.

Between her hoarse voice, her heavy limbs and broken fingers, Laura had managed to half speak and half write down what had happened to her.

It had taken her battered body several days to be strong enough for her doctors to discharge her. She had battled pneumonia and infections. The cuts on her feet had made walking difficult at first.

But the physical injuries had been nothing compared to the psychological ones.

The nightmares had started that first night. The flashbacks not long after.

But at least by the time she had been released from the hospital, Frank and Francis Garrett had been arrested.

It had been that fact that was the only thing that kept her going in those early days.

The fact that it was over.

And it *was* over.

Laura didn't think she could handle it if it wasn't.

There was no third man.

She would have known if there was someone else out there.

Only, there was one little thing bothering her about that.

She didn't think it was Frank or Francis who had grabbed her at her house.

She had convinced herself she was wrong, of course. Who else could it have been? And the Garrett brothers had definitely been there in the woods.

But the man who had been waiting for her in the house had been taller and more muscled.

She had fought wildly against him when he had wrapped his arms around her.

Even managed to twist free for a moment.

Then he'd been on her again.

Slamming her head into the doorframe.

The world had exploded into agony and she'd blacked out.

She hadn't woken up again until she was out in the woods.

So, it *was* possible that there had been someone else there during that time.

And Jack and Rose had said that what he was doing now was mirroring what the Garretts had done to her.

Abduction, rape, then that woman had been burned and cut and strangled, just like she had been.

Could it be true?

Could Jack be right?

Could there really have been a third man who had now come back for her?

If there was, would he get to her?

Jack said there were cops at her door and that she was safe, but was she?

If there was someone after her and he got her, then what did he intend to do to her?

She had a horrible feeling she knew the answer to that already.

No.

It wasn't true.

She wouldn't believe it.

Jack and Rose were wrong.

This had nothing to do with her.

There was no third man.

There wasn't, there couldn't be ... she began to sob.

* * * * *

12:26 P.M.

"You nervous about seeing them?" Rose asked as they parked

160

in front of Laura's parents' house.

"Mmhmm," Jack nodded. He was indeed anxious about seeing Mick and Karen Opal again after what he'd done to their daughter. He had avoided them after he and Laura had split. It had been close to the end of their senior year anyway, and then he'd been off to college. By the time he returned, the Opals had moved.

"Let's go get it over with, then." Rose climbed from the car and started for the front door.

The Opals' house was small, a single-story brick structure surrounded by an absolutely gorgeous front garden. Jack remembered that Laura's mother had adored gardening. When they were kids, they had loved eating fresh fruit and vegetables that Karen had grown. Then there were the flowers, hundreds of them in every color imaginable, all perfectly arranged. When they were dating, Jack had often picked bouquets of flowers for Laura from her mother's garden. Although on a smaller scale, Karen had recreated her magnificent gardens in her new home.

"You want me to lead the interview, since they probably aren't too keen on you?" Rose asked as she rang the bell.

"I'll start, but if they aren't too receptive to me, then you can take over," Jack replied, straightening his spine as footsteps sounded on the other side of the door and it swung open.

"May I help...?" Mick Opal broke off as he spied Jack, his face growing fierce. "Jack Xander. The man who broke my baby's heart."

"Good afternoon, Mr. Opal." Jack attempted a smile.

"Get off my property at once or I'm calling the police," Mick growled, already closing the door.

"Mr. Opal, please, I need to talk to you about Laura."

He huffed mirthlessly. "I wouldn't talk to you about Laura if you were the last person on the planet. You broke her heart," Mick said again.

"Mick, who's at the...?" Karen appeared beside her husband,

her face, so like Laura's, going stony when she saw him. "What is *he* doing here?" she asked her husband.

"Leaving," Mick answered.

"Mr. and Mrs. Opal," he tried again, convincing Laura's parents to let him in the door was turning out to be even harder than he had anticipated.

"That's it, I'm calling the police," Mick declared.

"I *am* the police," he reminded them. "Please, I wouldn't have come if it wasn't important. It's about Laura; I think she's in trouble."

This caused them both to pause. Karen's face grew pale. "Laura? In trouble?"

"What's wrong with her?" Mick was going with suspicious.

"Please, may I come in?"

He glanced at his wife, and when Karen nodded, Mick sighed and took a step backward to allow them to enter. They followed Karen into a small living room, filled with the furniture he remembered from their old house. Karen sat down on one of the two sofas, Mick sitting beside her, he and Rose taking the opposite one.

"This is my partner, Rose. And these are Laura's parents, Mick and Karen Opal." He made the introductions.

Karen merely nodded, her attention focused solely on him. "Have you seen her, Jack?" Her violet eyes were looking at him desperately, as though she were dying and he alone held the key to her salvation.

"Yes," he confirmed, knowing how scared and concerned Laura's parents must have been all these years, knowing their daughter needed them, but unable to go to her.

Karen gasped, her hands moving to cover her mouth. Then she dropped them to her lap as she asked, "Is she okay?"

He was unsure how to answer that. Laura wasn't okay physically or psychologically, but she was coping as best she could. He didn't want to worry her parents further though by telling them that she was struggling. "She's hanging in there," was what he finally settled on. "I know you haven't seen her in ten years."

Tears welled up in her eyes, and Karen nodded. "Did she call you?"

"No, I just stumbled upon her yesterday during an investigation. That's why I'm here. I think Laura may be in danger."

"In danger?" Fear flashed through Mick's eyes. "What sort of danger?"

"I think there may have been a third person involved in Laura's attack."

"Laura never mentioned a third man," Mick said, confusion lacing his tone.

"She may not have known. But I believe there was another man and that he's not happy that Laura was rescued. I think he wants to get his hands on her, finish what he started. He's been recreating her assault in her apartment building using random residents," he explained gently.

Shock marred both their faces. "No." Karen shook her head. "Laura's been through so much. You must be wrong."

"I don't think I'm wrong, Mrs. Opal," he said apologetically. "We need to know if you can think of anyone who could have been involved in her attack."

"You really think someone wants to hurt her?" Karen's voice trembled.

"Yes." He nodded. Unfortunately, he did. Holding up the sketch, he asked, "Do you recognize this man?"

"No," Mick replied. "I mean, he looks like he could be anyone, but not specifically."

"We told the police at the time that we didn't know anyone who would want to hurt our little girl. But Laura was in college, she wouldn't have told us everything that was going on in her life," Karen explained.

"I don't think she dated much, she was too busy studying and working," Mick added. "We met a few of her friends, they all seemed like great kids. And her roommates were all nice, too, no troublemakers."

"Did she have a particular friend she might have confided in?" Jack asked.

"Her closest friend was Matilda Warren, the girl who was killed," Karen responded. "I remember having to tell her that Matilda was dead. Laura was still in the hospital, she got so upset that they had to sedate her." Tears began to trickle unnoticed down her cheeks. "Seeing my baby like that was horrendous. What they did to her ..." She shook her head as though unable to comprehend it.

Jack struggled to reign in his fury. If he could get away with it, he would rip Frank and Francis Garrett to pieces with his bare hands. "I know. I've seen the pictures."

She shuddered. "I've seen the pictures, too—in court. But they were nothing compared to the real thing. I wanted to help my little girl so badly, but I didn't know what to do for her. Seeing her walk around in a daze and looking at me with those haunted eyes, it just broke my heart. That's why she left. She couldn't deal with her own grief, let alone everyone else's."

"Did she tell you she was leaving?"

"No," Mick answered quietly. "The day the verdict came back guilty, we wanted to celebrate. We hoped Laura would be able to get some closure, but she said she needed some time to herself. When we got back home, she was gone. She'd left a note, telling us not to worry and that she was okay but that she needed to be alone."

The trauma Laura had gone through had rippled out to touch the lives of everyone who loved her. "Was there anyone who came to the court who seemed to take a particular interest in Laura?" Jack asked.

"No. The court case was so hard on Laura, it was like she had to keep reliving what she'd been through over and over again. Those Garrett brothers got to keep hurting her, it wasn't fair."

Mick put an arm around his wife's shoulders. "All our attention at court went to supporting Laura," Mick explained.

"She was so fragile, so vulnerable," Karen cried quietly. "I just didn't know what to do for her. She wanted to call you, Jack."

"She did?" Jack was surprised, but also pleased—it was further confirmation that Laura still loved him, which meant he still had a shot with her.

"Yes, she did. She was just scared, she didn't want you to see her like that."

"I'm so sorry I hurt her," he told her parents imploringly.

"I know you are, Jack." Karen gave him a small smile. "I always knew that you were sorry. I told Laura so many times that she should forgive you."

"You did?" He hadn't known that, he'd thought Laura's parents hated him.

"I did. But I was Laura's mother, and if my daughter was angry with you, then I was, too. Laura was just scared to forgive you, in case she got hurt again."

"I hated you," Mick stated a little sullenly.

Karen waved a hand at her husband to silence him. "Jack, can you give us her address? So, we can go and see her?"

His heart breaking, he murmured, "I can't do that, I'm sorry."

"But if she's in danger then she shouldn't be alone, she'd be safer here with us," Karen protested. "And she needs us."

"I know she does, but I don't think Laura's ready to come home yet. She certainly wasn't pleased to see me, I don't want her to be angry with you for turning up when she's not expecting you." He attempted a smile to gentle his words.

"You just want time with her on your own so you can try to wiggle back into her good graces," Mick growled.

"Please, Jack." Karen ignored her husband. "I need to see my baby."

"I'm so sorry, but I can't tell you where she is. I can promise you two things, though," Jack stated seriously. "I can promise you that I'll talk to her and try to convince her to see you. And I can promise you that I'll keep her safe. I won't let anyone hurt her again."

* * * * *

6:49 P.M.

Rose was tired.

It had been a long day. When they'd finished up with Laura's parents, they'd spoken with the cops who had worked her case, who they hadn't had anything to add that wasn't already in the complete case file that they'd picked up on their way back from Laura's earlier in the morning. The two detectives hadn't seemed overly surprised when she and Jack had asked them about the possibility of a third person being involved in her abduction, but neither had they given a reason why they hadn't looked into it back then.

After that, they had met with Laura's sister, who had been just as angry with Jack as Laura's parents had been. Although, as with her parents, when they had told her that they believed Laura was in trouble, she had quickly moved past anger to focus on concern for her little sister. Rose had gotten the feeling that no one in the Opal family was really all that angry with Jack anymore, and that they all really in fact liked him—Laura included.

Then they had tracked down the remaining two roommates who had shared the house with Laura and Matilda Warren back when they were all in college. Neither of the women, both of whom were now married with toddlers, had spoken with Laura since she disappeared. And both had confirmed what Karen and Mick Opal had told them—if Laura had confided in anyone, it would have been Matilda.

No one had had anything to add to what they already knew. No one had recognized the man in the sketch. They were no closer to finding out who was after Laura than they'd been at the beginning of the day. Which was not good news for Laura.

Rose was looking forward to going home, taking a long, hot bubble bath, and then curling up in bed at a nice early hour. She was almost to her car when she saw someone standing a few yards away.

Her breath caught when she realized who it was.

It was Paige.

And she was standing staring precisely at the spot where she had been nearly killed almost six months ago.

"Paige?" she called as she hurried toward her friend.

Paige shouldn't be here, and certainly not on her own. She hadn't been back here since her attack, and coming here on her own could not be a good idea.

Her friend didn't respond. Didn't indicate in any way that she had heard Rose.

When she reached Paige, she saw that her friend's face was blank. Eerily blank. Expressionless. Rose was feeling totally out of her element. She should have waited for Jack to leave, come down to the parking lot with him. He would have known exactly how to handle Paige. Rose didn't have a clue what she should say to her friend.

"Paige?" she rested a hand on her shoulder.

Paige started, letting out a strangled scream, and turned huge unfocused eyes in her direction.

"It's okay, Paige. It's me. It's Rose," she soothed.

Reverting her gaze back to the spot where she'd been attacked, Paige was breathing way too fast and visibly trembling.

"Honey, what are you doing here?" Rose asked, wanting desperately to snap Paige out of her trance.

"I needed to see," Paige murmured so quietly Rose barely heard her.

"See what?"

"If I could come back here." Paige swayed and sunk to her knees.

Alarmed, Rose knelt beside her, taking hold of her friend's wrist to check her pulse. "Paige, honey, let me take you home. Is Elias there?" Paige shook her head. "Okay, then you're coming home with me." No way was she leaving Paige alone right now.

Instead of responding, Paige suddenly burst into a fit of hysterical sobbing.

Rose wrapped her arms around her friend. "Shh," she soothed. "It's okay, Paige."

Paige buried her face in Rose's shoulder. "What if I can't come back?" she cried.

"Come back where, honey?" Rose asked.

"To work. I want to come back, but what if I can't do it?" Paige sobbed.

"What are you scared will happen when you come back?" Rose was feeling helpless; what she wanted to do was call Jack or Ryan or someone who would know what to say to help Paige.

"This." Paige looked up at her. "I don't know what's wrong with me."

She brushed Paige's curly hair away from her face. "You don't know what's wrong with you? Paige, you were threatened, terrorized, and beaten nearly to death. What's wrong with you is that you're simply dealing with the fallout. And it doesn't help that he's still out there somewhere. But listen to me." She made sure Paige's brown eyes were focused on her. "If you're ready to come back to work, that's great; and if you're not, that's totally fine. Whatever you decide, I'm here for you. We're all here for you. Okay?"

"Okay," Paige sniffed.

"And you've done it now. You've come back here. Next time you come, it'll be a little easier and easier again the time after that, until it doesn't bother you anymore," Rose encouraged.

"Yeah, I guess you're right," Paige agreed, like the thought hadn't occurred to her before Rose had said it.

Rose tugged Paige to her feet. "Come on, I'll take you back to my place and we'll call Sofia, see if she can come and have dinner with us."

Paige allowed herself to be guided to Rose's car, and she helped her friend into the passenger seat.

"I have a headache," Paige murmured as Rose climbed into the driver's seat.

"I'm not surprised. I don't think it was a good idea for you to try that on your own. You could have asked Elias to come with you. Or me or Ryan or Jack or Sofia or anyone else," Rose admonished.

"I didn't know I was going to react like that." Paige rested her head back against the seat and closed her eyes.

"Yes, you did," Rose contradicted. "That's why you haven't come back before now. Only because you're going to be back at work soon, you thought you ought to do it."

Paige merely huffed.

"There's Tylenol in the glove compartment," Rose informed her. "Then text Elias and tell him you're going to be at my place. I don't want him getting home, finding you're not there, and worrying about you. Then close your eyes and rest."

After waiting to make sure Paige was going to follow her instructions, Rose picked up her own phone and typed a one-handed message to Sofia, briefly explaining what had happened and asking her to join them for dinner.

When she pulled into her garage fifteen minutes later, Paige seemed to have drifted off to sleep. Reaching over, she gently shook her shoulder. "Paige? Hey, we're here," she said softly. Paige's eyes blinked sleepily open. "How's your head?"

"Better," Paige acknowledged. "Thanks, Rose. For everything. Sorry I cried all over you."

"You're welcome and no worries, you can cry over me any

time you need to." Rose was pleased to see that Paige was obviously doing better; maybe she was better at handling hysterical people than she'd thought she was.

By the time they'd gotten inside and made a start on dinner— macaroni and cheese and a salad—the doorbell was ringing.

"I'll get it," Paige volunteered.

She returned a moment later with Sofia and Sofia's friend, Annabelle Englewood. "Hey, Rose." Sofia smiled at her. "Okay if Annabelle joins us?"

"Of course." Rose smiled back. "Hi, Annabelle."

"Hi." Annabelle smiled shyly back.

It wasn't that Rose didn't like Annabelle, she liked the younger woman just fine, it was more that she couldn't seem to connect with her. Rose knew that Annabelle struggled with major self-confidence issues, and that those issues affected the way she interacted with people. The only person Annabelle seemed close to was Sofia.

"So, how are you doing?" Sofia was asking Paige. "I can't believe you went there on your own. Why didn't you call me? I would have gone with you or Ryan would have or Jack or Rose. Why did you go on your own?"

"Rose already told me off," Paige replied.

"Well, good for her. That was really silly, you know. What were you thinking?"

"I guess I wasn't." Paige shrugged fitfully.

Sofia softened. "How're you doing?"

"How do you cope with him being out there?" Paige asked, refusing to look up from the tomatoes she was chopping.

"I try to keep busy and not think about it," Sofia replied grimly. "But he hasn't been violent toward me, it's *you* that he's a danger to."

This unknown man had been stalking Sofia for a couple of years now, long before they all met her. He had left Sofia gifts and flowers, called her and had even broken into her house when she wasn't home. Then he had disappeared, only to return six months ago when he got the idea in his head that Paige and Ryan were having an affair. Blaming Paige, he latched onto her and decided if she was dead, then Sofia's happiness would be ensured.

"Annabelle, how did you cope while Ricky Preston was still out there?" Paige asked Annabelle.

"I didn't," Annabelle answered simply.

"Having Ryan and Sophie helps," Sofia added. "You have Elias, and he's totally devoted to you. And maybe you guys might have kids soon."

"I can't get pregnant," Paige blurted out. "There were complications when I was attacked and I won't be able to have kids of my own."

"Oh, honey," she and Sofia said simultaneously, both moving to wrap their arms around a crying Paige.

"Why didn't you tell me?" Rose asked, knowing what a blow that would have been to Paige, who had dreamed of having children for as long as Rose had known her.

"No one knows," Paige replied. "Well, obviously Elias, but other than him, I only told Ryan."

For a long moment, the three of them just stood there. She and Sofia held Paige while she cried, while Annabelle stood awkwardly beside them. Her unusual eyes, which were so pale blue that they appeared white, were full of sympathy for Paige, but she wasn't comfortable offering comfort.

"Well, we are a depressing group, aren't we?" Sofia smiled ruefully.

"That we are." Paige gave a small chuckle.

"Actually, I had something I wanted to talk to you guys about," Sofia announced. "And since we're all here, this seems like the perfect time."

* * * * *

7:53 P.M.

"Hey, sweet pea, what are you still doing up?" Jack took baby Sophie from his brother's arms as Ryan opened the front door for him.

"She doesn't want to go to sleep for daddy," Ryan answered for the eleven-month-old baby.

"Sofia's out?" he asked as they headed for the kitchen.

"Yeah, apparently Paige decided going back to where she was attacked on her own was a good idea," Ryan grimly explained.

He winced. "It didn't go well, I take it?"

"Rose found her all hysterical. She managed to calm her down, though, and she thought it would be a good idea to distract Paige for a while, so she asked Sofia to go and have dinner with them." The concern for his partner was evident on his brother's face.

Jack echoed that concern. "Why didn't she ask someone to go with her? You would have gone; Sofia would have gone; Rose would have gone; I would have gone; anyone would have gone with her."

"Yeah, well, she's stubborn." Ryan sighed.

"Ryan, she goes back to work in one week, I don't think she's ready," he announced a little tentatively.

Ryan sighed again. "She has a lot going on."

"I know she does, but you don't want that distracting her. Getting distracted was what led to her getting attacked in the first place," he reminded his brother.

"Jack, she can't have kids," Ryan informed him.

"Oh ..." His heart went out to Paige. They all knew how much she'd wanted to have kids. Finding out she couldn't because of her attack would have been a major blow when she already had a lot on her plate.

Ryan rested a hand on Sophie's soft little head. "No one knows, only me and of course Elias, so don't say anything," he cautioned Jack. "She'll tell people when she's ready."

FOUR

"Yeah, I won't say anything," he assured Ryan, although knowing would add to his already existing concerns about Paige. Sophie's pudgy little hands began to pat his cheeks, and she gurgled excitedly. He smiled down at her. "You want some attention, huh?"

"I better go put her to bed. Don't want Mommy to be mad I let you stay up late," Ryan said as he picked up the baby. "I'll be right back, don't worry if you hear screaming, she's likely to protest a little."

Jack chuckled, feeling a twinge of jealousy as he watched how happy his brother was with his baby daughter. He wanted this. He wanted a home, a family, children. And he wanted it with Laura.

Which was all the more reason to wrap up this case ASAP.

Once this was over and Laura was safe, then he could work on winning her back.

While he waited for Ryan, he sent a quick text to Rose to check on Paige, and then checked in with the cops who were posted at Laura's door. By the time he had confirmation that Laura was still safe and Paige was doing okay, Ryan was walking back into the kitchen.

"So, I heard," Ryan announced.

"Heard what?"

"About Laura," Ryan replied with a slight eye roll. "I can't believe we never knew what happened to her."

"She didn't want anyone to know," he explained.

"Do you think Mom and Dad knew? They were still close with the Opals even after you two broke up, and after they moved."

"No, I don't think they knew. Laura told her parents not to tell anyone."

"So?" Ryan looked at him expectantly.

"So, what?"

Another eye roll. "Are you going to get back together with her?"

"Laura's still angry with me," he replied.

"Of course. What you did was stupid, but she'll realize that you were both kids back then and now you're both all grown up. She'll get over it because we all know she loves you. So, are you going to get back together with her?" Ryan asked again.

Jack hesitated. He wanted Laura back. Desperately. And yet, there was one thing that made him doubt that he was good enough for Laura. And it wasn't what had broken them up in the first place.

"Jack," Ryan began gently. "You never stopped loving Laura. We all knew it. You dated, but you never connected with any of those other women because deep down, you still believed that you would somehow get back together with Laura. Well, this is your chance. This is your chance to get back the only woman you've ever loved. Don't let what happened three years ago hold you back."

Jack was surprised that he had apparently done such a bad job at hiding that. He'd thought that his family and friends would simply think he was a little down about breaking up with his girlfriend. He'd never known that they'd figured out that more than that had happened on that vacation. But obviously, Ryan had known and Rose had known, and it was probably a safe bet that everyone else knew, too.

"You couldn't have really thought we were stupid enough not to notice the complete changes in your behavior?" Ryan arched a blond brow.

Actually, he had really thought that they hadn't known. Or maybe if he was honest, it was more like he had hoped.

"Okay, so maybe you did," Ryan chuckled. "But seriously though, Jack, you need to deal with whatever happened. If you want Laura back, then she's going to need to be your top priority. She's going to need a lot of help to deal with what she's been through. You don't want to be distracted by your own issues."

He considered this. It made sense, Jack decided. Laura would need therapy, and, more importantly, she would need support.

She needed someone who could be one hundred percent focused on her.

"So," Ryan was looking at him expectantly. "You want to talk about it?"

Although, Jack agreed that he was going to have to talk about it at some point—some point soon—he still balked at the idea.

Ryan sighed. "Okay, so you're not ready yet. But you better get yourself ready. You let Laura down once before, don't do it again."

He took the warning seriously. Jack didn't feel comfortable discussing what had happened with his family or friends. Nor did the idea of seeing a shrink particularly appeal to him, although it may end up being a last resort. But maybe he could talk to Laura. He didn't want to add to the heavy burden she was already carrying, but she might by the one person who truly understood.

"All right, I'm convinced," he assured his brother. "But you don't actually know what happened right?" he checked.

"No, I don't," Ryan promised. "I wanted to call someone and find out, but Rose said we shouldn't invade your privacy, that we should wait for you to tell us yourself. Although, I don't think she really thought we'd still be waiting three years later. Wow, I still can't believe Laura is back in our lives after all these years. I had the biggest crush on her in high school."

Jack was pleased with the lightened change in conversation. "I know. *Everyone* had a crush on Laura in high school. She was drop-dead gorgeous. She's still drop-dead gorgeous."

"Remember how much fun we used to have playing together as kids? You and me and Mark, Laura and Mary, the Jensons from up the block, and the Tinkers from around the corner. We used to get up to so much mischief."

"Yeah, we did. I think the whole neighborhood was thrilled when summer vacation ended and we all went back to school," he wistfully reminisced. The Laura they'd known back then was fearless, energetic, playful. She had sparkled. To see Laura now, too terrified to leave her apartment, trapped in a nightmare that she didn't know how to escape from, was heartbreaking. "Ryan, what they did to her ..." He trailed off shakily. It literally brought tears to his eyes when he thought of the hell those men had put her through.

"I know, Jack. I also know what it's like to see the woman you love battered and bruised and broken. But Sofia was never really broken, she was strong and she fought back and reclaimed her life. Laura is strong too. It might be a long road but she'll get there, she'll get her life back." Sympathy filled his brother's blue eyes. "Come on, I'm feeling in a reminiscent mood, let's go and look up some old photos of us as kids. Maybe you can use them with Laura to try and get her to remember just how great you can be."

"Worth a shot," Jack laughed. Anything was worth a shot. Because he was determined to get his girl back.

JULY 25TH

Why was she even bothering to lie in bed?

Laura knew she wasn't going to sleep.

Maybe it was because she felt somewhat safe in her bed. She could curl up, pull the covers over her head, and pretend she was in a little cocoon where nothing and no one could get to her.

That was exactly what she was doing right now.

She was also sucking desperately on her thumb.

Thumb sucking had been a bad habit she'd suffered from most of her life. She had sucked her thumb up until the age of about twelve, despite her parents many attempts to get her to quit, and the many taunts of her peers. Even as a teenager she had sometimes resorted to the habit when she was particularly stressed. Then following her abduction, the habit had returned as a coping mechanism. Sometimes it would be the only thing that could calm and soothe her when she was overwhelmed by fear and pain.

Laura knew she should break the childish habit. Having just passed her thirty-first birthday, she was much too old to still be doing that. But given that she lived here on her own so no one ever saw her do it anyway, it didn't really seem worth the bother.

Since sleep was obviously still out of the equation, maybe she should get up.

Only she wasn't sure she had enough energy to walk.

She had laid for hours on the floor in her living room, crying and panicking.

Then she had crawled to her bedroom and dragged herself up

and into bed.

She decided she may as well give standing a try. If she couldn't manage it, then she'd just stay here in bed. Maybe forever.

With grim determination, she pushed herself into a sitting position. Her head immediately protested, swimming viciously until it was all she could do not to moan piteously and sink back down onto her pillows. Laura fought against the dizziness until it subsided to a somewhat manageable level, and then she swung her legs over the side of the bed. Another sickening wave of dizziness swamped her as she stood. But again, it soon wore off enough that she could just make it to the kitchen on badly shaking legs.

Laura knew she needed to eat something.

One quarter of a piece of toast was all she'd eaten in the last twenty-four hours. And before that, she couldn't remember what she had last consumed.

She was just about to begin the mammoth effort of preparing some food when she heard voices outside her door.

"Relax," she admonished herself aloud. Jack had said there were going to be cops on her door. That must be who was talking.

Someone hammered on her door, and an accompanying voice called her name, "Ms. Opal?"

She forced herself to answer, "Yes?"

"It's Officer Lyle, we've been assigned to keep an eye on you, but apparently there's some raucous downstairs, so we have to go and check it out. More officers are on the way and we'll be back as quickly as we can. Ms. Opal, don't open the door for anyone while we're gone, and if anything happens, call 911 immediately," the officer ordered.

"Okay," she said because she knew he wanted a response.

Footsteps headed away from her door, and Laura went on wobbly legs to check the deadbolts were all in place. Before dragging herself to bed earlier, she had, of course, first had to lock herself back in.

Her gaze fell on the card Jack had left with his number on it.

She was sacred. She didn't want to admit it because admitting it was like admitting that he was right and this ordeal wasn't yet over.

Tentatively, she picked the card up.

Should she call him?

Taking the card with her, she returned to the kitchen and sank down into a chair.

Call or not call? She was still debating it several minutes later when she heard someone outside her door again.

Assuming it was just the officers returning, she didn't pay it much mind until the door handle rattled.

Someone was trying to get in.

Panic rushed through her.

The doorknob rattled again.

Someone definitely wanted in.

And it wasn't the cops.

Officer Lyle would have announced himself.

She grabbed the phone, her decision made for her, she dialed Jack's number.

"Detective Xander," his sleep-laden voice spoke in her ear seconds later.

"Jack," it was a whimper and all she could manage.

"Laura?" Instantly awake. "What's wrong?"

"There's someone at my door. Something happened downstairs. The officers had to leave. And then someone was trying to open my door," she explained in a rush.

"I'm calling more cops to come, okay?" he told her, and she could hear him moving about.

She took a deep breath. "Jack, I need *you* to come," she admitted.

"Already on my way," he assured her.

Jack said something else, but she didn't hear him—whoever was outside her door was pushing something underneath it. An envelope.

"Laura?"

"He put something under my door," she whispered haltingly, she was utterly terrified.

He muttered something unintelligible. "Just hold on; I'm on my way."

Panic pulsed through her again, she didn't want to be alone right now. "Jack, don't hang up, please."

"Wouldn't dream of it," he soothed. "I'll stay on the line with you until I get there," he promised.

Jack babbled away at her for the next ten minutes. Laura couldn't really make out any of the words he was saying, but the sound of his voice was like a balm on her fear.

"Laura, I'm outside your door," he said at last, giving a soft knock on her door so she would know it was indeed him.

Laura rushed the door, throwing open the deadlocks as quickly as her trembling hands could manage. Then she yanked the door open and all but flung herself into Jack's arms. For the moment, she was happy to just rest heavily against him, letting him hold her up, not thinking of anything other than that she was safe with Jack.

"It's all right, angel," he whispered in her hair, holding her tightly in his arms. "I'm here now."

Hearing him call her angel, his pet name for her since they were teenagers, again after all these years melted her heart. But it also annoyed her. She didn't want him to make her feel safe. She didn't want to still like him. None of that mattered. They weren't going to get back together, no matter how much Jack might want to.

Jack disengaged her arms from around his waist, keeping one arm supportively around her waist as he guided her away from the door so he could lock it behind them. "Are you okay?" he asked.

"Yes." But even she could hear the tremble in her voice.

His eyes raked over her as he shook his head. "Go and sit down before you fall down," he ordered.

"I'm okay, Jack," she protested.

Jack merely raised an eyebrow and prodded her in the direction of her couch.

Feeling worriedly light-headed, Laura thought maybe she better comply. So, as she sank down into the soft sofa cushions, Jack slid on a pair of gloves and picked up the envelope that had been pushed under her door. His expression grew dark as he looked at whatever was inside and Laura thought she didn't want to know what it was. Jack made a phone call, and then once he'd slipped his phone back into his pocket, he came back to her, standing in front of her and looking down at her.

"Come on, I'll make you something to eat." He took her good hand and pulled her to her feet, keeping hold of her so she didn't crumple into a ball at his feet.

Once he'd sat her down at the table, he set about rummaging through her fridge and cupboards. Deciding on soup, he took a can of chicken noodle, and set it to heat on the stove. Then he disappeared briefly, returning a moment later with the first aid kit she kept in her bathroom.

"I'm checking out your hand," he informed her as he took the chair beside her.

Ordinarily Laura hated when Jack was bossy, but right now she was so shaken that she was okay with him telling her what to do. Having him take care of her gave her a semblance of security that she hadn't felt in years.

So, she offered no protest as he gently took her hand, even though she usually hated for anyone to touch her, and unwound the bandage, wincing as he took in the burn on her hand. Using the contents of her first aid kit, Jack cleaned the wound, applied some antibiotic ointment, and re-dressed it. His touch was tender and careful as he dealt with her injury, taking care to cause her as little pain as possible. And the burn really did hurt.

"Your hand doesn't look so good, you know," Jack told her mildly once he'd set her hand gently back down on the table.

Despite the mild tone, Laura could see the concern in his eyes. "I know you can't go to the doctor, but what if I brought someone here to check it out?"

Unsure, Laura's instinct was to say no, but she agreed with Jack; the burn on her hand wasn't doing so well, and it probably did need to be looked at by a professional. "Maybe," she murmured tiredly.

"Good." Jack looked pleased with her response. He opened his mouth to say more but paused and pulled out his phone, glancing at the screen. "Sorry, angel, it's Rose. I already ignored her calls twice, and she knows I'm here, so she's going to be worried about you. I have to take this. Pop your head down and rest until your food's ready," he instructed.

Balancing his phone between his shoulder and ear, Jack moved to the stove to stir the soup, talking in a quiet voice to his partner while keeping one eye on her. When he saw she hadn't followed his orders, he frowned at her and motioned for her to lay her head down. With an inward eye roll, Laura did as she was told, folding her arms on the table and resting her head against them, letting her eyes fall closed.

Sometime later, Jack tapped her shoulder. "Soup's ready," he informed her. "You eat all of it," he ordered as he set the bowl down in front of her. "Here's some apple juice," he added. "This first, the sugar will help get your blood sugar up, and then you can have some water, I don't want you getting dehydrated."

Jack's fussing was irritatingly comforting. Laura knew she was safe as long as Jack was here.

Sitting across from her, Jack ate some soup, too. Neither of them spoke, settling into a comfortable silence. When she was finished—she ate every drop because she knew Jack was going to insist on it—he took their dishes, rinsed them, and set them in the dishwasher.

Then he set a glass of water and two pills on the table. "Painkillers," he told her. "Drink all the water."

Again, Laura did as she was told, noting just how out of sorts she was these days, given that she had never let Jack boss her around when they were kids.

Once she was done, he disposed of the glass, then sat across from her again. "Okay, angel, talk to me."

And to Laura's surprise, she did.

* * * * *

2:57 A.M.

If Jack had known getting Laura to talk was as simple as asking her, he would have done it two days ago.

It was like the tap had been turned on and words were tumbling out completely out of her control.

"I knew as soon as I opened my front door that something was wrong," she was saying. "You how you get that feeling sometimes?" She continued when he nodded. "But before I could do anything about it, someone grabbed me. I'd taken some self-defense classes, I managed to get away from him for a moment. But he got me. He slammed my head into the door and I must have blacked out."

Laura shuddered and Jack's concerns about her increased. She clearly wasn't doing well. She had been shaky and weak looking when he'd gotten here, barely able to remain on her feet. She was still wearing the same clothes she had been dressed in when he and Rose had been here yesterday morning. It didn't seem like she'd eaten anything, which was probably the reason why she was so wobbly on her feet. The fact that she was following all his orders didn't make him feel any better. The old Laura would never have let him boss her around like this.

"When I woke up, I was in this hole in the ground. My head ached and I wasn't wearing my clothes, only my underwear. I could tell that I'd been ..." She paused awkwardly, but she didn't need to say the word; he knew what she meant.

"I'm so sorry, angel." Jack wanted to take her hand, to offer her whatever comfort he could, but she clearly didn't like being touched, even though she had thrown herself into his arms when he'd arrived. However, she'd been scared then, she had needed reassurance. And she had also let him tend to her hand. Perhaps, given their history, she was comfortable enough with him to allow him to touch her. Tentatively, he reached out a hand and took her good one. She glanced at his large hand covering her small one, but she didn't pull away.

"I tried to get out, but I couldn't. Then they came."

The way she said it had his blood boiling. Frank and Francis Garrett deserved to suffer as horribly as they had made Laura suffer. "It's all right, angel, you don't have to tell me about what they did to you, I read the case file." Jack didn't want to hear Laura verbalize what he'd already read. He knew it would tear him up inside to hear her describe what she'd been through, but if Laura needed to get it out he'd listen, no matter what it would do to him—she came first.

Laura shivered and her violet eyes filled with tears. "Before those hikers found me, I knew I wouldn't last much longer. I was so weak. So exhausted from running through the woods. After they would finish ..." She paused and seemed to search for a suitable word. "... hurting me, they would tell me to run. They thought it was fun to chase me. They'd pretend to count like when you play hide-and-seek. I'd run as fast as I could, but I didn't have any shoes. My feet got so sore, but I knew I couldn't stop. But each time they hurt me, I got a little weaker, until I could hardly move at all. Then at night, they'd put me back in that hole in the ground. It was dark in there. And cold. All I could see was a small circle of stars above my head."

No doubt the reason for the stars left on Tarek Milford's ceiling, Jack thought. "Angel, are you sure there couldn't have been a third man?" he asked her.

The look she gave him clearly showed that she wasn't sure. "I don't know, Jack," she whispered. "The man in my house, I don't think it was Frank or Francis. I always thought that, only I told myself I had to be wrong. I never saw anyone else in the woods. Just the Garrett brothers and then those hikers."

"You didn't regain consciousness between the time you were knocked out in your house and waking up in that hole in the woods?" he confirmed. Laura nodded. "So, there could have been someone else there during that time. The police never found any evidence that you'd been in the Garretts' truck. Maybe this third person is the one who abducted you and took you to them."

"I didn't know that." Her huge, scared eyes found his.

"The police never told you?"

She shook her head.

"Did you tell the police that you didn't think it was either of the Garretts who grabbed you?"

"I don't remember." Laura closed her eyes and rubbed at her temples. "Everything around that time is kind of fuzzy in my head. I felt like I was walking around in a fog. I couldn't tell you hardly anything I did or said during that time. All I knew was that I was scared and hurting and desperately wished that I could pretend it never happened."

His heart ached for her. "I'm so sorry, angel. I'm so sorry that this happened to you, and I'm sorry that everything's been stirred up again. I'm doing everything I can to end this for you. But I need your help, Laura. Can I show you the sketch now? See if you recognize this man?" he asked tentatively, not wanting to upset her further.

Indecision battled in Laura's violet eyes. She gave the tiniest of nods.

He brought up the picture on his phone and held it up so Laura could see it. Her eyes darted to it and then jumped away. Then slowly, she moved them back and gave the picture a proper glance. "I don't think I know him." She looked deliberately away.

"But the picture is so vague, it's hard to tell."

"That's okay," he reassured her. "We're going to find this man, I'm not going to let him hurt you."

"There can't be a third man, Jack. I can't do this again. I need it to be over." Tears began to spill out, trickling down her pale cheeks.

Not caring whether she liked being touched or not, Jack stood and knelt beside her chair, pulling her into his arms. Laura stiffened instinctively, then gave a small sob and sunk down against him. Pressing her face into his chest, she cried. Her tears soaked through his shirt, but Jack didn't care; he just tightened his grip on her, stroking his hand up and down her back, attempting to calm her. When her tears finally dried up, Laura made no attempt to move out of his embrace, so Jack simply continued to hold her.

"Why do you cut your hair so short?" she asked at last, her voice muffled against his chest.

"It's a long story," he replied, not wanting to get into that now.

"I always liked your hair. It was so soft and silky." Then a shiver rocketed through her entire frame. "What did he leave in the envelope? It was him, wasn't it? This third man, the one who's been hurting people in the building. He was here tonight. He left something. What was it?"

Jack wasn't sure it was wise to answer her. He didn't want to upset her further, but they needed Laura if they were going to find this man, and every bit of information she had could help her to figure out who wanted to hurt her. He had called Stephanie to come and collect the letter and check it for fingerprints to compare to the ones from the other crime scenes. While Laura had been dozing at the table earlier, he had quietly slipped the letter out the door to the cops who were still posted there, so they could pass it on to Stephanie when she arrived.

They assumed that the man who'd left the letter had set things up to get the cops away from Laura's apartment so he could try to get at her. He had broken down the door to apartment 5J, then quickly disappeared, waited until the cops left Laura's floor then came up here and attempted to get inside. When he couldn't get in, he had left the letter instead. He was getting impatient. He'd thought he would have had her by now. Thought all his games would have sent her running from her apartment. But it hadn't. And he was obviously getting desperate.

"Jack?" Laura prodded when he didn't answer, lifting her head so she could see him.

"He left you a photo of the woman from your building who was kidnapped. And a note saying that you'd meet her soon."

She wiggled free from his grasp. "Oh, Jack." Her eyes were devastated. "She's suffering because of me. He only took her because of me."

"No, angel," he corrected firmly, tucking her long black hair behind her ear.

"Yes, Jack," she contradicted. "This is my fault. If I'd died out there, then she wouldn't be suffering right now."

"But all your family and friends would be suffering," he reminded her.

"They'd be better off without me," she whispered despairingly.

"No, Laura." He took hold of her shoulders and gave her a firm shake. "Your family loves you." He hesitated before saying, "Laura, I saw them. Your family."

She gasped, her entire body began to tremble violently. "You saw them?" she repeated.

"Yeah, I saw them," he confirmed.

"Are they all okay?"

"Yes, but they miss you, Laura. They want you back."

"I can't go back. You didn't tell them where I was, did you?" Her huge, saucer-like eyes bored into him.

"No, I didn't. But I think you should see them; I told them I'd try and convince you to." As he said the words, he was trying to gauge how likely it was she'd agree.

"Are they angry at me?" Laura's voice broke, fresh tears glittered in her eyes.

"No, angel, of course not," he assured her. "They love you." He paused, then decided he may as well lay his cards out on the table. "Laura, I love you, too."

Laura went completely still. Her face morphed into a blank mask, but her eyes remained alive, brimming with uncertainty. "Maybe you should go now."

"That's not going to change how I feel," he reminded her.

"And you telling me you love me doesn't change the fact that I don't trust you," she shot back.

That hurt, but given how he'd betrayed her trust in the past, he wasn't surprised. And the fact that she had asked him to come here, and allowed him to comfort her, plus the fact that although she was telling him to leave, her eyes were all but begging him to stay, were enough for him right now.

"Okay, angel, I'll go. For now," he added.

"Maybe it would be better if you didn't come back." Laura said the words, but didn't look like she believed them. "If you need something else from me, your partner could come instead."

Leaning forward, he kissed the tip of her nose. "Nice try, angel, but you're not getting rid of me that easily. You need me to earn your trust back; I'll do it. But let me make myself very clear: I am not going anywhere."

* * * * *

9:11 A.M.

He was getting annoyed.

Impatient.

He'd thought he would have her by now.

That Laura was as slippery as a fish.

She'd slithered out of his grasp once before, and now he

couldn't seem to get a hold of her.

He was sure that after everything he'd done in her building, she would have gone running out of that apartment she kept herself locked up in by now.

But the little witch hadn't budged.

And not only hadn't she budged, but last night she had actually called someone to come running to her rescue.

In the months since he'd finally tracked her down and been watching her, he had never seen anyone enter that apartment.

It was that cop.

Laura had called him and he'd come running.

The cops had only visited her twice. That was not enough time for a recluse like Laura to have connected with either of them. Which meant maybe Laura had known this cop before.

He had known Laura and she hadn't had any cop friends. Still, he'd only known college Laura—perhaps this cop was someone from her childhood.

Whatever.

He didn't really care how she knew this man, so long as the man stayed out of his business.

He did not want anyone interfering in his business again.

Those hikers had ruined things last time around.

Laura hadn't been in good shape by the time she'd been found. He'd almost been ready to kill her. He had been so close, only to have her snatched away at the last second.

That wasn't happening this time.

As much as he blamed the hikers for ruining his plans, he also blamed those idiotic Garrett brothers. How hard was it to keep one, twenty-year-old girl to themselves? He had been skeptical from the beginning about this idea of Frank and Francis to let her go running free and chase her around. He would have been a lot more comfortable to just keep her safely tucked away in the hole until the Garretts were ready to play with her again.

He hadn't touched her. Well, just once in his van before he'd left her with Frank and Francis. But he had enjoyed watching. Had enjoyed her screams. Had enjoyed watching the fight drain out of her. In fact, he had enjoyed it so much that he intended to do it all himself this time around.

Which was why he absolutely refused to have anything get in the way of his plans.

He had had to up the ante last night.

Laura obviously needed some more prodding before she'd leave that house.

And he couldn't wait for her indefinitely.

The police were already mostly on to him, especially if they'd latched on to Laura, which if they hadn't before, they certainly would have after last night.

So, he had decided he'd have to try grabbing her himself.

He'd gone back down to apartment 5J, then kicked down their door. It had been tight. He'd known that everyone in the building was on edge, and the Zeke family would respond promptly. So, he'd kicked and run, making it to the stairs before anyone saw him. He'd gone up and not down, in case anyone came after him. Then he'd waited till the cops who had been guarding Laura had gone running off to deal with the Zeke family. Once they were gone, he had made his move.

Unfortunately, just as he had first assumed, getting into Laura's apartment had been impossible.

While he was a little pleased that he knew Laura well enough to correctly predict her behavior, he was also annoyed. Annoyed that she had managed to thwart him again. Annoyed that he still didn't have her.

He had tried once more to scare Laura into leaving. He had slipped a photo of Audrey Nichols under her door. But his little game hadn't sent Laura running straight into his arms, it had instead sent her running straight into the arms of the cop who was hunting him.

Since Laura had still been unattainable, he had been forced to go back to the cabin and take his frustrations out on Audrey Nichols. He'd have to be careful about doing that. He couldn't afford to let his anger get the best of him and kill her before he got Laura there.

Laura needed to know the consequences of her actions.

She needed to know that the choices she made affected other people.

She had played God with his life and he was simply returning like for like.

She needed to see that these people from her building were suffering as a direct consequence of her.

She had to see Audrey die. There was simply nothing else to say about it.

Adjusting his binoculars, he was able to catch a glimpse of her through her window.

Laura was curled up in a chair by the window. She wasn't moving, she wasn't doing anything, she was simply sitting there staring into space. Well, if nothing else, he had certainly succeeded in scaring her.

Of course, that wasn't enough.

But her blank face and listless attitude were enough to satisfy him for now.

A slight worried frown creased his face as he continued to watch her.

She still hadn't moved a muscle.

Her eyes were open, so she wasn't asleep, but she was so still that for a moment, he panicked and thought she was dead. Had she committed suicide? Had he pushed her so far that she had ended things before he got a chance to do it himself?

But then he let out a relieved breath.

Something obviously startled her and she roused herself, stood and moved farther back into her apartment where he could no longer see her.

Whew, that was lucky. He would have completely lost it if

she'd already been dead.

That was it.

No more wasting time.

He had to get her now. Before it was too late.

But getting her was going to involve something a little more avant-garde. Something that the cops weren't going to expect. Something that was *guaranteed* to get Laura out of that apartment whether she liked it or not.

It was going to take a little logistical planning though.

So, there wasn't really any time to waste.

Quickly, he packed up his things and left the apartment, locking the door behind him. Then he left the building across the street from Laura's and headed home. He was going to be busy. But in the end, it was going to pay off. He was going to get Laura.

* * * * *

11:56 A.M.

"How's Laura doing?" Rose asked as Jack pulled up his car beside hers. They were at the prison where Frank and Francis Garrett were serving out their sentences. They'd driven out here—the prison was about three hours away—in separate cars, because Jack had some family business to attend to this afternoon.

Since they hadn't driven together, she hadn't had a chance to find out how his visit with Laura had gone. While Jack had been dealing with Laura last night, Rose had enjoyed dinner with the girls. They had spent the majority of the evening discussing Sofia's interesting proposition.

She had just said goodbye to her friends, since Sofia had offered to drive Paige home, when Stephanie had called. The crime scene tech had let her know that she had just received a phone call from Jack saying that the killer had been right outside Laura's door. The fact that he'd set up a disturbance downstairs to get the cops away from Laura so he could make a play for her and leave her a letter was further proof that they were correct; this was all about Laura.

"Not that great." Jack looked and sounded extremely concerned. "I don't think she's eating or sleeping, it's like she's in a trance—shock, I guess. I'm just not sure that she can make it through much more of this."

"She called you last night, though; that's a good sign," Rose encouraged.

"Yeah." A small smile wiped away some of the anxiety from her partner's face.

"It doesn't seem like she's angry with you anymore."

"I don't think she's still mad at me, but she did say she doesn't trust me," Jack told her.

"Still, when she was scared she reached out to you," Rose pointed out.

Jack nodded. "She did let me take care of her. And she practically threw herself into my arms when I got there." Jack looked as pleased as punch about that. "She let me check out her hand and she even opened up a bit about what happened to her. She definitely trusts me to keep her safe, it's just her heart she doesn't trust me with," Jack finished grimly.

"So, what are you going to do about that?" Rose had some misgivings about Jack's apparent all-encompassing enthusiasm to reunite with Laura. Perhaps it was because she had never known them as a couple. She wanted Jack to be happy, and she knew that he wanted a relationship and a family, but he still had unresolved issues that had thus far prevented him from seriously dating. Add to that that Laura had been through hell and had enough issues to fill the ocean, and she just wasn't entirely convinced that him getting back together with Laura was what was best for either of them.

"I told her that I'm going to win her trust back," Jack answered. "I told her that I wasn't going anywhere, and I'm not."

Rose didn't have a chance to say more because they entered the prison, signed in, handed over their weapons, and were escorted to an interview room while some guards went to retrieve Frank Garrett.

They had decided to tackle Frank rather than Francis Garrett. Even though he was the older of the brothers, according to Laura's statement, he seemed to be the less dominant of the two. When detailing her assault, she had stated that Francis was the one who appeared to garner the most enjoyment from inflicting pain on her. Meanwhile, Frank had been more interested in raping her. While he had taken part in torturing her, it was always at the instruction of his younger brother, and most of the time he was happy to simply rape her and then hold her down and let Francis have his fun.

Hopefully, with his brother out of the way, they might have a chance at getting something useful out of Frank.

Time was quickly ticking down for both Laura and Audrey Nichols.

The killer's risky move last night indicated just how desperate he was getting. And since his little game hadn't gotten him any closer to Laura, he was probably going to up the ante. His increasing impatience could not spell out anything good for Audrey, who they were having no luck in locating. The obvious location for the killer to have taken her, given that Laura was his real goal, was the place where she had been taken when she'd been abducted. As soon as the link to Laura had been made, they'd sent officers to check out the woods near where Laura had been found, but it was hundreds of acres of dense woodland, and so far, there was no sign of Audrey Nichols or their killer.

She noticed how stiffly Jack was sitting in his chair, his hands clenched into fists on the table in front of them. "Are you going to be able to do this without throttling him?" she asked softly. Rose couldn't imagine how much anger and hatred Jack must feel toward Frank Garrett for what he had done to Laura.

"Yes," Jack replied tightly. "Because as much as I want to rip him to shreds, finding out who's a threat to Laura now is more important."

Rose nodded, but she wasn't convinced. If she needed to send Jack out of the room because his anger was getting too much, she wouldn't hesitate to do it. As he'd just said, finding out who was a threat to Laura right now was the most important thing.

The door behind them opened and two guards led in a shackled man in his mid-thirties. Frank Garrett was surprisingly good-looking; he had wavy, brown hair, large, light-brown eyes, and he was lean and wiry, but strong looking. The only thing that ruined his looks was a crooked nose that had obviously been broken somewhere along the way, and a couple of chipped teeth.

Frank studied them silently as he was shackled to the table. He dismissed Jack promptly, but his eyes travelled Rose's body slowly, pausing at her breasts, then he gave a small smile as his eyes met hers. Rose had to force herself not to shudder in revulsion.

"All right, Mr. Garrett, we'll make this brief," Jack began once the guards had left the room. "We know there was a third person involved in the abduction of Laura Opal. We want that person's name."

"Ahh, Laura," Frank's voice was almost melodic—he was not what Rose had been expecting in a reclusive lunatic who chased a woman through the woods and repeatedly raped and tortured her. "She was hot, and good in bed–well, not technically bed," he added with a chuckle at his own joke. "I miss her," he said that almost wistfully, like he did truly miss Laura.

Jack remained stone-faced. "We're not here to talk about Laura."

"Oh," Frank said with mock surprise. "I thought you wanted to know about her abduction."

The man was obviously clever; no wonder his defense that he was so scarred by a childhood of isolation, neglect, and abuse that he couldn't tell right from wrong, had failed.

"We're here to talk about you and whomever you were working with," Jack said with forced calm.

Apparently, Frank correctly interpreted the reason for Jack's tension. "So, you want to talk about me and my brother? I don't see how you can talk about us without talking about Laura, too. She's so pretty, isn't she? A total hottie," he goaded.

Jack didn't respond to his taunts. "We know there was a third person involved, Mr. Garrett," he repeated. "Laura said the person who grabbed her in her home wasn't you or your brother. And we know that she was driven out to the woods by someone other than you two, since she was never inside your truck. We're not asking you *if* there was a third person involved, we're asking you *who* he is."

"Maybe we rented a van or something." Frank was visibly amused. "And Laura was knocked out when she was taken, so I'm not sure anything she said can be taken too seriously."

"Someone has been recreating her attack," Jack continued. "Since we know it's not you or your brother, it has to be this third person."

"Maybe it's just some nut who found out what happened to her," Frank suggested, feigning helpfulness. "It wouldn't be all that hard to find it out. I think you're looking for some sort of copycat."

"How did you meet Laura?" Rose asked.

The question caught Frank by surprise, apprehension flickering quickly through his eyes. Then he covered it. "She caught our eye one day—as I said before, she is *hot*. What man could look at her and not want her, am I right?" he addressed this to Jack, who simply glared. "See?" he chuckled, returning his attention to her. "Your friend agrees with me. And let me tell you, she felt every bit as good as she looked."

Frank was deflecting. Attempting to avoid having to give them any information by distracting them with talk about Laura that he knew would agitate them. So far, it wasn't working. Rose wasn't going to get drawn into his games, and Jack was managing to keep his cool. Just.

"Where?" she asked Frank.

"Where, what?"

"Where did you see her? You said that she caught your eye, so where were you when you first saw her?"

Unable to come up with a convincing lie, he went with a simple one. "I don't remember. I was probably too engrossed in watching Laura to pay much attention to where we were."

She furrowed her brow in confusion. "Oh, I was under the impression that you and your brother never left your father's property. That was part of your defense, wasn't it? That you were traumatized by never being allowed to leave, by being abused, et cetera, and that was why you weren't responsible for what you did to Laura."

Shrugging disinterestedly, he said, "Maybe she was out our way."

"No." Rose shook her head. "Laura had never been there until she was kidnapped. She went to school, she worked, she hung out with her friends; she didn't go traipsing through the woods three hours away from where she lived."

"Whatever." Frank was starting to become irritated.

"So, we've established that you and Francis never saw Laura until she was brought to your property," Rose summarized for him. "So there has to be someone in-between, right? Someone who you guys knew who also knew Laura. Someone who didn't like Laura very much."

Frank said nothing. Clearly, he wasn't having so much fun now that his games weren't having any affect.

"So, who was it?" Rose asked. They only had a small window where this mystery man could have come into contact with Laura. If he'd known her while she was still in school, her parents or Jack would have noticed him, which meant he'd met her somewhere in the couple of years she'd spent in college.

"You didn't know many people," Jack prompted when Frank didn't respond. "Maybe it was a relative?" They both watched him closely for any tell that they were on the right path. But Frank was good. He wasn't giving anything away. "We're going to look into every relative, every acquaintance, anyone you've ever come into contact with," Jack warned him.

Rose decided she may as well attempt to appeal to the obvious like, or perhaps lust, he had for Laura. "Someone wants to kill her." She paused to see if her words were having any impact. "This man is after her and he's not going to rest until he has her. He knows where she lives and he's been re-enacting what you and your brother did to her. What do you think he's going to do to her when he gets his hands on her?"

"Maybe she deserves it," Frank suggested, his smirk returning.

Jack went completely still. His entire body tensed. Rose was about to send him from the room before he did something they'd all regret, but then he relaxed. "Are you scared of him?" Jack asked.

That made Frank mad. "I'm not afraid of anyone," he snapped.

"I think you are," Jack contradicted. "I think you're afraid of what he's going to do to you if you give him up. When I find him, I'm going to mention to him that you were very helpful."

Then Jack stood and headed for the door. Rose followed. Behind them, Frank was yelling and screaming his protestations, but they both ignored him. Once they were in the hall, Jack slammed his fist into the wall. Rose couldn't help but wince, but Jack didn't seem to feel the pain that would no doubt appear once he calmed down.

"Laura did not deserve what those men did to her," he fumed.

"Of course, she didn't, Jack. Frank only said that to upset you. But, Jack, what he told us will help us find this man. If he thinks that Laura deserves what she's getting, then he's obviously angry with her. Angry enough to abduct her and have her tortured, and then come back for her after all these years. I'll go back and talk to Laura's old roommates to see if they know of anyone who may have been angry with her. Then when you finish up with Mark and the rest of your family, we'll go back to Laura."

＊ ＊ ＊ ＊ ＊

11:56 A.M.

She needed a plan.

Audrey was in pain, but she couldn't let that slow her down. He had been violent with her earlier—hitting her and kicking her and ranting about some woman called Laura, who he blamed for ruining his life.

He had raped her, too.

Then he'd taken her clothes with him, leaving her in just her underwear.

She supposed it was just another way to keep her under control. Maybe he was hoping that if he kept her nearly naked, she would be too scared to run if the opportunity presented itself.

If that's what he was thinking, he was sadly mistaken. If Audrey got a chance to run, she was taking it. She didn't care if anyone saw her nearly naked. In fact, she didn't care if anyone saw her completely naked if it meant getting out of here.

Right now, all her focus was on finding a way from this room.

She wasn't thinking about being abducted or raped or beaten—there would be time for her to process all of that later. If she didn't get out of here, she wouldn't have a later.

He was going to kill her.

Of that, there was no doubt.

He hadn't said it in so many words, but his intention had been clear in everything he had said and done.

He was just waiting until this Laura got here.

Audrey didn't know who Laura was, but she knew what the

woman was in for.

This man hated her. *Hated* her.

Whatever he was going to do to her, it was nothing compared to what he would do to this Laura.

But she couldn't worry about that right now.

She had to weigh her options.

She had searched the house time and time again, but there was no way she was getting out of it without the key.

Which meant she would have to attempt to get the key when the man came back next.

However, she wasn't sure that was really a feasible option.

Both times, he'd come back only to assault her then left immediately afterward. There was no time for her to try to sneak it away from him. The man got down to business with her as soon as he walked through the door and he didn't stop until he left. There was no way she would be able to get out from underneath him and find the key in his pocket without him noticing.

And even if she got the key, how would she be able to get to, unlock, and get out of the door?

Simply put; she couldn't.

Which left waiting until this Laura arrived.

Either the man was going to kill them both here, or he was going to take them someplace else to do it. Whatever his plans, it gave her some options.

If he was planning on moving them, then that would give her, and Laura, the best opportunity of escaping. He would have to have the door unlocked; he would have to get them into a car; he would have to drive them; he would then have to get them back somewhere secure. At any of those junctions, she might be able to make a break for it.

Even if he kept them here, there would still be two of them against his one.

At least if Laura was conscious.

What would Audrey do if she wasn't?

Even if Laura was a small woman, there was no way Audrey would be able to drag her deadweight along with her in an escape attempt.

But could she leave the woman behind, knowing what he was going to do to her?

Audrey honestly didn't know the answer.

She would never normally leave someone behind, but what if it was the only way to ensure her own safety? Not just safety, but her life. He wanted Laura, anyway, so it might work.

Still, it wasn't likely that Laura would be unconscious the whole time. Even if she was when she arrived, he would want her awake for what he was going to do to her. He liked to hear their screams of fear and agony.

So that meant that at some point, both of them would be awake and able to try something.

Unless he had them both tied up.

This man wasn't stupid.

Surely, he wouldn't allow them any opportunity to get the best of him.

Which meant that really, her options were non-existent.

Audrey didn't want to face facts, but the facts were that her chances of getting out of here except in a body bag were slim to none. *Very* slim to none.

She was going to die here.

She knew it; she was just in denial.

But she couldn't live in denial forever.

For the first time since she'd woken up in this hell, she curled up into a little ball in a corner of the cabin and cried.

Then resolutely, Audrey stopped her tears as a thought occurred to her.

She had already searched the cabin for something to use as a weapon so she could prepare herself to jump the man as he came through the door, but she had come up empty.

Perhaps, though, she may be able to find something suitable to cut through whatever he was going to use to bind her, and she was sure that at some point he would tie her up again. Then when he tied her up, he would think that she was secure and out of commission, which if she could get free, would give her the element of surprise.

Even something like a nail might be useful.

Depending on what he used, it might be a long shot.

Still, it was the only shot she had.

So, she started her search.

* * * * *

11:19 P.M.

"How did things go with Brian?" Rose asked as they met up outside Laura's apartment building.

"All clear," Jack informed her. The whole family had let out a collective relieved breath earlier this afternoon when eight-year-old Brian's tests to see if his leukemia had returned came back negative. His youngest brother's little boy had battled the disease for a couple of years before he finally went into remission. At the moment, he was still having checkups every six months, and as the time for his tests grew closer, the entire family grew tense. But now that Brian was in the clear again, they could relax for another few months.

"That's great." Rose smiled.

"You make any progress?" he asked as they headed into the building.

"Not really," his partner sighed. "I spoke with both of Laura's other roommates again and neither of them could think of anyone who hated Laura. They couldn't even think of anyone who disliked her. They said she was sweet and hardworking, and everyone got along with her."

Of course, Jack had already known that. Laura was the

sweetest person he'd ever met. "He had to come across her at college—I would have noticed anyone suspicious. We'll talk to Laura again."

"Think she's going to be happy to see you?" Rose cast him a sideways glance.

"I hope so." Jack wasn't entirely sure whether Laura would even let them in the door.

"Jack," Rose began carefully, "are you sure about Laura?"

Frowning, he asked, "Sure about what?"

Before Rose could reply, they arrived at Laura's floor, where the two cops were still standing outside her door, chatting away in quiet voices.

"No problems?" Jack checked in with the two young officers.

"Nope," one replied. "We've been knocking on the door at regular intervals, just to make sure she's doing okay."

"Good, and thanks." Jack let out a relieved breath, pleased that nothing had happened today. Although, he knew it wouldn't last. This man would come back at Laura again. And he was worried about just what he'd try next. It would no doubt be something bigger and more dramatic than what he'd done so far. He knocked on the door. "Laura? It's Jack. Rose is with me. We need to talk to you."

He listened to see if she was moving about in there. It was late, but he didn't think Laura slept much, so she probably wasn't in bed.

"Laura?" He gave another knock. If she didn't open the door soon, he'd try phoning her; he had her number now since she'd called him the other night.

"Go away, Jack," a voice spoke quietly, right on the other side of the door.

"It's important, Laura," he pressed.

A long pause, then Laura spoke again, "Then Rose can come in."

"No, Laura." He nipped that idea in the bud immediately. "I'm coming in. I want to check on you and on your hand. Now open the door."

He heard her sigh, but then he could make out the sounds of the deadbolts sliding undone and the door inched open. Laura stood before them, looking as worn out and disconnected as she'd looked the last time he'd seen her. But she'd changed her clothes and her hair was damp, so she appeared to at least be going through the motions. At least some of them, he thought as his eyes travelled her body in an assessing search. She still wasn't eating, by the looks of it.

"Come on, let's get you something to eat." He took her uninjured hand and led her to the dining table, gently pushing her down into a chair. "Rose, did you have dinner?"

"A sandwich a few hours ago, but I could go for something else." Rose walked into the kitchen. "I'll make something, Jack, you check her hand. You like omelets, Laura?"

"Yes," Laura replied.

"She likes them with just cheese and tomato," Jack added with a small grin at Laura. He knew she didn't like him acting as though he knew her perfectly, even though they both knew he did, and he was hoping that his gentle teasing might lighten her mood a little.

"And Jack likes cheese, tomato, bacon and mushrooms." Laura gave him a small smile of her own. "But don't you two have more important things to do than just coming over here to feed me?"

"We have to talk to you about a few things, but we can do that while we eat," Jack answered. If Laura couldn't take care of herself right now, he was more than happy to step into the role and do it for her. And with food being taken care of, he left Rose in the kitchen and went to retrieve Laura's first aid kit again.

Back in the kitchen, Laura offered no protests as he unwound the bandage. The skin on her hand was bright red with oozing blisters. Luckily, the burn wasn't too big, and on the back of her hand, not the palm, but it looked like it needed professional medical care. When he'd re-dressed the wound, he looked at Laura.

"No, Jack," she said immediately. "I can't go to the hospital. I'm sorry. I know I should, but I just can't."

Then he was going to call Mark tomorrow and have his youngest brother come and look at her hand. Mark was a trauma surgeon, so burns were not his specialty, but he was a doctor and knew more about burns than the rest of them. "We talked before about bringing a doctor here to check it out. Before, you said maybe, but I think your hand is serious enough that it warrants a doctor's visit."

He could see her debating it internally, but eventually she gave a resigned nod. "Okay."

Relieved, he said, "Good. Isn't that painful? Have you taken anything for it today?"

"It hurts," Laura acknowledged, "but I'm good at compartmentalizing pain. I've had a lot of practice."

Thanks to the hell those men had put her through. Jack had struggled to keep his cool while interviewing Frank Garrett earlier today. The man was scum, slime, filth. He deserved death. A slow and painful death. If he could've gotten away with it, he would have killed the man in a heartbeat.

"What happened to *your* hand?" Laura asked, her gaze on his bruised knuckles.

Slamming his fist into the wall at the prison hadn't been the smartest thing he'd ever done. But the anger simmering inside him had been threatening to bubble over and he'd needed to do something to relieve the tension. "It's nothing," he answered vaguely, standing to go and get Laura some painkillers.

"Did you hit something?" she asked.

He was saved from having to answer that when Rose set three plates down on the table. "Dinner's served."

"Once you've eaten, you can take some aspirin," Jack told Laura, setting the pills and a glass of water down beside her.

But Laura wasn't to be distracted. "Why did you hit something, Jack?"

"Eat," he ordered, taking a mouthful of his own meal.

Laura obediently ate a little of her omelet, then repeated her questions, "Why did you hit something?"

Obviously, she wasn't going to let it go, so he may as well answer her. "Rose and I visited Frank Garrett this morning."

Every ounce of color drained from her face, and the hand holding a forkful of omelet halfway between her plate and mouth began to shake. "You saw him?" her voice trembled more than her hand.

"Yeah," he answered softly. "We needed to see if he'd give up the third man."

"Did he?" Laura's eyes seemed to grow larger in her pale face.

"No, I'm sorry, angel," he replied apologetically. He would do anything to end this for Laura, only he couldn't, because they didn't have enough information yet.

"Did he say there *was* a third man?" Laura asked.

"No, he wouldn't confirm it, but there was, Laura, you know we're right. He said that maybe you deserved what had happened to you, that you deserved what was happening now, which implies that whoever's behind this blames you for something," Jack explained. "Can you think of anyone who you had an argument or a disagreement with or any sort of problems with at all while you were in college?"

Laura gave a minute shake of her head. "What else did he say?" she whispered, although she seemed unsure that she wanted to hear the answer.

"Nothing, Laura, he just made some taunts about you to try and upset us," Jack told her. It had worked, too. Hearing that man even say Laura's name had been enough to make Jack want to lunge across the table and wrap his hands around Frank's neck like he and his brother had done to Laura.

Setting down her fork, Laura pushed her plate away from her.

"I can't eat anymore."

"You've hardly had any; you need to eat to keep your strength up," Jack protested.

"Really, Jack, I can't eat anymore." She was still shaking, and she looked like she might throw up at any moment.

"All right," he agreed.

"I'm sorry, I have to ..." Laura trailed off as she stood on wobbly legs, seemingly unable to gather enough strength to come up with an excuse, and left the room as quickly as she could manage.

"Do you want me to come with you?" Jack called after her.

"No," came the reply, and then a door slammed shut.

Jack muttered a curse under his breath. "We should have prepared her for the idea that we were going to be talking to the Garretts rather than springing it on her, so she had time to get used to it. If we can get her calm enough to focus, she'll be able to figure out who this man is. He's so angry with her—she can't have crossed paths with him and not have noticed him."

"Unless he's some sort of stalker whom she's never even met," Rose suggested.

"No." Jack dismissed the idea. "He's so angry with her, he had to have real actual contact with her. He blames her for something, so they definitely met somewhere along the way."

"Jack, about Laura ..." Rose began tentatively.

"What about her?"

"Are you sure? Are you sure that you want to get involved with her again? She's clearly not the same person she was back then. Jack, I like her, she's sweet. And I most definitely feel sorry for her after everything she's been through. But, Jack, she's messed up. Totally understandable, but are you sure you're ready to handle that? She needs a lot of help if she's going to get her life back. Are you up for it? Because we're not talking some mild issues to work through, she is on a whole other level, she's like a fruit loop ..."

Rose broke off as they heard a gasp.

They both turned to find Laura watching them.

"Oh, Laura, I'm sorry, I didn't mean it like that," Rose began to babble apologetically.

Laura turned on her heel and disappeared.

"Jack," Rose turned devastated green eyes on him. "I didn't mean it the way it sounded. I totally get why Laura's messed up. Who wouldn't be after going through what she has? And you know I love Paige and Sofia, and both of them are still suffering the effects of what they've been through. I am totally on board in helping you help Laura, so long as you are one hundred percent sure that it's what you want. I just want you to be sure, since she's ..."

"A fruit loop," Jack supplied dryly. He would have been angry with Rose if he'd thought she meant it.

"That was a poor choice of words." Rose's cheeks heated in embarrassment. "You want me to talk to her, explain?"

"No, maybe you'd better go. I'll talk to her." Jack thought he'd have a better chance of calming Laura down on his own.

"Jack, I'm so sorry," Rose implored.

"I know you are," Jack assured his partner.

"I truly didn't mean to upset her. I'm an idiot," Rose groaned.

"Yeah, you are," he agreed mildly. "You go on home and I'll call you later."

"Okay," Rose agreed in a small voice.

Leaving his partner, Jack headed for the bathroom where Laura had taken refuge and found the door locked. He could hear running water coming from inside. It seemed like she was in the shower.

"Laura?" he knocked on the door. "Let me in."

JULY 26TH

12:31 A.M.

"Laura?"

She ignored him.

She didn't want to see him right now.

She didn't want to see anyone.

Rose was right.

She was a fruit loop.

She had never thought about herself in that particular term, but she couldn't deny it fitted her.

She was crazy. A complete and utter mess.

"Laura?"

It had been a mistake letting Jack back in.

Both physically into her apartment and into her life again.

She was sinking further and further down.

It wasn't fair to drag Jack down with her.

He had his faults, but even she had to admit he was basically a good guy.

He deserved better than her.

He had been banging on the bathroom door ever since she'd fled in here.

She sought solace in the shower.

She was sitting on the floor, curled up in as small a ball as she could make, with the water pounding down on her.

She had the water turned on cold, though.

She'd done that before.

The first night after she'd been released from the hospital. Her parents had taken her home to their house, and she had climbed

209

JULY 26TH

12:31 A.M.

into the shower. Staying in there so long that she used up all the hot water.

At first, of course, the cold water had made her shiver, her body coming out in a mass of goose bumps.

But then she'd started to go numb.

Not just her body, but her mind, too.

She had liked that.

The feeling of numbness. Nothingness.

Sometimes when she felt overwhelmed, like now, she liked to do it again.

Numb was so much nicer than terror.

"Laura, let me in." Jack was still at her door. "I'm worried about you."

Shouldn't he have given up and left by now?

Why was he being so persistent about her?

Like Rose had said, she was no catch.

Jack was gorgeous and kind and caring, cheating notwithstanding, he could have his pick of any number of women.

Why did he want to waste his time with her?

Just because they had a past?

So, what?

They hadn't been together in fourteen years, much longer than they'd been a couple, almost longer than they'd known each other.

He certainly didn't owe her anything, even if he had cheated on her.

He should just go and leave her alone.

"That's it," she heard Jack mutter.

A moment later, she heard some jiggling and then her bathroom door swung open.

"What are you doing?" Jack demanded.

Laura didn't bother answering, just rested her head on her knees.

"Arrgh!" Jack yelped as he reached above her to turn off the water. "This is cold, what on earth are you thinking?"

That she didn't want to feel afraid anymore, that she didn't want to feel anything anymore, that was what she was thinking.

"Damn, you're like ice," he said as he touched the back of his hand to her cheek.

Why couldn't he just go and leave her be?

The more he hung around, the more she got used to the idea of having him around.

And that was a mistake.

He left for a moment, returning with a stack of towels. "Come on, let's get you warmed up." He wrapped a fluffy towel around her and lifted her out of the shower and into his arms. Carrying her into her bedroom, he set her down on the bed. "We better get you out of these wet clothes before you catch pneumonia."

Instinctively, Laura tensed. If Jack took her soaking wet clothes off, he would see all her scars. No one other than the doctors at the hospital had seen her scarred body. Not even her mother had seen it, and her mother had taken care of her after she'd come home from the hospital.

With broken fingers on both hands doing even simple, everyday tasks had been difficult. Having her hands so badly damaged had been the worst thing they had done to her. At least, the worst of the physical things. The rape had been the worse of the worst, because it had left her feeling so violated and filthy. But the snapping of the small bones in her fingers had been excruciatingly painful, and having her nails ripped out had been even worse. She had passed out from the pain the first time Francis had done it.

Her nails had eventually grown back normally, and her broken fingers had healed well, and these days you couldn't even tell that they had been injured.

Unlike when you looked at the rest of her body.

Then you could read what had happened to her like a book.

"No, Jack," she protested, teeth chattering. She was starting to feel the effects of the cold; her whole body was shaking uncontrollably.

"I'm sorry, angel." Jack was already pulling off her socks, "But you're already freezing, we have to get you dry and warm before you get sick."

Laura scrunched her eyes closed so she wouldn't see Jack's face when he saw her body. But even without being able to see him, she could feel him tense as he removed her sweatpants and sweater. When he had all her clothes off, he didn't bother redressing her, simply grabbed another towel and began vigorously rubbing her all over. When he was satisfied she was dry, he wrapped her in another towel, and then a blanket and picked her up once more, carrying her through to the living room, turning on the heat, and sitting down with her in his lap. Laura burrowed closer against him, tucking her face into the crook of his neck, trying to let his body heat help warm her up.

"Why did you do that?" Jack asked. "Was it because of what Rose said?"

Shivering too much to speak, Laura simply shook her head. Her need to feel numb hadn't really had anything to do with Jack's partner. She had been feeling overwhelmed long before then.

Apparently not believing her, he continued, "Because Rose didn't mean it. We have two friends who have been through traumatic experiences and it messed both up, so she totally gets it. It was more about me than you, anyway. She knows you're going to need a lot of help and she just wants to make sure that I'm up to giving it to you because I've been a little depressed lately."

That caught her attention. Jack was always so calm, so confident, so in control that Laura couldn't imagine anything pushing him to the point of depression. She lifted her head from his shoulder to look up at him.

"Nothing for you to worry about." Jack smiled down at her. Then he grew serious. "Laura not only *can* I be here for you, but I *want* to be here for you. Whatever you need, whenever you need it. You've struggled for ten long years on your own, don't you think it's time to let someone help you?"

Was it?

She truly didn't know the answer to that.

She had spent ten years trying things her way and it obviously hadn't gotten her anywhere.

Maybe it was time to try someone else's way?

Taking her silence as evidence that she was at least thinking about it, Jack continued, "Do you trust me, Laura? You said before that you didn't, but I think maybe you trust me more than you realize."

Laura wasn't sure about that.

Did she trust Jack to keep her physically safe from harm? Yes. Did she trust Jack to take care of her? Yes. Did she trust Jack not to hurt her again? No. Well, maybe not no, maybe more like she wasn't sure. She didn't think Jack would intentionally do anything that wasn't in her best interest.

How had he managed to gain so much of her trust back in just a couple of days?

A week ago, she wasn't even thinking about Jack Xander. He was just someone from her past. And now … now …

Well, now she wasn't sure what Jack was. But she couldn't deny he was something. And if he had managed to wiggle into her life this quickly, what could he do in a few more days?

But Laura had the feeling that Jack's question about trust had to do with something specific he had in mind.

* * * * *

12:57 A.M.

"Laura?" Jack prodded. "Do you trust me?"

"Yes and no," she answered him honestly.

He smiled. That was an improvement. Just a few days ago, she'd told him she didn't trust him at all, now he'd been upgraded to a half and half. With just a little more time with Laura, he was convinced he could get all the way up to a yes.

"But you know I want what's best for you?"

"Yes," she agreed.

"Then let me take you outside," he said.

Absolute horror washed over Laura's face and she would have fallen off his lap if he hadn't been holding on to her. She struggled in his grip, but he kept a firm hold—she wasn't going to run from him. They were going to deal with her problems together.

"Let me go, Jack," she begged, fighting him frantically, like a trapped animal.

"No," he told her firmly. "Just think about it. We can do it together."

She was shaking her head so quickly, her black hair went swishing around her face. "I can't," she whispered desperately.

"But you've been outside since your abduction, right? I mean, after you were released from the hospital, you went home and to court and I'm guessing a few other places?" He continued when she nodded. "So, it's only since you left home and came here that you became agoraphobic. Maybe you can go outside, you haven't tried it, angel," he coaxed.

"No, I, uh, I don't think, I'm not sure, I …" Laura stammered.

"What if I carry you?" he pressed. Jack wasn't sure attempting to take Laura outside was a good idea, but he had to do something. The way she was disconnecting from reality, withdrawing further inside herself, was scaring him. He had to do something, and this was the only thing he could think of that might snap her out of it.

If he was honest, he also wanted to prove to Laura that she needed him. That he could be there for her. That she should rely on him. He was desperate to win her back, and if he could help Laura work on her phobia, it would have to give some points in his favor.

"Come on, you can do it," Jack encouraged. "How about we go and get some clothes on you?" He stood with Laura in his arms and walked with her to the bedroom. Setting her down, he retrieved some dry clothes from her closet and handed them to her.

As the blanket he'd wrapped her in earlier dropped down, exposing her shoulders, he caught sight of her scars. Jack had thought he'd been prepared to see them; he'd seen the pictures of what her injuries had looked like just after she'd been found, so he'd thought seeing the scars eleven years later wouldn't be all that hard.

He'd been wrong.

Seeing all those round pink circles from the cigarette burns, and the words that you could still make out on her back, had left him shaking with anger. Poor Laura would be forced to relive her attack every time she looked at her own body.

"Need any help?" he asked her when he saw she hadn't made any move to put her clothing on.

"No." Laura's voice trembled, as did the rest of her, although now she appeared to be shaking from fear and not from cold.

"Pop your clothes on," he instructed, then gathered up the wet clothes he'd discarded earlier. "Two minutes," he warned, as he went to put her things in the washing machine. He had ended up using a credit card to open the lock to her bathroom when after at least ten minutes of calling her, she had refused to let him in. Jack hadn't been expecting to find her huddled in the bottom of the shower, letting cold water stream down all over her.

When he returned to her room two minutes later, Laura was dressed and standing in the middle of the room looking terrified. Still, the fact that she had complied and put on her clothing had to be a good sign. Jack was still worried that what he was about to do was not a good idea.

Before either of them could change their minds, he snatched

her up and walked determinedly to the front door. Laura was completely still in his arms, her arms locked around his neck.

"I'm opening the door now." Jack kept his voice as soft and gentle as he could manage, all the while his heart was pounding with dreaded anticipation. "I'm going to take a step into the hall," he informed her.

As he stepped them out of her apartment, Laura whimpered.

"It's all right," he soothed. "It's done, we're out. You're out of your apartment."

Now that that first awful step was out of the way, and Laura hadn't burst into flames, Jack's confidence grew, and with long strides, he headed for the stairs. It seemed like the smart idea to keep her moving. If they stopped and waited for the lift, it would give Laura time to dwell. Taking the eight flights of stairs two at a time, they soon emerged into the lobby.

"Laura?" Connor Newman, one of the doormen, came rushing over. "Is she okay?" Concern was written all over the man's face.

"She's okay," Jack replied for Laura. "We're just trying something."

"She's agoraphobic, she can't be outside," Connor admonished.

"So far, she's made it from her apartment all the way down here," Jack informed him somewhat distractedly. His attention was focused on Laura. Her breathing was ragged, her eyes were clenched shut, and she was worryingly pale. Still, they'd come this far, so Jack wanted to follow through.

"We're going to go outside now." Jack spoke softly in Laura's ear.

"I don't think that's a good idea," Connor protested. "Look at her, she doesn't want to, take her back to her apartment."

Ignoring him, Jack walked the remaining short distance to the glass doors and then out into the night. A warm, gentle breeze wafted over them. The summer sky was clear and dark, dotted with thousands of merrily twinkling stars. The moon shone brightly, adding its own light to the glowing streetlights and car lights.

However, Laura didn't appear to be enjoying the beautiful night.

In his arms, she was gasping for breath now. He could feel her heart beating wildly against his chest; her forehead was pressed against the side of his face and he could feel it beaded with sweat.

She was in full panic mode.

Cursing his own selfish desires to be Laura's knight in shining armor and force her to do something she clearly wasn't ready for and in which he clearly held no expertise, Jack whisked her back indoors.

"It's okay," he crooned in her ear. "We're back inside. I'll have you in your apartment in no time, just try to hold on."

"I told you that wasn't a good idea," Connor yelled after them as Jack darted for the stairs.

Once again, he paid no heed to the doorman as he rushed Laura back up the stairs and into her apartment. Balancing Laura, he managed to lock the deadbolts behind them, then stood for a moment, giving his own pounding heart and ragged breath time to calm.

Well, that was a disaster. He was an idiot for attempting that on his own. Laura quite clearly needed professional help. What had he been thinking?

Right, that once again, it was all about him. It was that thinking that had led to him hurting Laura in the first place.

Not sure she would want to still be in his arms, Jack set her gently down on the sofa and sat beside her. Laura immediately crawled back into his lap, pressing her trembling body against him, and clinging to him like he was the only thing in the world that could help her right now.

Slowly, the tension inside him ebbed. He'd been selfish and stupid, but Laura hadn't pushed him away.

"Shh, angel," he murmured as he began to stroke her hair,

enjoying the way the silky strands of Laura's gorgeous hair slid between his fingers. "Try to relax. I'm sorry. I'm so sorry for making you do that, you're not ready, I shouldn't have forced you."

Jack wanted to promise that he wouldn't do that again, but he remembered his boss' warning that if it came down to it, that Belinda would have her forcibly removed from her apartment and put in a safehouse.

"There you go, good girl." Laura was beginning to calm, her breath still hitched but it was returning to normal. Picking up her wrist, Jack checked her pulse, it was still too fast but had slowed substantially.

"When I was out there," Laura began in a ragged whisper, "when they were raping me and hurting me, I could feel the leaves and the grass beneath me, the fresh air, the wind, the sun, the clear blue sky, the stars at night, the birds, the streams; I hated it all."

Jack rubbed her back. "I'm sorry, angel," he said because he didn't know what else to say.

"Francis," she continued, "he enjoyed every horrible thing he did to me. His eyes ..." She shuddered and he tightened his grip. "They were so evil. His face would light up with excitement. I'd try not to scream, because he liked it when I did, but sometimes the pain was so bad that I couldn't help it."

Jack was fighting to keep his cool. Laura didn't need his anger right now; she needed his support. She needed him to just be here and listen and offer whatever small comforts he could.

"And Frank, he was almost worse. Sometimes when he raped me, it was so rough it would leave me bleeding, but sometimes he was gentle, like we were lovers instead of me being their prisoner. I hated that the most." Tears were streaming down her face, which she had buried against his chest. "I fought them at first, as hard as I could, but, Jack," she lifted her tear-stained face and looked at him with such earnest self-recrimination that his heart clenched, "I gave up. I just laid there and let them do all those horrible things to me. I let it happen. I let them rape me and torture me. I was weak and pathetic. I should have fought them every time. I shouldn't have stopped. What was wrong with me?" She sobbed helplessly.

"Oh, angel." He brushed at her wet cheeks with his thumb, knowing exactly how she had felt. "Baby, that's not true," he rebuked firmly. "You were not weak and pathetic, and you did not *let* those men do anything to you. You did what you could but they were bigger and stronger than you, and you were badly injured; there was no way you could have done anything to get away from them."

Laura just sank back down against him, tucked her face into his shoulder and sobbed her poor little heart out. Jack let her cry, let her get it out, and just held her. Whispering pointless consolations in her hair and rubbing her back and just holding her so that she would know she wasn't alone anymore.

When at last she fell silent, Jack gathered her up, and as she immediately curled closer, he carried her into the bedroom. Pulling the covers back, he laid her down and then tucked her in.

"Jack, no," she gave her head a tired shake.

He stroked her hair away from her still damp cheeks. "Yes," he contradicted. "You're exhausted, you need to rest."

"I'll have nightmares," Laura whimpered.

"I'm going to stay. I'll sleep in the chair." He pointed to a comfortable looking armchair in the corner. "So, if you wake up from a nightmare, I'll be right here, okay?" Jack didn't want to overstep his bounds, but he wasn't comfortable leaving Laura alone in her present state.

"Okay," she agreed, her eyelids fluttering closed as though she didn't have enough strength left to keep them open. "Jack?"

"Yeah, angel?"

"Thank you."

As she drifted off to sleep, Jack pressed a tender kiss to her forehead, then dragged the armchair closer to the bed and settled in to it. The night hadn't been a total disaster. Taking Laura outside had been a mistake, but it did seem to have brought them closer together.

Content, Jack closed his eyes and fell asleep.

* * * * *

9:07 A.M.

"Jack, is she okay?" Rose all but rushed her partner when he walked into the conference room.

"Relax, Rose." Jack wore both a large smile and the same clothes he had been wearing yesterday. "Laura's not upset with you."

"Did you spend the night?" she asked, totally shocked. Laura hadn't seemed angry with Jack anymore, but neither did she seem ready to jump into bed with him.

"In a chair beside her bed." Jack laughed at the look on her face. Her partner was certainly chipper this morning, but despite his evident good mood, concern still lurked in his blue eyes.

"You didn't say that she's doing okay," she pointed out. "How is she?"

"Not all that great," Jack admitted. "She blames herself for being hurt so badly because she thinks she didn't fight back enough and just gave up."

"Which is as ridiculous as you blaming yourself for her attack, and I hope you told her so," Rose declared. What was it with victims blaming themselves? Paige and Sofia did it, too.

"I may have pushed her a little too far," Jack confessed.

"How?"

"I took her outside." Jack looked sheepish.

"What on earth possessed you to do that?" Rose demanded, perplexed.

"I don't know. I thought it might snap her out of that depression she was sinking into, and I thought if I could help her overcome that, then ..."

"Then it would help you get closer to her," Rose finished for him. "Jack, that was pretty stupid," she reprimanded. "Isn't she dealing with enough right now?"

"I know, I know. At least one good thing came out of it."

She arched a brow.

"I stressed her out enough that she was exhausted enough to actually sleep."

She chortled. "I don't recommend trying that again next time you want her to sleep." Then she grew serious. Laura was at least physically safe for the moment, but she wasn't going to remain that way if they didn't find this guy. He'd struck again. "Jack, I have bad news."

His face fell. "What?"

"A couple in the building across the street from Laura's were attacked," she explained.

Puzzled, he asked, "What does that have to do with our case?"

"The apartment that he went for is on the ninth floor, you can see directly into Laura's from the windows," she told him.

"So he could watch her." Jack's face grew dark. "It was getting too dangerous to be in her building, so he had to change tactics to keep an eye on her. You said a couple was attacked—what did he do to them?"

"Thankfully not too much. The couple was Derek and Liza Triton, both in their early eighties. He broke in shortly after he put that letter under Laura's door. The Tritons were in bed, they heard someone breaking in, but he was quick, knocked them both out and then tied them up before they could do anything. They came to in the closet. Tried to get free but couldn't. Said they could hear him, though, ranting about people interfering in his business, and how no one was going to save Laura this time."

"So, it's definitely him, then." Jack looked dejected, like there still might have been some hope that it was purely a coincidence.

"Yep, and fingerprints confirm it," she added. "Stephanie went straight there as soon as the report came in."

"How'd the couple get out of the closet?"

"When the man left, they just started banging on the wall," Rose replied. "Eventually, one of the neighbors came, broke the door down and found them."

"The couple have anything else to add?"

"Just that the man was angry that he still didn't have Laura, and that since what he'd done so far hadn't gotten her out of the apartment, he was going to have to go with something bigger."

"I don't like the sound of that."

Rose didn't, either. Something bigger was no doubt going to lead to more casualties. "Why now?" Rose wondered. "Why come for her now? I mean, he obviously wants her dead, so why wait nearly eleven years? You think he's waiting for an anniversary?"

"No, I think he just couldn't get to her before now," Jack replied.

"Still, you'd think he could have gotten to her early on. I mean, no one was looking for a third man, they thought it was over, they thought they had the men who hurt her."

"Yeah, but getting to her would have been too hard," Jack explained. "I don't think she would have gone anywhere alone those first few months. And then, she just disappeared. I think it took him all this time to find her. And now that he has, he doesn't want her getting away again. He won't give up until he kills her."

Jack's theory made sense. And she agreed that killing Laura was this guy's top priority.

"I think we should look into Kirby Tam's past, see if it matches up with Laura's while she was in college," Jack announced.

"I thought forensics discounted Kirby, plus he was in custody when Audrey Nichols was abducted. And he hasn't gotten bail yet, so he's still with us, which means he couldn't have put the letter under Laura's door or broken into the Tritons' apartment," Rose reminded her partner.

"I know all of that, I just don't think we should discount Kirby just yet. We know that whoever this third man is that he's worked with others in the past. He brought the Garretts in to do most of his dirty work. Perhaps he's doing the same thing this time. Kirby could be working with someone again. He could have been watching during Jessica Elgar's assault and she just never realized he was there. He could have been watching during all the attacks, including Laura's. Just because she never saw anyone in the woods doesn't mean he wasn't there."

Doubtful, Rose didn't think that Kirby was their guy, but she knew that Jack was desperate to find any direction to pursue. "I guess it can't hurt to look into it."

"Other than that, we're just going to have to go through Laura's life with a fine-tooth comb. Everyone she knew in college, every professor, everyone she worked with, all her friends, boyfriends of her friends. Every single person."

* * * * *

1:02 P.M.

"Knock, knock."

Laura knew it was Jack at her door even before she heard his voice.

"I brought lunch," he called when she didn't immediately let him in.

With a weary sigh, she unlocked the deadbolts. Laura wasn't in the mood to let Jack in, but she knew he wasn't going to go until he saw her, so she may as well get it over with.

"Hey," he beamed at her as soon as the door opened.

"Hey, Jack," she returned listlessly. Leaving him to lock back up, she dragged herself to the couch and collapsed onto it.

"You doing okay?" Jack was standing in front of her, peering down at her anxiously.

"Not really," she admitted. For some reason, she kept giving Jack truthful answers when what she wanted to do was tell him she was fine and to leave her alone.

He knelt so they were eye to eye. "Angel, what am I going to do with you?" His voice was full of tender affection. "I bet you haven't eaten today or taken anything for your hand. Sit tight and I'll go get some water and painkillers."

She caught his hand as he stood. "No, just stay here with me, please." She tugged and he complied, sitting down beside her.

Laura was so conflicted when it came to Jack. Part of her wanted to throw him out of her home and her life and never forgive him for hurting her all those years ago. And the other part of her wanted to admit that she had already forgiven him and beg him to stay with her and never leave her side.

"Here, you need to eat something."

Jack passed her a sandwich, which looked about as appealing as a pile of mud. Shaking her head, Laura moved closer to Jack and rested her head on his shoulder. She wanted to crawl into his lap like she had last night.

Ordinarily, she would have refused to have any part of Jack's plan to take her outdoors. It was ludicrous. She couldn't leave her apartment. But she was in such a fog that for some reason, she had allowed him to do it. As she had predicted, it had been a bad idea. When the fresh air had hit her, it was like it had ripped the breath from her lungs. Flashbacks had assaulted her, throwing her back in time to the woods.

Only this time, the flashbacks had been different.

Well, not the flashbacks, but her reaction to them.

She hadn't been alone.

Jack's strong arms had been around her, holding her against his hard chest as he'd whispered soothing reassurances in her ear. She'd been too shaken, too busy focusing on attempting to breathe, to make out the words, but just the sound of his voice had been enough to help calm her. When he'd set her down, her battered mind had wanted nothing more than to seek solace from the one person that made her feel safe, and so she had climbed into Jack's lap, resting against him, soaking up his strength.

From the safety of Jack's arms, she had admitted to him things about her attack she had never confessed to anyone else. Not to the police, not to her parents, not to her doctors, not to the psychiatrist her parents sent her to.

What was it about Jack that was different?

What was it about him that had her allowing him to touch her, to hold her, that had her crying all over him? After that first time she'd woken up in the hospital and thrown herself into her mother's arms, not a single person who wasn't a doctor or nurse administering medical care, had laid a hand on her. And yet several times now, she had sought comfort in Jack's arms.

She hadn't even offered a word of dissent when he had proclaimed that he was spending the night.

"I never stopped loving you, Laura." Jack was stroking her hair, letting it slide through his fingertips.

"What we had was never real," she contradicted. "If you had really loved me, then you could never have cheated on me."

"You know that's not true," he gently reprimanded. "Sometimes we hurt the people we love."

"Maybe we didn't know what love was. Maybe we were simply young and naïve to think that what we had could last forever," she mused. Back then, Laura had had her whole life planned, down to the very smallest detail. But that had all changed the day Jack had come to her and told her that he had cheated on her and the girl was now pregnant with his child. He had been so adamant that that didn't mean they had to break up. That he wanted to raise his child with her. That they could still have everything they'd ever dreamed.

But of course, they couldn't.

He had broken her heart and her trust, and she didn't know how to put them back together where Jack was concerned.

So, she'd told him to go. That they were over and done with. That she never wanted to see him again. That she hated him.

And she'd meant it. Then.

Now, however, she wasn't so sure what she wanted.

"Laura, I'm the first to admit that what I did was stupid and selfish and that I hurt you terribly, but I loved you then and I love you now. I want you back."

It annoyed her that hearing him say that had her heart all fluttering. "Even if I still loved you, and even if I could learn to trust you again, it doesn't matter; I'm not the same person that I was back then. Once you spend a little time around me, you'll realize that. You'll realize that I'm not what you want. I can't go outside, I can't be touched, I suffer from insomnia and nightmares and flashbacks. I'm not really relationship material."

"That's not true, angel," Jack challenged. "Last night you crawled into my lap and cried in my arms. You opened up to me. You let me try taking you outside, granted that was a mistake, but you let me try it. I'm still in love with you, Laura. I know everything that you've been through and I still want you. I want to help you through this."

"I like to be alone," she stated, but even she could hear the lack of conviction in her voice.

"No, you're trying to punish yourself—that's not the same thing as wanting to be alone," Jack told her firmly. "You were all alone out there in the woods, and for some ridiculous reason, you blame yourself because you couldn't fight off two men twice your size, and add to that you were injured, so your chances of escape were even further diminished. You felt helpless and scared and all alone and now you want to punish yourself because you couldn't get over it in five minutes. I don't care how long it takes you to work through it, I'm here for the long haul."

The thought of not being alone was enticing, and yet Laura

couldn't even contemplate getting better. She just didn't have the strength to do it. Even for Jack. All she wanted was just to climb into bed and sleep and never get up again. She didn't want to spend another day trapped in this living nightmare of fear and helplessness and utter despondency. Life just wasn't worth living if all you were doing was simply existing.

With her bed too far away for her exhausted body to reach, Laura sought the next best thing. Or perhaps, if she were honest, her overburdened mind and body sought the one thing it really wanted. Crawling into Jack's lap, Laura just closed her eyes and rested.

* * * * *

11:46 P.M.

"You should go on home, Rose," Jack told his partner. "No point in us both being a wreck tomorrow."

"Are you going home? Or to Laura's?" his partner asked.

"Neither." Jack shook his head. "We can't have long left before he makes his big play to get her. He hasn't done anything in a couple of days, which means our time is running out. I'm going to stay here for a while and work through people from her past."

Jack wasn't just worried about Laura's physical well-being. If they didn't get this man soon, he was also extremely concerned about her psychological well-being. She was shutting down. Giving up.

Although, ironically, the more she shut down, the more she lowered her defenses and the more she began to lean on him.

Despite her declarations at lunch that they had never really been in love, and even if they were it wouldn't work out because she was too messed up, she had once again come into his arms for comfort. It had been hard to leave her to come back to work. In fact, he wouldn't have left her had it not been for such a good cause.

"Francis Garrett said something that intrigued me," Rose was saying.

"Yeah?" After his lunch with Laura, he and Rose had made the six-hour round trip back out to the prison to speak with Francis, hoping they'd have more luck with the younger brother than they'd had with the older. They hadn't. Francis Garrett was very different from his brother. He was a pure psychopath. He enjoyed inflicting pain on others and did so without an ounce of empathy or remorse.

"When you were asking Francis whether Laura was his and Frank's first victim, he said no she wasn't *their* first victim, the way he said it made it sound like the brothers had done this before, but whoever brought Laura to them hadn't."

He nodded. "Which could explain why he was so non-hands on with her, be took her there but he didn't do anything, except perhaps rape her while she was still unconscious."

"Which means he had to know the Garretts well enough to know what Frank and Francis were doing and to take someone to them that he was angry with because he knew what they'd do to her. Where are we on relatives?" Rose asked.

"Humphrey Garrett, their father, was an only child, both parents deceased, and he was raised the same way he raised his boys. Their mother disappeared when the boys were young, we don't know what happened to her after that. The mother had four brothers, so it's going to take us a while to get through them all," he replied. "You're not going to go home, Rose?" He repeated his earlier question. He'd already kept his partner up late last night because of Brian's doctor's appointment that the whole family attended together, and he didn't want to keep her out late two nights in a row.

"I'm staying," she assured him. "We've got to get that girl of yours safe."

"Thanks." He shot her a grateful smile. "What about if you go through the Garretts' relatives, and I'll go through people from Laura's college days, since I'm more likely to be able to pick out people Laura may have connected with."

For the next couple of hours, they worked away in silence. Jack went through the list of students who had taken classes with Laura, checking for any with criminal records who stood out, but the problem was their killer didn't seem to have a record. Which meant not only did he not show up in any of their databases, but he was probably also extremely adept at fitting in. He'd be the kind of person that when his friends and family found out what he'd done, they'd all be saying they were so surprised because he was such a good and kind man.

Rose yawned and looked up from her computer. "Okay, Jack, I think we should call it a night. I can hardly keep my eyes open, it's nearly two o'clock, and we don't want to miss something because we're both exhausted."

"Yeah, okay," he reluctantly agreed just as his phone rang. Hoping it was Laura, he snatched it up. "Hello?"

"Jack, it's Belinda, you better get over to Laura's building immediately," his boss' anxious voice came down the line.

"Why? What's wrong?"

At his tense tone, Rose paused in gathering up her belongings to listen in to his side of the conversation.

"A call just came in reporting a bomb in her building."

The air seemed to leave his lungs in a rush. "He's trying to force her hand." Jack thought he said it aloud, but maybe he only thought it.

"Jack, will she leave her apartment if the cops on her door ask her to?" Belinda was asking

"No." He grabbed his keys and gestured for Rose to follow him. "She's probably only going to open her door for me. And *if* she lets me in, and that's still a big if, I'm going to have to drag her out. I'll call her from the car, Rose and I are on our way."

"What was that all about?" Rose asked as they headed for the car.

"He put a bomb in Laura's building," he answered quickly, already dialing Laura's number.

"Jack?" her groggy voice answered after only a couple of rings.

"Laura, I don't want you to panic," he began, trying to keep his own panic in check.

"What's wrong?" her voice bordered on shrill, as, of course, she panicked.

"I need you to let the cops outside your door take you outside," he ordered.

"What? No," she protested immediately.

"Laura, he put a bomb in your building, you *have* to get out," he explained. Whether she liked it or not he was taking her out of that apartment.

"No, Jack, no, I can't," she babbled hysterically.

"I'm going to be there soon, okay?" He tried to soothe her. "I'll take you outside myself. But you have to open the door for me as soon as I get there. Promise me, Laura," he insisted.

"Promise," she all but sobbed.

"All right, angel, try to prepare yourself, I'll be there in maybe fifteen minutes."

"Think she's going to let you in?" Rose asked as he hung up.

"I honestly don't know," he replied.

The drive to Laura's apartment was the longest, most stressful fifteen minutes of his life. The scene in her street was like something out of a movie. Cop cars and fire trucks littered the street. People were evacuating, streaming away from the building in question, chattering, mostly animatedly, although a few looked more grumpy than interested.

Leaving the car, they sprinted for the building, where they were stopped by a cop they didn't know. "Sorry, no one's allowed to enter this building," he informed them.

Explaining as quickly as he could without being rude, "We've been working the crimes that have been happening in the building. The victim the guy who planted the bomb is really after is still in here."

The cop nodded. "Yeah, someone explained the whole thing to me, apparently she won't come out of her apartment."

"She's agoraphobic," Jack informed him. "She should open her door for me, though."

Eyeing him shrewdly, he asked, "You her boyfriend?"

How Jack wished he could say yes to that. "We're old friends."

"You got a couple of minutes. I got a battering ram being brought in. Given her condition and what she's been through, I don't want to traumatize her, but getting her out before this building blows is my top priority, and I only got another twenty minutes left on the timer."

"He set a timer?"

"Yeah, it was the ticking that attracted the attention of the guy who found it."

"How many floors are evacuated already?" Rose asked.

"Pretty much everything," the cop told them.

"All right, we'll go get Laura." Jack was already running for the stairs, reaching her door in record time. "Laura, it's Jack, let me in," he hammered on her door.

"No."

"Laura, I am not leaving this building without you," he warned. "If you stay here until it explodes, then I'm going to be right here with you." Jack thought it was best not to mention that the police were going to forcibly break down her door and remove her if she didn't come with him, no need to stress her more.

"Jack, no, go, get out."

"Then open up and let me grab you," he bargained.

"Jack, I can't," she whimpered. "I'm sorry."

"Laura, open the door now," he instructed sternly.

A moment later, it opened and Laura's petrified face peered back at him. He didn't have time to reassure her or soothe her fears; her safety was the priority right now. Grabbing her, he threw her over his shoulder and he, Rose, and the cops who'd stayed by Laura's door, all headed back downstairs.

In the foyer, Jack froze.

Something felt wrong.

Why would the killer, who'd gone to so much effort to grab Laura, risk blowing her up in an explosion?

He wouldn't.

He had been watching her. He had to know that she was agoraphobic and that he'd have to play it big to get her out of her apartment. He had to also know there was a chance she couldn't come out.

The bomb had to just be a distraction. Simply a way to force her outside and then grab her unnoticed in the chaos created by the evacuation.

"Why did you stop?" Rose demanded.

"He's out there, waiting for her," he explained.

"You think the bomb's just another game?" Rose asked.

"Yes, let's get her to the car and away from here." Jack adjusted Laura so she'd be more comfortable, sliding her down so he could cradle her in his arms, rather than having her draped over his shoulder. "Just hold on, angel," he said softly, "we're about to go outside, but I'll get you someplace safe as soon as I can."

While Rose quickly explained to the captain of the bomb squad what they believed was going on, Jack stepped out into the warm night. And almost immediately, the night erupted into confused bedlam.

Bullets began to whiz through the air.

People screamed and ran for cover.

Jack threw himself and Laura to the ground, covering her with his body.

He'd been right.

The killer was here.

He'd known that they'd drag Laura out of her apartment by force and he was waiting for them.

Rose and a couple of other cops came down beside him.

"Jack, you two okay?" Rose had to yell to be heard through all the noise.

"Yes. He's shooting at her." Jack was breathless with fear for Laura. This man wasn't going to stop until she was dead.

"Here're the keys to the patrol car just over there," the cop beside him gestured and passed him a set of keys. "It's the closest car, try to get her to it while we cover you."

Almost unwillingly, Jack readied himself to snatch up Laura. Half of him wanted to stay where they were. Partially hidden behind a row of bushes, with him on top of Laura, the killer couldn't get to her. The second they moved, he could get off another shot. However, staying where they were wasn't an option. He could be wrong about the bomb, it might not be just a distraction, it could kill all of them when it exploded.

"On three," someone murmured. "One, two, three."

Grabbing Laura, who was completely limp, although from fear and not because she'd been shot, Jack suspected, he and Rose darted toward the car. The cops around them fired off shots in the direction of the shooter, and Jack was able to throw Laura in the back and dive into the driver's seat before any more bullets were fired from the killer.

With tires squealing, Jack maneuvered the car as quickly as he could through the crowded street. Heart racing, pulse pounding, breathing hard, Jack had to fight to focus on driving so he didn't have an accident.

That had been close.

Too close.

It wasn't until they'd gone a few streets from Laura's building that he slowly started to calm down.

"That was close," Rose echoed his sentiments.

"Yeah, it was. Hopefully, they catch him." Surely, they had to,

Jack thought. There were so many cops there and the killer was only one man; the odds were stacked firmly against him.

But the killer wasn't one to give up that easily.

As Jack turned a corner, the night once again erupted into gunfire.

JULY 27TH

3:08 A.M.

Laura couldn't move. She seemed to have lost complete control of her body. It was like she had been turned to stone.

"Laura, get down," Jack screamed at her.

Bullets continued to whizz by the car, but she was powerless to move. Then suddenly, Rose was flattening her down against the back seat.

"Keep her down," Jack was yelling to Rose.

"Yeah, I got her, Jack, just focus on driving," Rose shouted back.

Above her, the back window shattered as a bullet pierced it, sending a million tiny glass shards raining down on her and Rose.

Laura couldn't believe this was happening. Just being outside her apartment was enough to send her into a blind panic, but someone had tried to blow her up, and someone was shooting at them. Her heart was beating so hard and fast, it felt like it was going to break right through her chest. She could hardly draw enough air into her lungs to keep oxygen flowing through her veins.

She should have stayed in her apartment.

She didn't care if she died in a bomb explosion. Only, Jack had said he wasn't going to leave her. And she couldn't let him die just because she didn't care if she did.

"I think you lost them." Rose cautiously sat up, brushing the glass off herself and Laura.

"Laura, are you hurt?" Jack demanded.

She was unable to make her voice work. And she was unsure

how to answer that, anyway.

Rose's hands were on her, quickly skimming her body in search of injuries. "She's okay. She's just in shock."

"Because we took her out of her apartment," Jack murmured.

"Well, we can't take her back there now, so I hope you have a plan." Rose let out a deep breath, calming herself.

"Yeah, I know where we'll take her; she should be safe there until we can figure out who's after her," Jack replied.

"You were right, he was watching us, waiting for us to deliver her right to him."

Tuning out their voices, Laura tried desperately to calm herself. She was still lying across the back seat where Rose had pushed her. Her eyes had been clenched shut ever since Jack had thrown her over his shoulder and carried her from her apartment, and she pressed her face against the smooth seat and tried to imagine that she was safely tucked up in her own bed. She pictured her soothing blue walls, her warm cozy feather quilt snuggled around her. She had spent months making that colorful patchwork quilt. It reminded her that before her abduction, her life had been bright and happy.

"Jack, are we almost wherever it is we're going? Laura is shaking like a leaf." Rose's voice cut through her panicked fog.

"Laura, honey," Jack's voice was soothing, "we're almost there, okay? Try to concentrate on your breathing, try to slow it down. Just hang in there a minute more, then I'll get you back inside."

It didn't matter, anyway. Going back inside wasn't going to make things better. They could never go back to the way they'd been before. Jack and Rose had shattered her carefully constructed protective little bubble.

"I'm going to call and see what's going on at the apartment building, see if anyone got anything on the shooter. I'll meet you inside," Rose announced once the car stopped.

"Hey, angel," Jack was suddenly beside her, stroking her hair. "Let's get you inside." He gently gathered her into his arms and lifted her from the car and almost immediately, Laura felt herself begin to calm. She was still shaking, still struggling to draw a decent breath, but she'd regained control of her limbs, and wrapped her arms tightly around Jack's neck, clinging to him. For some reason, Jack seemed to possess the ability to make her feel safe.

He carried her quickly toward a building, a door opened and light spilled out into the dark night. He whisked her through it and they were back indoors, but it didn't feel right. This wasn't her home. Laura kept her face tucked against Jack's shoulder and her eyes tightly closed.

"Is she okay?" an anxious male voice asked. The voice was familiar, but Laura was too upset to try and place it. "Do we need to call an ambulance?"

"She's in shock, she hasn't been outside in ten years," Jack replied. "The baby's not here, right? If he manages to find Laura, I don't want anything to happen to Sophie."

"Relax," the voice soothed. "She's at Mom and Dad's, they said they can keep her until we sort things out."

"Can you get me some blankets? She won't stop shaking."

Her relief at being back inside was being overshadowed by the presence of so many people. It had been ten years since she had last been around people and meeting so many all at once was overwhelming. Laura wanted desperately to be back in her apartment, but she knew it was impossible—a killer was waiting there to get her.

Jack sat, cradling her in his lap. "It's okay, Laura, we're inside now, try to calm down," he soothed.

"Here you go," a female voice murmured quietly.

Laura felt blankets being wrapped around her shoulders, and she pressed herself closer against Jack, trying to absorb his body heat.

"Are you sure we shouldn't call an ambulance?" the male voice still sounded concerned. "She doesn't look so good."

"It's just going to freak her out more." Jack's voice rumbled in his chest.

An ambulance was the last thing Laura wanted right now. A trip to the hospital would just bring back horrible memories. And the hospital would be full of people. Too full. She couldn't handle that on top of everything else. She lifted her head to convince Jack she was okay, but his hand pressed her head back down to his shoulder.

"Don't open your eyes right now, just rest," he ordered gently. "I texted Mark in the car and he should be here any minute, he can check her out," Jack assured the other man.

"How's she doing?" Rose asked.

"A little better. Anything from the explosion?"

"Things are still pretty crazy over there," Rose replied. "I told them we'd be by later today."

"Did they find who was shooting at us?" Laura pried open her eyes, squinting at the bright light.

"No, I'm sorry, Laura." Rose patted her shoulder apologetically.

"But you're *going* to find him, right?" she persisted desperately. She wanted her life back, only she wasn't sure now what life that was. Did she want the life she'd been living for the last ten years back, or did she want the life she'd had before she'd been kidnapped?

"Yes," Jack answered firmly. "We are going to find him."

"How can you know that for sure?" Laura wanted assurances that this would soon be over, only she knew no one could give her that.

"Because I won't stop until I find him," Jack replied, fierce determination in his voice. "I won't let anyone take you away from me."

If anyone was surprised by his possessive tone, they didn't show it. She'd known Jack wanted her back from the moment he'd first appeared on her doorstep, and he'd told her several times that he was still in love with her. The problem was, she wasn't sure she wanted him back. He'd broken her heart once before and now her heart was a lot more fragile than it had been back then. She wasn't sure she could cope with him breaking it all over again. For the moment, at least she was just going to let his forceful yet unfounded assurances reassure her. "Okay," she whispered and wearily laid her head back down on his shoulder.

"Are you going to be all right?" Jack asked, voice gentle again.

"Yes." She tried to sound as convincing as her pounding heart would let her.

"Are you sure?"

"No." Laura chewed on her bottom lip to keep her tears at bay; she didn't want to cry in front of strangers.

"Anything I can do to make things easier for you?"

"Just find him and arrest him," she begged. Although what she really wanted was whoever was after her dead. Laura didn't think she could go through another long drawn out trial.

"We will," Jack promised. "And until we do, you should be safe here."

"Where is here?" She lifted her head from his shoulder to finally take in her surroundings. They were in a cozy sitting room, the walls were a warm yellow color, the furniture was simple and well worn, but added to the homey feel.

"My brother Ryan's house. He's a police officer now, too, so one of us will stay with you at all times. I mean it, Laura," he added when he felt her tense. "You are not to go anywhere alone until we catch this guy."

Reluctantly nodding her acquiescence, since she knew he was right, she relented. "I don't like it, but okay."

"Good." She felt Jack's shudder of relief. "All right, you remember Ryan, and this is his fiancée, Sofia," he made the introductions.

"Hey, Laura." Ryan smiled at her. Of course, she remembered Jack's younger brother. They had known each other all their lives, played together as children, gone to school together, gotten into trouble together. She had been so carefree back then, having no idea what life held in store for her.

Ryan held out his hand to shake hers. Laura was still apprehensive about physical contact, with anyone other than Jack, it seemed, since she kept finding herself in his lap. Still, she reached out a trembling hand to shake Ryan's. "Hey, Ryan, so you and Jack both followed in your father's footsteps. What's Mark up to these days?"

"He's a surgeon, married with four kids," Ryan replied.

"And you're engaged, huh? With a baby?"

"Yep," he grinned. "The wedding is next month, on Sophie's first birthday."

"That's a nice way to celebrate her birthday." Laura smiled back, hoping it didn't come out all wobbly.

"Yeah, well, the day she was born wasn't a good one, so we wanted to change that and make it special for her, for when she's older." Ryan's blue eyes grew dark. "It's a long story," he added when he saw the confusion on her face. "Jack will fill you in once things calm down."

Would he? She asked herself. Would he stick around long enough? Would she let him stick around long enough?

"You look like you could do with a nap." Sofia smiled warmly. She had wavy red hair, sparkling silver eyes, and an easy manner that put Laura at ease. "The spare room is all made up."

"No, thanks," Laura answered quickly. The prospect of nightmares was too much to deal with right now.

"You need to rest, angel," Jack reminded her gently. "You've barely slept in days."

"I don't want to," she protested, and was saved from having to defend her position when Ryan glanced at his phone.

"Mark just pulled up in the driveway, I'll let him in," Ryan announced.

"You agreed to let a doctor check out your hand," Jack told

her in way of explanation.

She had, unfortunately, and since she knew Mark, it was preferable to a stranger. However, there were already more people here than she was comfortable with.

"Hi, everyone." Mark walked into the room a moment later. "Hey, Laura, long time no see." He gave her a warm smile.

"Hi, Mark." She attempted to smile back.

He knelt in front of her and set down a small bag on the floor beside him. "Jack, pop her down so I can check her over."

Laura nearly opened her mouth to protest the idea of moving out of the safety of Jack's arms, but stopped herself and allowed Jack to slide her off his lap and onto the couch. Mark took her pulse and blood pressure, checked her temperature, then listened to her heart and lungs, before moving on to her hand. Carefully, he examined, cleaned and redressed the wound.

"How bad is it?" Jack asked once Mark was finished.

"Second degree burn, full thickness in some areas. I know that you're agoraphobic," Mark addressed her, "but if you can manage a trip to the hospital, I'd strongly recommend it. I'd say you're bordering on needing a skin graft."

She turned panicked eyes on Jack. She could *not* manage a trip to the hospital.

"Shh," Jack soothed before she even said a word, apparently correctly interpreting her panic. He sat beside her and wrapped an arm around her shoulders, and she leaned into him. "Does she have to go?"

"No, not yet. But she really has to have it checked out, as burns heal the skin can contract, on the back of her hand that could mean she wouldn't be able to fully close it. I'm also concerned about infection, so I'm going to put her on antibiotics. Since I know she can't go outside, and since you guys are a little preoccupied with keeping her alive, I brought some with me." He pulled a bottle from his bag. "I'm going to come and check on you again tomorrow," he informed her. "Other than that, Jack, she needs rest. Make sure she eats and drinks plenty of water."

"Will do." Jack nodded.

"Call me if you need anything at all. If she starts having panic attacks, or she feels like she can't cope, I'll bring some sedatives," Mark said quietly to Jack.

No way would she be taking any sedatives. Although, the thought of deep, uninterrupted sleep was tantalizing.

"Thanks, Mark," Jack said.

"Yeah, thanks, Mark," Laura echoed.

"No worries," Mark patted her shoulder. "Stay safe, guys."

"I'll walk you out," Ryan told his younger brother.

"All right, now you get some rest," Jack pronounced once Mark had left.

"I really don't want to," Laura almost begged.

Jack tucked her hair behind her ear, his fingertips lingering on her cheek. "You heard what Mark said, you need to sleep."

"I don't want to go up to bed," she pleaded.

"Why don't you just lie down on the couch here then?" Jack persisted. "Just close your eyes and rest for a little while? We'll all be here with you, you won't be alone."

"I ..." she hesitated.

"Please," Jack said softly. "You need sleep."

"Okay," she relented. "But only down here on the couch."

"Okay." Jack lifted her up, then laid her back down on the couch, covering her with the blankets. "Close your eyes and try to clear your mind," he murmured, sitting on the floor beside her and stroking her hair.

"You're not going anywhere, are you?" Her eyes wanted to close but she was fighting it.

"I'm not going anywhere," Jack assured her. "I'm going to be sitting right here."

"Promise?"

"I promise. Try to relax."

"I can't," she whimpered. "Every time I close my eyes, I'm

back in the woods."

"Don't think," he told her. "Just get yourself comfortable." He waited while she wiggled over onto her stomach and put her thumb in her mouth, then he began to rub slow circles on her back. "Now just focus on me."

That was exactly what Laura was worried about. Her focus had become all about Jack Xander. He comforted her, made her feel safe, calmed her when nothing else could. How was she going to live without that when this was all over and she told him to go back to his life and forget about her?

* * * * *

10:59 A.M.

"We need to figure out who he is and how he's connected to her abduction, or we're never going to find him." Jack was starting to feel desperate. This guy had come after Laura twice now, killed someone, abducted someone, attacked four others, fired a gun into a crowd of people, and they were no closer to finding him.

He cast a glance at Laura who was still asleep on the couch. Or rather, who was *finally* asleep on the couch. She had tossed and turned, half dozing in a fitful slumber for hours before exhaustion had taken hold and she had drifted off to sleep.

"Maybe who we're looking for has nothing to do with when she was kidnapped," Ryan suggested.

"Could be he's just some psychopath playing with her," Xavier Montague, a friend and colleague of theirs, suggested. "It wouldn't be hard to look her up and find out what happened to her."

Jack shook his head. "No, this guy was somehow involved in her kidnapping. He knows things about it that he couldn't have known unless he was there."

"How do you know that?" Ryan asked, raising a skeptical brow.

"The stars," Jack replied, "that he left on the ceiling of the first victim's apartment were to taunt her."

"How so?" Xavier asked.

"When she was out there and they were assaulting her, she would lie there and look up at the sky and feel helpless and weak. Then at night, they'd put her in this hole in the ground, and all she could see was a circle of stars above her," he explained. "So, he knew enough about her and what she went through to know that that would shake her."

"All right," Ryan nodded, "so she was twenty and in college, so it has to be …"

His brother never finished his sentence because Laura let out an ear-piercing scream and bolted upright. Jack darted to her side, grabbing her shoulders and giving a gentle shake. Laura swung her arms wildly, frantically fighting against him. "Laura, hey, it's okay. It's Jack. You were just dreaming," he said as he tried to hold her still without hurting or scaring her.

Her arms dropped back down, and she was gasping, struggling to catch her breath. "Jack?"

"I'm here," he assured her. He pulled her into a hug, and she leaned into him, pressing her face against his chest. "You were just dreaming, angel," he repeated.

For a moment, she just rested against him, bringing up her thumb to suck on as she calmed herself. She'd had that habit since she was a kid; he remembered how hard her parents had worked to break her of it. Apparently, she had picked it up again following her assault. When she was ready, she gently pulled herself away, surprise and a hint of trepidation flashed through her eyes when she saw that there were more people here than when she'd fallen asleep.

"This is Xavier, he works with Rose, Ryan and me, and his girlfriend, Annabelle," Jack made the introductions.

"Another babysitter," she murmured.

"I need you safe, Laura," he told her unapologetically. He couldn't deal with the idea of anyone taking her away from him and he didn't care if she and everyone else knew it.

"But safe from whom?" she pondered, nodding absently.

"We were just discussing that." He took her hand and led her to the table where Rose, Ryan, Xavier, Sofia, and Annabelle were still seated and gently pushed her down into a chair. "It had to be someone you came into contact with back then."

"But who?"

"You didn't know the Garrett brothers, right?" Ryan asked. "You'd never seen them anywhere before?"

Laura shook her head and was unable to hide her repulsed shudder at the mention of the men who had ruined her life.

"Are you sure?" Ryan pressed.

Annoyed now, she snapped, "Don't you think I would have told the police at the time if I'd met Frank or Francis Garrett before?"

"Sorry, Laura, I'm not trying to upset you," Ryan soothed. "I was just confirming that this man we're looking for is the middle man, connecting the Garretts to you."

"Why does there need to be a middle man connecting the Garretts to me?" Laura challenged. "It was just random."

"They killed your roommate and grabbed you as you were entering your house," Jack reminded her. "They could have taken your roommate or anyone else, but they waited for you."

Her face went pale. "It could still have been random," she protested weakly. "This could be random." Her violet eyes travelled the group seeking affirmation.

"You know it's not, Laura. This guy knows you, he knows specifics about you and what you went through." Jack hooked a finger under her chin and tilted her face so she was looking at him. "He was involved; he knows enough to put stars on the ceilings of his victim's home because he knew that would upset you."

"You were in college then, since you never met the Garretts you probably met this guy before, maybe you even knew him well. Can you think of anyone from that time in your life who might have done this?" Xavier asked.

"No, of course not." Laura looked indignant. "I would have remembered if I'd ever met a psychotic stalker killer."

"He might not have seemed psychotic at the time," Jack reminded her. "Try to think of anyone who stood out in some way. A boyfriend who didn't take the breakup well. A guy who asked you out and you turned down. Someone who might have been hanging around you."

"I don't know. I don't know anyone like that. I never knew anyone like that. I don't know," Laura said helplessly, tears brimming in her eyes.

"Okay, okay," he calmed her, catching her flailing arms. "Let's take things slow. Any bad breakups?"

She shook her head. "I only dated two guys while I was in college. I wasn't ready to get involved in another relationship after …" She trailed off and stared at him uncomfortably and once again, Jack hated himself for cheating on her and ruining what they'd had. "So," she continued, "I kept busy with work and studying; I always thought there was time later to date."

"And things ended well with both of those relationships?" Jack persisted, pushing away his guilt as it wasn't going to help Laura right now.

"Well, the first guy was cheating on me." Her cheeks reddened. "So, I broke up with him. I guess that's not ending well, but he certainly wouldn't have had any reason to be angry with me about it. And with the second guy, it was mutual."

"Can we have their names?" Rose asked. "We'll check them out just to be sure."

Laura frowned but nodded. "Arthur Wilcox and Ken Lincoln."

"Okay, do you remember anyone hanging around you? Maybe

followed you around, kept popping up places you frequented. Maybe someone who kept calling you or sending emails or texts or letters?" Jack persisted. The answer was there; she just had to figure it out.

"No, there was no one like that."

"Anyone who asked you out but you turned down?"

"I got lots of offers." Laura's cheeks heated in embarrassment once again. "But like I said, I didn't date much, I was too busy."

"Anyone stand out amongst the guys you turned down?" He fought against a surge of jealousy at the idea of other men asking Laura out, which was ridiculous, given he was the reason they'd broken up; but nonetheless, he didn't like it.

"No." But she'd hesitated, her brow scrunching as something obviously occurred to her.

"What is it? Do you remember someone?"

"Maybe." She looked up at him uncertainly.

"You need to tell us, Laura, it might be important."

"It's probably nothing," she cautioned.

"I'm sure you're right," he agreed. "But it also could be something."

"He was my psychology professor. He was married, he had a kid, but he asked me out several times. I kept telling him no, that I didn't date married men, but he kept asking. In the end, I told him if he didn't leave me alone, I'd go to his wife and tell her what he was doing, but I never got a chance."

"What happened with him?" A glimmer of hope lighted in him with this potential direction.

"Nothing," she shrugged. "I got kidnapped and dropped out of school and never heard from him again."

"What was his name?"

"Axel Christenson."

He exchanged glances with Rose. "Axel Christenson?" he repeated.

"Yes."

"Laura," he began gently, "did you know there's an Axel Christenson living in your apartment building?"

Her eyes narrowed in confusion, then widened in fear. "All this time, he was living right in my building?"

"At least for a while," he replied softly. They'd been so close. Spoken with the man. He had inserted himself into their investigation by pretending to find the letter he himself had left.

"No." She shook her head desperately; she was breathing way too quickly, bordering on hyperventilating.

"Try to calm down," he cautioned.

"Laura, what do you remember about Axel Christenson? Did he ever seem violent or unstable?" Rose asked.

"No. I don't know. I never really paid attention. He was persistent in asking me out, but I didn't know he was crazy. Is my interrogation over now?" Frustrated, Laura stood and stormed to the other side of the room.

Jack followed her. "It wasn't an interrogation," he assured her.

"It certainly felt like one." She looked close to tears again.

"I'm sorry, Laura, I know you're going through hell right now, and I don't mean to make it harder for you." Gently, he took her shoulders and turned her to face him. "I just want to find out who's doing this to you."

She sighed. "I'm sorry, I know you do. It just feels like it's starting all over again, and I thought it was over. I want it to be over. I *need* it to be over."

"And soon, it will be," he assured her.

"And then you'll be gone," she whispered softly.

Before he had a chance to remind her he wasn't going anywhere, Rose interrupted. "Jack, we should stop by the precinct on the way back to Laura's apartment building, run the names she gave us and get contact details so we can arrange to meet with them."

"Yeah, okay," he reluctantly agreed. He wanted to stay here and convince Laura that even when this was over he wasn't going anywhere, that he was going to earn her trust back so they could be a couple again. But realistically, he had a better chance of convincing her after he'd caught the man trying to kill her.

"You're leaving?" Panic was written all over Laura's face.

"Just for a little while," he told her.

"But ... but ... I ..." she stammered. "I ... need you here."

"I'll be back here with you soon," he promised. "And while I'm gone, Ryan and Sofia and Xavier and Annabelle will be here with you. You'll be safe."

"I'm sorry," she pulled away physically and emotionally. "You have work to do and I'm being silly. I'm more than used to being on my own, so go, I'll be fine. Sofia, where's the bathroom?" She was dismissing him.

"I'll show you." Sofia shot him an apologetic glance as she followed Laura from the room.

Staring after them, Jack knew that Laura was pushing him away because she was both scared and wary of being hurt again, but still, it stung, and he was starting to wonder if after everything he had done and everything she had been through, she was ever going to be able to open herself up to the possibility of the two of them getting back together.

* * * * *

2:26 P.M.

"Wow, this place is still crazy," Rose said as she and Jack parked their car at the end of Laura's block.

Crime scene techs were bustling about everywhere. Residents had been allowed back into the buildings, and in the full light of day, the carnage left behind by last night's chaos could be fully seen.

One person had been killed, and six others, including a cop, had been injured by the killer's bullets. Three of those hurt had received minor injuries; two received serious injuries, and one was in hospital in critical condition. They hadn't told Laura this yet. She was struggling enough as it was and she didn't need to know right now that this man had hurt more people in his mission to get her.

They had fared better on the bomb front. As Jack had predicted, the bomb was merely a distraction, meant to ensure that Laura was forced out of the building. He couldn't risk killing her on the odd chance she wasn't forcibly removed in time, so the blast had been small. It had damaged only the two cars it had been set between and had been filled with confetti.

Forensics would probably take a couple of days to come in, but they didn't really need them at this point. They already knew that it was the same man who had been terrorizing the apartment building to get to Laura.

They were mainly here to check out Axel Christenson's apartment.

So far, they had been able to count out both men Laura dated in college. Ken Lincoln had been diagnosed with a brain tumor a year after Laura's kidnapping and had succumbed to the illness eighteen months after that. Arthur Wilcox had married an English woman and the two had moved to London four years ago; he hadn't been back to the country since.

"We were lucky to get Laura out of here alive." Jack glanced at his watch for about the millionth time since they'd left Ryan and Sofia's house.

"But we did get her away alive, and she's safe at your brother's house," Rose reminded him. "She's in good hands, try to focus."

"I am trying," Jack grimaced. "It's just hard when she panics because I'm leaving her."

"I know, but right now we have a viable suspect—let's confirm it's him so we can arrest him," she encouraged. If they didn't end this soon, she wasn't sure either Laura or Jack were going to make it.

Rose was still feeling awful and embarrassed by upsetting Laura the other night with her badly worded, badly timed comment. When things calmed down, she intended to apologize and make it clear that she was here for Laura, whatever she needed.

Jack's adoration for Laura, the way he looked at her, the way he couldn't stand to be away from her, was getting Rose thinking. She'd always thought there was plenty of time later to find the right guy, get married and have a family. But Paige's situation was getting to her. Paige had thought there would be plenty of time later to have kids, and now she would never have children of her own—at least, not biological ones. Rose didn't want to end up missing out on happiness just because she kept putting it off until later. With Jack all but back together with Laura, she was the only one of her group of friends still single. Perhaps it was time to do something about that; she didn't want any regrets in her life.

"Detectives." Connor Newman rushed over to them as soon as they entered the lobby. "How's Laura?"

"She's all right, Mr. Newman," Rose assured him. The man seemed to be the only person who Laura had any contact with. "Are you and Laura friends?"

"I guess as much as she has friends," the man agreed.

"But you know about her past?" Rose pressed.

"Only that something had happened to her to make her agoraphobic. I collect deliveries for her, groceries and things, so she doesn't have to see anyone."

"Why did you help her?" Rose didn't think that Connor was involved, but she wondered why he had gone out of his way to help someone he didn't even know.

The man shrugged. "Because she asked me to. Poor girl, I felt sorry for her, she was all alone." Turning shrewd eyes on Jack, he continued, "Until you, anyway. She let you take her out of her apartment. You like her. She obviously likes you, too; she let you spend the night. You knew her before."

"Yes, we grew up together," Jack replied.

"You dated." It wasn't a question. "You broke her heart."

"She told you about that?"

He gave a wry smile. "Nope, got four daughters of my own and eight granddaughters, I can tell." Connor grew serious. "Don't hurt her again."

"I won't," Jack said just as seriously.

"Mr. Newman, what do you know about Axel Christenson?" If anyone in the building was going to know about the man they were after, it would be Connor Newman.

"Is he the one responsible for all of this?" Connor demanded.

"Perhaps," Jack nodded. "How long has he lived here?"

"Almost a year," Connor replied. "I remember vividly the day I first met him."

Jack arched a brow. "Why was that, Mr. Newman?"

"He came in to see about an apartment, it was one next door to Laura's, now that I think about it. When I told him someone had just signed a lease for it, he went berserk. I told him we had other apartments available, but he really wanted that one. I thought it was odd at the time, but I never guessed it was because he was obsessed with Laura." Connor looked truly shocked and shaken.

"Did he say why he wanted that apartment?" Jack asked, looking horrified by the thought of Axel Christenson being so close to Laura for a whole year.

"He said he liked an apartment that was in the middle and not corner ones, he said he didn't like to be too close to the ground or too high. Like I said, I thought it was odd, his reasons for wanting that apartment didn't really make sense, but then again," Connor shrugged, "some people are just odd."

Lucky that apartment had already been taken. Who knew what Axel would have done if he'd been able to get that close to Laura. If Rose had to guess, she would have thought Axel would have looked for a way to break through an adjoining wall so he could get access to her. If he could have found a way to keep her quiet, he could have done whatever he wanted to Laura whenever he wanted and no one would have been any the wiser.

"But he took one of the other apartments?" Rose asked.

"Yeah, apartment 6D," Connor confirmed.

"What do you know about Axel?" Jack all but barked.

Rose knew he was stressed, but he was going to have to calm down. Laura was safe for now and Jack needed to be focused and calm if they were going to find Axel Christenson and keep Laura safe.

"I don't see a lot of him, and when I do, he's always pretty rude. He never says hello, never really acknowledges me at all. But I wouldn't have guessed he was capable of this ..." He gestured at the building. "He just seemed snobby."

"What about family?"

"I don't know of any. He lives alone, no girlfriend that I've seen, no visiting kids either," Connor replied.

"Friends? Visitors?" Jack continued.

Connor shook his head. "No visitors that I've seen. I mean, I'm not the only doorman, but when I'm here, I haven't seen anyone come or go from Mr. Christenson's apartment."

"Do you know what his job is?"

"I believe he's a college professor. Psychology, I think." Connor looked disgusted at the fact that someone who lectured people in psychology could turn out to be a psychopath.

"Any problems between Mr. Christenson and the other residents?"

"Nope, not that I know of. Work and home seem to be all he does. He's pretty structured—usually leaves in the mornings and arrives home in the evenings at the same time every day. I've seen him greet other residents in the lobby, exchange pleasantries, but that's about it. No one's complained about him."

"Can we go and see his apartment now?" Rose asked.

"Warrant?" Connor asked.

"Got one." Jack handed it over.

"Then go find something to nail that monster," Connor declared as he handed over the keys.

* * * * *

10:31 P.M.

"Here you go." Sofia stood in front of her, a steaming cup of tea in her hands. "Drink this, maybe it'll warm you up a little, you haven't stopped shaking since you got here."

"Thank you," Laura murmured, taking the cup, grateful for the gesture but knowing that nothing was going to warm her up. She wasn't normal cold. She was cold with a numbing horror that filled up every inch of her being. Nothing could warm that kind of cold.

She hesitated, well maybe that wasn't true, she thought to herself. Maybe something could warm that kind of cold, more like *someone*. She was pretty sure Jack could. But Jack wasn't here right now. He and Rose had left hours ago to go back to her apartment building to see how things were progressing there after the explosion. And even if Jack had still been here, she wasn't convinced it was a good idea to keep letting him comfort and calm her. She couldn't allow herself to get used to that because soon he would be gone from her life once again.

"Don't worry, Laura, he'll be back soon," Sofia seemingly read her mind.

She nodded distractedly. Unfortunately, soon wasn't soon enough. Despite her uncertainty in all things Jack related, she still wanted him here by her side, keeping her overwhelming terror at bay.

At least he hadn't left her alone. He'd left her in the watchful care of Ryan, Xavier, Sofia, and Annabelle. Two police officers ought to make her feel safe, but still she yearned for Jack. It was odd, though. After ten years spent alone in her apartment, never seeing a living soul, she felt comfortable and at ease with Jack's family and friends.

"Paige?"

At Sofia's surprised exclamation, Laura lifted her head to see a pretty brunette entering the living room.

"What are you doing here?" Annabelle asked.

"Ryan called, explained the situation," Paige replied.

"Are you sure you're okay to be here?" Sofia was looking at the woman with concern.

"Yes." Paige nodded, a little defensively.

"You're not supposed to be back at work yet." The worry in Sofia's eyes was mirrored in the eyes of everyone else in the room.

"I'm back at work next month, which is really next week." Paige sounded frustrated and shot the others an irritated frown. Then she turned her gaze in Laura's direction. "You must be Laura. I'm Paige, Ryan's partner."

She grimaced slightly. "Another babysitter." She wasn't mad, she wasn't a cop, and she couldn't keep herself safe. If she was honest, she was touched that Ryan and Sofia, Xavier and Annabelle, and Paige had given up their time for her. She was, however, wondering what had happened to Paige that had everyone in the room watching her with thinly veiled concern.

Paige grinned. "Can never have too many of those. Especially given the circumstances," she sobered.

A shiver of fear rocketed through her, and Sofia's arm quickly wrapped around her shoulders. Paige was right. This man had already killed, abducted, and assaulted in his quest to get to her. Then when that had failed, he had tried to break into her apartment, almost killed them in an explosion and shot at them. Plus, he may have been involved in her kidnapping. Laura was glad Paige had come.

"What about a game of charades?" Xavier proposed suddenly.

"I love that game." Paige's grin was back, and she came and

plopped down on the sofa. "You like charades, Laura?"

Her family had played charades every Christmas when Laura was growing up; she wondered whether they still did. "I haven't played in a long time," she answered.

For the next thirty minutes, Laura let the others' laughing and playful theatrics distract her. As she watched them, she drew strength from them and started to wonder whether she'd made a mistake locking herself away. If these people, most of whom she'd only just met, could offer so much comfort just by being there, then how much comfort could her family who loved her have given her?

Laura's head snapped up as there was a knock at the door.

Ryan, Xavier, and Paige all rose, guns drawn.

"Stay here, Laura, don't move from this room unless I tell you to," Ryan instructed. "Paige ..."

"Yeah, I got her, you two do the door." Paige nodded, positioning herself between Laura and the living room door as Ryan and Xavier left the room.

Sofia once again wrapped a comforting arm around her shoulders. "Ryan won't let anyone hurt you, neither will Paige or Xavier."

She nodded unsteadily. Laura believed that, but still, she wished that Jack was here. And that scared her. She knew it was a bad idea to let herself get too attached to him. Too used to relying on him. And yet, all she could think of was Jack. Maybe that meant ... well, she wasn't sure what that meant, but maybe ... just maybe.

The seconds ticked into minutes and the swirling anxiety in her stomach grew.

"It's only us," Ryan finally announced, re-entering the room, and Paige lowered her gun.

"Who was it?" Sofia asked.

Ryan shot her a troubled frown. "It was a package. For Laura."

Panicked, she asked, "For me? But no one knows I'm here."

"Someone does," Xavier told her gently.

She struggled to keep her breathing even. "What's in the package?"

"You want me to open it for you?" Ryan asked, his blue eyes, so like Jack's, examining her carefully.

She gave a shaky nod and watched as Ryan slipped on a pair of gloves, then sat at the dining table. Paige, Annabelle, and Sofia joined him. Xavier remained standing by the door, his expression alert as though he expected a threat to walk through the door at any second. Given that someone had dropped off a package here, she guessed he could be right.

"You okay, Laura?" Ryan asked when he realized she hadn't joined them at the table.

"Yeah." She forced herself to stand, willing her legs to hold her up, and managed to make it to a chair before her knees buckled.

Using a knife, Ryan cut the tape sealing the box and eased it open, peering inside. With a gloved hand, he reached inside to pull something out. "You recognize this?"

An ice-cold shiver raced through her. She opened her mouth but no sound came out.

"Laura?" Paige's hand gripped her shoulder, shaking gently.

She drew in a harsh breath. "It's mine," she whispered, staring at the delicate gold chain Ryan was holding in his hand. Her eyes were drawn to the diamond cross. Her parents had given it to her for her eighteenth birthday. "I was wearing it when I was abducted." She was fighting not to hyperventilate. "The police never found it. They searched the Garretts' house, but it wasn't there. I thought I must have lost it in the woods. It was a gift from my parents. I thought I'd never see it again."

"Hang in there, sweetie." Paige kept a hand on her shoulder, squeezing lightly.

"Is there anything else in there?" Annabelle asked.

Her head snapped up to hear Ryan's answer.

He grimaced. "Sorry, Laura."

"What?" she asked but was sure she didn't want to know the answer.

"It's photos."

Her heart dropped. "Photos of what?"

He raised an eyebrow.

"Of them raping me," she answered her own question.

"I'm sorry, honey." Ryan looked pained.

She attempted to hold on to control. "How many of them in the pictures?"

"Three. And you."

"So there really is another man." Laura could feel the color draining from her face as reality sank in. So far, she'd been clinging to denial. She had needed to believe that what had happened to her was in the past. But she couldn't do that any longer. There had been three men who had assaulted her, not two, and that other man was clearly intent on bringing her past crashing into the present.

"Are you okay?" Sofia was peering at her worriedly.

No, she wanted to answer, but instead, "I think I'm going to go lie down." She needed to be alone. No, she corrected herself, what she really needed was Jack to come back. The only place she was going to feel safe was in Jack's arms. And she so desperately wanted to feel safe. She missed that feeling so much. Had always taken it for granted before her abduction.

She rose on shaky legs, and Ryan stood with her. "You want me to come up with you?"

She was grateful, but having Ryan there wasn't the same as having Jack. "No, but thanks."

"What about I call Mark and ask him to come back and bring you something to help you rest?"

"No, I don't want to take anything." She ignored the concern in his eyes, mirrored in the eyes of the others. She paused at the door. "Ryan?"

"What do you need?"

"Maybe you could call Jack?" She attempted to control the tremble in her voice but failed dismally. "Ask him to come back here as soon as he can?"

"Done. Call out if you need anything. I'll be up to check on you soon." His calm voice soothed her a little.

She managed to make it up the stairs before her legs gave out, and she sunk down onto the top step, dropping her head to her hands. Tears were pricking the backs of her eyes but she held them back. She didn't want to give this man the satisfaction of making her cry.

Laura wondered whether it really could be Axel Christenson who was doing all of this. She didn't see why he would. So, she wouldn't sleep with him because he was married and had a baby at home. That was no big deal. Nothing that should cause him to hate her so viciously. Surely her rejecting him couldn't have been enough to make him orchestrate her abduction and rape. Or enough to make him hurt people just to get to her. And where had he been these last eleven years? Waiting? Waiting to come back and torture her some more?

Images of those horrible days flashed across her mind.

She forced them back with years of practice. Imagined herself picking them up one by one and putting them in a drawer, then closing and locking it. It was what she always did when the memories got too overwhelming.

Nauseous, she pushed herself upright, leaning against the wall for support and headed for the bathroom. She was reaching a hand for the doorknob when someone grabbed her. A hand clamped over her mouth. An arm wrapped across her chest, pinning her arms to her side.

Panic swelled inside of her. Laura could almost feel it stretching out its tentacles to fill every inch of her frame. As fear took over, she lost control of her body. In her mind, she was back in the woods, lying helplessly as the Garrett brothers assaulted her repeatedly.

A chuckle rumbled in the chest she was pressed against. "I see nothing's changed. Still too cowardly to fight back."

Tears seeped from her eyes. He was right. She was a coward. She'd done nothing to prevent herself from being raped and tortured. And she was doing nothing now to save herself. He was going to take her—where, she didn't know. But to do what to her, she certainly did know. And she was going to let it happen because she was scared frozen.

Another chuckle. "Come on, we better hurry before your cop buddies come to check on you."

As he started to drag her, Laura could feel herself starting to pass out. Her vision began to fade, and her body sagged. Caught off guard, the man holding her stumbled, his hand dipped from her mouth as he tried to stop himself falling.

On autopilot, Laura let out an ear-piercing scream.

Growling in frustration, the man released her, shoving her violently and she went crashing into the wall. Still not in control of her body, her face took the brunt of the impact, pain radiating out across her cheek.

Panting, she struggled for control, and her legs turned to jelly.

Then Ryan was there, holding her up. Xavier rushed past them and into the room where the man had fled.

"He went out the window," Xavier announced a moment later.

"Go after him, I got Laura. Take Paige." When Xavier was gone, Ryan turned his attention to her. "Laura? Honey, look at me."

But she couldn't. Her head was spinning mercilessly.

Keeping hold of her with one hand, his other grasped her chin, giving it a firm shake. "Laura, come on. I need you to focus. Are you hurt? Do I need to call an ambulance?"

Steadying herself a little, her hands reached up to grab fistfuls of Ryan's shirt, clinging desperately. "I'm okay," she whispered.

"Do you know who that was? Do you know who attacked you?"

She clenched her eyes closed and managed a nod. She thought she did, anyway; she was pretty sure she recognized the voice.

"Who was it?"

"I think it was Axel Christenson," she answered, unable to believe that her worst nightmare was coming back to life. She fought to push down a sob, but it half escaped.

Ryan pulled her into a hug. "If you need to cry, go for it, don't hold back on my account."

Laura allowed herself to draw comfort from Ryan's arms, but she wasn't going to cry. Not until this was over. Or at least until Jack was here and it was his hard chest she was leaning against, his strong arms around her, cocooning her in a bubble of warmth and safety.

JULY 28TH

12:41 A.M.

"Where is she?" Jack demanded, running frantically into his brother's house.

"Calm down," Ryan ordered.

"I can't calm down, someone broke in here and attacked her." His heart had been beating wildly ever since his brother had called to tell him what had happened. "I thought she'd be safe here. I need her safe. Where is she?"

"She's upstairs with the girls," Xavier replied.

"Alone?" he asked incredulous. "No offense to Sofia and Annabelle, but I don't think they're going to be much help if that guy comes back."

"Relax," Ryan ordered again. "Paige is up there with them."

"Paige is here? Is that a good idea? She's not supposed to be back at work yet." Jack was out of his mind with fear and concern for Laura, but that didn't automatically override his concerns about Paige.

"I'm keeping an eye on her, Jack. Try not to worry about Paige, just focus on Laura right now. She's safe for the moment, but, Jack, you really need to calm down before you go see her. Right now, she's holding it together, better than I thought given everything she's been through, but she's hanging on by a thread. If you go running up there in a blind panic, you're going to push her over the edge. Jack," his brother waited till he met his gaze, "she's counting on you to keep it together."

He forced himself to take deep, calming breaths. "Okay, what do we know?"

"Not a lot," Xavier answered. "Laura thinks that it was Axel Christenson who attacked her, but she's not positive. Stephanie's on her way here to collect the photos and necklace and see if he left anything behind."

"Did you get a good look at him?"

Ryan shook his head. "When we heard her screaming, we ran up immediately, but he was already out the window. Xavier and Paige chased him, but he was already in a car and driving off down the street. And no, they didn't get the license plate."

"I'm going to go see her now." Jack couldn't stand to be away from her for another second. He was aching with the need to hold her in his arms. He repeated to himself over and over to keep his cool, but he wasn't sure he'd be able to; it tore him up inside knowing that Laura still wasn't safe.

He knocked softly on the door, since he knew that his brother's partner would be keeping watch. A moment later, it inched open and Paige gave him a quick once-over, presumably ascertaining whether he was holding it together before she let him see Laura. Apparently, he passed because Paige took a step back and swung the door farther open.

Inside the room, Laura sat on the edge of the bed, holding herself stiffly, and looking completely and utterly alone, even though Sofia perched on one side of her and Annabelle on the other, both chattering away, attempting to lift her spirits. Laura was pale, her violet eyes glazed with shock, unable to completely hide the tremble in her hands, which she held clutched tightly together in her lap.

"Laura?"

She turned instantly, tears immediately welling up in her eyes. When he held out his hand, she came to him, wrapping her arms around his waist, and pressing her forehead against his chest. He brought her closer, one hand cradled her head, threading his fingers through her silky black hair; his other rubbed her back, stroking the length of her spine, feeling her quake beneath his touch.

"We'll leave you two be." Sofia shot him an understanding smile.

"Try to get her to rest," Paige murmured quietly in his ear. Then louder, "Ryan, Xavier, and I are right downstairs, so there's nothing to worry about," she reassured Laura.

Once they were alone, Jack gently pulled Laura back so he could see her. He kept hold of her shoulders as he searched her face. "Are you okay?"

She nodded, but he could see a bruise already forming on her left cheek. "He hurt you," he growled.

Again, she nodded, but wouldn't speak. The blank, empty look in her eyes was scaring him. He'd seen it there before, after the incident with Rose. Last time, he'd been able to make it go away, but he wasn't sure this time he could.

"Laura?" He hooked a finger under her chin and tilted her face up so her violet eyes met his. "We're going to get this guy, you know that, right?"

Another nod, but she let her eyes drop.

"We're going to end this," he assured her.

She shook her head. "No," she whispered so quietly he hardly heard her. "It'll never end. It never ends." She said it so wearily, it broke his heart.

Unfortunately, he understood that all too well. "I know, honey."

Laura must have read something in his voice because her head snapped up, eyes confused. "You really do know."

"Come here." Jack led her to the rocking chair and pulled her down into his lap, rocking them both gently, as much to soothe himself as her. He drew in a deep breath and let it out slowly, preparing himself to tell the story he'd never shared with anyone else. Laura waited patiently as he readied himself, resting her head on his shoulder and taking his hand, entwining their fingers.

"I never told this to anyone else," he began at last. "A couple of years ago, I was away on vacation, visiting with the family of the woman I was dating at the time. One morning, she was catching up with some friends and I went to run some errands. I went to the bank and ..." he had to pause to take a calming breath, "and three armed men came in." Laura squeezed his hand and he found the strength to keep talking. "There were thirteen of us held hostage for a little over five hours. The longest five hours of my life." His voice was unsteady. "The police eventually took them down, but not before four innocent people were killed." His voice cracked now and Laura pressed herself closer against him. "Two of the hostages killed were a mother and her three-year-old daughter."

"Oh, Jack." Laura's devastated eyes looked up at him. "I'm so sorry."

He plowed on, even though he knew the words he was about to say might push Laura away forever. "I didn't do anything to stop them. I just sat and watched as those men shot four people. I couldn't do anything to stop it from happening," he repeated brokenly. He'd never forgiven himself for not doing something to keep those people alive.

"What could you have done?" Laura asked softly. She hadn't pulled away; in fact, she had raised a tentative hand to his shoulder and was kneading softly.

"I'm a cop, I should have done *something*," he replied.

"Did you even have your gun on you?"

"No."

"Did you do what you thought at the time was your best move to get everyone out of there alive?" Her voice was calm, rational.

"Yes."

"Then nothing that happened was your fault," she said evenly.

He disagreed. "I felt so helpless, Laura." His voice was still wavering. "I just sat there and watched them shoot those people. The little girl's screams as she watched her mother killed before her eyes, I've never forgotten them. Sometimes I wake up in the night hearing them. She wouldn't stop crying after they killed her mother, so they shot her. I was sitting beside her, trying to console her, when they shot her. I had her blood all over me, in my hair ..." He trailed off, unable to say more.

With gentle fingers, Laura brushed away tears from his cheeks. "Why did you tell me this?"

"Because you feel alone." He struggled to compose himself. He had shared his biggest shame with her because he needed her to know that he truly understood. "You think no one else understands what it's like to feel completely and utterly helpless. I wanted you to know that you aren't alone, that I understand." Praying she wouldn't pull away, he lifted a hand to cup her face. Fear flashed briefly through her eyes, but she didn't move. Taking it a step further, he gently traced his fingertips across her cheek. Laura flinched and he froze, not wanting to do anything to scare her away. After a moment, she turned her face a fraction of an inch and leaned into him, and his fingers found her lips. Slowly, her eyes rose to meet his and in them he saw an intense longing. Carefully, not breaking eye contact, he dipped his head ...

"Knock, knock," a voice spoke from outside the door.

The moment over, Laura darted up from his lap, and positioned herself on the opposite side of the room. As far away from him as possible.

Jack sighed. "Come in, Stephanie."

The door swung open to reveal CSU tech, Stephanie Cantini. "Hi, Jack. And you must be Laura." Stephanie turned sympathetic eyes in Laura's direction. "I'm Stephanie, I work with Jack and the others, I'm crime scene."

"Nice to meet you, Stephanie." Laura's voice was calm, but her eyes were tiredly wary. After locking herself away for ten years, she was coping remarkably well with meeting so many new people all at once.

"How're you doing?"

"I'm okay," Laura answered, but she wrapped her arms

protectively around herself.

"I already collected the photos and necklace and checked out where he attacked Laura in the hall," Stephanie told them.

Jack had to fight to hold down the anger that bubbled inside him at the thought of this man taunting Laura, hurting her, terrifying her.

"I'm sorry, honey," Stephanie continued softly, "but I need to take your clothes. He may have left something behind when he grabbed you."

"My clothes?" Horror was written all over Laura's face and Jack pictured all her scars. "But I don't have anything else to wear. All my clothes are back at my apartment. And I can't handle going outside right now." Her breath was coming way too quickly.

"Shh." Stephanie was at Laura's side before Jack had a chance to move. "It's all right, honey. Sofia sent up some clothes for you to wear. It's okay." She put a gentle hand on Laura's shoulder. "Shh, it's okay."

Laura took a couple of deep, shuddering breaths, attempting to calm herself. "I'm sorry."

"Hey." Stephanie gently grasped Laura's chin. "You have *nothing* to be sorry for. Do you hear me?"

"Okay," Laura agreed in a small voice.

"Okay, then." Stephanie nodded, she released Laura and handed her an evidence bag. "Pop your clothes in there." She picked up a stack of neatly folded clothes. "And put these on."

Laura took the clothing and bag from Stephanie's hands, made it to the door and then froze in her tracks. "Can I change in here?" Her cheeks heated in embarrassment. "Can you two just close your eyes? I'm kind of scared to go to the bathroom on my own to change. I'm …" *Sorry*, she'd been about to say, but instead shot Stephanie a look.

Stephanie smiled. "You're a fast learner. And of course, you can, honey."

They both closed their eyes, and a minute later, Laura

announced, "I'm done."

Stephanie took the bag. "I'm going to get this back to the lab. Jack, I'll call you if I get anything. Laura, try not to worry, I know these guys, they'll keep you safe."

"I really like your brother's fiancée," Laura announced once Stephanie had closed the door behind her.

"Sofia's pretty great," he agreed.

"And Ryan and Mark are as sweet as ever. I missed your family." A wistful sigh escaped her lips.

When this was over, he intended to see if he could manage to help her mend fences with her own family. "I hope there's someone else in my family you missed, too." He tried to keep his voice light, but it came out heated and a little husky.

Her pulse pounded in the hollow of her neck. "There is."

He wanted to take it further, but he knew Laura wasn't ready yet. "You need to get some sleep," he told her gently, leading her toward the bed.

"No." Panic flared in her eyes. "I don't want to sleep. I can't. Not right now."

He understood her fear and almost held his breath as he asked, "Do you want me to stay with you?"

Uncertainty replaced the fear in her eyes. "On the bed with me?"

"We won't do anything, Laura. We'll just sleep," he assured her.

"Will you hold me?" her voice wobbled.

He nodded once. "If you want me to."

She hesitated. "I want you to." She shuddered. "In your arms, it's the only place I feel safe."

Hope flooded through him—maybe a relationship with Laura wasn't such a lost cause after all. When she'd been scared, she'd asked for him to come. When he'd come, she'd allowed him to comfort her. When she needed to feel safe, it was his arms that she sought.

"Then that's where you'll be." He drew her to him, holding her tight against his chest. Her arms came around him, clinging tightly. He picked her up and carried her to the bed, where he set her down and then stretched out beside her. He lay on his back and gently pushed her head to his shoulder, his arm around her brought her close.

Laura held herself perfectly still, and Jack was just about to tell her that it was okay if this was too much for her right now, when she let out a weary sigh and relaxed into him. Tentatively, she brought up a hand and placed it on his chest, then ever so slowly, melded her body closer against his.

She was almost asleep when she looked up at him. "Why do I feel safe in your arms?"

"Because you are."

* * * * *

8:41 A.M.

He was so close now, he could almost taste it.

Axel had been waiting so long for this, it was hard to believe it was nearly time.

Revenge really *was* sweet.

That Laura was too pretty for her own good. The way she walked around flaunting her looks, practically inviting every man she saw to do it with her. And then when he'd taken up her invitation and asked her out, she had turned him down flat.

And not just once.

He'd asked her out several times and each time she told him no. Apparently, she was too good to do married men.

So, he'd been married; so what?

That didn't mean he couldn't get a little on the side.

His wife hadn't touched him after she had gotten pregnant. In fact, in all their years of marriage, and they'd been married a good fifteen years or so by the time he'd met Laura, she was only ever interested in sex when she was ovulating. That woman was obsessed with having a kid.

So, he had started looking elsewhere for his sexual gratification.

Axel had *never* had a woman turn him down.

Until Laura.

And not only had Laura had the audacity to turn him down, but then she had gone to his wife and told her about his indiscretions.

What unmitigated gall!

Who did Laura think she was to go interfering in his personal business?

What went on between him and his wife was none of her concern.

Because of Laura's meddling, his wife had left him. And taken his son with her. Then his witch of a wife had lied to a judge, convinced him that he had abused her and was a threat to their baby and gotten full custody.

Laura had started the game between them; he had simply taken it to the next level.

Surely, she couldn't complain about that.

So, Axel had taken her on a little trip.

He hadn't been prepared to kill the roommate. He hadn't known anyone was going to be there. Not that he'd been all that upset about killing Matilda Warren, and really, it was all Laura's fault, anyway.

She had put up a fight that first day, and he'd had to knock her out in order to take her. Having her unconscious and all to himself had been too great a temptation to resist, so he'd finally gotten to do her. That time in the van had been the only one, and only to satisfy himself that he got every woman he wanted. Then he had delivered her into the hands of his nephews, Frank and Francis Garrett.

The brothers were his older sister's children. His sister had only been married to Humphrey Garrett for a few years before she had fled, unable to take any more of the abusive recluse who hated women. Humphrey had beaten his wife, regularly locking her in the cellar and leaving her there for days, until at last, she couldn't take it anymore and she had simply left and disappeared.

Axel had still been a teenager back then, but as he got older, he had started going and checking on his nephews from time to time. From the first time he visited, it had been clear that Francis, in particular, was every bit as sadistic as his father was. Frank was just a follower.

Still, it had been a shock the time he'd gone out there and found his nephews ripping out the fingernails of a woman they had tied to a tree. Although he wanted no part of their torturous games, the thought of turning them in simply never occurred to him. Then when Laura had outed him to his wife and he had lost his son, it had seemed like the natural thing to do to take her to his nephews to receive her punishment.

Frank and Francis were supposed to call him when she was close to death so he could come and finish her off, but instead he had received a phone call from them saying that Laura had been rescued.

He'd been robbed.

Twice.

First, he'd lost his family and then he'd lost his chance for revenge.

It had taken him nearly ten long years to finally track her down since the tricky little thing had disappeared. He'd wanted to grab her immediately. But first she'd been in the hospital and then her family had hovered constantly around her, and then she was simply gone.

His patience had paid off and eventually he had managed to track her down. When the apartment next door to hers had come up for rent, it had seemed like the answer to his prayers. He'd conjured up ideas of breaking through the wall and grabbing her and being able to do to her whatever he wanted, whenever he wanted. Only, it hadn't worked out that way. Still, being in her building had been a great way to learn about her, and thus to hatch his plan, which was now in its final stage.

Inserting himself into the police's investigation had been fun. Pretending to find the letter left by the killer had been a spur-of-the-moment decision, and he was glad he'd made it. Getting up close and personal to the people hunting him was exhilarating. They hadn't had a clue that they were talking with the very man they were looking for.

The explosion diversion had nearly worked perfectly, and it probably would have if it hadn't turned out that Laura was old friends with the cop. He wondered if the police had enjoyed the confetti. He'd thought it was an appropriate filler for his bomb since this was, after all, a celebration.

Then those cops had bested him a second time at that house. He had paid some kid to drop the parcel off and then while Laura's cop friends were busy grilling the boy, he had snuck in through the back. He hadn't had to wait long for Laura to isolate herself. But perhaps he had goaded her a little too far. The stupid girl had nearly passed out. It had caught him by surprise and he'd stumbled, then she'd screamed and he'd had to abandon things again.

Soon though, he'd get her soon.

And he had everything all set. He even had one final game all lined up for Laura. Once he'd introduced her to Audrey Nichols, he was going to let the woman go running off into the woods. Then it was a race for him and Laura. If she found Audrey first, he would kill her quickly; however, if he found Audrey first, then the woman would suffer a slow and painful death.

And then for all the trouble she had caused him, the final painful death would be Laura's.

* * * * *

3:15 P.M.

Running his fingers through her hair, Jack looked down at Laura, who was still fast asleep in his arms. Her head laid against his shoulder, her breath whooshed across his neck, and her hand rested on his stomach. She was finally getting some good rest and he didn't want to disturb her.

Jack was also a little concerned that when Laura awoke, she would begin to pull away emotionally from him again. The attack had shaken her, and once again, she'd been willing to allow him to offer comfort. Bit by bit, she was opening up to him, but she was still wary about getting too comfortable with having him around.

He, however, was feeling much better about things. Refreshed from some decent sleep, his mind was clear and sharp. If Laura needed time before she was ready for a relationship, then he would give it to her; they had all the time in the world to take things as slowly as she needed.

He had also been formulating a plan on how to catch the guy who was after Laura. Obviously, he'd been watching them, followed them here to Ryan's house, so maybe they could get him to follow them someplace else.

Someplace that was important to him.

Someplace where he felt connected to Laura.

The place where he had taken Laura when he kidnapped her.

It might take some doing to convince Laura to go back out there, but she was desperate to bring an end to this, so he thought he should be able to …

All of a sudden Laura began to thrash wildly, caught in another nightmare. "Laura?" He eased her off his chest and back onto the mattress, then sat up and grabbed her shoulders, shaking her. "Laura, wake up."

She whimpered pitifully, and then screamed as she sprung

awake. Still caught in her dream, she fought wildly against him; her gaze was wild and disoriented.

"It's okay, Laura." He was struggling to catch a hold of her arms, and narrowly avoiding being hit in the chin. "Laura, it was just a nightmare, you're safe now. You're safe."

Panting hard, she stopped fighting him, her hands clutching at his shirt as she fought to regain control. "I'm sorry," she murmured at last, "did I hit you?"

"I'm fine," he assured her. "Are you?"

She jerked a nod. "Sometimes my dreams feel so real that it's like I'm still in them when I wake up."

"It must be so terrifying to wake up scared and alone." He tucked her hair behind her ear and hoped he wasn't being too obvious.

She raised an eyebrow. "I'm glad you were here," she conceded. "How long was I asleep?"

He checked his watch. "Over twelve hours."

"Wow, I must have been more tired than I thought."

"You needed the rest." He cupped her face in his hand and she immediately leaned into him, raising a hand to cover his, her violet eyes staring longingly into his blue ones. Before either of them could change their minds, he kissed her, soft and gentle, and she returned the kiss without hesitation. When he finally broke away, she studied him seriously. "What?" he asked.

"I don't know what to do about you. About us." She started to move her thumb toward her mouth, but stopped herself and clutched her hands tightly together in her lap.

"What do you *want* to do about us?" He brushed a finger back and forth across her lips.

Her pulse pounded in nervous anticipation in the hollow of her neck. "I want to find a way to get back what we had before."

Before he could respond, she slipped out of the bed and headed for the door. Following her, he was almost giddy with relief and joy, and he had to remind himself not to get distracted.

For the moment, he had to focus on her safety, on finding who was after her, then they could make a start at sorting out everything else.

"Hey, Laura, you're looking better." Sofia smiled at them as they entered the living room.

Laura smiled back. "I didn't realize how tired I was."

"I'm glad you were able to get some rest." Ryan pulled out a chair for Laura and set a sandwich down in front of her.

"So am I," Jack ventured carefully, aware that what he was planning may end up pushing Laura away. "Because I have an idea."

Catching the change of tone in his voice, Laura shot him a wary glance. "What?"

"I was thinking, while you were sleeping, about how we can get ahead of this guy."

"And …?" Ryan prompted when he didn't continue.

"He tracked you down, he tried to get to you and when he couldn't, he used us to bring you right to him. When that failed, he followed us here, tried again to get to you, only that didn't work out either. So, I was thinking maybe we could get him to follow us someplace else …" He trailed off, aware of Laura's increasingly horrified expression.

"To the place where Laura was taken when she was kidnapped," Ryan finished for him.

"He went to a lot of effort on all of this. He knew where Laura was, he could have found a way to just kill her straight out, but instead, he went to such elaborate lengths to make this dramatic. If he wants a big explosive finale, what better place than where this all started?"

Laura was nearly hyperventilating. "You want me to go back outside? And not just outside, but to the place where I was raped and tortured?"

He knelt beside her. "Laura, honey," he put his hands on her shoulders.

She shrugged off his touch. "Don't touch me. How could you even suggest that to me? You know what they did to me out there, how could you even think about making me go back?"

His hands hovered uncertainly above her. "I just want to end this for you."

Open betrayal was all over her face as she met his gaze directly. "I told you *everything* about what happened to me there. I opened up to you, you said you understood, but if you really did, you would never ask me to go there again."

He took her hands, tightening his grip when she attempted to pull away. "I do understand, Laura. I do understand what I'm asking you to do, but I'm asking you to do it anyway so we can stop this guy before anyone else gets hurt, including you."

"I can't do it." Tears were spilling down her cheeks. "I think I'm going to pass out."

"Head between your knees," he murmured, pushing her head down. When her breathing had slowed a little, he gently sat her back up. "I don't mean to hurt you, Laura, you know that."

"But you are hurting me. Don't make me go back there," she pleaded.

"I don't want to, angel." She was breaking his heart and he had to remind himself that he was doing what was in her best interest. "But we have to end this, and this is the only way I can think of to do it, and do it quickly. Laura, he's not going to stop until you're dead, this way we can get ahead of him, this time we can be the ones in control. You won't be alone. I'll be with you, and so will Rose and Ryan and Xavier and Paige. Please, Laura, please say you'll do this, please trust me." This was a crucial step toward a relationship. If Laura couldn't learn to trust him again, then no matter how much they both wanted things to work out, it was highly unlikely that they would.

Slowly, she nodded her head a fraction of an inch, then she was throwing her arms around his neck, her tears flowing freely. "I do trust you, Jack, but I'm scared. I don't know how I'm going to be able to make myself go there again."

"We're going to do it together," he told her, holding her close. "You're going to do it by trusting me, by leaning on me and letting me help you." He kissed the top of her head. "We're going to do this together," he repeated.

* * * * *

6:03 P.M.

Legs tucked up against her chest, arms wrapped around them, her long black hair falling in a protective shield around her face, Laura had her eyes clenched closed and was trying to focus all her energy on breathing.

A hand closed around her shoulder and Jack's voice rumbled beside her, "You can do this, Laura."

They were in the car on the way out to the place where her life had been ruined. Despite Jack's insistences that she could do this and that they'd do it together, she wasn't convinced she could. It had taken Jack almost an hour to coax her out of the house and to the car.

Unlike the last two times he'd taken her outdoors, this time he hadn't just picked her up and carried her out; this time he'd wanted her to trust him. He'd gone slowly, allowing her time to gather her reserves of courage. When her chest had felt like it was going to explode from her wildly beating heart, he'd talked with her, about anything and everything, until she was ready to move on.

Now that they were in the car on the way there, it was all Laura could do to focus on keeping herself breathing. Jack was talking away with Rose, Ryan, and Paige, planning exactly what they would do once they arrived. They'd decided it would be best if Xavier remained at Ryan's house with Sofia and Annabelle on the odd chance that the killer hadn't seen them leave and made another attempt at breaking in to get to her.

Time seemed to float away into nothingness. All Laura was thinking about was sucking in one nauseous breath after another. Her thumb was in her mouth in an attempt to remain even somewhat calm, and her head was resting against the window, the cold glass soothing her burning forehead.

"Laura?"

Jack's voice broke her concentration, and she choked on the breath she was drawing and erupted into a coughing fit. Jack just rubbed her back and waited until she regained control of herself.

"We're here," he told her once she'd managed to get her breathing back to a semblance of normal.

"I'm sorry, I can't do this," she whispered desperately. She wanted to be anywhere but here.

Taking hold of her chin, he turned her face away from the window. "Look at me, Laura." Jack waited until she reluctantly lifted her lids. "You said you trust me, I believe in you, I know you are strong enough to do this."

Locking her gaze onto Jack's bright blue eyes, which seemed to almost hypnotize her, she nodded. When his hand firmly encircled her own, she let him pull her from the car.

As the fresh air hit her, so did a barrage of memories. The Garretts laughing at her and mocking her, burning and cutting her, raping her over and over until she wished they would just kill her and end it all. Her knees buckled under the weight of the memories, but Jack was right beside her, his arm wrapping around her waist and keeping her upright.

"It's all right, Laura," he soothed.

"I can't make them stop." She pressed the heels of her hands to her eyes as though she could physically stop the flashbacks. "I can't make the memories stop."

"Yes, you can," Jack contradicted confidently. "You don't have to do this alone, I'm right here with you."

A whimper was all she could muster as a response.

"Keep your eyes closed," Jack instructed. "And take a deep breath. Okay, now hold it and count to ten, and then slowly let it out. All right, good, now I want you to think of something that makes you happy …"

Laura pictured last night, lying in Jack's arms, the reassuring beating of his heart beneath her ear, knowing that she wasn't only safe with him, she was also loved and cared about, she was important to him. Jack knew that she'd been weak and pathetic and helpless, and he wanted her anyway. The tightness in her chest eased a little.

"Feel better?" Jack asked. He continued when she nodded. "Okay, now imagine yourself taking a photo of that, and every time you feel overwhelmed, you just look at that photo."

"Thank you." She looked up at him gratefully. Last night when she'd awakened wrapped in Jack's arms, feeling safe and secure for the first time in eleven years, all her doubts about whether or not a relationship with him was a good idea had fled. She couldn't hold something that he'd done when he was a stupid kid against him forever. When this was over, she wanted to see where things led with him.

"You're welcome." He pressed a kiss to her forehead. "I told you that you don't have to do this alone, I'm right here with you every step of the way. There's a cabin just over there, think you can make it?"

She nodded and tried to pull away and stand on her own, but Jack wouldn't release her.

"Remember, we're doing this together, Laura."

With Jack's arm still around her, Laura made her way to the cabin on wobbly legs. She let out a weary sigh of relief when the door closed behind them and they were back inside.

Jack helped her to the couch and sat her down before turning to his friends. "I'll stay here with Laura while you guys go and check the place out."

The others exchanged glances. "Actually, Jack," Rose began,

"we thought it might be better if one of us stay here with Laura."

He frowned at his partner. "Why?"

"If you're right and he's followed us out here, then you staying here with her is exactly what he's expecting," Ryan explained. "We came out here to get ahead of him, give ourselves the advantage, and we want to keep it, so maybe Rose should stay with Laura, and you, Paige and I will go see if he's here."

"I don't know ..." Jack wavered.

"Do you trust me to keep her safe?" Rose asked.

"Of course." Jack nodded emphatically.

"And you don't want to do anything that could potentially put her life at risk, do you?"

"Of course not."

"Then let me stay with her. I won't let anything happen to her."

"Okay," he agreed reluctantly.

"What?" Laura's head snapped up. "You're leaving me?" At the moment, Jack was the only thing keeping her sane; she was petrified she would fall apart if he left her.

He crouched in front of her so he could look her in the eyes. "Only for a little while."

"But you promised we'd do this together," she whimpered.

"And we are going to do this together." He took her hands. "But unfortunately, they're right about this. I'm too emotionally involved with you, I can't be objective, I'd be endangering your life, and that I won't do. You'll be safe with Rose. And Ryan, Paige and I will be back before you know it."

"I don't want you to go." She clutched desperately at his hands.

"And I don't want to go." He took her face in his hands. "We're ending this tonight. When he comes, we're going to get him before he has a chance to get close to you, but if by chance he does get near you, then Rose will be here to protect you."

"All right," she agreed, only because it seemed she didn't have a choice; they'd already made up their minds. "But hurry back, please."

Jack leaned in and kissed her. "I'll be as quick as I can."

She watched Jack, Ryan, and Paige depart, then curled herself up on the couch and began to suck her thumb, attempting to calm herself. Rose filled the silence with mindless chatter, but Laura was barely listening, instead counting the seconds in her head until Jack returned. Outside it began to rain, the rhythmic drumming of the rain on the roof matched her thumping heart. It had been raining the night she was kidnapped. Raining the day she had been found, too.

A bump somewhere out in the dark night had both her and Rose jumping. Rose went immediately to the window, trying to make out the shadows.

"What was that?" Laura asked.

"I don't know, but I don't like it. Go," Rose commanded, "hide in the closet and don't come out unless Jack or I tell you to, promise me."

"I promise," Laura nodded solemnly.

"I mean it." Rose raised an eyebrow. "Jack will kill me if I let anything happen to you."

"I promise." She nodded again, more emphatically this time.

Rose slipped her gun free then paused, "Hey, Laura."

"Yeah?"

"I'm sorry I called you a fruit loop." Her eyes dipped in embarrassment. "That you still get up every morning considering everything you've been through is a miracle."

"I …" Laura never finished the sentence. The cabin door was suddenly flung open, a shadowy figure fired off a shot, and Rose's green eyes flew wide open in shock. Blood foamed from her mouth as her gun clattered to the floor, and half a second later, Rose dropped down beside it.

* * * * *

7:35 P.M.

Running.

Audrey was running.

Partly because she didn't know what else to do and partly because moving helped keep her otherwise paralyzing fear at bay.

The man had been driving her around in his car for what seemed like forever, although she guessed it had been close to forty-eight hours. It had just been getting dark when he'd returned to the cabin, tied her up and thrown her in a box in the back of his white van. The box hadn't been airtight, nor had it completely obscured her view. If she pressed herself up to the top, she could see through the crack between the sides and the lid, and through that, out a window in the side of the van.

Audrey couldn't maintain the position for very long; with her wrists tied behind her back and hogtied to her bound ankles, she wasn't very maneuverable. Still, for short periods of time she would do it, and would stare out the window and watch the sky get darker and darker until slowly it started to lighten again.

They'd driven to somewhere noisy and busy. The man had muttered about if this didn't work, he didn't know what would. He had left her for a while and she had thumped as loudly as she could manage, but no one had heard her. Then the man had returned and they were off again, a bevy of gunfire had nearly scared her witless, but she had fought to keep her carefully controlled calm.

The idea of him taking her somewhere else before the arrival of this Laura woman he was all worked up about hadn't occurred to her. For a little while, it had thrown her. Did his apparent change in plans mean good news or bad news for her? Audrey wasn't sure, but she knew she wasn't going to give up. She was not a quitter.

Audrey had managed to find something to use that might help

her get free later. *Might,* she emphasized to herself. She had found a pin, like the kind you used in sewing. It was probably no good against the plastic zip ties he'd tied her up with, or ropes, but it could have worked against duct tape. She might have been able to push it through and make a small hole and then work from there.

In the end, it had become a moot point.

After the gunfire, they'd driven through what seemed like a residential neighborhood where they had come to a stop. They'd been there for hours; it grew light and then dark and then light once more. And then they were on the move.

They'd driven here.

To these woods.

Darkness was falling again.

The man had finally stopped his van, opened the back, and then the box inside which she was stuffed.

He had lifted her out, set her on the ground, and cut her bindings with a knife.

Audrey had been petrified that he had given up on the whole Laura thing and decided to just do whatever he'd been going to do to the other woman to her instead.

But he had simply smiled at her, told her to run, and that he'd see her soon.

And so, run she had.

At first, it had been awkward. After so long bound and squashed in a small place, her limbs were numb and useless.

But that hadn't stopped her.

Not knowing whether the man was behind her, she cleared her mind of everything else except moving.

She had barely noticed when a thunderstorm hit.

Thunder rumbled, lightning lit up the woods for terrifying seconds where she was sure the man would spot her and come for her, rain poured down, drenching Audrey and the world around her making things slippery.

She lost count of how many times she fell.

All that mattered was that she kept on moving.

And she did.

Until she ran headlong into something warm and solid and human.

The person she had run into lost their balance, and the two of them tumbled to the muddy ground.

Fearing it was the man, Audrey fought as hard as she could. Swinging her fists and her legs.

"Ow," the person beneath her yelped as Audrey's fist connected with her face.

Before she could process that the voice was a woman's, someone had tackled her and was pinning her on her stomach against the ground.

"Paige, are you all right?" A tall man knelt beside the woman. "Where'd you get hit?"

Paige propped herself up on her elbows. "In the face."

"Let me look." He shone a light in the woman's face, and probed the area she indicated. "That's going to leave a bruise, but I don't think anything's broken, we'll ice it as soon as we can."

"Jack?" The voice of the man holding her down sounded concerned.

"She's fine," Jack assured him, helping Paige to her feet. "Who was that?"

She was rolled onto her back. "It's Audrey Nichols." The man sounded surprised.

How did they know her?

Audrey's panic levels spiked back up.

Should she fight them?

What good would that do? There were three of them and only one of her. And she was hurt.

Then the man above her eased off her and said the words she'd been longing to hear. "It's okay, ma'am, we're the police, you're safe now."

Dizzy with relief, she sank back against the wet grass. She was saved. Somehow, the police had found her.

"Are you hurt, ma'am?" the cop beside her asked as he shrugged out of his jacket and wrapped it around her near naked body.

"Just some bruises," she managed to choke out, fighting back tears of utter joy. "The man who took me, he's after someone named Laura." They needed to find that woman before the man got her.

"Yeah, we know," Jack replied grimly. "Ryan, you okay here while I go back and check on Rose and Laura?"

"Of course," Ryan replied. "We'll head back to the car and radio for an ambulance and backup."

Jack nodded and jogged off, quickly disappearing into the rainy woods.

"Can you walk, ma'am?" Ryan asked her.

Her body was sore, stiff, bruised, and exhausted; she wasn't sure she could take another step. "I don't think so," she replied.

"No worries." He gave her a comforting smile. "I got you." Lifting her easily, he began the trek out of the woods. "Just so you know, the paramedics are checking you out, too," he said over his shoulder to the woman.

"What? No, I'm fine," Paige protested.

"Six months ago, you sustained injuries that nearly killed you; you get checked out," Ryan shot back.

"You're not the boss of me, Ryan," Paige retorted.

"Well, isn't that a mature comeback," Ryan laughed.

The sound of their argument was oddly soothing and Audrey sank down into Ryan's arms and simply reveled in being alive.

* * * * *

8:12 P.M.

Too terrified even to scream, Laura just stood there as the dark figure took a step into the cabin. A sheath of light fell across him and she knew they had been right.

"Hi, Laura. We were interrupted last time; this time I think we'll be able to settle some old business." Her old college professor, Axel Christianson, took another step toward her. "I see my friends and I made quite an impression on you." A gleeful smile lit his face. "It was your fault, you know. You never fought back, you just laid there and let them hurt you over and over and over again."

Laura tried to speak, tried to tell him that she had fought at first but it did no good. Still, she knew he was right. She was weak and pathetic, and she still wished she had died out there in that forest, that those hikers had never stumbled across her half dead body.

He chuckled. "Never mind, I like it better that way. I never forgot that day in the van; it was magical, the best day of my life. I'd love to take my time, savor every second, but those cops are still out there, so we're going to have to make this quick."

As Axel came closer, Laura could see his blue eyes sparkling with lust, his breathing already heavy in anticipation. She wanted to run, to scream, to fight with every ounce of strength she had, unleashing the anger over what the Garretts had done to her that she had kept under strict control the last eleven years.

Yet, she found herself powerless to move.

She just stood there while Axel threw her over his shoulder and laid her down on the bed. The torrential pounding of the rain outside seemed to enter her brain; it's rhythmic beating became almost hypnotic and she found herself able to perfectly recreate the deep blue skies of that summer. In her head, she saw the tiny white clouds chase each other across the endless blue that almost made your eyes hurt if you tried to stare at it too long. Then there were the bigger clouds that morphed from one thing to another as they drifted more slowly in the sky.

She was so wrapped up in her imaginings that she hardly

noticed Axel pull off her jeans, but as his fingers traced their way up her legs and found the elastic waistband of her underwear, one of the clouds suddenly changed into Jack's face. Jack had said that she was strong enough to do this, to finally fight her demons once and for all. He had said that they were going to do it together, and even though he wasn't here right now, maybe there was still a way he could help her.

She pictured in her mind the photo she'd taken of the place that made her feel happy, just as Jack had instructed her to do when she felt overwhelmed. Imagining Jack's arms around her now, she drew strength and comfort and slowly the fog in her mind lifted a little and she could think. Last time she'd been alone, but this time, Jack and the others were here with her. They couldn't be that far away; they'd be back soon, and all she had to do was keep herself alive until they returned.

By now, Axel had removed her sweater and was fumbling with the clasp on her bra. Summoning strength she hadn't known she possessed, Laura lashed out with her arms and legs simultaneously, connecting with Axel's chest and groin, not hard enough to cause any real damage, but enough to catch him off guard.

Throwing herself off the bed, Laura made a dash for the door, but Axel recovered quickly and fired off a shot. Waiting for pain to explode out from somewhere in her body, it took Laura a second to realize that Axel had aimed for the light globe, not her, and plunged the small room into darkness.

"Ah, it seems like we *are* going to have a bit of fun, after all." Axel clapped his hands excitedly.

Dropping to her knees, Laura knew that her one hope of getting out of here alive lay on the floor over by the bed. Doing her best to ignore Axel's account of the 'fun' they had had that summer as she crawled as quickly as she dared toward Rose's body. In the pitch black, unable to see where she was going, she banged headfirst into a piece of furniture, causing a bang that seemed amplified in the quiet cabin. She pressed one hand to her mouth, the other to her cheekbone that was already sticky with blood, and held her breath as she waited for Axel's hands to close around her neck and crush the life right out of her.

"Well, this certainly is a bundle of fun," Axel cheered. Apparently, he was happy to drag this out for as long as he could. "I was always sorry I missed out on the hunt, that I never got to chase you in the woods. Well, I guess we're making up for it now."

A rumbling peel of thunder announced a coming burst of lightning and Laura took cover behind a chair and prayed that Axel wouldn't see her. She needed to get to that gun, but to do so, she needed to keep Axel distracted. If she could keep him talking, it should keep him sufficiently occupied so she could keep moving undetected. The prospect of talking to the man responsible for what had happened to her made her feel physically sick, but she'd already found the strength to fight back once, that empowered her to try again.

Taking a deep breath, she asked, "Why? Why did you do it?"

"Because of what you did." His voice turned to a vicious snarl.

"What did I do?" she asked, edging her way toward the sofa.

"You know what you did," he snapped.

"I said I wouldn't have sex with you because you were married with a family." She tensed her muscles, preparing herself to move after the next flash of lightning. "Why would that make you hate me enough to do this?"

"You did more than that." Axel's face looked manic as Laura caught sight of it as bright light briefly illuminated the room.

Continuing her quest when the room fell dark once again, Laura hardly noticed when she crawled over the tiny shards of glass that had rained down when Axel had shot out the light globe. The pain in her knees and hands was nothing compared to the giant knot of fear that gripped her heart and made her feel like the mouse being played with by the cat.

"You went to my wife," Axel was ranting. "Told her everything. She left me, took my son, convinced a judge I was abusive, and she got full custody of him. He's eleven years old now and I haven't seen him since he was one. You thought you were so perfect, so high and mighty, playing God with my life, costing me everything. You deserved everything you got."

She was so close to the gun now, she just needed to keep him talking a little longer. "How did you know the Garretts?"

"They're my nephews." His voice grew smug once more. "Their mom was my older sister. She ditched them when they were young, couldn't stand their lunatic dad, so I used to look in on them from time to time. Imagine my surprise when one day I go to check on them and I find they have a little visitor."

"What they did to me, it wasn't the first time?"

"Far from it," Axel laughed. "With two loser parents, I thought they deserved to have their fun. Then when you played with my life, I thought it was only fair that I play with yours."

"You knew—you knew what they were doing and you never tried to stop them. That makes you as bad as they are."

"Little Laura, always so prissy and perfect," Axel sneered.

Finally reaching the bed, Laura lay down on her stomach and eased underneath it, inching her way toward the other side. Feeling around, her hand brushed against Rose's and she had to bite on her lip to stop a sob escaping. At last, her hand clasped the item she'd been searching for. With a deep breath, she tried to steady her nerves, she was only going to get one chance at making this work.

"I never went to your wife," she announced.

"Liar," Axel screamed.

As another peel of thunder crashed above them, Laura's muscles tensed and as a bolt of lightning temporarily lit the room, she sprung up and fired, hitting her target right between the eyes.

The room bathed in darkness once again, and Laura heard the thud as Axel's body hit the floor and found she had once again lost the ability to move.

It felt like hours that she stood there listening to the rain. Occasionally, lightning would light the blood-splattered room, but Laura liked it better in the dark. It felt safer.

She'd just killed a man. The fact that he was a psychopath who had organized her kidnapping, killed people, and who had been about to rape and murder her, didn't seem to factor in. All she could think of was that she'd just taken a life.

She didn't hear Jack come in, although she supposed he must have spoken. All she could hear was the sound of the gunshot ringing in her ears.

The first she realized he was there was when he gently eased the gun from her hands, wrapped his jacket around her shoulders, and picked her up, carrying her from the room and out to the car, where he laid her on the back seat, resting her head in his lap.

Laura was numb by the time a swarm of paramedics and police officers descended on the cabin. Jack handed her over to a pair of medics, promised her that he would meet her at the hospital, then disappeared into the cabin.

She didn't believe him, though.

How could he ever want to see her again? His partner was dead because of her.

She was going to go back to her apartment, lock herself back inside, and return to the life she'd been living the last ten years, completely giving up any notions of a happy future with Jack or anyone else.

* * * * *

10:42 P.M.

He stood and watched the flashing red and blue lights of the ambulance as it rushed off down the road. Jack had been torn between riding with Laura to the hospital and remaining here until things were wrapped up. In the end, he had decided to stay, unable to leave while his partner's body still lay inside the cabin.

As the lights were swallowed up in the dark night, Jack turned and headed back toward the cabin, pausing at the door, trying to convince his brain that the scene before him was real. He had attended hundreds of crime scenes in the years since he joined the police force, but this was the first ever where the murder victim was someone close to him.

Inside, the carnage looked surreal. Lights had been set up, giving the room an eerie glow. Axel's body was still lying where it had fallen. The glass from the shattered light fixture still littered the floor. Paige was crying in Ryan's arms over by the bed. Rose's body was covered with a sheet, but it didn't matter, the picture of his partner's lifeless corpse was forever burned into his mind.

"You doing okay?" Ryan suddenly appeared beside him.

He nodded absently; he'd been in a haze ever since he'd returned to the cabin to find Rose and Axel dead, and Laura standing in the middle of the room staring blankly into space.

"How's Laura?"

"Still in shock." Just as she had been since he found her. Laura hadn't heard him arrive, even though her name had been the first word he uttered upon discovering the carnage. After quickly checking to confirm that both Axel and Rose were dead, he'd gone to her, asked her if she was okay, but she still hadn't heard him. She hadn't realized he was there until he had gently taken the gun from her, wrapped her trembling form up in his jacket and carried her from the room. "I'm going to go to the hospital to be with her once we finish up here." He shook his head to focus his dazed mind. "So, how did it go down?"

"There'll be time to go through this later," Paige said softly. Her eyes were red and puffy. Paige had been just as close as he had been with Rose. Jack had no idea how any of them were going to get through this. "Go to the hospital; Laura needs you."

"I can't until they ..." Jack trailed off, his eyes glued to the bloody sheet.

Exchanging glances, Ryan gave Paige a nod. "Looks like he caught them unaware, shot at Rose, got her in the back, right through the heart, and she died instantly," Paige explained. "Laura's clothes are by the bed," she continued carefully, her brown eyes studying him. "Did you ask her if he raped her?"

The queasiness in his stomach intensified. "I asked her." As soon as he'd found her dressed in nothing but her underwear, he'd been afraid that Axel had forced himself on her before she shot him.

"And?" his brother prompted.

"And I don't know, she didn't answer, she didn't answer any of the questions I asked her, she was in shock. I asked the EMTs to get the doctors at the ER to do a rape kit on her." He was working hard to keep his voice neutral. He wasn't sure how Laura was going to cope with all of this—taking a life, no matter how justified—was something that haunted you.

"Well, whether he did or not," Paige continued, "Laura must have fought back, managed to get away. Axel Christenson probably shot out the light. Laura had cuts on her hands, knees, and face, so it makes sense that she was crawling in the dark across the glass from the globe and crashed into something. It seems she made it to Rose's gun ..."

"Maybe she got the gun at the beginning," he suggested. "If she was near Rose when he ..." He trailed off, unable to finish the sentence.

"Maybe," Paige nodded slowly. "But I'd say unlikely. If she had the gun at the beginning, Axel would have taken it off her when he took off her clothes. Or he never would have had a chance to take her clothes off because she would have shot him right away."

"I guess," he agreed, reluctantly acknowledging Paige's logic but still desperate for a scenario that categorically precluded Laura being raped.

"Assuming she got Rose's gun after she fought him off on the bed, she was able to get a shot at Axel, lucky she's such a good aim or she'd probably be dead now, too."

He was barely able to breathe. He had come so close to losing her. If her aim had been only a little off, she would have missed her chance and Axel would have killed her. He couldn't help but picture how terrified she must have been, crawling across the floor in the dark, desperately trying to get to the gun so she would have something with which to protect herself against this maniac. Jack was hoping that the knowledge that she hadn't been helpless this time, that she had fought back and saved herself, was going to be enough to help her through this.

"At least he's dead now," Ryan murmured. "Laura is safe."

Safe but probably petrified out of her mind, he thought. Alone in a sea of people. The ER would be busy and Laura would have to draw on reserves of strength he wasn't sure she had left. The paramedics had given her a sedative; he hoped it was enough to calm her panic and keep it at bay until he got there.

Guilt was beginning to crush him as he pondered all the things he ought to have done differently. He ought to have found Axel Christenson sooner; he ought not to have brought Laura out here; he ought to have been the one to stay with her; he ought to have gone with her to the hospital and not made her face that alone.

"Can I have a minute alone, please?" he asked Ryan, Paige, and the CSU techs who were busy collecting evidence.

"Are you sure?" his brother asked.

"I need a moment to say goodbye." Jack's eyes were once again riveted to the bloody sheet covering his partner's body.

"Okay." Ryan nodded to the CSU techs who left their equipment and filed out the door.

"Want me to call the hospital and check on Laura?" Paige asked.

"Yeah, thanks. Tell her I'll be there as soon as I can."

Once alone, Jack bent over and pulled back the sheet, staring down at Rose. She lay face down, her red hair spilled out around her head, the jagged hole in the back of her white turtleneck the only indication that something was wrong. He burned with rage at Axel Christenson's cowardice. Shooting someone in the back was the lowest of low.

He knelt and gently eased Rose onto her back, cradling her head in his hand. Laura had survived, she was still alive, and he still had a shot with her, but at the expense of his partner's life. A tear splashed down onto Rose's cheek, then another and another, until he was sobbing quietly.

JULY 29TH

6:03 P.M.

She ignored the ringing phone.

It would be Jack.

Again.

Laura had already ignored several dozen phone calls from him. He'd filled up her answering machine, but she'd stopped listening after the first message. She didn't want to hear his assurances that he'd be over as soon as he could. It was better to make a clean break of things. She didn't need him to come in person to tell her that it was over, that he couldn't forgive her for getting his partner killed.

As much as she didn't want to admit it, hearing his voice still offered comfort it shouldn't. If just his voice could comfort her, then having him here in person was sure to be more than she could deal with right now.

Everything that had happened last night was weighing down on her. The events replayed themselves relentlessly in her mind. Rose dying right in front of her, Axel almost raping her, shooting him. Every time she thought about killing Axel Christenson, her heart felt like it was being tied in a knot.

She pulled the covers tighter around herself. She'd been in bed ever since she returned from the hospital in the early hours of the morning. At the hospital, she had let the doctors stitch closed the gash on her cheekbone, clean the cuts on her hands and knees, and tend to her burn, but when they had said they wanted to do a rape kit on her, she had flatly refused. There was no need for one, Axel hadn't raped her, although he would have if she hadn't managed to fight him off. She'd considered telling the hospital staff that it wasn't necessary, but all she had really wanted was to get back home.

She had also flatly refused when they told her they wanted to keep her in the hospital overnight under observation. Instead, she'd signed herself out and taken a cab back to her apartment.

Reaching her fortress, she had locked herself in, thrown off the scrubs the doctors at the hospital had given her to wear since the police needed her clothes as evidence, and pulled on a pair of her favorite pajamas, then climbed into bed. Jack's first call had come shortly after.

Someone knocked on her door and she jumped a mile.

She knew who it was even before they called out. Since she hadn't buzzed anyone into the building, it had to be someone her doorman would be comfortable letting in, and the only person who knew where she lived and who her doorman knew was Jack.

"Laura?" Jack's voice called as he hammered on her door. "I know you're in there, let me in, we need to talk."

She pulled the covers over her head and ignored him.

"Laura?" he persisted. "I need to see that you're okay, please let me in."

She had hoped that the fact that she hadn't answered or returned any of his calls would have been a big enough hint that she didn't want to talk to him.

He banged on her door more insistently. "Laura, I'm just going to break your door down if you don't answer."

Assuming he was joking, Laura stayed right where she was, tuning out the thumping and his increasingly desperate pleas for her to open the door.

She narrowed her eyes in confusion when she heard a strange buzzing noise. Reluctantly climbing out from under the covers, she followed the sound to the front door. She slid the five deadlocks undone and pulled open the door to find Jack kneeling on the floor in front of her, removing the screws with his drill.

He flashed a smile at her. "I didn't want to hurt myself breaking down the door."

Refusing to allow herself to be drawn in by his adorable dimples and endearing grin, Laura turned and was about to close the door once more when Jack grabbed her wrist.

"Laura, wait, please." He turned her to face him. "Please, I just want to talk to you."

She knew she'd regret it even as her mouth was forming the word. "Fine."

Jack followed her back inside her apartment, where he relocked all five deadbolts, then took her hand and led her to the couch. "Are you okay?" he asked as he gently pushed her down.

Not trusting herself to talk, she simply nodded.

His blue eyes went fierce. "Before you shot him, did Axel rape you?"

She suppressed a shiver. "No."

Visibly relaxing, he sat down beside her. "I was afraid he'd hurt you and it would be one more thing that you'd have to …"

"Why did you come here?" she interrupted. It was too hard having Jack here and this was hard enough as it was, she needed him gone.

"I told you I'd come," he reminded her. "Actually, I told you I'd meet you at the hospital, but when I got there you'd already checked yourself out." A hint of reproach was in his tone.

She stood to dismiss him. "Look, I don't want to talk right now, I just want to be alone."

He jumped up and blocked her path as she tried to escape to her bedroom. "What's wrong? I thought we were doing okay. You shouldn't be alone right now, I want to stay with you."

Tears welled up in her eyes. "How can you even stand to look at me?"

"What?" Genuine confusion filled the blue eyes that looked down at her.

"Rose is dead," she reminded him.

"I know." Pain flashed across his face, but the puzzlement was still there. "And?"

"And your partner is dead because of me," she finished. No longer able to hold back her tears, they burst out in a noisy sob.

"Listen to me." Jack took her shoulders in a firm grip. "What happened to Rose was *not* your fault."

His words only made her cry harder, so Jack gathered her into his arms and sat back down on the couch, setting her in his lap, his arms wrapped tightly around her. She gave herself permission to let go of all the doubts and insecurities and entwined her arms around his neck and clung to him as she wept. Jack's hand stroked up and down her back, his other cradled her head, and she drank in his warmth and strength. She lifted her head from his shoulder to peer up at him. "Don't you blame me?"

"Of course not."

Searching his face to judge the sincerity of his words, and deciding he was being truthful, she nodded. "Okay."

"You believe me?" He sounded surprised by her apparently easy acceptance of his words.

She was a little surprised herself that she had been able to believe in him, but so far Jack hadn't lied to her once, even when it had hurt and upset her, he had maintained his honesty. "You asked me to trust you and I do. You've never lied to me before. Even when you knew what you were going to tell me was going to hurt me."

He tipped her face up, and gently kissed away the last of her tears. Then his lips found hers, kissing her deeply and passionately.

"Thank you," she whispered when he finally pulled back.

"For what?" he asked, his thumb lightly brushing around the stitches on her cheek.

"For helping me find my way to the path to start getting my life back. I know I have a long road ahead of me, but at least I have hope, and before you came back into my life, I didn't. Thank you."

Jack smiled down at her. "You're very welcome." Then he dipped his head to kiss her again. "Now, please tell me you had the hospital check the burn on your hand."

Resting wearily against Jack's chest, she nodded. The doctor at the hospital had wanted her to meet with a plastic surgeon, and she had reluctantly agreed to go back tomorrow for an appointment. "I have to go back; will you go with me?" Laura reached for Jack's hand and entwined their fingers.

"Of course, I will." Jack lifted their joined hands and pressed a kiss to hers. "Come with me to dinner at my parents' house. Ryan and Sofia will be there, and Mark and his family. My parents are dying to see you again, they always loved you. Plus, I have a surprise for you."

Laura opened her mouth to protest and to express her wariness at just what his surprise may be, but he pressed a finger to her lips.

"You said you trust me, Laura," Jack reminded her. "You know I'd only ever do something that I believed to be in your best interest, so just trust me."

* * * * *

8:21 P.M.

"You okay?"

They were sitting outside his parents' house. Laura hadn't said a word since they'd left her apartment. It hadn't taken too much coaxing to get her to agree to the family dinner, but as soon as they opened her front door, she had clung to him so tightly he couldn't walk. Once he scooped her up into his arms, she relaxed a little, and he got her to the car as quickly as was physically possible.

Now she turned huge violet eyes to him. "I'm not sure I can

do this. I want to go home."

He reached for her hands; he couldn't get enough of touching her. "You'll do fine."

Doubtful, she responded, "I can't even walk outside on my own, you have to carry me."

"So, what? You're coming out of your apartment and that's great, I'm so proud of you."

"I'm not just going to be able to get over this instantly," Laura warned him.

"I know that, angel," he assured her. "We'll get you counseling and whatever else you need. Laura, we can take things between us as slowly as you need to," Jack promised her.

Laura took a deep breath and let it out slowly, looking thoughtful now. For a horrifying moment, Jack felt his heart practically stop, convinced Laura was about to end things, to say that she didn't love him, that she wasn't relationship material, that she just wanted to be friends.

Would he walk away if it was what Laura wanted? Could he?

Would he stay and fight for her? Was that fair to Laura to do?

But then the hands that he still held squeezed tightly, and Laura's face lit up in the first proper smile he'd seen since he found her again. "I don't want to take things slowly, Jack. I wasted ten years of my life being scared and alone; I don't want to be anymore. I was wondering whether maybe you would want to come and stay with me for a while? I feel so much safer when you're around, and you're kind of good company," she said shyly.

He kissed her; he never wanted to stop kissing her. "I would love to come and stay with you. And not just for a while. Forever." He released her hands and reached into his pocket, pulling out a small velvet box.

Her eyes flew from the box to his face. "Jack, are you proposing?"

He grinned. "Yes and no."

Her brow crinkled in surprise. "Yes *and* no?"

"I bought this back in high school," he informed her. "Laura, I always knew that I wanted to marry you, I've always been in love with you. So yes, I am proposing but not today. When I do, I want everything to be perfect. So, be ready, it's coming soon and when you least expect it. Are you crying?" he asked, dismayed. He'd thought she would be pleased.

"Yes. But happy tears," Laura assured him. "I really missed you. I love you, Jack."

He kissed her again and then somewhat reluctantly glanced at his parents' house, wishing now that he'd stayed home with her and kept her all to himself. He brushed away the last of her tears. "We better go in, they're waiting for us."

Laura tensed immediately, small tremors began to wrack her body, and she gave a little whimper.

"It's all right, Laura. I'll carry you inside, and you've been to my parents' house hundreds of times. Plus, you know everyone in there except Mark's wife. It'll be okay." Climbing from the car, he went around to Laura's side and scooped her up. "So," he waited until her eyes found his, "when I come and stay with you, do I get the spare room or your room?" he waggled his eyebrows.

She laughed, as he'd hoped she would. "My room, but just for sleeping. I still want to wait for our wedding night."

Whether intentionally or unintentionally, she had just told him how he had to win her trust back. Fifteen years ago, when she'd told him that, he'd stupidly gone and slept with someone else, but now he wanted to wait. He wanted to do whatever made Laura happy.

Inside, his family swarmed around them, his mother all but dragging Laura from his arms as they all covered her in hugs. Jack knew Laura didn't like to be touched, by anyone other than him it seemed, but she didn't protest his family's demonstrative affections.

Leaving Laura with his family, Jack pulled Ryan aside. "Are they here?" he asked his brother.

"Yep, waiting in the other room," Ryan replied. "Does she know?"

"No."

"You think she's going to be okay with it?"

"I hope so." Jack went to retrieve Laura. "Hey," he took her hand, "ready for your surprise?"

Instantly uncertain, she replied, "I don't know."

"Trust me, Laura," he reminded her as he guided her through the house and down to the kitchen.

Laura froze when he opened the door and saw who was standing there. Last night, he had called Laura's parents, explained to them everything that had happened and asked them to come to dinner tonight. He had promised them he would do his best to convince Laura to come.

At the sight of her daughter, Karen Opal gasped, tears brimming in her eyes. She took a tentative step toward Laura, who squeezed his hand so tight he nearly winced, and stepped back.

"It's okay, angel," Jack encouraged.

"No." Laura shook her head wildly, released his hand and spun toward the door.

Worrying he'd done the wrong thing, he should have told her, prepared her. "Laura, wait."

With her hand on the doorknob, she stopped.

"They're not angry with you."

"Baby, you thought we'd be angry with you?" Karen sounded distressed.

"How could you not be?" Laura was crying now. "I just left. I never called or anything."

"We were never angry with you, baby; we understood that you were traumatized. We missed you and we were worried about you, but we weren't angry," Karen assured her daughter.

Ever so slowly, Laura turned back around to face them, her eyes moving from her mother to her father. She didn't move toward them, but neither did she back up.

Gauging Laura's reactions, Karen came toward her again. This time Laura remained still. And then her mother sobbed and threw her arms around Laura. Laura didn't return the hug but Karen didn't seem to mind. Then Mick, who had remained silent, staring at his daughter like she might be a mirage, joined them.

Catching his eye as he watched the family, Laura gave him a small smile to let him know she wasn't mad at him for blindsiding her with her parents' visit. Jack was under no illusion that things were going to be smooth sailing for Laura now. She had a very long road ahead of her, but at least she wasn't doing it alone anymore. What she'd been through would never leave her, but hopefully she could learn to live with it and not let it rule her.

As the evening went on, Laura grew more and more relaxed.

Having other people around her helped her not to dwell so much, but it also wore her out. When they moved to the lounge room after dinner, Laura sat down in his lap and rested heavily against him. The shock and horror of the last few days, plus the adrenalin overload of last night, would take a while to work itself out of her system.

"So, Laura," Sofia suddenly spoke, "you're a psychologist, right? You counsel kids?"

"Yes," Laura's voice went immediately tentative.

"I inherited a fair bit of money when my family was killed," Sofia explained. *Fair bit of money* was an understatement. Sofia was inconceivably wealthy. "And I've been thinking about what I wanted to do with it. I already spoke to Paige and Annabelle and Rose." Tears sparkled in Sofia's eyes as she mentioned Rose.

Jack didn't think that Rose's death had really sunk in yet. It was hard to believe that he wasn't going to see her when he walked into work. Or that he couldn't just text her to ask her something. Or that they weren't going to hang out together with their friends. It also bothered him that Laura blamed herself; another reason to hate Axel Christenson.

"And I wanted to open a center for women and kids who are

victims of violence," Sofia continued. "I used to run a women's shelter, but now that I have more money to put into it, I want to expand it, and I was hoping you'd be involved, that you'd come and work there as a counselor once I get it up and running."

Laura was stiff in his arms. "I don't know that I'm the best person to be helping others, given how badly I reacted to what happened to me."

Everyone in the room frowned reproachfully at her, but Sofia spoke before Jack could. "Laura, I'm going to be honest with you because we're probably going to be related, and besides that, I hope we'll soon be good friends. So, you know that's ridiculous, don't you? Just because you were a twenty-year-old psychology major who was brutally assaulted, you're not allowed to become agoraphobic? Honey, what you went through was horrific, cut yourself a break. I think the fact that you can truly empathize with other victims would make you an awesome counselor. So, are you in?"

A shudder rocked through her and Jack tightened his grip on her. Laura snuggled closer, then sighed, "I'm in."

A collective sigh of relief flittered through the room and Laura rolled her eyes, but Jack just tilted her face toward him and kissed her. Already, Laura was making steps toward getting her life back. And he had gotten everything he'd ever wanted.

Jane has loved reading and writing since she can remember. She writes dark and disturbing crime/mystery/suspense with some romance thrown in because, well, who doesn't love romance?! She has several series including the complete Detective Parker Bell series, the Count to Ten series, the Christmas Romantic Suspense series, and the Flashes of Fate series of novelettes.

When she's not writing Jane loves to read, bake, go to the beach, ski, horse ride, and watch Disney movies. She has a black belt in Taekwondo, a 200+ collection of teddy bears, and her favorite color is pink. She has the world's two most sweet and pretty Dalmatians, Ivory and Pearl. Oh, and she also enjoys spending time with family and friends!

For more information please visit any of the following –

Amazon – http://www.amazon.com/author/janeblythe
BookBub – https://www.bookbub.com/authors/jane-blythe
Email – mailto:janeblytheauthor@gmail.com
Facebook – http://www.facebook.com/janeblytheauthor
Goodreads – http://www.goodreads.com/author/show/6574160.Jane_Blythe
Instagram – http://www.instagram.com/jane_blythe_author
Reader Group – http://www.facebook.com/groups/janeskillersweethearts
Twitter – http://www.twitter.com/jblytheauthor
Website – http://www.janeblythe.com.au

sic enim dilexit Deus mundum ut Filium suum unigenitum daret ut omnis qui credit in eum habeat vitam aeternam

CPSIA information can be obtained
at www.ICGtesting.com
Printed in the USA
BVHW031731130423
662310BV00005B/74